# ENOCH'S PORTAL

A Stephan Raszer Investigation

## PORTAL

# A.W. HILL

CHAMPION PRESS, LTD.

CHAMPION PRESS, LTD.
VANCOUVER, WASHINGTON

ISBN 1-891400-58-4

Library of Congress Control Number: 2001091756

Manufactured in Canada 10 9 8 7 6 5 4 3 2 1

THIS BOOK IS DEDICATED TO MY BROTHER.

# AUTHOR'S NOTE

Vaclav Havel, President of the Czech Republic, makes a fictional guest appearance in the latter part of this book. With the exception of those quotations specifically attributed to him, all the words spoken by his character are my own poor attempt to mime his incalculably precious voice, and the actions given him are purely fictitious.

# ACKNOWLEDGEMENTS

Although "Enoch's Portal" is a work of fiction, I have taken a great deal of care to portray my fictitious cult and its adherents accurately in comparison with their real-life analogs. In this effort, I have received invaluable assistance from the following individuals and scholarly works:

John R. Hall and Philip D. Schuyler, "The Mystical Apocalypse of the Solar Temple," in *Millennium, Messiahs and Mayhem,* Thomas Robbins and Susan Palmer, editors. London: Routledge, 1997.

Massimo Introvigne, "Ordeal By Fire: The Tragedy of the Solar Temple," © 1995, Academic Press Limited.

Bertrand Ouellet, Director General, Centre d'information sur les nouvelles religions; Montreal, Quebec, Canada.

Beyond these contributions, I wish to make special acknowledgement of the value of my continuing exchanges with Professor John R. Hall of the University of California at Davis, the narrative insights of Ms. Jane Goldenring and the enthusiastic sponsorship of my friend and colleague, Chris Desmond.

This book is for three "Mercuries," whose work aided and abetted Stephan Raszer's flight: Dr. Stephan Hoeller of the Ecclesia Gnostica of Los Angeles, Robert Anton Wilson, and the late Professor Ioan Culianu of the University of Chicago, whose insights will resound long after the echo of his assassins' bullets has died away (be warned: the Invisible College will find you out!)

# PROLOGUE

## AL JIZAH (GIZA), EGYPT
## JUNE 21, 1993

"She's coming," whispered Fourché, the reverberant tomb lending silver to his fine voice. He flicked a wriggling millipede from his wrist and reflexively wiped its discharge on his trousers. "Can you smell the sea?"

"It's the salt." The second man's pounding heart betrayed his position on Fourché's left, his face obscured in the absolute darkness. Like Fourché, he spoke French with the lilting accent of the south. "The salt on the chamber walls. It overpowers even the bat droppings!"

A third man, seated at Fourché's right elbow, gave a snort and fumbled in his canvas pack, not intending to be heard.

"No," Fourché objected. "Not the walls. Not the stink of vermin, or rot, or the iron of fear on your breath, Jean-Paul. How is it that my acolytes have forgotten the smell of their own birth? Sweet *Stella Maris!* She's coming for the *Seven Sages,* the last of the great ones. Outside these ancient walls, over the eternal Nile, Sirius is rising and the end of time begins. Once the Seven have left, it will be up to us to close up shop on earth."

There was a loaded silence and an awkward shifting of positions. The interior of the Great Pyramid began to resonate almost imperceptibly. The man on Fourché's left – the one he'd called Jean-Paul – cleared his throat. They were all believers, but it was one thing to believe and another to see. Directly ahead in the darkness, the airshaft inclined thirty-nine precisely engineered degrees from the mid-point of the niche on the south wall of the Queen's Chamber. In a matter of minutes, if the prophecy held true, the eight-inch square shaft would fill with focused light from the Dog Star in the *Canis Major* constellation, and that river of light would carry home the spirit stuff of those seven sons of Horus who had carved the Sphinx and offered mankind the solution to its riddle. Mankind had rejected the offer, and now, neither Fourché nor his two companions intended to waste any tears over its damnation. They had other plans for their own souls.

The three men seated shoulder-to-shoulder on the rough, limestone floor, mingling fetid sweat and holy dread, had been assigned by The Lodge to witness the transit of the planet's last protectors. Of the three, only Fourché could claim to have seen miracles in his time. This should not have influenced the performance of their shared task, except that miracles engender an envy of the most fanatical sort. The man on Fourché's right mopped his brow. There was precious little air in the chamber, and the humidity was better than ninety percent.

The hum within the Pyramid's pitched cavities became a rumble, and the rumble shook stone dust from the gabled roof of the narrow chamber. The stone of cathedral, and megalith, and mound, when excited by sacrament, has a scent all its own, a scent so deep and primal that a man will either make it his own or run from it in babbling, dog-eyed terror. It is the smell of stardust, the perfume of the natal cosmos. The man called Jean-Paul shuddered as it entered his nostrils, and in the closet of darkness, where no one but God could see him, he crossed himself in atonement for what he was about to do, just as he'd been taught to do as a boy. He turned to his mentor as a faint, sourceless glow touched the chiseled outline of his face, and spoke softly.

"I will carry on the work. By all that is holy, by the *Rose-Croix* and the line of Jacques De Molay, I will see that the others you've chosen are delivered. And I will see you in Paradise…"

Fourché turned to his protégé, a question on his lips that his heart had already answered, and felt the garrote slip around his neck and contract with a brutal snap, forcing the air from his windpipe, denying him the breath to deliver an *"Et tu, Brute?"* The sentence was executed with the antinomian zeal of one who has been trained to hold the flesh in low regard; Fourché, even as victim, could not but be impressed. Within seconds, his legs ceased to kick and he lay still on the damp stone. Jean-Paul turned away as the assassin repacked his weapon.

"Let's go," said the killer. "The guards are paid only until sunrise."

Jean-Paul hesitated. "Should we not wait?"

"No. Heaven will do its work in spite of us."

They fumbled for the exit passage. It wouldn't do to switch on a flashlight while still in the Chamber, for to look on their master's body could bring nothing but bad luck. But suddenly, there was light all around them, reflecting off the polished walls as if from the face of the moon. Brilliant light of full artic blue, like the light that blinds high altitude climbers. The two men dropped to all fours and scurried through the passage like children caught trespassing.

Outside the Great Pyramid of Cheops, an armed Egyptian guard shifted his weapon and glanced toward the southeastern horizon, over the slums of Cairo and the Red Sea and Sinai beyond, where the rising Sirius spun a helix of light toward the monument.

The guard blinked, and the night was dark again.

# 1

## SOUTHEASTERN FRANCE
## DECEMBER 21, 1999

WHAT WAS MOST striking from the air was the purposeful arrangement of the bodies. The reports in Lyon had described the victims as "gathered around a campfire," but it was clear from six hundred meters that they formed a pattern, a sort of starburst around the nucleus of the still-smoldering pyre. The prosecutor winced and hissed with disgust as his zoom lens framed the charred forms of three children, one of them not more than an infant. He counted fourteen bodies in the star formation and two more fallen in the drifted snow not far beyond, coronas of blood about their heads. He was dismayed to see that these two – who, for some reason had not joined the circle – wore the uniforms of Swiss gendarmes.

He directed the helicopter pilot to remain at present altitude a while longer, and racked his focus to take in the surrounding landscape of dense pine forest and Alpine foothill. They were in the *Vercors,* a wilderness area southwest of Grenoble, known mostly to backcountry hikers and Nordic skiers. The day, 21 December, was the Solstice, the dark opening of the timeless feast of *Sol Invictus,* which, by a neat ecclesiastical sleight-of-hand had been replaced by Christmas. The place chosen for the ghastly ceremony was *La Serre de L'Aigle,* The Eagle's Talon, a rocky, treeless pass through the high country.

Glancing at his military survey map and then back at the overview, the prosecutor squinted through the glare and gleaned the overlaying pattern. The human wheel was enclosed in a topographical trinity consisting of three landmarks well-known to students of French antiquity: The Black Mount, the Devil's Well and *le Trou de L'Enfer,* the Mouth of Hell. A uniformed French policeman came to the prosecutor's side in the port of the helicopter and squatted with an emphatic groan.

"The wind is picking up!" he shouted through cupped hands. "We should get down, unless you're onto something."

"They're in the center of a triangle," said the prosecutor. "Or perhaps—" He pointed toward the brilliant blue sky to indicate a third dimension. "—A pyramid."

The policeman grunted. "I'd rather die in a bordello."

"Yes, Louis, but then you would die without grace."

With a motion to the pilot for a minute's more time, the prosecutor returned to his camera.

THE REGION KNOWN as the *Vercors* took its name from the root *carra,* charcoal, and for centuries the peasants here had made a living by creating fuel from the burning of timber. The prosecutor could not help but ponder the connections as the helicopter dropped lower and the odor of charred flesh and cedar ash entered his nostrils.

He had been in his kitchen, savoring the aroma of his wife's simmering *pot-au-feu* when the call came from Grenoble. "They're at it again," the chief of police had said mordantly before proceeding to read him the contents of the note that had been pinned to a tree at the crime scene. "Those that come into Thee," it read, "have the *same gate,* and through that *same gate* descend those that Thou sendest. Behold, we offer bodies and all worldly goods if it will please Thy angels to dwell within us and we with them. Woe be unto earth, for she is corrupted."

It would later be determined that the message paraphrased a quotation from the works of the 16th century alchemist John Dee, attributed by Dee to the apocryphal Hebrew prophet Enoch, whose visions had found their way into a host of millennial scenarios. The note had been signed with a woodcut of the little glyph, now familiar to French authorities, known as the *Monad,* a footed cross mounted by a circle and a semicircle; a symbol of Mercurius, god of transit within and between all worlds. The insignia was followed by the name of that strange order to which these poor pilgrims had inexplicably given their faith: *Le Temple du Soleil.*

The Temple of the Sun.

AN ICY GUST shook the helicopter, raising a last flick of flame from the embers below, and the prosecutor ordered a landing. As the product of

twenty years of stringent French academic standards, he knew that these
voyagers had not been the first to ascend to *La Serre de L'Aigle* on a spiritual journey. The place had been the trailhead of an Alpine crossing used
by the Knights Templar on crusade during the luminous 12th and 13th centuries, during which the powerful and hermetic order operated under papal
aegis as the outfit charged with insuring the safe conduct of pilgrims to and
from the Holy Lands.

Not far from where the prosecutor stood was the small village of
*Saint Pierre de Cherennes*. There, in 1310, fifty-four Templars had been
burned to death by order of King Philip "The Fair." The last known Templar Grand Master, Jacques De Molay, followed his cohorts to the stake
four years later. For both King Philip and Pope Clement V, the Templars,
with their huge cache of gold and much-rumored secret knowledge, had
come to threaten the hegemony of Church and State. The Order was ac-
cused of misusing its holy mission to the East to consort with Saracens and
pagans, and of sympathizing with anti-Roman heretics like the *Cathars of the
Languedoc,* who believed that the body was little more than a container for a
spirit that ached to return to God. It was even charged that in Templar
ritual, the severed head of the goat-man Baphomet was worshipped, and
that the Templars were sodomites whose initiates were required to thrice
kiss the anus of a black cat.

The most explosive rumor was that the Templars had been privy to
the existence of a hidden royal lineage – *the Prieure de Sion* – sired by Christ
himself in consort with Mary Magdelene, who after Calgary had carried
their child to the Port of Marseilles, whence he had then fostered the
Merovingian line – the line of Clovis. However farfetched, the idea must
have put the rulers of France in a lather. The Templar Order was dissolved
and had vanished in visible form by the 15th century, but the prosecutor
knew bastard variants had survived under cover of Europe's profusion of
Masonic and Rosicrucian fraternities. He also knew, as did his colleagues at
Interpol, that a 1995 missive from the mysterious leaders of *Le Temple du
Soleil* had promised that precisely fifty-four of its members would make
"the transit," presumably to join their 14th century forbears. Twenty-three
had died on a farm in Switzerland, and nine within a gated compound in
the Laurentian Mountains near Montreal. The prosecutor could account
for sixteen more here, in the shadow of the helicopter's strobing rotor. He
sprinted over to a pair of plainclothes detectives who were standing over
the stiff bodies of a woman and child, coutured like matching mannequins
in the display window of a *16th arrondisement* boutique.

"Is Fourché here?" he called out. "Have you found his body?"

One of the detectives took the prosecutor's arm and led him to a corpse on the other side of the fire. Louis, the French cop, stumbled alongside, shaken by the carnage.

"Have a look," the detective said drolly, pointing to the body of a man burned beyond recognition. "The lab in Lyon will tell us, but the overbite looks familiar."

"For the sake of these children, let's hope you are right."

"Who is this man, Fourché?" asked Louis, the police attaché.

"The less you know about him, Louis, the better," answered the prosecutor. "To know of his work is to be absorbed in the mystique of death, and I can tell you, it is not a pleasant occupation." They turned away from the disfigured corpse and walked closer to the remains of the fire, in which could still be seen the detritus of post-modern ritual: scorched champagne bottles and melted prescription drug vials.

Those around the fire had died three times: by asphyxiation (plastic bags covered their heads), by gunshot – point blank to the head – and finally by the torch. The scene stank of gasoline that had been used to anoint the bodies before the final conflagration. It stood to reason that the police officers, who displayed only gunshot wounds, had performed the service and then shot themselves. Or did it? Among the dead were many of good standing and high station: a psychotherapist, an art teacher, a mayor and the jet set scion of an internationally famous sportswear manufacturer. Whatever despair had fed their act, it was not want of material comfort. This was not Jonestown.

Most of the victims, including the man tentatively identified as Luc Fourché ("Luc the Fork" to Interpol), the cult's putative co-founder, had gone to their maker wearing the white silk robe emblazoned with the red crusader cross of the order, a fact which lent weight to the prosecutor's theories about their choice of location. Two days after the discovery of the bodies, he received an anonymous letter care of the Interior Minister's office, purporting to be a sort of manifesto. It said, among other things, "death is not what we take it for," and it provided a forwarding address for the recently deceased: The "White Lodge" in the double-star system of *Sirius,* the Dog Star. Exactly how they traveled there was anybody's guess.

Interpol remained unconvinced that those who had died at *La Serre* were willing players in some sort of continuing historical drama, and wanted the case handled as a murder investigation. But the prosecutor had seen things on the mountaintop that had burned themselves onto his cortex and stolen his sleep.

Before leaving the scene, he had knelt with Louis to examine the bodies of 34 year-old Marie-France de Villiers and her five year-old daughter. Even in death, the girl's tiny hand remained folded into her mother's. Beneath their scorched white robes, they wore identical cashmere coats with fox fur collars. As the prosecutor considered this, the sound of sleigh bells jangled the brittle mountain air, and he looked up to see that a horse-drawn *traineau* carrying five bundled tourists had paused on a slope about two hundred meters distant. The police on the perimeter of the crime scene waved them away, but the prosecutor's thoughts were momentarily diverted from forensics. A few kilometers away, in the fashionable chalets of *Villard de Lans,* there were other women in fur, sipping hot wine and celebrating *la belle vie.* The woman at his feet was one of *them.* How, where and why had her detour occurred? He recalled an e-mail alert he had received two months earlier from a persistent private investigator in Los Angeles, and reproached himself that when one is dealing with the lunatic fringe, one had best pay heed to those who traffic there.

The prosecutor returned his trained eye to the corpse. Louis leaned over Mme. De Villiers' torso and tugged gently on the black plastic bag that covered her head. It had snagged on the chain of a silver pendant that she and some of the others wore around their necks, a pendant bearing the image of a two-headed eagle.

"Masons!" Louis exclaimed, himself a member of a venerable policeman's lodge.

"Maybe…and maybe not," said the prosecutor.

Once freed of the chain, the bag slipped off easily. The prosecutor felt his intestines contract. Although there was a bullet hole in the center of her fine, high forehead, her eyes were fully open and her ice blue face was frozen in a beatific smile. Louis turned to uncover the head of the tiny girl at her side. Her face bore an identical expression.

OVER THE FOLLOWING week, in the safety of his office, the prosecutor revisited the tableau again and again in his mind's eye. As holy as church bells at midnight, and as awful as plague bells. On the Thursday following Christmas, he phoned Louis, who was holding all the evidence collected at the crime scene in the police vault.

"The note we found at *La Serre,* Louis, and the letters that came in through the Interior Ministry; fax it all to that investigator in Los Angeles. Yes, Raszer, Stephan Raszer, I believe. Americans have a certain kinship with heretics, don't you think? Perhaps it is he who can shine some light on our mystery."

# 2

## PERCEVAL

*The problem of opposites called up by the 'shadow' plays a great — indeed the decisive — role in alchemy, since it (alchemy) leads in the ultimate phase of the work to the union of opposites in the archetypal form of the hierosgamos or 'chemical wedding.' Here, the supreme opposites, male and female (as in the Chinese yang and yin) are melted into a unity purified of all opposition and therefore, incorruptible.*

— Carl Jung — "Psychology and Alchemy"

STEPHAN RASZER SMILED and began counting down from one hundred as the toffee-skinned masseuse jackhammered his buttocks with the heels of her hands. He was reasonably adept at meditation but found it difficult to relax when an erogenous zone was being worked. It was important that he buy at least forty minutes of serenity before he got on the plane, and an old anesthesiologist's trick was as effective a mantra as any: count down from a hundred; by eighty-nine, you're out.

He'd just begun to drift when the back of his eyelids went hot pink and it occurred to him to query Chandra, the half-Ethiopian masseuse whose touch he'd driven ninety miles for, on the subject of dualism. He rolled his head to the side; his sinuses had cleared and the scent of eucalyptus and seasoned redwood entered his nostrils. Chandra was on his tailbone, a good time to get the truth out of her.

"You're a spiritual person, right Chandra?"

"I try to be," she answered softly.

"But," Raszer continued, "you're also a body person. You're totally connected with the physical."

"Un-huh."

"Ever feel any conflict between the two?"

"No, Raszer," she said with a smile. He was her only regular who managed anything but small talk, who actually *sought* her opinion. "Body is the antenna of spirit. You don't tune the antenna, spirit can't go out or come back in." She did some *shiatsu* on his lower spine, a trouble spot for Raszer, who spent a great deal of time hunched over arcane texts with enigmatic scripts. *Shiatsu* was good pain in practiced hands and Raszer was not averse to pain, in measured doses, if it promised illumination. It had been good enough for Catherine of Sienna; it was good enough for him.

"Did you ever hear of the Flagellants?" he asked her.

"No. Is that some new, hardcore nasty boy band?"

"Ha! It will be soon if it isn't already. Historically though, they were a loose-knit movement of medieval penitents who protested the corruption of the church by scourging themselves in public. A lot of them were rich ladies in sackcloth. They believed they could free the spirit by mortifying the flesh."

"Kinky," she said, and moved down to his feet.

"And then some. But it's an old idea: body and soul at war."

She worked the pressure points on his feet expertly, producing more colors: turquoise, sienna, burnt orange. When she laid into his left ankle, there was an explosion of scarlet. She felt him flinch.

"You been rock climbing again, Raszer?"

"Just some boldering at Joshua Tree. The ankle's bad, huh?"

"I should give you a wrap if you're going off on another crusade."

"No time, darlin'. I've got to get back to Tinsletown."

"Turn over, then. I want to get at that third chakra."

"That wouldn't be the one under the towel, would it?"

She shook her head and snorted, not for the first time in their three-year acquaintance. "Here I am, trying to put you on a higher plane—"

"Good sex *is* a higher plane, don't you think Chandra?" He rolled over while she held the towel over his midsection.

"Can be. With the right person."

Raszer was half tempted to sit up but reminded himself that he was there to relax. He took a deep breath to slow his words – when Raszer was not either physically engaged or sedated, his mind tended to roil with thought, and the words sometimes came out so fast and hard that people took it for a polemic.

"But now," he said, "that limits ecstasy to the confines of a correct relationship. I'm talking about savoring everyday *eros*. It's tantric. You and I may never be lovers, Chandra, because that would end what we have, but that doesn't mean I can't get a buzz from the way you smell when you walk into the room."

CHANDRA PAUSED, HER hands hovering above his solar plexus, and took note of the faint throb in her belly. For an instant, she considered locking the door. She took in his long, lean frame; more that of a cowboy aesthete than a weight trainer. She lingered over his bony, borderline handsome face, with its hawk-like nose and wide, slightly insolent mouth, the only androgynous brushstroke on an otherwise masculine canvas. She studied the steel gray eyes and close-cropped sandy hair that would soon enough match the eyes. She read the old white scars on his wrists.

"THE THING IS—" Raszer continued, slurring a bit. Chandra, immobilized, had not moved her healing hands from their position above his center, and the inadvertent *Reiki* effect was taking him to the bottom of a deep well. "—that as soon as we begin to feel the serpent uncoil, we want to jump somebody's bones instead of nursing it the way the Sufis and the Russian love mystics teach. *Sex magic.* It's…"

A fraction of a second before Raszer's eyelids had fluttered and dropped, Chandra had detected a faint glimmer in the iris of Raszer's right eye.

CHANDRA'S TOFFEE CHEEKS darkened to molasses. She did not posses Raszer's peculiar knack for drinking deeply without getting drunk, and she felt a bit ashamed of how ready she'd been to "end what they had." Perhaps he hadn't noticed; after all, it was only a fantasy. She was about to begin again, on his fingers, when he took her brown hand briefly in his and whispered, "…good stuff…"

RASZER EMERGED LIMP from the spa a half an hour later and lit a cigarette to put an edge on his seventy-five dollar satori. A good massage on the eve of beginning a new assignment was one of his many rituals, but he was forever worrying that if he got too comfy, he might decide to skip the wars and stay home. That, in truth, was never a possibility, least of all in the matter of the Temple of the Sun. Raszer was driven to know what made people leave the farm, and toward what blazing, end-of-the-rainbow epiphany they ran. How else was he to confirm that it might be safe for him to set out past the gates as well?

Three months after receiving the faxed materials from the French prosecutor, Raszer had gotten word that an American woman named Sofia

Gould might be "in trouble" with the French-Canadian sect. The lead had come from Sid Jaffe, a Hollywood client whose teenage son Raszer had retrieved from a saucer cult encamped on Mount Whitney. Jaffe was a skiing buddy of Sofia's husband, Lawrence Gould, CEO of Empire Pictures, Corp., a mini-major studio with corporate roots in Canada. Gould was as American as a Hollywood mogul can be, but Sofia was of French-Canadian descent, a minor actress whose budding career had been effectively nipped when Lawrence Gould carried her away to Hollywood as his child-bride. Gould was fifty-two, Sofia half that. From all evidence, she was a hothouse flower that had not taken well to transplantation.

Raszer had sent a message back through Jaffe that he was aware of the Temple's history and m.o., and he might be able to help. Two days later, Lawrence Gould, acting through his attorney, requested Raszer's "credits," which Raszer took to mean his *bona fides* as a private investigator. Though it might have suited his impish humor to do so, he did not include in the package his own acting roles in such classics as *South Beach Crazy!* or *Caged Desire*. That, as far as Raszer was now concerned, had been another man. That was before his day of reckoning.

"DO YOU LOVE your wife, Mr. Gould?"

The introductory meeting had been arranged in Lawrence Gould's oak-paneled office atop a Century City high-rise. The whole thing had nearly fallen apart over the issue of time. Raszer did all his research at night and rarely rose before ten. Gould, like most executives, was nervous if he hadn't closed a deal by nine. In style, temperament and predilection, few men could have been less alike, and it was clear from the start that Gould viewed retaining Raszer as only slightly less distasteful than hiring a divorce detective out of a seedy Hollywood walk-up.

"Yes. I do. Isn't it obvious, Mr. *Razzer?*" Gould pronounced the name with a short "a," as in *raspberry*. There was a hint of disdain, not only in the deliberate mispronunciation, but in the way the silk-suited mogul had fingered Raszer's business card, as if he feared the ink would rub off and effect some awful mutation.

"It's *Raszer*. Rhymes with *laser*. *Stephan* rhymes with *even*."

"Sorry," Gould said absently. He was clearly more concerned with the blinking light on his phone, one of eight incoming lines. "Is it Eastern European? Doesn't sound Jewish…" Raszer smiled and lowered his eyes. "Anyhow, why do you ask? If I love my wife?"

"Because," Raszer said, doing his best to connect, "if she's in as deep as you think she is, it's a good bet that only something just as deep will bring her out."

"Well then, if it's love she needs, why should I pay you six grand a week?"

"Because I can go places you can't, Mr. Gould. And wouldn't want to. And because I've made a career of why people like Sofia run away from—"

"People like me," Gould interrupted, finally in attendance. "What can he be offering her, Raszer? This *guru* of hers – this new age con artist?"

"Whether he's a con artist or a prophet, he can only offer her what she thinks she doesn't have. It's for you and me to figure out what that is."

Raszer went reflexively for the cigarettes in his pocket, then squelched the impulse when he saw there wasn't a single ashtray in the room. He drew a deep breath of recycled office air, heavy with lemon oil and imported wood, and settled back into the chair. Why was he suddenly nervous? It was because Gould was taking his measure; not only the measure of his dress (a collarless knit shirt, black, and loose-fitting khakis) or his appearance (fit, but decidedly not L.A. buff), but of his worth, of which Raszer was never entirely sure. Gould had the look of a cop who has "made" a perp.

"A tough question," Raszer said, "if you don't mind."

"Sure, shoot. Hey, didn't you—" Gould rubbed his chin, trying to place his recollection. "Do people tell you, you look like Steve McQueen?"

Raszer snorted. "Not often enough. Listen, your wife is clearly looking for something. We both agree, if it's the same group that the French and the Canadians are after, that she's looking up the wrong tree. But if she's not in danger, and she wants to stay up there, are you prepared?"

"To let her go?" Gould reached for the framed photograph on his desk and turned it toward Raszer. "Would you?"

The woman in the photograph had the eyes of a saint and the mouth of a harem girl. Black hair fell in ringlets around an alabaster face. Raszer was more moved than he'd expected to be.

"She's not mine to let go," Raszer answered, "but I need you to know, sir, that even if I can adjust her course, it may never be the straight and narrow."

"Can't you – what's the term of art? Detox, er...*deprogram* her?"

"You're talking about an 'exit counselor.' An e.c. usually works from a presumption of fraud. I'm a tracker. I assume people know where they want to go but get lost along the way. Spiritual hunger is not an eating disorder, Mr. Gould, and your wife…well, I can't just reinstall the old software. If I can show her the real face of this organization, though, she may well *want* to come home."

"Jesus," Gould sighed. "I don't even know what fucking religion they practice. She's been chanting lately. What is it, some Hindu thing?"

"They seem to pitch mostly to disillusioned Catholics."

"Christ," said Gould, whom Raszer guessed had not had a religious thought since his *bar mitzvah*. "Why couldn't she have joined the Scientologists? At least they do career counseling." Raszer accepted the invitation to laugh. "What is it, exactly, that they believe, Mr. Raszer?"

"The letters found after Grenoble are a smorgasbord of New Age gospel and Rosicrucian mysticism, but that's all for public consumption. I'm sure there's more to it. The danger for Sofia is that they also seem to have a huge persecution complex, and with good reason. There are five separate task forces in eight countries investigating banking, bribery, arms trafficking—you name it. You know what happens when true believers feel surrounded, right? Waco. Jonestown. Do you know the story of Masada, Mr. Gould?"

"I'm a Jew, aren't I?"

"Well, I wouldn't presume to know, sir."

"Right, but listen, for six a week, I don't want a lot of mystical *mishegaas*, okay? I want to know if my wife – or my bank account – is in danger. And I want to know about this little French *putz*, Luc…"

"Fourché, who your wife claims to have met in Cannes. There's a problem with him, though, Mr. Gould."

"What's that? And for chrissakes, call me Larry."

"Interpol has four different files on Luc Fourché. Four files, four different men, one of whom died in Grenoble. You don't have a photograph, do you?"

"No, but I can sure as hell describe the son of a bitch."

"Good," Raszer said, getting up. "We'll get to that." Gould rose as well, and Raszer leveled his gaze. "One more personal question, Larry. Are you concerned that your wife and this man are having an affair?"

Gould considered the question, as if for the first time. "Not a chance," Gould answered a little too quickly. "Not her type."

"Everything okay in the bedroom then?" Raszer was out of line but had to ask. The difference in their ages made it look like a showcase marriage.

"Let's put it this way, Mr. Raszer; it's as okay as her moods and my schedule will allow. Any more personal questions?"

"There's an old bit of Jewish folklore, Mr. Gould. Romance your wife at least once a week, preferably on the eve of the Sabbath. Otherwise, the Devil may step in and father your evil twin." Raszer extended his hand and smiled empathetically.

Gould warily accepted the extended hand. "I've got a personal question for you."

"Shoot," Raszer said, leaning back onto the big mahogany desk.

"You come highly recommended, but you have an unusual, some might even say 'suspect,' profession. You say you're not a deprogrammer. Hell, you look more like a priest. Why do you do this?"

Raszer smiled. He didn't mind being called to account. "I suppose because faith is too important an issue to be left to the preachers. People are hungry, and they're swallowing a lot of stuff they shouldn't, but the hunger is real. You wanna know my ulterior motive? I'd like to know if there's anything out there worth believing in."

"So, you're what? A spiritual racket-buster?"

Raszer laughed. "I may have to get new business cards."

"There must be easier ways for a bright guy to make a living."

Raszer lowered his head. "You've put your wife's soul in my hand. When I was nineteen…"

Gould had folded his hands, ready for the pitch.

THE MEETING HAD taken place on April Fool's Day. Now it was Father's Day, another marker in time. Raszer leaned into the wobbly pine railing of the old spa's deck and chuckled, recalling how Lawrence Gould had responded to his confession as if half-inclined to ask for his check back. His mind was on the memory, but his eyes were on the saloon-style doors of the little haute Western restaurant across the rutted dirt road. The restaurant had a good bar, with a wine list suited to the well-heeled industry types who trekked up from L.A. to get patted down and mud-plastered. Raszer had once found a particularly good *Sancerre* there, and now he started thinking about its cold, flinty slap against the roof of his mouth. He took a last drag on his cigarette.

RASZER HAD CONCLUDED the meeting saying, "Stay in touch, Mr. Gould. If Sofia is A.W.O.L. for more than twelve hours, let me know immediately. Meanwhile, I'll start digging." Raszer had gripped Lawrence Gould's hand, and it had then been his turn to take the other man's measure. For all his stature, the studio head had a damp, weak handshake. It had seemed to Raszer that Gould was not at all sure that he could best the Temple's offer for his wife's affections.

RAZSER DITCHED THE cigarette and headed across the road toward the swinging doors, stopping mid-path to observe a mule deer in the scorched chaparral. The canyon smelled of sage and eucalyptus. He was in Ojai, a sleepy cowboy town about ninety miles north of Los Angeles that came alive once a year to host, of all things, an avant-garde classical music festival. Ojai was nestled in a magnificent transverse valley, reputed to be streaming with telluric potency, and had served as the location for *Shangri-La* in the Ronald Coleman version of *Lost Horizon*. It was also the home of the Krotona Institute, founded by the self-styled sorceress Madame Blavatsky, queen of the 19th century parlor occultists, and it was the Institute's library of arcane texts — as well as Chandra's hands — that had drawn Raszer north on the eve of his departure for the Old World.

Aside from his chronically offended ankle, Raszer felt as fit as he had in more than a year. He'd been on a two-week crash diet that consisted mostly of soy protein and wheatgrass, but where he was going, the fashionable abstemiousness of Southern California would seem as distant as the stars. His hiker's frame and the ruddy flush induced by the sulfur baths suggested good health, but could not entirely mask the deep fissures born of prior excess. When Raszer was not nursing his lost sheep, he was often in need of being nursed.

The place he had come for succor was called Windsor Hot Springs, and the eponymous vein gurgled and steamed sulfurously from a gash in the woods about a hundred yards north of the main building. On that spot a few years ago, the spa's founder and his young son had been killed instantly when the limb of an oak, sawed just short of the breaking point long before by a rare bolt of California lightning, chanced to fall at that moment on the unsuspecting pair as they knelt to inspect the source of their fortune.

*Fortune.* The word danced like Shiva across Raszer's mind as he caught himself staring into the woods. These woods of the West, with their scrub oak, mesquite and tinder-dry brush that crackled underfoot, were different from those back east that he'd known as a boy. There, he'd found himself drawn again and again into the forest's wet, loamy embrace in pursuit of a phantom.

He was just eleven when he first saw — or thought he saw her, darting from mossy tree trunk to lush bracken like a pre-pubescent Morgan le Fey. As he entered adolescence, she assumed more womanly proportions, and his trips to the Hundred-Acre Woods took on an erotic flavor. He would leave the forest with a sweet ache in the region of his solar plexus, and sometimes with an odd but not unpleasant tingling in his nipples that made him feel ashamed. For a time before his thirteenth birthday, he had harbored a secret and terrible fear that he was growing breasts and turning into a woman, but he kept going back anyway. As much as the Woman of the Woods frightened him, she was also his first love.

SOFIA GOULD WAS, likewise, a phantom. Tall and swan-like in bearing, she had an unsettling ability to slip in and out of Raszer's field of view. She had the substance of quicksilver. Her dark beauty was of another century, possibly even another consciousness. She was a beauty for men who loved the ideal of beauty as much as its corporeal expression. In appreciation of this, Raszer found unexpected common ground with her husband.

He had begun his assignment with routine surveillance. Outwardly, it was no different from the work of a divorce dick shadowing an adulterous wife, although the betrayal observed is far more profound. Cult adherents, Raszer had found, exhibited body language and behavior that was either furtive or brazenly purposeful, and this behavior said a lot about their level of devotion. Sofia displayed neither. She simply attended to her life – whether it was prayers to the Virgin at a grotto in Malibu Canyon or visits to her erstwhile agent at ICM – with the practiced detachment of a Parisian shopkeeper closing up for August. It seemed to Raszer that she was already somewhere else – that he was tailing a ghost.

On May 1, he had followed her home from a late afternoon trip to an herbalist on Montana Avenue in upper Santa Monica, and then lingered outside the gates of her Mandeville Canyon home long after she'd vanished through the portico. He sat in his car and gripped the wheel, trip wires snapping in his mind. The jasmine on her trellis, the gables of her Tudor home, the red mailbox at the end of the drive: all had become numinous, haunted by her desire for rebirth and his uncertain pledge to abort it. Although he hadn't yet said the words to Lawrence Gould, Raszer was convinced that Sofia was preparing to die. He came to that conclusion even before getting independent confirmation that the Temple was organizing another field trip.

He left his car as dusk fell and moved quietly around the tall hedge to the west side of the house, where she kept her private bedroom and shaded patio. Raszer hopped the wrought iron fence, landing inside the hedge in a crouch. Fifty yards away, a Mexican gardener was stringing party lights around the shrubbery. Raszer crept to the house and pressed his body into the brick, just beside the frame of her bedroom window.

Sofia was seated at her vanity table, her body masked by the mirror, the right side of her face faintly visible through the lace, haloed by the flicker of a votive candle. Her lips were moving as if in prayer, the right eye open but unseeing. On her vacant reading chair, a book lay open on its face: a history of the Cathar heresy.

The gardener plugged in an extension cord, and the little white lights sprung to life *en masse,* casting the window in an antique glow. Raszer pivoted on his weak ankle and lost his footing. His head bobbed into the frame, and he caught the glint off a surgical blade Sofia held poised in her right hand. She registered the movement and froze, her eye suddenly focused.

Raszer dropped to all fours. He scurried along the hedge until he reached a narrow canal that passed beneath a chain link fence and emptied into the wash and concealing foliage of the canyon. It was possible she'd seen him, but not for long enough to imprint.

Raszer circled back to his car. Two weeks after that, Sofia Gould disappeared, and it was now Razser's job to track her down.

AT 39, RASZER could reasonably claim that he had snatched a personal victory from the jaws of disaster. He had overhauled his identity from the spare parts left after a failed marriage, a venomous custody battle and an acting career that he had determinedly blown away along with numerous powdered substances. His last attempt at professional redemption had led to his being unceremoniously escorted off the Paramount lot. In the midst of his headlong plunge, he had nearly lost his daughter, Brigit, to a rare liver disease. He'd been only blearily aware that she was ill, even thought they had once been thick as thieves. Soon after that, Raszer collapsed. The fall was not a result of Raszer's failure as an actor. It happened due to an act of sabotage perpetrated on himself, by himself. It happened because, in Raszer's words, his life "wasn't right."

When his daughter survived and recovered, he considered it an act of grace. He staggered to his feet, finding himself with a strange flaw in his right eye and a hunger that had been there all along: his desire for what the ancient Greeks had called *gnosis;* direct knowledge of the divine. It was a rarefied passion, shared variously by mushroom-eating shamans, Platonic philosophers and a few odd physicists. To fund his quest, he set about rebuilding the bridges to L.A.'s new money that he hadn't burned beyond repair, and designing a gig that would pay him reasonably well to search for faith in that sprawling, centerless Bedouin camp by the sea. He knew what it was he wanted to do, but there were currently no listings for "Grail Knight" in the Employment Section. He found it instead while browsing the L.A. Weekly Personals:

```
To His Supreme Holiness Chakra Khan: If
my daughter is with you, please send her
home. I will do anything. I will even di-
rect your movie. Charitably, Gordo.
```

The ad had been placed by Gordon Wexler, a successful director of made-for-TV movies, who was fond of quoting New Age aphorisms and had once commented favorably on one of Raszer's performances. It seemed his lonely teenage daughter had taken his enthusiasm for a charismatic stuntman-turned-yogi to the adolescent extreme and run off with the guy.

Raszer tracked her to a trailer camp near Sedona and earned her oily guru's trust posing as a disciple of Carlos Castaneda. For a week, he sat reverently at Chakra Khan's feet, then took the girl to the red rocks for two days and nights on a makeshift vision quest, after which, she accompanied him home to L.A. On the rocks, she told her grateful dad, she'd come to understand that we are never far from God's embrace. Raszer took the success for what it was: beginner's luck. But he'd found a worthy use for his acting skills and a serviceable m.o.: *defrock the false and the true stands naked.*

Raszer was now the sole proprietor and one of only two employees of a highly specialized detective agency that he called, in a wry imitation of West L.A.'s emporiums, Raszer's Edge. The wordplay and its homage to Somerset Maugham worked because his firm was dedicated to a very peculiar kind of missing persons search. In L.A., you had to have an angle and the more acutely it was carved, the better your chances for cutting through the milky haze that lay over the city on most days.

On the first couple of jobs, he winged it in the time-honored style of Hollywood, where you are what you say you are. Then he buckled down, took the required 300 hours for a P.I. license and hit the books and the Internet for a solid year. He spent three months in the Sangre de Cristo Mountains with a Hopi tracker. From the Salvadoran ex-Marxist guerilla fighter who tended his neighbor's pool (and now aspired to bourgeois normalcy), he learned to use a knife. He studied the *Corpus Hermeticum, The Zohar* and the writings of Plotinus. He underwent a reasonably intense course of Jungian therapy with what was left of his Screen Actors Guild medical insurance. Along the way, he read the Bible for the first time.

Raszer presented himself to clients as a shepherd, and he never took a fee unless he was fairly certain that the sheep had stumbled into barren pasture. He disliked terms like, "cult victim," and referred to the objects of his searches as "strays." He understood people like Sofia Gould; how they were haunted at every turn by Peggy Lee's plaintive *is that all there is?* Raszer was an outsider, too, and outsiders understood both the hunger for inclusion and the desire to flee. The world is too much with them.

The key to Raszer's fascination with *terra incognita* may have lain in the yellowed stack of vintage *Fantasy* comics that he still kept in the hall closet, or in the H. Rider Haggard novels he'd read as a boy. It had assuredly burgeoned with the biography of Sir Richard Francis Burton he'd encountered at twenty-one. Burton, the prodigious British explorer, secret agent and linguist who had shocked Victorian sensibilities with the first English translations of *The Kama Sutra,* had been Raszer's most enduring hero. It was in Burton's journals that he had first run across the word *gnosis*. There were also the events of his 19th year, the events he had summarized for Lawrence Gould. That was the year his phantom lady reappeared in a new guise and demanded a price much higher than a walk in the woods.

A more recent impetus behind Raszer's curious enterprise lay in his exclusion four years prior from his father's last will and testament. The old man, who'd fashioned himself as a Kerouac-style vagabond, had deserted his family when Raszer was five, appearing only in tantalizing cameos throughout Raszer's youth. On his death, he finally cut the cord; *I make no provision in this will for my only son, to whom I have left other gifts.* From that moment, Raszer felt himself to be, essentially, an orphan, and now he received handsome fees to track down kindred souls. With each dollar he collected, he earned back small pieces of the legacy his father had denied him.

On the day Lawrence Gould sent him off to find his Sofia, Raszer had felt an uneasy sense of fruition. He had sacrificed goats with Satanists and waited on desolate hillsides for the arrival of flying saucers, all for the sake of a good bounty and a peek behind the veil, but this was the case he'd rewritten his life for.

THE TEMPLE OF the Sun was far and away the most secretive organization Raszer had ever been asked to penetrate. Its geographical roots were in the Lake Leman district near Geneva, Switzerland, from where it had spread to France, French Canada and even Australia. One Canadian official had recently suggested that the cult was involved in money laundering, bank fraud, arms trafficking and even acts of political terrorism, but these charges were frequently leveled against sects in an attempt to flush them out or frighten them into dissolution. This particular gang was operating in a murky area where the line between murder and suicide was obscured by the smoke of sacrament. The word "occult," Raszer knew, meant neither "magical" nor "supernatural," but simply…hidden.

Raszer had been off the payroll for a week when Sofia vanished on May 12. Despite the urgency of Raszer's warnings, Gould had not wanted to fork over another week's salary for photographs of his wife reading martyrdom histories in the Malibu hills, even though he had found the scalpel in her vanity drawer and a sun sign drawn in blood around the date of June 20 in her diary. He decided instead to put her in the hospital, and that must have done it. She took only a single suitcase-full of clothing, and left the big house in Brentwood otherwise undisturbed, but for a puzzling note laid upon his pillow.

It was two days before Gould could bring himself to phone Raszer. Gould seemed embarrassed, maybe even ashamed. Perhaps he hadn't taken the conjugal advice and now felt like the Devil's cuckold.

"Don't blame yourself, Lawrence," Raszer counseled. "From what I've learned, these people have a serious pitch. Let's just get on this before she gets too far."

"I read on the net," Gould stammered, "that Princess Grace was in with these nuts. They say it's what got her killed."

"There's no question we're dealing with very expensive snake oil here; if snake oil it is."

"What the hell is a Cathar? Some weird sex cult?"

Raszer allowed himself a private smile. Religion was easily the least understood aspect of human endeavor, *except* perhaps for sex.

"A medieval Christian-Dualist sect from the South of France. They believed that the material world was the creation of the Devil. The Church trumped up charges of sexual perversion, and the Pope's armies wiped them out, down to the last man, woman and child. Why?"

"I mentioned a few weeks ago that maybe we should try again to have a kid. Sofia's got some plumbing problems but most of the doctors seem to think it's psychosomatic. She said that as a Cathar, she couldn't bring a child into this world."

"That's really important, Lawrence. Read me the note."

"It's not much," Gould said. Raszer could hear him unfolding it and sensed the man's big hands were shaking. "It says, *Dearest Larry. Try not to hate me too much. I have tried so hard to live in your world, but it's dark all the time, like a drug-sleep I can't wake up from. Where I'm going, the light is brilliant and clear. Pray for me, if you can. Did you know that the most beautiful word in the English language is oblivion? Love, Sofia.'"*

"Shit," Raszer blurted, forgetting his bedside manner.

"What the hell is this, Raszer?"

"It's a suicide note, Lawrence. Written five weeks in advance."

"Fuck me."

"You said she'd tried once before."

"Younger. Maybe fifteen. She's got the scars on her wrists."

Raszer tugged unconsciously at his own sleeve, craving a smoke.

"This isn't going to be easy, Larry, but I will find her."

Over the following weeks, the two men had spoken often, Gould always anxious to know what Raszer had come up with, and Raszer usually offering the same response, "Hang tight, Lawrence. I need to pin her down." He would not board a plane until he had located Sofia down to a square block and was certain that his approach would not trigger flight. Reliable data was very slow in coming.

Raszer had made one startling discovery that not even the task force in Lyon had stumbled on. He played out an obscure lead from a jailhouse informant in Montreal, and learned that the present-day Temple was a schismatic offshoot from a crypto-Masonic lodge formed in 1970 that had called itself the Reformed Temple. Its founder had been a former Gestapo member, known to travel in the clandestine world of European secret police organizations. The virulent bloodline of the Reformed Temple could be traced all the way back to the Germanen Order, a theosophical lodge founded in 1912, counting among its initiates a young Adolph Hitler. It seemed an odd legacy to have engendered the loyalty of a rich American girl with a Jewish surname. What did all this Aryan mischief have to do with Sofia's 12th century soulmates, the martyred Cathars of Montsegur? And was the Temple's pitch earnest fanaticism or highbrow con? Who, if anyone, would profit by the death of these innocents?

RASZER STEPPED THROUGH the saloon doors into the little bar and ordered his white wine, then reconsidered.

"Scratch the Sancerre," he corrected the leather-skinned bartender. "Make it scotch, over ice."

On the borderlands that Stephan Raszer had made his beat, easy political and ethical distinctions dissolved, and everyone played a high stakes game of "button, button; who's got the button?" The "button" was nothing less than the Elixir of Immortality, and in its quest were made some strange bedfellows.

Raszer scanned the rack for his favorite bar scotch. "White Horse, please."

He had left himself the evening to return via the 101 to L.A. and cross the last few t's before a noon flight, first to Montreal, then to London before continuing to his final destination. A scant two weeks earlier, the prospects for pinning down Sofia before her solstice date with the reaper had seemed bleak. His leads had dried up, informants dummied up. He'd been very close to turning the case over to Interpol, though he feared that was as good as signing her death warrant. Cult suicides were often precipitated by the perceived proximity of the "Inquisition." He had narrowed her possible location to three venues: Martinique, Tenerife or Prague, but it was not until he put his own ass fully on the fire that things got cooking. They reached a boiling point when a man named Stocker Hinge returned his phone call.

Hinge was an erudite and somewhat controversial researcher in the field of "emerging religions." He was a "mole" and had written his best papers from deep inside the sects he'd penetrated. He also had an odd thing for limericks. Raszer had been initially reluctant to enlist one of his own kind in the quest. Finally, he'd had no other choice. On June 1st, Stocker Hinge phoned Raszer from a private line in his office at the *Centre pour L'Observation des Nouvelles Sectes* in Montreal, the city that was purportedly the current base of the Temple. Hinge's message was brief and cryptic, "I may have something for you, Stephan. I'm going to introduce you to a man we'll call Mr. X."

"Why not Mr. Ed, the talking horse?" The cloak and dagger stuff always tickled Raszer. Hinge missed the joke.

Hinge went on to propose a risky gambit that would put Raszer at the center of the ceremony and advance Mr. X's agenda, as yet troublingly undefined. All that was clear was that he held a grudge and wanted to stick it to his erstwhile comrades. For his part, Hinge would get a vicarious peek behind the velvet curtain, *sans* any risk. He probably intended to use Raszer's experience as the basis for his next paper, but it didn't matter. In agreeing to the plan, Raszer got the information he needed. Sofia Gould was in Prague, capitol of the Czech Republic.

SHOOTING PAST THE Technicolor green soybean fields north of Camarillo, Raszer dropped his vintage Avanti into third gear just to hear the engine's sweet protest. He fumbled in the glove box for a tape and popped in Geoffrey Oryema, the Ugandan Leonard Cohen. The sound system in Raszer's old coupe was high-end mono, and he'd searched long and hard for the components – he thought the idea of stereophonic sound in a moving vehicle with a noise floor of 80 db was a joke.

The throbbing body rhythms of the African music brought Raszer back to the massage table and the honeyed overtones of the kalimba evoked the remembered scent of a South African sojourn: sweet, grassy air, musk oil and hashish. For less than an instant, he flashed on damp, coffee skin in a hut near Mmabatho, and felt a tingle in his groin, recalling the way the *Lesotho* girl had lifted her dyed skirts and opened herself to him without the slightest hint of Western shame. The sense memory of her sex took Raszer tumbling again across space-time to a remote Coptic monastery in Egypt.

*There it is again.* The residual vibration of sex and the trailing perfume of the oceanic feminine were inseparable in Raszer's mind from his groping attraction to mystical experience, notwithstanding the fact that women had a habit of dangling his feet over the fire. Women wanted something from him, of that he was certain, but he'd lost the memory of what it was. He no longer heard the secret language they spoke, though he was sure he once had. Back then, in the woods, before his nineteenth birthday.

He downshifted at the Hwy. 134 junction, and eased over into the right lane, heading down through the Cahuenga Pass into Hollywood and his Whitley Heights home office. There would undoubtedly be another binder-full of briefing papers for him to read over dinner, prepared (the papers, not the dinner) with consummate skill by his research assistant and other half, Monica Lord.

# 3

## THE LADY OF THE LAKE

*Women who seek to be the equal of men lack ambition.*

— Timothy Leary

MONICA LORD LICKED her finger and dabbed a drop of carrot-ginseng juice off the front of Raszer's briefing book. She affixed a Post-It note, *Hope it's a page-turner. See you when the cock crows. M.,* and set the binder on the bar where Raszer typically took his dinners. The bar stood at about a seventy-five degree angle to an enormous picture window that looked southwest toward the canyon. Sometimes, when they'd done a good day's work and Raszer didn't have to burn the midnight oil, he would make margaritas in time for them to toast the setting sun. He'd remove the frosted glasses from the freezer and dredge them in sea salt before straining the concoction, to which he always added mescal, into them. Monica had known Stephan Raszer for seven years and could still remember when he'd been more inclined to rim his margaritas with crystal methedrine.

The man she now worked for was a recalibrated version of the intense but miscast actor for whom she'd agreed to put aside her journalistic goals and play publicist. He was the same material, but newly infused, like an inert gas that fluoresces when current is applied. Counter to the norm in so many "recovery stories," Raszer had not abandoned all his vices in a Calvinistic purge. He simply abandoned the compulsive excesses that had led to his fall, excesses that, to Monica's way of thinking, were the sidecars of perfectionism. Now, Raszer kept his bad habits as proof of fallibility, like the flaws deliberately left in a Persian rug so as not to offend God.

Monica had been there during Raszer's brief to B-movie phase in the early 90's, a time when Roger Corman noticed him, and casting agents compared him to a young Steve McQueen. And she'd been there throughout his long fall, though she did not flatter herself that she had, in any sense, caught him. Nobody could have caught Raszer; his trajectory was pre-plotted. But she remained, always, within earshot of his screams.

She was there when the parts stopped coming and he could no longer afford to pay her, but did anyway, with VISA's he collected like baseball cards and traded for a month's grace at a time. She had by then acquired a handful of other clients whose fees paid the rent on her North Hollywood efficiency. She was there when the liquor and the dope made him abusive and pathetic, and every audition was faced like an appearance before the Star Chamber. She was there when his wife, a rich man's daughter from the east, slapped a restraining order on him and took away the one human being who *never* questioned his worth: his five year-old soul child, Brigit. And she was there when they rushed him into Cedars Sinai, his heart rate pushing one-ninety and a look on his face that said, "Let it come down."

MONICA WALKED THROUGH his house like an actress on her marks, switching off the floor and table lamps that augmented the plentiful natural light. Raszer hated overhead lights, preferring small, defined pools of illumination that drew the eye and invited reveries. In the narrow hallway, she paused for a moment outside his bedroom, where the main source of light was a stained glass window depicting Galahad's vision of the Grail. He had spent the proceeds of a three-month gig on it. Raszer was like that. The rest of the room was unfurnished but for a futon.

Why had she remained in the orbit of a man once so manifestly determined to crash and burn? Monica guessed that it was because he was the most interesting person she had ever met. And though she wouldn't have copped to it then, it might also have been on a hunch that his collapse would yield a supernova.

She turned off the hall light. A ray from the retiring sun found the pane of stained glass, precisely in the spot that Raszer and his general contractor had argued over, and the beam refracted off the Grail like the time-lapse blooming of a gilded rose.

THEY HAD MET in the bar at the Hollywood Roosevelt Hotel, where she had come for a meeting with a hot young movie executive who'd dangled a job in the studio's press relations department. The executive was late, and she had graduated from iced tea to gin and tonic, the first step to saying, "fuck it." The indignity of her situation was not entirely relieved by the glamour that surrounded her. She had studied to be an investigative journalist, and now she faced a career of making turkeys look like peacocks. She'd brought a book along so as not to look unoccupied and there-

fore undesirable. A strand of her long, straight, newly streaked hair fell
over an eye and brushed the open page. She pushed the hair back from her
face and held it there while completing the paragraph, unconsciously letting a shoe drop to the floor as she did when reading at home. A gentle
tingle in her tailbone caused her to look up, and she caught a guy at the
end of the bar admiring her. After a beat, she tugged reflexively on the
hem of her skirt and pretended to continue reading.

The executive never showed, but she and Stephan Raszer each had
three more gin and tonics and spent three hours in the lobby bar of the
Roosevelt. She'd been wrong to presume that he'd been ogling her thigh.
Well, *no*. He *had* been looking at her thigh, but as part of the whole package, and the package had suggested to him someone who wanted to be
someplace else. There was this thing with Raszer, and it was there even
before his epiphany. Sex was not separable from identity. When he looked
at her, even now, he drank in the whole punchbowl, and subverted in a
heartbeat the feminist notion that relationships can be compartmentalized.
Still, they had never been lovers, and, except for one time when they'd
gotten stoned on bootleg absinthe, they'd never gotten past first base.
*Fucking*, Raszer said, was for strangers, for whom it offered the only path
to intimacy. He and Monica had not been strangers, even at the first.

Raszer adored women. They either adored him back or were furious
with him. He saw something in women that most of them didn't see in
themselves, something holy and forgotten.

"*Eve* was the first initiate," he'd once said. "She got a bad rap." Then
he'd smiled and added, "I've always liked girls who stick their noses where
they shouldn't be."

ONE DAY, AFTER Raszer's Edge had been in operation for about a
year, Monica found herself on the Internet, pulling down data on a resur-
gence of Aryan Nation activity in eastern Oregon. An aromatherapy candle
burned at her side. "English Rose for Inner Beauty," the label said.

Raszer wandered in to find his cigarettes and check on her progress.
He glanced at the screen.

"Think our little skinhead's in Oregon?"

"Could be," she said. "I see the same pattern of petty theft up and
down the Cascades."

Raszer leaned in to sniff the candle and gave a snort. "That's not
what a rose smells like. A woman's scent is the only aromatherapy I'll ever
need."

He'd walked away without another word, leaving her, as usual, wondering whether he'd uttered something flagrantly crude or cryptically sublime. Later, he gave her a translation of 12th century troubadour poems by *Chretien de Troyes* for her birthday, and she began to see where he was coming from. After that, she was never again able to write him off entirely as a sexual throwback, if indeed she ever had – not even when he told her that a green sweater-dress she sometimes wore made her ass look, "as supple as the green signal hills in Somerset." There were bawdier sentiments than that in the *Song of Solomon.* Raszer was a throwback, all right, but of another sort. That there was a connection between his apotheosis of the feminine and the weird visions he'd had since adolescence had, of course, occurred to her, but she knew it was not quite that pat.

IN THE HOSPITAL following his big dive, with IV tubes running to both wrists and EKG and EEG taps all over his body, he told her of his brush with the infinite, and he revealed to her what three years later he revealed to Lawrence Gould.

"When I was nineteen," he told her, in a voice rendered flat by the sedatives, "I came close to joining a monastic order." She held onto his hand and scooted a chair nearer his bedside.

"The Holy Order of the Anthropos. Founded by three black sheep: a renegade Catholic priest, a Jewish mystic, and a Muslim doctor. It wasn't flaky, but it definitely wasn't orthodox. I was in my second year of college, studying acting so that I could be rich and famous and self-actualized, but there was a part of me that, well— This thing hit me like a bolt from the blue. It seemed so fucking true, this idea that all the spokes had a common hub. I went home for Spring Break and announced that I was leaving the material world for a retreat in upstate New York. My mother freaked. In those days, nobody was thinking that way. It was 'morning again in America," junk bonds and Madonna, remember?"

Monica remembered, though less objectively. She was a child of Ronald Reagan's deification of capital. She noticed what seemed to be a dark spot on the iris of Raszer's right eye. A broken blood vessel, she reasoned. From the stress.

"The whole fucking world came down on me," he continued. "My friends, relatives…my childhood shrink. I stuck to my guns, but it got to me. There was also a part of me that wasn't *ready* to leave the world. The Order wanted me to give up everything: *sex, red meat and psychotropic substances* – three of my favorite things. Not to mention *ambition.* I started to tear down the middle. I remember feeling it start *right here,* on the top of my head. On the day I was supposed to go back to school, I cracked up. I mean a seismic, *San Andreas Fault* sort of a crack-up. They had me on Thorazine for more than a year. It was somewhere in there – maybe on a day when they thought they could get away with reducing my medication – that *She* came again."

Monica blinked and waited for elaboration. "Anyhow," he concluded, abruptly jumping an eon of experience, "I got better. I finished school and eventually made it out here. I tried to stay on task, even when I saw that friends who had it all were more miserable than ever. I did okay…until recently."

Before she left that day, Monica saw the dark spot in his eye flare like an ember.

After that day, Raszer wasn't scared anymore. He took up rock climbing, sometimes persuading her to come along. One day, on Suicide Rock near Idyllwild, she asked him why the truth couldn't be as plain to see as the rock face an inch from her nose. "Because," he said, "God likes to play hide 'n seek, only we're always 'it.'"

THE SUN'S LIGHT dropped below the windowpane, and Monica turned from Raszer's room. She walked into the front room, which faced Whitley Drive and served as their office, and clicked off the rocker switch that powered all the auxiliary communications equipment, leaving the main computer on. A small galaxy of blue and green LED's twinkled off.

She instructed the Mac to wake Raszer at six with Beethoven's *Eroica* Symphony. Then she armed the security system, locked the twin deadbolts and stepped out into the dusk.

RASZER PULLED INTO the driveway of the three-bedroom Spanish in the scrubby, laurel-scented Hollywood Hills. He had come to prefer Old Hollywood to the trendier Westside turf because he thought it held what little residue of real magic the city had left to offer.

If you drove up Beachwood Canyon to the Hollywood reservoir with the right light throwing the desert succulents into relief, you could still feel a bit of the cheap alchemy the town had once promised. From the shadowed corners of these little bungalows had once emerged would be Gene Tierneys and Katharine Hepburns, their parted lips painted full and blood red to accent smiles as white and fine as any prized courtesan's. They were tiny things, mostly, but possessed of a towering, carnivorous ambition to be transformed from the cow town girls they knew they were into the goddesses they knew they ought to be. And Hollywood, like all places of alchemical potency, had been host to grotesque excesses – its Black Dahlias, its Fatty Arbuckles – existing right alongside its most sublime creations.

They still came west: the restless, the shadow-children, the formless looking for form and an awful lot of them still lived in Hollywood. So did Stephan Raszer. Hollywood, he sometimes mused, was a *golem* factory.

Raszer's office reflected the fastidiousness of a CPA cluttered with the bric-a-brac of an eccentric archeologist. Whatever order existed was Monica's doing. Raszer hadn't been able to handle being managed by his wife, but he took it from Monica. He called her his *Supergirl Friday*, even though he knew it was a button-pusher, but she got the joke all right. Besides being a superb digger, she had become, by default, the firm's marketing rep. Raszer possessed a chameleon's knack for blending with even the most exotic surroundings, but he was a lousy salesman. It was often Monica who generated the leads, which he followed. She rooted them out in everything from FBI and Interpol bulletins to society columns. The rich could afford to be seduced away from the material world by the promise of Paradise, for they could always come back to Laguna Beach if *Shangri-La* failed to materialize. Raszer never scoffed at them. Saint Francis had been a rich man, too.

The motley appearance of their office belied the sophistication of the telecommunications and computer hardware they'd installed over the past two years; they could interface with virtually any bureau or police agency worldwide, and could do everything from photo enhancements and fake i.d.'s to credit checks, not all of which was entirely legal. Monica had written most of the programs, and used her networking skills to reel him in from more than one brush with disaster, the most recent of which had come at the hands of an angry mob of celebrants at a bogus Santeria Mass in Barbados.

HE DISARMED THE security system and passed through the house, turning on just enough lamps to see his way, though he knew his way well. He dropped his book bag on the sofa and headed straight for the bar, where she'd left the binder with the day's briefing on the results of her research. There was a half-empty bottle of a decent *Medoc* and a covered cheese plate with what remained of a good-sized slab of dry, Spanish *manchego*. He poured himself a glass, sliced off a piece and hoisted himself onto a stool to review her work.

The latest entry was on top, but the binder was an inch-and-a-half thick with three months' digging into the origins, doctrine, personnel and criminal history of The Temple of the Sun. While Raszer tended to focus on belief systems and ritual, as befitted the man who'd have to slip into the party without having his invitation questioned, Monica's bent was facts, and particularly facts that tended to build a case *against* legitimacy. It was the muckraker in her, and it was also because she'd had a close encounter with L. Ron Hubbard's *thetans* when younger. She was adversarial; Raszer was circumspect.

"Look first," he'd counsel her, "for what *attracted* our stray in the first place. Once you've got that, you can deconstruct it."

He took a sip of wine and opened the binder. Her summaries were duplicated in his e-mailbox, and the bold-faced items were links useable for further exploration on the Internet. As always, she'd provided a title:

## WHY THE TEMPLE IS IN PRAGUE

M.L.6/16/00 – Prague, Czech Republic. Former imperial city of Bohemia. Long-held association with the occult, esp. **alchemy**, **Rosicrucianism,** and **kabbalah**. It was in the Old-New Synagogue (Jewish Quarter) that **Rabbi Low** was said to have conjured the **Golem**, a 16<sup>th</sup> c. Jewish "Frankenstein." Prague was ruled by the Austrian **Hapsburgs** from 1589-1918. Occult activity reached peak with **Emperor Rudolf II** (1576-1611), patron of alchemists like Doctor **John Dee**, astrologer to Queen Elizabeth & creator of the **Monas Hieroglyphica**, the symbol found on the suicide note at Grenoble. Dee came to Prague in the 1580's, accompanied by his "skrier" and probable charlatan, the earless **Edward Kelley**. (Here Raszer scribbled in the margin, *No. Kelley was a skunk but not a charlatan!*) Using Kelley as a medium, Dee had deciphered an angelic language he called **Enochian**, so-called because originally revealed by the angel **Uriel** to the Hebrew prophet **Enoch**. Dee used the language in his alchemical attempts at **theurgy**, the restoration of mortal flesh to its original angelic essence. Dee performed his experiments in the **Powder Tower** at Hradcany Castle. Dee also brought with him a rare document now known as the **Voynich Manuscript**, attributed by Dee to **Roger Bacon**. Others have claimed it to be the legendary **Cathar** treasure, smuggled out of Montsegur with the aid of the **Knights Templar**, or even the papers found by Father Sanieure at **Rennes le Chateau**. Written in an indecipherable script, it has been called "the most mysterious manuscript in the world." Many attempts to decode it, including Dee (see Appendix 3C – "The Alchemical Cookbook," a thesis by your cover, Professor Noel Branch). In 1973, at the heart of the Watergate scandal, Nixon and Kissinger directed the NSA to convene a top secret symposium on the Voynich. Is this a link to right-wing **Masonic** groups, like **SAC, P2** or the **Grand Loge Alpina**? In any case, Dee got booted out of Prague and died a pauper, while the Hapsburgs reigned on for 400 years. Nazis and Communists held court from 1918 until 1989, when came the Velvet Revolution and **Vaclav Havel**.

Raszer lifted his eyes from the page and sliced off another hunk of the pungent, salty cheese. There were another six pages of annotation, but they'd covered all this in depth a hundred times. The bit about Nixon and the Voynich M.S. intrigued the hell out of him, and he made a note to himself to re-read Noel Branch's paper on the oddball document, for it was *as* Professor Noel Branch that Raszer would gain his *entre* to the ceremony now about to commence in Prague. Before closing the binder, one other item regarding John Dee caught his eye:

John Dee was reputedly the first spy in Her Majesty's Secret Service. He signed his missives to the Virgin Queen with the code name: **007.**

Monica had come up with that one on her own. It was things like this that affirmed for Raszer that truth is indeed stranger than fiction, and the world a sphere of endless fascination. He picked up his wine glass and retired to the library.

"PASSPORTS, TICKETS, ITINERARY and contact list. You're three hours in Montreal for the meeting. Mr. X's driver will meet you at the airport and take you to the *St. Casimir* address, where Stocker Hinge will join you. After the powwow, you're back to the airport for the Virgin Atlantic red-eye to London. Jeanette will see you off from the Terminal B bar. On Monday, the British Air flight gets you into Prague just before noon.

"Don't eat salad for two or three days until your stomach acclimates. The lettuce is full of pesticide even though they say it's far better than it used to be. AIDS awareness is not what it is in the major Euro capitals, and they're having their own *summer of love* over there," Monica paused, finally, to catch her breath. "Be a good boy," she admonished.

Raszer saluted and accepted the updated binder. It was 7:50 a.m. and the *Eroica* was still ringing in his ears.

"Now, Dr. Branch," she began again, "let's get you into character one more time."

MONICA HAD GOTTEN in at 7:03, radiant from a three-mile run through Griffith Park, and found Raszer sprawled across the Moroccan cushions on the floor of his library. An antique copy of a strange collection of arcane theorems, *The Monas Hieroglyphica of Dr. John Dee* lay at his side, open to a hand-drawn rendering of the symbol itself.

"Did you sleep?"

"Yeah. Enough," he'd said groggily, and smiled. The morning light through the French doors leading to his patio and herb garden had caught her just right. Penelope in a slit skirt. "You look good."

Monica nodded toward the book. "What is it exactly, Raszer? That glyph?"

"The Monad? It's a 16th century stab at a unified field theory of existence. It's what physicists nowadays would call a 'simplex,' describing the act of creation; the sequence by which material reality unfolds from the void, from the *prima material.* Astrologically, it's the copulation of the sun and moon under the influence of Mercurius, the god of transit between the universes. It enfolds both male and female principles."

She shook her head. He was wired at seven a.m. "It's a sex symbol?"

"Sort of. Alchemy is full of sexual metaphor – the *semen solaire* and all of that. Only it's not, uh, Dick and Jane. The perfected human can have sex with himself."

"Bet you'd like that," she said. "You want an espresso?"

"Triple." He rolled off the cushions and stretched like a big cat.

"So what's the connection?" she prodded. "From what I've read, Dee seems like a humanist, a guy who wanted to bring, I don't know, some kind of magical wisdom into the world. What does that have to do with suicide and infanticide?"

"You're right," Raszer said, levering himself up from a lotus position. "He was. I don't get it, either; unless what they're about is *reversing* the sequence. Dee was part of this intellectual underground – hell, maybe the *founder* of it – of heavyweight scholars and mystics who called themselves 'The Invisible College.' They thought that the whole Catholic-Moslem-Jewish rift could be healed in a global religion based on ancient Egyptian wisdom – an end to religious warfare."

"Like the Sufi ideal," Monica said. "The many paths lead to the One."

"Right. They asked people to turn on to the angels in their midst, and tune out the bigots in the Church and the universities. Now, based on the documents we've seen, our Templars in Prague seem to think they're in some way linked to the tradition, but something's wrong."

"Yeah," she said. "They're not busy being born. They're busy dying."

"Dee was trying to open up a channel from Heaven, but—"

"Maybe they want to go back. Maybe that's what the Sirius thing is about."

"That's not supposed to happen before Judgment Day. In the scriptures, there are only three instances of true ascension."

"Jesus, Mary," Monica said. "And who else?"

"Enoch, the prophet. And his book is apocryphal. I confess, I'm stumped."

"And you're going as a Temple *credente* and renowned expert on Renaissance alchemy? And Professor Noel Brach is supposed to be a native Canadian to boot?

"Got a ringer this time, eh?" Raszer followed her into the kitchen.

"Well, you've got an eleven hour flight to figure it all out."

"Okay, let me get caffeinated, then do your thing and prep me once more."

THEY SAT AT their respective desks, opened their notebooks and began the practiced ritual of bestowing the identity he would carry for the duration of his mission. He lit an American Spirit cigarette and opened his briefing book. She sat in front of him, parking her long legs on his desk. Her feet were bare.

"Hello, Mr. Noel Branch, Professor of Renaissance Philology at the University of Quebec, academic liaison and elect *auditore* for The Temple of the Sun—wow!" Monica flipped the two-toned bangs out of her face. "You've got some issues. Sodomized by a parish priest at twelve...that accounts for some anti-Catholic bias."

"Forever changed the way I hear, *thy rod and thy staff, they comfort me.*"

Monica winced. "Twice reprimanded by the University regents for practicing 'sex magic' with the co-eds."

"Now I'm warming to my role."

"But you've also done some *serious* work."

DR. NOEL BRANCH was a Temple 'officiator' who was due in Prague on Monday to chronicle the cult's next voyage for posterity. According to the shadowy Mr. X, the Temple of the Sun had a number of such carefully selected *auditores* in academia and business, and no final journey was undertaken without a witness from outside the circle present. It had occurred to

Raszer that the function might serve a legal as well as a historical purpose, as the *auditore* would be able to attest in any court – whether earthly or celestial – that the participants had willingly turned over their estates and given up the ghost.

In any case, it was an honor to be so selected, and it must have come as a profound disappointment to Professor Branch to be informed by his "section chief," Mr. X, that he would not be going to Prague, after all. He was to be dispatched on sabbatical to a writer's cabin (presumably a Temple "safe house") in the Canadian outback, where he was to write a grand history of the neo-Templar movement in the 20th century. Stephan Raszer, who had finally found an honorable use for his acting talents, was to take his place.

"NO TELEPHONES THIS time, Raszer," Monica directed, admonishing him with her bare right foot. He lost his focus momentarily while considering that her toenails had gone from mauve to chartreuse, "other than secure lines. These people are way too sharp; they're the cult equivalent of a German multinational. We'll talk by e-mail – keep your Powerbook batteries charged. I'm bouncing off two or three satellites before I get to you, and if they do get into your files, everything will lead them back to a server I've set up in Montreal."

Raszer dragged the cigarette down to the filter and crushed it. "And Mr. X has certified through Hinge that none of the gang in Prague has ever actually met Branch or knows what he looks like?"

"If we can believe him."

"Well, that part fits," Raszer affirmed. "Branch is a sort of *consigliere;* he has to keep his nose clean. Mr. Ed probably set him up to have total deniability. How long does he think we can keep the real Dr. Branch in the woods?"

"Three days, max," was her sober reply. "The professor's no dummy. Fortunately for us, he's a womanizer and he's used to following Mr. X's orders. It's up to Jeanette to keep him entertained and sedated. I wouldn't want her job."

"That's okay; she probably wouldn't want yours. Women like Jeanette are danger junkies."

"She's still a woman, Raszer. If she goes, the whole bridge falls down."

DESPITE MR. X'S assurances that Branch was being generously compensated for his compliance, Raszer had felt the need to buy some extra insurance. That's where Jeanette Molineux had come in. Out on the perimeter where Raszer lived, there were a handful of hired guns that cared about karma, old souls who had seen their minds blown in the sixties and seventies and then scabbed over in the mercenary eighties. Jeanette was one of them; wise, witchy and not at all afraid of death. She'd already died a thousand times. Raszer was to rendezvous briefly with her in Montreal, before she boarded a small, private plane and headed for Thunder Bay as Noel Branch's escort and amanuensis.

He was also to have in Montreal his first and only face-to-face meeting with his two co-conspirators. Mr. X had something to give the detective, and wanted to handle it personally and with secrecy worthy of an Israeli commando strike. Raszer had determined that his own code name for the meeting should be "Wilbur." He hoped he would get a chance to press Mr. Ed for his motive, and for an answer to the one question that no amount of background work had answered. Had Luc "the Fork" Fourché, the man Lawrence Gould claimed had spellbound his wife, really died last December on a Grenoble mountaintop, or was he too, in Prague, preparing to play master of ceremonies.

"LET'S TALK ABOUT Sofia," Raszer said. "Any contact with her husband?"

"None. Gould was worried enough to blow off a lunch with Sumner Redstone. He's sure she's in way over her head."

"I'm sure he's right," Raszer snorted. "And we're six days and counting until the summer solstice." He stood and put his hand on Monica's big toe. "And the police? Anything on the wires to indicate they're on this?" She shook her head. "Not the Swiss? Or the French?"

"Girl Scout's honor. That prosecutor in Lyon, he may have an inkling, but he's on our side. The police, no."

"Well," he said, "we'll have to let them in sooner or later. Now's not the time. I want to find out how these people get the cream of Europe's jet set to pay for their own executions."

Monica drew her knees up to her chest. She was sometimes not sure if Raszer took evil seriously enough.

"You don't think, Raszer," she said softly, "there's the slightest chance that Sofia has fallen for this guy and plans to scam her husband out of a lot of money?"

"No," he answered. "Not at the moment."

"Gould's twice her age, not especially charming and very rich. And she's—" Monica scrunched up her mouth. "An actress."

"I don't think she's that kind of gold digger."

"You're not falling in love with her, are you? Like that old movie...*Laura?*"

"Dana Andrews," Raszer nodded. "No, but I'm not numb, either. I can see how she could be somebody's *Beatrice*. And I'm not as cynical as you are, *Miss Gen X, I missed the 60's and I'm bitter*. Did we ever hear from her doctor?"

"Yeah. He was a little leery of discussing Sofia's file, so I got Gould on a conference call. No exotic drugs, just common stuff like Zoloft and Prozac. But there's a twist. Sofia Gould hasn't had a normal menstrual period in six years."

Raszer cocked his head and squinted. His mental hard drive temporarily full, he started down the hall for a shower and a shave.

"Raszer," Monica called out. He turned. "Remember when you told me about how the Gnostics believed that we all had a God-spark in us, left over from the *Fall?*" Raszer nodded. "If people believed that, there'd be a revolution."

"The mighty would fall. I think that's what Jesus had in mind."

"And the alchemists...their cover was turning base metal into gold, but what they were really about was more subversive, because *gold* was those hidden God-sparks. And John Dee and his friends were...gold diggers!"

"I'm going to miss you," he said.

"See, I'm not so cynical, Raszer. My world just isn't lit up like yours."

"Now, you're beginning to understand Sofia's choice."

The telephone rang and Monica jumped. She put the receiver to her ear.

"Yes, Mr. Hinge, he's here. I'm just about to get him to the airport. Would you like to speak with him?" She activated the speakerphone.

"Hello, Stocker," said Raszer. *"Ca va?"*

"A Siamese twin from Des Moines...had suffered a wound to the groin...He couldn't perform, and his wife was forlorn, so he asked his twin brother to join."

"You're getting better, Stocker. I only cringed a little. May I take it as a sign of burgeoning friendship that you try your limericks out on me?"

"If you like," Hinge replied, "but friendship is so *banal*. In this enterprise, we are closer to blood brothers."

"Okay, brother. Everything clear up there?"

"I've got a sick mother," Hinge answered in the familiar Quebecois accent, "but other than that, yes. I'll meet you at the house."

"I'm sorry about your mother. How's our Mr. X?"

"Remarkably cool, considering he's not in a witness protection program. And your girl, Jeanette; does she know what she's in for with Dr. Branch?"

"She can take care of herself." Monica rolled her eyes. "See you in a few hours, Stocker." Raszer hung up the phone, somewhat reflectively, and turned to his assistant. "I'd better get ready, partner."

Monica tugged on his shirtsleeve like a bell chain. "One more thing, Raszer," she said soberly. "I can see how Sofia might be drawn into all this history and ritual, but I still don't get the secret police and neo-Nazi connections we've found all over the place. There are more spooks in this story than in a John Le Carre novel."

"Well," he came back, "ask yourself: what objective could an age-old sect that calls itself a 'chivalric order' have in common with the agents of aristocracy?"

"I don't know." She made a grandiose gesture and giggled. *"World domination?"*

"Don't start laughing yet. It's Europe, not Peoria. It's not a 'Coke or a Pepsi' situation. It's all shadow play. *The enemy of my enemy is my friend.* Look, we know that one of the Temple's parent groups was heavily stocked with SAC members in the 70's. Sometimes *State* enlists *Church* to lend it legitimacy. And sometimes good enlists evil in order to compete with indifference. I'm not sure what they're up to, but when Hitler sent his chief archeologist to Montsegur to dig for the Holy Grail, he said something about how seriously Europeans take magic."

Raszer hustled down the hall, but Monica wasn't finished. "Oh, lord and master?"

"Yes?"

"There's a pound of premium, low-fat beef jerky in your duffle bag; in case you get an anxious moment where you can't smoke."

"Jerky I have. At peace I am. You're the best."

"And I did another link-page for you. On the whole Sirius thing."

*"When?"*

"This morning. Before my run."

"Eat your heart out, *Double-O Seven.*"

RASZER STOOD BARE-CHESTED before the steamy bathroom mirror, razor in hand. He was entering middle age, the age of fathers and salesmen, but his skin fit his bones well. Only he could still see the unformed, fear-ridden homunculus that his father had deemed unworthy of love.

Taped on the mirror was a photo of a nine year-old girl squinting into the autumn sun. "Hello, angel," he said aloud.

She lived in Mystic Seaport, Connecticut with her mother, who was rich enough to have benefited from the services of a celebrity divorce lawyer. *Fortune*, he thought again. If he'd had this gig then, he might at least have kept her in the state.

He went with the blade for that difficult place on the upper lip, just under the nose. "Shit!" he hissed as the blood seeped out.

Raszer was about to reach for the toilet paper when he was stilled by the awareness of a thread of light *emanating* from the flaw in the iris of his right eye; a finely focused beam, as when a magnifying glass is held at the proper angle to the sun. The flaw, usually black and opaque, had recently shifted violet. He turned his head and the beam tracked his movement.

At that moment, Raszer lost his equilibrium and clutched the basin. He lost his bearings in the familiar world and thought he heard himself cry out. The seizures had gotten worse and more frequent. He raised his chin with effort and saw, in the mirror in the light of his eye, not his own face but that of a graying old harlot whose mouth curled mordantly. An unfiltered cigarette hung from her crimson lips, and flecks of blue dotted her hair. It was not, in any typical sense, a hallucination. Modern times have no name for it, which was one reason Raszer feared he was again going crazy.

The hag spoke harshly. *"The door swings both ways, Sherlock. Don't let it hit you in the ass on the way out. Caw! Caw!"*

"Go 'way!" Raszer growled, as if drunk. *"Whatyouwantfromme?"*

"Everything," she creaked. Then she was gone and he was bleeding.

RASZER OPENED HIS eyes to find himself in the limo on the way to LAX. He groaned. Had he even said goodbye to Monica? The car phone on the limo's rear deck burped. He lifted the receiver to his still-ringing ear.

"How are you feeling?" Monica asked.

"Okay…a little shaky. Was it—"

She drew a breath. "I peeled you off the bathroom floor again."

He squinted, trying to focus. "Shit. It's almost as bad as my tequila and gold dust days."

No, Raszer. This is scarier. You seen anybody about this?"

"I have. They don't have a cure for a rebellious right brain."

"I've got Lawrence Gould for you. Can you handle him?"

"I'll have to. By the way, something I forgot: see what you can find out about the insignia; you know, the two-headed eagle they found on the victims. It may be Masonic, but I know I've seen it somewhere else, too."

Monica put Gould through and he spoke over a squawk box. He wanted to confirm Raszer's intent to have Sofia back by next Saturday. He ended the call by saying, "Get it done, Raszer. I want my *life* back."

Raszer wondered if Gould had made a Freudian slip. He checked his watch. Once Montreal was behind him and he was trans-Atlantic, he'd be able to wash down a Halcyon with a good claret and go gentle into the night. It was June 16. For Sofia Gould, next Saturday would be too late.

# 4

## THE INITIATE

*Inside this new love, die*
*Your way begins on the other side*
*Become the sky*
*Take an axe to the prison wall*
*Escape...*
*Die, and be still*
*Stillness is the surest sign that you've died*
*Your old life was a frantic running from quietness*
*The speechless full moon comes out now*

— From a 13th century poem by Rumi, *Quietness*

SOFIA GLIDED DOWN the *U Kozi*, a broad street that runs from the *Stare Mesto*, the Old Town, into the *Josefov*, the still older Jewish Quarter. June 16 was warm in Prague. Warm enough for a fine layer of sweat to form, even under loose cotton garments. Anyone watching would have described Sofia's movement as gliding; as if she were being drawn through the sidewalk crowd on a thin cushion of air. Her tall, sapling form, the long, untended black hair and the simple white dress that was not much more than a nightgown: all gave the appearance of a penitent.

Sofia had a destination and stopped briefly at a pomegranate stand to inquire in broken Czech, *"Prosim. Jak se dostano do,* uh, St. Agnes' Convent?" The ageless fruit seller gestured up the road toward the Vltava, the great waterway that bisected the luminous city and had once brought the spice trade to this land-locked country.

Sofia floated on. She broke her forward gaze for an instant to observe a passing girl with bells on her sandaled toes and exaggerated blue makeup. It took her back to a Polaroid she'd seen in her parents' photo album. Had she been born two decades earlier, she might have been a flower child. In the 1300's, she would decidedly have been a novitiate, eager to give her body and soul to Christ. As it was, she had been born to a time when children were expected to fathom *laissez-faire* morality at an age when they might have preferred the comfort of dogma.

Her father, a gifted writer, was a Jew who had fought his way back from depression to establish a credible reputation and a third marriage in middle age. He wedded a French-Canadian girl, a minor actress who relinquished her own career in order to tend his wounds, and then retreated into her own brand of reactive Catholicism to sop up the pain of his philandering. Sofia was their only child.

From the first, she sought out her father's light. He called her his *little Hokhmah,* and told her it meant that she was wise beyond her years. Despite her mother's disapproval, he took her with him to smoky writers' salons, and by the age of fifteen she'd been seduced by two of his younger friends.

At sixteen, her mother caught her with an opium pipe in one hand and a penis in the other, and sent her off to convent school. Her father, though not an observant Jew, asserted his patrimony and argued against immersing Sofia in the "Roman Circus," but Sofia's fate was sealed. Off she went to the Sisters Of The Sacred Heart in *Sainte-Anne-de-la-Perade,* a village south of Montreal. There, gathered furtively around a strobing candle with her dorm mates, she first learned of the ecstatic brand of Christianity. It was better than drugs. It was better than sex. It was sex with God.

It was during Sofia's exile at Sacred Heart that an intense young Cistercian monk called Brother Paul first observed her. Prior to his vows, his name in the world had been Jean-Paul Millais, and it would not be long before he took yet a third. The Cistercian Order had been founded upon the fervent medieval devotion to the Virgin, and that was what had drawn him. In the present age, however, Brother Paul had found that the privations required in her name were far too lax for his liking, and that Catholic orthodoxy left the mystic in him hungry.

The Cistercian monastery was separated from the convent by a thick wood of spruce and quivering aspen, into which Sofia would come twice weekly for her penance. She had now learned – more from the older girls than from pious study – of the more sensational devotions of the female saints. Agnes and Catherine and Hildegard and Theresa; and she was given to understand that the gifts given her in the flickering darkness had to be paid for in the light if she were to retain the favor of the Queen of Heaven.

And so she came to the woods with two other girls of similar bent, girls who – like her – had pasts to answer for, and they cut switches from the low-hanging bows of spruce, and freed their shoulders from the straps of their uniform dresses. Brother Paul would kneel, hidden in the brambles a stone's throw away, and hold his breath as the tall, slender Salome with the head of tangled black hair dropped to her knees and lowered her forehead to earth.

After two years, Sofia's father won his wife's assent that their daughter could come home and rejoin the stream of normal life. But nothing resembling normality was ever to be Sofia's lot. On the day he was to fetch her, she sat on her bunk with bags packed and waited until finally drifting off to sleep at midnight. She learned the next morning that her father and another passenger had been killed in a car crash. The passenger was his mistress, a girl a year older than Sofia. At that moment, Sofia's mind left her body behind. Bodies suffered; she'd had enough of that.

She went off to college two years later, still fragmented. Despite her cerebral nature, Sofia no longer had an interest in the intellectual life. The whole edifice of academia seemed to her oppressively masculine, devoid of the numinous hum she'd felt at Sacred Heart. She was prone to impulsive moves, not the least of which was her abrupt decision to leave college for an actors' workshop in *Trois-Rivieres*, as if to somehow redeem the aspirations of her neglected mother. She leased a one-room flat near the river, became a vegetarian and started attending weekly seminars on homeopathic healing that were held at the community theater. At one of those sessions, she joined the mailing list of an organization called *Adytum*. As she stood at the foot of the stage, leaning over the sign-up table, she was watched from the wings by the now lapsed Brother Paul, the driving force behind *Adytum*.

Her dark, good looks landed her parts in a host of Canadian indies, including a small but memorable role in *Jesus of Montreal.* That was how Lawrence Gould, newly appointed CEO of Empire Pictures, came to fall under her spell. He took an interest in her career and found her better parts. In turn, she helped him cope with his divorce and sometimes cooked for him. She thought it was exceedingly kind for a rich, powerful man like him to invest in damaged goods like her. Sofia had no idea what the rest of the world saw. When Gould moved his offices to L.A., and called for her, she came. She married him, and now, she had left him cold.

SHE ENTERED THE quiet grounds of St. Agnes' Convent and smelled the nearby Vltava River's sweet soup of rainwater and vegetal decay. Prague was a noisy city, but here, in the 13th century cloister, there was only gurgling of water and the murmuring of stone. She quickly found her way to the west transept entrance to The Church of the Holy Savior. Her destination was a small chapel that she had been told contained an especially beautiful pieta. Sofia still talked to statues of the Virgin; she'd been doing it since Sacred Heart. Occasionally, they talked back.

As she knelt, she recalled the words whispered to her that night in Cannes a year ago; words that had altered her life. She'd attended the film festival with Larry, her husband of barely six weeks, and they were at one of those parties in the hills that attracted everyone from dispossessed royalty to proponents of the host or hostess' current *cause celebre*. Sofia, in floor-length black velvet and without a hint of makeup or jewelry, had been a hit. The dress and her ectomorphic form, as well as her raven, waist-length mane, made her seem even taller and more impressive than she was. Her delicate ivory skin and dark Jewish eyes lent her a sort of Pre-Raphaelite beauty that more than one man at the party would have liked to violate. She stepped out onto the terrace to look over the lights of Cannes and escape the smoke and was drawn to a beautiful marble fountain mounted by a sculpture representing the ascension of the Virgin, a trophy no doubt pillaged from some abbey by the owner's noble forebears.

For just the time it took for a brushed velvet breeze up from the *Croissant* to blow a strand of hair across her face, she felt something like pure, unadorned happiness – happiness *without* the usual background radiation of anxiety to remind her of her essential sorrow. Just as quickly as it had come, it left, and she was left staring at the ecstatic face of the Virgin, a face freed at last from the prison of flesh. *Lucky girl*, she'd thought.

That was when Luc padded up behind her on cat's feet. She was aware of someone's presence only from the hum in her spine.

*"Pardon, Madame..."* He spoke with a sweet, reedy voice. "Are you a devotee of the Lady?" His English was good and almost unaccented. His bow tie was loosened and lay against a bone-colored silk shirt, and in his hand he held an icy bottle of *Comte de Champagne*. Sofia had steeled herself for another assault – *where was Larry?* She decided to give him one chance and spoke sincerely.

"The Lady has been a friend to me for a long time."

The man nodded and his eyes twinkled with what seemed like understanding, so she allowed herself to relax and accept a glass of champagne. He gestured toward the fountain.

"The facsimile you are admiring, it may give the peasant some small comfort, but what if I told you—"

She cut him off sharply. "You're wrong; it's not a facsimile. A Barbie Doll is a facsimile. The artist may have meant it to be a resting place for her spirit. How can you look at it and not feel that?"

He stepped back an inch and bowed slightly. "Ah, so you are a latter-day hermetist? Bruno said much the same thing. I will speak to you then as one who knows." Sofia took a sip of champagne and looked out beyond the lights to the black Mediterranean as he continued. "What if I told you that she is as real today as she was two thousand years ago, and that you needn't confine yourself to speaking to her through statuary? What if I told you that being in her embrace is only a heartbeat...a breath...away?"

While speaking, he'd folded his fingers around her bare arm with a gentle certitude, and she felt the gooseflesh rise beneath his hand and on the back of her swan-like neck. After a beat, he released her arm and tipped his head.

"I beg your pardon," he said. "We have not been introduced." The man once known as Brother Paul said that his name was Luc Fourché, and that if she cared to see them, he would show her the gardens.

SOFIA LEFT THE Chapel quietly, as if to leave no evidence of her coming, and headed for her assignation. It was 3:45, and she was to meet Luc on the Charles Bridge at four. In the year since Luc entered her life, she'd accepted in her heart almost everything he had taught and promised her, but she held onto her statues as a fail-safe. She picked out a colorful cab from the nearby taxi rank and directed the driver to the far side of the Charles Bridge.

The clandestine character of the meeting had been necessitated by the exquisite sensitivity of their undertaking. Each of the Seven was housed in a separate sector of the city, and at the moment Sofia felt very much alone. Something was eating at her, and she needed the reassurance of her Master's voice.

She had been waiting on the bridge, in the shadow of Saint Augustine's black effigy, for nearly an hour, when a huddle of Swiss tourists parted to let Luc through. All around her on the broad pedestrian thoroughfare wove the renaissance festival that was post-Communist Prague; shaggy minstrels in bell-bottoms, painters of Kafka's dark alleys and hawkers of all sorts of talismans. Her gaze had been fixed on a flock of white swans adrift near the west bank of the Vltava, but she had turned reflexively from the wrought iron railing just as he came into view.

He walked briskly toward her, oblivious, even dismissive of the throngs of people that separated them. Luc struck her as a man without peripheral vision. He was a flame burning its way down to a fuse; his eyes were polished emeralds.

"The Norman conquest cannot have been this complicated," he said irritably, once he'd arrived at her side. "I've been on the telephone with Caudal for more than an hour, and they still haven't cleared us. I detest bureaucrats!" This, Sofia supposed, was his way of apologizing for keeping her waiting. "At least this much is confirmed. Tomorrow will be our first night in the Tower. The guards have all been paid and the equipment has been moved into the basement. The process takes four nights if Dee's formula holds true."

Sofia raised her dark eyes to the edifice of Hradcany Castle, looming over the river from the palisades just to the northwest. "God, Luc," she whispered, "How *did* you manage it? An army couldn't storm that thing, but *you* got us in."

"We are an ancient regime, Sofia, with friends in very high places. If I told you how many of our own hold office in Europe, your mind would shatter from the shock."

She gestured toward the castle and the block of government buildings on the west end.

"What about *him?*" she asked. "The poet statesman?"

"*Havel?* Sadly, no. He is one of those men who nurses the utopian vision that died in 1948. But some in his service? *Oui. Absolutely.*" She turned to him, snatching a long-stemmed rose from a passing vendor. On her nod, he paid the man with some reluctance. The moment's pause gave her a chance to observe him; the fine nose, the slightly intemperate little mouth. It was easier to size him up when his eyes were not on her. His eyes swallowed her whole. When they were off her for long, she began to have doubts, as she did now.

"So, tell me, my dark rose," he said, "why was it so urgent that you see me? You know how busy I am with the preparations."

She swallowed hard. "I'm not sure I want to go through with it."

Momentarily, Luc was too startled for words. *"The transit?"* he sputtered. "But surely you know that it's too late for second thoughts. Operations would have you shot and thrown in the Vltava."

"No, no!" Sofia protested. "I want that more than anything. It's the business with my husband. I just—"

He cut her off. "Don't tell me you're afflicted with moral qualms on the eve of ascent! Ten million dollars amounts to a Christmas bonus for your avaricious Jew."

"This is me, Luc," she bristled. "My choice. He shouldn't be punished for it any more than he already has been. I thought you were an illuminated soul, Luc – not a common thief."

With savage reflex, without concern for the passing crowd, he struck the side of her face, drawing blood from her lip. Then he calmly reached into the front pocket of his suit coat and handed her a handkerchief with the monogram *LMF.* She dabbed at the blood as if she knew the drill and turned back to the railing.

"We exist, you and I," he said, with the labored tenderness that always follows habitual abuse, "in a sphere beyond good and evil. Certainly, beyond law. Do you honestly think Heaven cares if your husband is relieved of the interest on his usury? We are angelic beings, Sofia, and all around us is the work of the *Demiurge.* From the moment of your birth, the world has fit you like a poorly made pair of shoes. All that lies ahead here is sickness and corruption. But now, you know another place. The White Lodge, *cherie.* There, the glass slipper will fit."

"What will they do with the money?" she asked without affect.

"Keep the Inquisition at bay for another year. Secure the fidelity of a few dozen judges and prosecutors. And perhaps, be able to offer another group of the elect their freedom, before the conflagration comes. And it is coming, Sofia."

"What do I have to do?"

"A fax will go out tonight, informing your husband that you are being held by our rivals in Australia, the same schismatics who questioned my design and nearly destroyed the Temple after the new regime took over."

"Why Australia?"

"To divert the authorities from looking for you in Prague, my dear. To neutralize our enemies. And because Caudal and Golden Circle ordained it.

She turned and moved within an inch of his nose, her lower lip swollen from the blow. "And if he pays, you won't send me home, will you?"

He touched her cheek. "By the time the last bank transfer is made, you will be in Paradise."

Sofia looked for any hint of guile or pretense or uncertainty in his eyes and found none.

"What will it be like to die? Will I suffer?"

"Does a rose suffer when its petals fall, Sofia? What would be the point, when there is another rose budding behind?"

"Then I will be a rose," she said. Nearby, a busker began to play a simple tune on his recorder, and the sun dropped a notch, casting the spires of Prague in autumnal gold.

"I don't like those men you have guarding me, Luc. They look like thugs."

Luc chuckled, and it threw her. She'd rarely heard him laugh.

"They *are* thugs. The light is meaningless without the dark." He kissed her chastely on the forehead. "I'll see you tonight, as planned." Just before disappearing into the milling crowd, he turned. "Oh, there is something else. There will be one more of us; an *auditore* from the University of Montreal who is to witness our operation and report back to the Circle. *He* is supposed to be an expert." He shrugged. "They will never trust me completely."

Sofia returned her eyes to the river. A single white swan sailed out from underneath the bridge, and she wished she could ride on its back. Maybe that's what death would be like. Closing her eyes, she imagined being borne up on white wings.

MR. X HUNG up the pay phone, lowered his head and began the four block walk back to the offices of the investment firm that fronted for Temple operations in Montreal. The Temple had consumed his life for the past ten years, as well as most of his ample estate. As a *Level 7 Chevalier,* he was privy to all but its most deeply held secrets, and it was one of these secrets that seven years ago had set him against his brethren in the Golden Circle. Now it was time to even the score.

The phone call from Stocker Hinge had confirmed that the American detective was in the air and that the plan was in motion. He was quite certain that Raszer, in spite of his preparation, had no idea what sort of world he would enter when he finally walked into the Powder Tower, the site where John Dee and Edward Kelley had once practiced their secret alchemy – the site selected by the Frenchman, at enormous risk and expense to Montreal, for the 20th century's boldest experiment. But that naiveté would make Raszer more effective as an operative, or so Mr. X believed. If all went well, the elaborate ransom scheme that he had persuaded the other members of the Golden Circle to approve would backfire and blow the infested Montreal Temple sky high.

They were such fools, really, in their venality and their pig-headed, Bavarian determination to quell the Australian insurgency. Only he knew where all the money was and sadly, these days, it was money, not restoration, that mattered. It had not been so when *compagnons* like himself ran the Lodge. It had not been so when Fourché had set the course, with a *savoir-faire* born of his uniquely privileged sense of history. Now, he was gone, a victim of treachery, replaced by a corporate elite that counted souls as capital and a pretender who sought to be the New Age Enrico Fermi. Only a miracle would summon him back, and Mr. X intended to foment it.

Interpol would be persuaded that the Temple had overreached and proved itself patently criminal, but Mr. X – known to his colleagues as Philippe Caudal – knew that the true Temple would always be, no matter who was handling earthly administration. As for the opportunistic little Frenchman, he would fall victim to his own hubris. He had gained his position through his mentor's murder, and now would reap what he'd sown.

Caudal smiled. The Master would have been proud of him. The Master would have wanted his Temple purified.

# 5

## BLIND MAN'S BLUFF

MR. X'S CHAUFFEUR was waiting just inside the gate displaying a hand-printed sign emblazoned with Raszer's code name, "WILBUR." Raszer approached and saluted.

*"Monsieur Wilbur?"* the driver asked with a Gallic earnestness that made the name sound almost genteel.

*"Oui, bonjour."* The driver looked about for something to carry and, seeing nothing, reached out of habit for Raszer's briefcase. "I've got it. My bags are checked through to Prague." He paused as the driver examined him, and then said, "Take me to your leader." Once in the car, Raszer lit a cigarette and slid open the glass partition that separated them.

"St. Casimir, is it?" he asked casually. "It's pretty over on that side of the river, don't you think?"

"Oh, yes. Very beautiful," the man replied dryly, without turning from the wheel.

Raszer's eyes scanned the front seat for a clipboard, a dispatch form – anything that might bear the name of his mysterious host. There wasn't so much as a scrap of paper in sight. He offered the driver a cigarette, accepted his refusal and pressed on.

"Your employer; um, *Monsieur. . .?"*

The driver let the moment pass without comment and then, making a sharp right turn toward the bridge, answered matter-of-factly, *"Oui?"*

"Ah, never mind," Raszer conceded. "I'll meet him soon enough." He hadn't expected the chauffeur to reveal anything, but he had to try. Raszer had learned the hard way that the most critical bits of information often slipped out by way of the most elementary human error, such as dropping one's guard while making a right turn.

On the approach to the bridge that spanned the Saint Lawrence and led to the wealthy bedroom communities of the Palisades, the driver pulled over. He turned and looked at Raszer with the practiced servile nuance that always prefigures some great inconvenience.

"I'm sorry, sir, but my instructions are to blindfold you before we cross."

"Is that *really* necessary?" Raszer objected, knowing he would not prevail.

"If you refuse, I am to take you directly back to the airport. Please."

The driver came around to Raszer's door and fixed the black sash firmly. As the car started up again, Raszer felt paradoxically at ease. For one thing, it relieved him of the obligation to observe, and gave him leave to contemplate. For another, Raszer was not entirely unfamiliar with the use of blindfolds as a sensual enhancement. The car phone bleeped once and the chauffeur snatched it to his ear.

*"Allo?...Oui...Oui. Il est avec moi...oui, monsieur."* He passed the receiver back through the partition and waved it in front of Raszer's blindfold. "It is for you, sir. *Monsieur* Hinge.

Raszer felt for the phone and cradled it against his head.

"Wilbur here. Is this from the horse's mouth?"

"There once was a dick from L.A.," said the wry voice on the other end, "who tunneled all night and all day—"

"Not today, Stocker. You didn't tell me we were playing 'pin the tail on the donkey.'"

"Yes, the blindfold; just go along, Stephan," Hinge said calmly. "Mr. X is a little paranoid; probably with good reason. There are a few unsolved murders in Montreal that bear the Temple's signature. I don't imagine he wants to be the next."

"Where are you calling from?"

"I'm at the hospital with my mother. There's been a turn. They don't know that she'll make it through the week."

"God, I'm sorry, Stocker." Raszer wondered briefly how Hinge had the pluck to compose a dirty limerick at such a time.

"Stephan, I'm not far, but I may not be able to get there before you have to leave for the airport. I apologize."

Raszer cursed under his breath. "Do what you have to do, partner. Does Mr. X know?"

A beat passed as the limo lurched over a speed bump.

"Yes," Hinge answered. "Just proceed as planned. He'll soon tell you everything you need to know. If I don't make it, we'll talk as soon as you arrive in London."

"I'll be fine. Tell your mom to fight the good fight."

"I will. I hope her doctor's not a Temple member – I'd sooner have Dr. Kevorkian."

THE GRADE OF pavement beneath the limo's wheels changed to a well-poured blacktop, and the driver eased into a gentle slalom. They were ascending into what must have been a developed residential area. He lowered the passenger window and listened. It was quiet except for birdsong and the tenor thrum of new tires on asphalt. The limo turned onto a steep driveway, and then continued for what seemed an eternity before slowing to a stop. Raszer inhaled deeply. He could smell the vapor of saltwater borne on the updraft from the riverbank below and taste the robust tang of pine trees all around.

"You may remove your blindfold, *Monsieur*," the drive said.

Raszer peeled off the sash and blinked into the cool shadow of a carport. Across the well-tended lawn was a fine but not ostentatious house, built of stone in the style of a French country manor. The driver came around to his door and opened it.

"Please come with me, sir. My employer will see you in the garden."

Raszer smoothed the wrinkles on his sportcoat and drew in the surrounding landscape with his newly restored vision. They seemed to be at the highest point of the Palisades, the city of Montreal stretched out to the north, across the river. He was led into a pretty garden of hibiscus and local wildflower and then to wood-frame changing house beside the kidney-shaped pool.

"Please have a seat inside, *Monsieur* Wilbur," the chauffeur directed, guiding him to a wooden bench in front of the only window. He opened it and lowered the shade to block any view of the exterior. He switched on a Tiffany table lamp, opened a leather attaché he'd carried from the car and handed Raszer a fat manila envelope. "My employer thought this might be of some use to you."

Raszer accepted the dossier and dropped onto the bench with a sigh of puzzlement. The driver withdrew politely and shut the door, securing the deadbolt lock. It wasn't the way Raszer had expected things to go.

After a few minutes waiting, Raszer unclasped the envelope and pulled out the slim, leather-bound briefing book that looked to have been assembled with care. The file contained the personal data and selected published papers of Dr. Noel Branch, as well as the photograph that had previously been e-mailed to L.A. Branch was a slightly effete-looking fellow of 43, with a Roman nose, large eyes and an oddly crooked smile. Other than general weight, height and a certain cerebral intensity, there was not much physical resemblance to Raszer. This wasn't supposed to matter, as the man leading the party in Prague – referred to only as "the Director" – had reportedly never met Noel Branch. Nonetheless, Raszer had prepared a minimal disguise: his hair would be grayed and pomaded back, his eyebrows darkened and his eyes outfitted with a pair of costume bifocals.

The external touches would complement the *real* disguise, which lay in Raszer's inborn ability to slip into another skin. Raszer genuinely believed – and had, especially since his crack-up – that the psyche resident in one human "vehicle" might fairly easily jump into another and take the wheel. Paradoxically, this perception of one man's essential *likeness* to another had the effect of setting him apart, because most people cherished the notion of their absolute uniqueness. In any case, the photograph of Noel Branch in the Director's version of the briefing book would be of Stephan Raszer in full character. Mr. X had seen to that.

Under a section of the dossier labeled "Food and Drug Allergies," he noticed a listing of penicillin and other ergot derivatives. That would include certain *entheogens* – psychotropic drugs like LSD. A compendium of Branch's scholarly writing, including the paper on the Voynich Manuscript that Monica had cited, followed. The second and larger section of the book was labeled "Operation Rudolph." Raszer would get into that on the plane.

Outside, a stirring was followed by approaching footsteps. Raszer heard a wrought iron chair being drawn to the window. As the person sat, Raszer caught the trace fragrance of an herbal *eau de cologne* and ripe cheese from a recent lunch.

*"Pardonnez-moi, mon Pere,"* Mr. X said, "it has been several years since my last confession." The voice was muffled and metallic, altered by way of some device. Under the circumstances, though, the droll humor was comforting.

"Mr. X, I presume?" Raszer asked.

*"C'est moi, Monsieur* Raszer. *Bienvenue* Montreal. Your crusade is a worthy one. I am available for your questions."

"You're aware that Stocker will probably not be joining us."

"Yes, but I know he has prepared you superbly, and that you are already something of an adept of the hermetic arts, *non?"*

"An amateur," Raszer replied.

"We are all amateurs, Mr. Raszer. All but the Ascended Masters. But you do have a kind of gift? Or so Mr. Hinge has told me."

"A gift for getting drawn into situations like this may not be such a great survival tool. Tell me about Operation Rudolph." It bothered Raszer that Mr. X knew of his dubious psychic abilities. He'd discussed it with

Hinge in order to establish rapport with the esoteric researcher, but there was no reason for Stocker to have informed X, unless it was considered an occupational skill. When Raszer was bothered by something, he squinted hard. He was squinting now, even in the dim light.

As a result of Mr. X's late arrival, they had, at best, another twenty minutes and X's responses were cagey. Raszer had picked up little more than some Temple argot and a few useful Noel Branch anecdotes.

*"Monsieur,* what exactly is your position in the Temple hierarchy?"

"I am a Chevalier of the Alliance, as you may know; beyond that, I handle the money, and it's the money that will bring them down. It was once used to buy scholarly research, publications, influence – now, it's hoarded for its own sake. They have discovered that death is profitable."

"Who are *they?"* Raszer asked? "What am I up against?"

"If I told you the whole truth," Mr. X replied, "you might be persuaded that the odds against your success were insurmountable. Suffice it to say that your Watergate scandal was a lipstick stain compared to this."

"That's the reason for the spooks? The Gaullist secret police and—"

"When you wish to obtain something contraband, Mr. Raszer, you cannot do it overtly. Espionage and the occult are inextricably linked. Men drawn down dark alleys are of a type, whether they are looking for microfilm or magic beans."

"How do I make contact with the Director?"

"He will contact you; at the hotel," X replied. "It's our practice to keep the *auditore* in the dark until his services are required."

"And the Director's name is?" Raszer had to take his shot.

"Whatever is currently convenient."

"But not Luc Fourché?"

"If it suits him," X said. "But know one thing: whoever Fourché once was, he is now among the Ascended Ones."

"How strong is Sofia Gould's bond with the Director?"

"Any separate identity she had," Mr. X answered in his watery, metallic voice, "has now merged with her desire to create a new one. Imagine a painter who has been without sleep for a month in thrall to his creation. The Director will have convinced Sofia that her death will be her life's masterpiece."

Raszer swallowed hard. "Are these people capable of murder outside their own ranks?"

"That would come under the authority of Defensive Operations. Not my area. As a general rule, I think not. It's a bit like the Mafia. You are in grave danger only if they let you in and *then* you betray them. This, as you can appreciate, is my position. With the outside world, they must maintain the illusion of a civil relationship. You, *mon ami,* will be walking the line."

"What is the importance of Sirius? I'm aware of the associated myths, but surely, your people can't believe in literal transport to another star system. Is it a kind of spiritual metaphor?"

"No more so than Heaven. Have you not studied the Masonic *oeuvre?* Sirius and the craft? Well, in any event, it is beyond the scope of your assignment. One day, in better times, we may speak of these things."

The chauffeur arrived. It was time to go to the airport, but before Mr. X took his leave and Raszer was freed from the cabana, the older man leaned forward to the window for a final word. He was close enough for Raszer to feel the heat of his breath and identify the cheese as Roquefort. The cologne he could not place.

"You'll find a Canadian passport in the dossier. I have taken the liberty of opening an account for you at the Czech National Bank, in the name of Noel Branch, of course. Operations engages heavily in bribery, and you may find at some point you need to outbid them."

"I don't generally take money from more than one employer at a time, *Monsieur,*" Raszer said. "It tends to complicate things."

"Use your judgment. In any case, Mr. Hinge will inform you of the account code at a later time. You will not be able to contact me. All communication must be through Mr. Hinge." He stood and cleared his throat through the electronic aqualung. Raszer heard the rustle of fine silk.

"Mr. X?"

"*Oui?*"

"Why are you helping me?"

"It is quite simple, Mr. Raszer. They murdered the only man I ever loved. Good luck, sir."

Raszer listened to the footsteps die away in the direction of the manor house before the door swung open and his blindfold was reapplied for the trip to the airport. Without having yet set foot in Prague, he knew already that this job would be unlike any other.

JEANETTE WAS WAITING, as arranged, at the cocktail bar just outside the Virgin Atlantic lounge. She was drinking a rum sour and seemed utterly out of place in her full body leather and cowgirl pumps, a cascade of knotted red hair falling to her tailbone. She spun around when she spotted him in a mirror.

"Hey, baby," she said, taking Raszer's hands and pulling him to the bar, "long, long, long fucking time, huh?"

She had once been almost shockingly beautiful, a Queen Mab in torn blue jeans, but damage had been done and now there was a deep weariness around her eyes. Nobody in Raszer's generation had expected to live past thirty and when they invariably did, they either had to reinvent themselves or wander like misfits, cheated of the tragic death that the atomic age had promised.

"You look good enough to bring down the House of Lords," he told her.

"Nah, I'm past my prime, but you...*Mm-hmm.*"

Raszer ordered a scotch. "I've missed you. And I owe you big time for this one. So, tell me, what do you make of Noel Branch?"

"He's a little boy with wrinkles," she replied. "Totally obsessed with the 16th century. He called me his *amanuensis.* Too bad he's not on our side."

"So you've hit it off. Good. Now don't get high or have sex with him if you can help it. There's some real *thanatos* operating here, Jen. I get the feeling that life is about as precious to these people as a used condom." Raszer's drink arrived, and he set his worn leather shoulder bag, heavy with books, on the stool beside her. "By the way, I read in his profile that he's got an ergot allergy, so if you do have to go into your medicine kit, make sure it's kosher stuff. Alkaloid family, indoles—"

Jeanette pivoted on her stool to fish through Raszer's bag, pulling out his John Dee biography and setting it on the bar. The cover bore an illustration of Dee whispering in the Queen's ear.

"Cool. Do you think they were really lovers?"

"If not on earth, then in eternity. She was the one who kept him out of The Tower of London."

She flipped idly through the gilded pages, pausing on a full-page plate with a lithograph of the monad symbol. Four stools to her left, a gnomish, bald-headed little man, wearing a bone-colored jellaba, hoisted himself up to the bar and ordered a 7-Up. Raszer lit a cigarette and regarded him obliquely. It wasn't altogether unusual to see a dervish in Montreal International, as the city was second only to Geneva in holding syncretistic gatherings and New Age symposiums, but Raszer habitually kept one eye on the door, and the little guy seemed to have appeared at the bar without having come in. From his manner of dress and the weightless grace of his movements, Raszer guessed him to be a Sufi master.

"So," Raszer said, returning his focus to Jeanette, "you'll contact Monica twice a day with the palm unit. If it fails, get to a pay phone and use the secure line. You know there's no phone in the cabin" She nodded.

Raszer leaned in close, forehead-to-forehead with her, whispering as if to a lover. "If he gets on to you, go for the brainstem and put him out cold. Then get the hell away from the cabin and call the RCMP number Monica gave you, okay?"

"Aye-aye, sir!" she said teasingly. "Do I have to do his brainstem?"

"Just be careful. I need four days."

"I'll be fine, Darlin'," she said, draining her cocktail. "Hey, that Mr. Hinge of yours. Now there's a dapper dude. Looks good, smells good. Wouldn't mind jumping his bones."

"Really? I figured him for a wonk."

Her eyes widened. "You haven't met him, Raszer?"

"I saw him speak once…from a distance. I was supposed to meet him today, but he didn't show. His mother's dying. Odd, but I haven't felt the need. I feel like I know him pretty well."

Raszer heard the squeak of a spinning barstool and raised his eyes to the dwarf dervish. He was sipping his 7-Up through a straw and staring unguardedly at the book that lay open in front of Jeanette. The corners of his little mouth curled up. Raszer made eye contact and lifted his highball glass in a toast to a kindred soul. Jeanette turned to look over her shoulder, and the dervish's eyes twinkled. If he was a Sufi, he no doubt recognized a sister of the craft. She turned back to Raszer, a knowing smile on her wide, mischievous mouth.

"You caught one, Raszer. Don't let him go until he shows you the end of the rainbow."

"Pardon me," the little man called out. "Pardon me, sir, but I couldn't help noticing your book. You wouldn't be, by any chance, a prospector?"

"Come again?" said Raszer.

"A seeker after gold?"

"Do you know of a nearby vein?"

"There may be one," the man answered, "in Prague."

"You don't say. I'm headed to London, myself."

"Ah. Say hello to the Queen for me." Raszer smiled and the two men's eyes found a common wavelength. "Just bear in mind what Bacon said, *'Don't pretend to any gold other than Our gold.'* Should you ever find your-self in Prague, there is a very wise man you might want to seek out. A rabbi. May I give you his name?"

"Of course," Raszer answered. The little man hopped off his stool, walked down and placed a folded scrap of paper in Raszer's hand. "Thank you," Raszer said without dropping his gaze and felt two warm fingers curl inside his palm.

"Be very careful, sir," said the little man.

In a swirl of loose gown, he was out the door, his movement like a quantum stutter, a violation of time. Raszer unfolded the scrap. It read, *Rabbi Scholem, Old-New Synagogue, Praha 3Z656.*

"Yes," Jeanette said softly. "You be careful. You're my last hero."

"Magic for the people," Raszer said. He kissed the corner of her mouth, slung the satchel over his shoulder and headed for the gate.

THIRTY-FIVE THOUSAND feet over the lights of Halifax, Raszer drifted gently into a drug-induced sleep. He didn't really need the pills, but since he couldn't yet skip over space and time like a Sufi, he gratefully accepted second best. Raszer felt that mankind and pharmacology had enjoyed a long and symbiotic relationship, and he gave some credence to extant theories about the effect of entheogens like *soma* and *psylocibin* on the development of consciousness. The book on John Dee had long since dropped to his lap, and the first cabin steward had dimmed the lights. In his cozy semi-consciousness, Raszer was still struggling to connect the dots between Dee's arcane alchemical theorems and what was about to occur in Prague. Now something was scratching at the foggy perimeters of his mind, like a mouse in a bedroom wall. Whereas he was now accustomed to encounters like the one he'd had in the airport bar, the hallucination back in L.A. had bugged him. The *hag*. She had been a little too brusque and familiar with him, and he found himself offended by her presumption of intimacy. Who did she think she was, anyway? He had given her walking papers twenty years ago, after his first trip to the snake pit.

He had come to rely heavily on the intuitions of others in his work and his life, but he had little faith in the veracity of his own visions. The last time he'd listened to "voices," he'd ended up on the wrong side of the looking glass. It was as the velvet curtain finally fell on his waking mind that he felt something bump into his footrest. His eyes fluttered open for just an instant to see a tall, gaunt man settle back into his seat across the aisle. Raszer shuddered reflexively and then dropped into blackness.

THE MAN FROM Defensive Operations sipped his cognac and glanced across the aisle at his neighbor's lap. The Professor's finger still lay extended on top of the page he had been studying. A strand of his graying hair had drooped from his otherwise neatly brushed coiffure and rested atop the gold frames of his bifocals. The chapter concerned Dr. Dee's attempt to decode the Voynich Manuscript. The NSA report commissioned by the U.S. government in 1974 was still classified TOP SECRET, but there were those who had known of the manuscript's importance long before the Americans had taken an interest. The tall man gave a habitual twist to the double eagle's-head ring on his finger and switched off his own reading light, the better to observe the faint glow of indigo pulsing from beneath Raszer's eyelid.

# 6

## King's Road

THE YOUNG MAN awoke with semen on his bed sheets. His first sensation was shame; a knee-jerk fear of discovery on laundry day. That was followed immediately by a puzzled irritation. He hadn't had a wet dream for quite a few years. He was, after all, 19. Girls were no longer out of his reach. But it was the third image fragment crossing his cortex that blew him out of his bed, out of the realm of ordinary adolescent anxiety and down to the kitchen to filch one of his mother's Pall Malls. He had had a visitor.

Her hair had been blue-black, a hue he'd seen before only in the plumage of certain tropical birds or possibly in the coat of a panther. She had said unspeakable things and uttered curses in a language that he could only describe later as pre-existing time itself. Her body was strong and olive-colored, and her odor had the sweet pungency of figs. It was with him still as he sat smoking. He had ejaculated inside her. She had his seed.

Over the next few months, she came to him several times. Once he got over the fear of harm, he began to long for her nocturnal calls, and since he could not predict when she would come, he began to lose sleep. One night, his mother found him writhing on the bed, clutching his swollen sex organ and screaming in what she would describe to the psychiatrist as "something like Arabic."

Upon reciting a handful of words she remembered, Dr. Eliot Benezra, an erudite man, said calmly, "That's Hebrew. It's archaic, but it's Hebrew. Do you know what it means, son?"

"No."

"It means, 'I will serve you forever.'"

The boy's mother found his stash of pot, and he could not convince her that drugs were not the source of his hysteria. The visitations stopped abruptly on the night his bedclothes were saturated with another fluid — blood from his own wrists. It was not until many years later that he learned about Succubae. Devils, like gods, come in both genders, equally intent on propagating their own kind.

RASZER SLEPT THROUGH the landing at Heathrow and awoke with a firm nudge from the flight attendant. He shook off the lingering Halcyon haze and unconsciously glanced across the aisle. The tall man's seat was empty, and most of the passengers had deplaned. He wrestled his over-stuffed garment bag clumsily out of the narrow coat rack and scooped up his shoulder bag. On the way through the terminal, he got in the way of a young girl taking flash pictures of her boyfriend's arrival in London, and Raszer flinched reflexively at the sound of the shutter and raised his satchel to cover his face. He had not allowed himself to be photographed in over two years, a significant concession for an ex-actor.

In his hurry, Raszer missed a step on the way down to the taxi rank and came down hard on his weak left ankle. "Shit!" He could gauge the damage from the degree of pain; he'd be limping now for three or four days. He hobbled to the taxi and threw his baggage in. The low-grade pain sent a shot of dopamine into his bloodstream and made him think of his friend Petronella. She was the primary link in Raszer's long-held association of London with kinky sex. She had a way of conjuring his demons and then blowing them out like birthday candles. Maybe he'd call on her to-night, if she still worked at the little place in Knightsbridge.

London was hot, too hot for June. It had been, for a very long time, his favorite city, but he had to concede that London did not wear summer well. It was an autumn city, meant to be savored on a cool day when the amber light lingered on the ivory facades of the old row houses, and the leaves rustled dryly on the primeval oaks in Green Park. When the sun burned, the air turned clotted and hazy and the city lost its definition. There was one appealing side effect, though: some old, giddy madness seized the British when the weather was warm enough to compel the re-moval of one's outer garments. It drove them into the parks, where they exposed as much skin as British modesty would allow, and all of a sudden every shop girl became the Lady of Shalott. He caught a glimpse of a bare midriff and green eyes as the black taxi blurred past Hyde Park on its way to South Kensington. The driver negotiated Hyde Park Corner and headed west down Knightsbridge toward Queen's Gate.

The operational reason for Raszer's stop in London was to adjust to the time zone before he hit the ground running in Prague. Jet lag is no small impediment to clear thinking, let alone to the sort of ruse Raszer hoped to pull off. The layover would also allow a twenty-four hour period for pullback in the event that his meeting with Mr. X resulted in a betrayal of his mission to the Temple enforcers.

The taxi came to a stop. After years of hotel hopping, Raszer had finally settled on a venue that suited him. The Atheneum was stalwart and The Halcyon was idyllic, but his home away from home in London had become the Kensington Gore. It was a smallish place on a pleasant tree-lined thoroughfare, and the entire front bank of rooms had French windows that opened to the street and looked out on the Iranian Embassy. The rooms were Spartan, with bare wooden floors, washstands and not a hint of Victorian frou-frou, but they were sunny, tasteful and immaculately clean. The entire staff, from manager to kitchen boys, seemed to be gay, a fact that aroused no prurient interest in Raszer but seemed to account, at least in part, for the fastidiousness and efficiency of the operation. If he wanted a bottle of Lynch-Bages 1988 at two a.m., it was at his door in fifteen minutes. And for London, a city where the rate of inflation was directly relatable to the number of Saudi oil barons currently in residence, it was cheap.

After checking in, he set up his Powerbook and modem and ordered a cup of Earl Grey. It was 5:30 p.m. He hammered out an e-mail to Monica, then peeled off his wrinkled clothes, took a quick shower, and set out with Monica's binder under his arm for the Grenadier Pub, hidden not far from his doorstep in the shady, haunted mews behind the old Berkeley Hotel. After the long flight and lingering effects of the Sufi encounter, he felt the need to anchor himself with the mother's milk of lukewarm English bitter and some casual flirtation with the barmaids.

He found a booth in the backroom of the former soldier's quarters and ordered a pint and a plate of bangers. It was as good a time as any to get his stomach ready for Eastern Europe. He opened the binder and began to read the new brief Monica had prepared in the early morning of the day of his departure.

## SIRIUS B, ISIS, AND THE DOGON

M.L.6/17/00 – Ancient Sumerian myth tells of the appearance of **Oannes,** an androgynous fish-god who brought advanced wisdom to Babylonia. A strikingly similar myth seems to have sprung up among the **Dogon** people of Mali, descendants of Lemnian Greeks who had intermarried with the indigenous tribes. According to Dogon legend, the **Nommo** was an amphibious deity of surpassing intelligence who had come to earth from the orbit of **Sirius B,** the dwarf companion of the Dog Star, to rescue man from the error of death. Western science did not possess telescopes powerful enough to confirm the existence of a double-star system until the 19$^{th}$ c., but Dogon pictographs make it clear that the tribe knew of Sirius B long before. Furthermore, the myth asserts that the Nommo's home was on a small planet, the **Digitaria seed,** the existence of which is now also accepted by scientists. The Nommo taught that humankind had originated on the Digitaria seed as a perfect, androgynous creature, and still had curled within his brain the fetal forms of both male and female. The Nommo made a communion of his flesh and blood (Nommo means "to make one drink"), and was crucified by the Dogon shamans, who kept the secret wisdom for themselves. Eventually, the secrets are passed to the covetous priest-kings of Egypt, who encode them in the legendary Book of **Thoth,** also known as **Hermes Trismegistus,** the founder of the Hermetic Tradition that survives in all serious schools of magical knowledge. Thoth is associated with **Horus,** divine son of the dismembered **Osiris** and his sister-bride **Isis,** the "Woman clothed with the Sun," who is represented in Egyptian cosmology by none other than Sirius, whose heliacal rising signaled the annual flooding of the Nile. It is conjectured by some that the rebel prince **Moses** took his own version of the fish-god's wisdom to the Promised Land, where it reached its apotheosis years later in the coming of the messiah, **Jesus Christ.** Like the Nommo, Jesus shared his body and blood, and like the Nommo, he was crucified. If all this sounds too wild, consider that the early Christians adopted as their symbol the sign of the **fish,** and that the "Woman clothed with the Sun" is the description given by **St. John** to the descending / redeeming Mother of Christ in the **Book of Revelations.** More to come on the Isis, **Magdalene, Templar** connection.

Raszer closed the binder and bit off the end of a smoky banger. Monica had done an excellent gloss on the material, worthy of medieval scribes. There was just enough depth and insinuation to blow a tiny hole in anyone's tidy conception of things, and that was exactly the point of having her do it.

Emerging an hour later into the dusky, cobblestone alley, he felt a cozy buzz at the base of his skull that did not completely dispel his anxiety about the job. He could not stop going over the details, and he knew it was time to quit thinking ahead or behind and start existing in the absolute, present, unfolding moment of time. It was then that he made up his mind to track down Petronella.

PETRONELLA POPE WAITED tables at Menage á Trois, a trendy little bistro on Beauchamp Place that, local talk had it, Princess Di had frequented in her Sloan Ranger days. Petronella seemed to get fired and re-hired with some regularity, and Raszer had a sense he'd always find her there. Pet was 32; younger below the neck and older around the eyes. Physically, she was every male baby boomer's mid-60's mod-girl wet dream, complete with enormous and excessively made up green eyes and a helmet of henna colored hair with sheepdog bangs. She still wore black kid leather miniskirts, the look so out-of-date it was *retro chic*. It brought derision from females – until they got to know her – but from men, well. Pet was the original British bad girl, with a head full of vices that were particularly Anglo-Saxon. She was also a genuine British witch, complete with pentagram earrings, hooded red cloaks and a Chelsea flat full of Wiccan paraphernalia. Petronella was the one person Raszer knew personally who had actually copulated on the alter stone at Stonehenge. Somehow, he was sure that her accomplice had been wearing horns.

He took a small table in the corner and watched her for a while. She was absolutely Zen in her performance of her simple tasks. He hid his face as she brushed past him with a platter full of escargot. As the trail of garlic found his nostrils, he cleared his throat and said, "Hey gorgeous. Got a date for Sabbat night?"

She stopped in her tracks, without turning around, deposited the snails dutifully before her charge, and then rushed back and plopped down onto Raszer's lap. "You bastard! Why didn't you tell me you were coming?"

"I was afraid you might have a fella," he said, feigning indifference.

"I do," she replied, going into Cockney, "but he don't please a girl the way my fancy man do."

Raszer noticed the restaurant manager scowling in the rear and eased her off his lap. "Would you make me a bone chilling martini, Pet? Up. Dry as Moab."

She smoothed her skirt and curtsied as best one can in a skin-tight leather skirt. "It's Beefeater this year, right?"

"No, I'm an unfaithful slut. I've gone back to Bombay."

He sipped a second one before she finally quit at one a.m., and savored the way the cold, clear syrup shot straight to his forebrain and effectively anesthetized all the little demons of doubt. Gin was an increasingly rare treat these days; he could no longer afford serious hangovers. They were gone with the other forms of self-abuse he'd swept out of his life when God promised him a second chance.

Later, he lay on the four-poster bed in her flat, feeling pleasantly numb but for the tingle in his tailbone. Her back was turned to him but the closet door was ajar and he could see her reflection in the full-length mirror. He loved to watch her undress, as much as – and probably because – she loved to do it. It was not a striptease. Each article of adornment, from the classic white silk blouse and black elastic suspenders to the silver serpent bracelets on her left wrist, was removed with a slow-motion sensuality that held an element of narcissism. Every so often, she would turn her head and cast a glance his way, as if to say, *Aren't I a peach?* And she was.

Raszer felt a strangely thrilling uneasiness moving up his spine, like the imagined serpent in a Kundalini yoga exercise. He knew that Pet would call upon something atavistic in him; that's what witches did. He could feel it waking now. If there had been a Church of Latter-Day Flagellants, Petronella would be a charter member, though she might have used it more as a dating service than as a means to piety. She wanted to be spanked, and she required a steady supply of refined and paradoxically gentle men who understood that this did not mean also that she wanted to be battered. When she folded herself over a man's knee, it was to say, "for this moment – and this moment only – I yield to your hand, but you'd better play by the rules." It was, she had once told Raszer, "the only thing she wanted." She had, as far as she knew, never reached orgasm by any other means.

When she finally presented herself naked before him, it was with a sense that the curtain could now be raised on the theater of forbidden longing. He knew not to undress (one of her things). She liked him fully clothed. She laid her head on his chest, and he caressed her hair as he glanced about the room for evidence of change. The African ceremonial masks were still hanging there, as was the pagan tapestry showing the Morris dancers. He ran his fingers down her spine to the perfect cleft of her ass and felt her arch toward him.

"Raszer," she whispered into his neck.

"Yes, baby."

"Take me down."

"We'll go down together," he said.

On the street beneath Petronella's candlelit bedroom window, the tall man from Defensive Operations lit a cigarette. On hearing the first slap of flesh against warm flesh, he smiled sardonically. True to his reputation, Noel Branch was again toying with sex as sacrament. When the girl moaned to God, Josef De Boer became shamefully aroused and bit his tongue until the blood had left his genitals. *Waste of time,* he said to himself. Branch would cause no breach in the Temple's walls tonight. He turned and walked hurriedly away.

RASZER LEFT HER sleeping soundly at 2:30 a.m., a delicate bow of a smile on her face. In repose, she was as virginal as Snow White. He bent down to kiss her forehead, took a rose from her vase and laid it on the pillow under her nose. Then he doused the lights, locked up and left. In the dark and silent street, he felt again the aching pressure on his diaphragm that he remembered from the woods of his past.

He was turning off the Chelsea Embankment when he heard behind him the singular *crack* of a heel against pavement. He limped into the center of the street, his ankle throbbing. From out of nowhere, a minivan shot by and someone yelled, "Watch out for Spring Heel Jack! He's lurkin' about this time o' night!"

After the sputter of the four-cylinder engine had left his range of hearing, silence fell again like the fog sitting stagnantly over the Thames. Raszer turned from Heyne Walk onto Oakley Street, heading for Kings Road and a taxi.

It was a mostly residential area of old brownstones and narrow mews that curved off into the darkness. On this unseasonably warm night, not even darkness could offer relief. The oaks that lined the street seemed to be holding their breath for fear that with the slightest movement they would break out in a prickly sweat like the one that lay over Raszer's neck. Ever since the plane, he'd had a nasty feeling he was being tailed.

He was about to reach for a cigarette when he heard it again. This time it was more like a scrape or scuff – boot leather dragged over pebbled concrete. He turned back to his right, crouching slightly, and thought he saw the fringe of a yellow scarf pulled into the blackness behind a parked lorry. There was an exaggerated after-image of the scarf that caused him to question his senses. Something unreal about it, as if his mind had grabbed hold of something that had not yet fully come into being. Just like Bohm's theory, he thought. Things don't simply *exist*. They *unfold,* moment by moment, from the "implicate order," the plenum, the extra-dimensional Godmatrix. Sometimes, there were fore-echoes of their coming.

Raszer remained in a crouch and moved slowly toward the curb, head rolled slightly to the left, eyes cast sidelong to the right and rear of the lorry. He padded to within six feet of the truck's rear bumper. There was no way to see through to the rear – the back windows had been blacked out – so he bent from the waist and folded his head down to meet his shins and peer underneath the vehicle. Spaced about twenty-eight inches apart in fight-or-flight stance behind the lorry was a pair of ornately stitched cowboy boots. Raszer was well aware that he was unarmed. When he was operational, he carried a seven-inch blade strapped to his shin, and, in his shirt pocket, a little plastic sheath containing six needles coated with a paralytic agent. Depending on where they were applied, these could either stun or induce cardiac arrest. Neither was available to him right now.

He slapped his hands hard against the front of the truck and feigned right. The move had the desired effect. His pursuer shot off to the left and Raszer caught up with him, seized the dangling yellow scarf and slammed the gasping cowboy into a brick wall at the mouth of St. Kevin's Mews. Raszer's knee torpedoed the man's groin at the same time his right index finger found a pressure point on the side of his neck. If the guy was a pro, Raszer would have, at best, five seconds to disarm him. This was no pro.

While his would-be assailant was on all fours, puking bile, Raszer fumbled through his burgundy kid leather jacket and matching trousers and, finding nothing, pulled the man off his knees and sat him back against the wall.

"Who the fuck are you and why are you following me?"

Only now did Raszer get his first good look at whoever, or whatever, had tailed him from Pet's flat, and his immediate thought was that he'd just roughed up one of her kinky playmates. Maybe even the boyfriend she'd referred to at the restaurant. He was dressed like an exile from the neo-punk scene two blocks north on Kings Road. His head was completely shaved, its shape narrow and delicate like the sculpted, hairless renderings of African queens you see in museums. There were multiple gold rings piercing the ears, the left nostril and the plump lower lip. Raszer didn't feel like guessing what other body parts might also bear decoration. The over-large eyes betrayed neither fear nor menace, but the extravagantly long lashes completed an androgynous portrait that was both oddly reassuring and deeply chilling.

"I'm a walk-in," the man said calmly, after he'd caught his breath.

"Bullshit," spat Raszer.

"Ah," continued the stranger in an eerily emasculated voice, "you know the term, then."

Raszer collapsed back against the wall and lit a cigarette. "Sure. Webster's New Age Dictionary defines a 'walk in' as a higher being who assumes human form in order to complete a spiritual assignment or bring a message. How am I doing?"

"Bravo," the man said. "You've defined me. Now look at me. What else could I be?"

Raszer flicked an ash and pushed his hand through his damp hair. "We're not doing too well with my first question. Let's try number two. Why were you following me?"

The stranger pushed himself up from the wall and assumed a vaudeville posture. For a moment, Raszer thought he was about to break into a music hall routine.

"I thought you were one of us."

Raszer, never one to dismiss the possibility of gaining knowledge from the absurd, decided to play along. "And why is that?"

The stranger's left arm dropped as if given slack by a puppeteer, and he pursed his lips and shook his head like a schoolmarm. "Because of this!" He lifted his left leg and shook his foot from the ankle, the sashayed around an eight-foot diameter circle, dragging the left foot like a cripple. "I have a limp, too, you see. Many of us do. We all carry some physical imperfection that allows us to be recognized by those we want to be recognized by."

Raszer tossed his cigarette into the shadows of a former stable yard.

"I can see now," said the man, resting his chin in his palm, "that yours is only temporary. Had it before, though, haven't you?"

Raszer advanced on the tall, elongated figure, his patience wearing thin. Whatever this encounter was, it was hardly innocent.

"Do you know my name?" he asked.

"Who is the King of Kings?" the man shot back, like the Mad Hatter on Ecstasy. The stranger threw back his head, fluttering his long lashes, and laughed. "Why, the Queen of Queens, Matthew!"

Raszer staggered. He felt the cold rush through his bowels as if he'd just been given an ice water enema. Before his psychic makeover, before his checkered acting career, before the crash at 19, his given name had been Matthew. Matthew Ross. The androgyne's elegant fingers went for his inside jacket pocket, and at that, Raszer leapt behind him and clamped his forearm around his neck.

"Who are you, goddamnit?"

The stranger removed a tiny breath spray atomizer from his inner pocket and pumped two shots into his mouth. "Oh dear, a Doubting Thomas. I told you; I'm a walk-in."

"From what planet, asshole?" Raszer demanded, throttling him.

"Thertainly not Thirius!" the man gasped. "Want me to prove it to you?"

"Sure."

In less time than it took for the word to escape Raszer's lips, the body in his grip went completely limp. As he struggled to keep the dead weight from slipping through his arms, his right hand inadvertently grasped the creature's crotch, where in place of the usual lump of male genitalia, there was something akin to a codpiece. Cradling the body, Raszer dropped to his knees and set the head down gently and warily. He checked for a pulse and detected none. All color had drained from his pursuer's face, and his flesh was as cold as if he'd been in the morgue for two days. Dangling from the lobe of his left ear, the last and largest of seven ornaments, was a solid gold replica of John Dee's Monad.

Raszer was suddenly aware that his hair was on end.

He remained on his knees until he saw the light go on in the upper unit behind the mews, and then hobbled out of the alley and made a bee-line for the lights of Kings Road. He reported the location of the "body" anonymously from a red phone box at the corner and then hailed a taxi as quickly as he could.

ON MONDAY MORNING, Raszer sat on the edge of his narrow bed in the Kensington Gore and waited for the taxi that had been called to take him to Heathrow. He was rolling something over the fingers of his right hand, in the manner of a magician doing a coin trick, but the object he held was the walk-in's golden earring. It was theft, of course, but he felt somehow certain he would be forgiven if he ever ran into the creature in this world or the next.

Before having dropped off to a fitful sleep, in what little had re-mained of the night, Raszer had flipped open his laptop, switched on the modem and accessed the British Telephone "switcher" he and Monica had arranged for. It in turn had routed the call through another modem located in an obscure machine shop in Holland Park, from there to a server in Montreal, and finally on to Hollywood.

Monica's last e-mail came up slowly. It informed him in the matter-of-fact cool blue of cyber-speak that a ransom demand had been issued to Lawrence Gould. A ten million dollar "charitable donation" to something called Eternity Corporation would prevent his "assets from being severely devalued." The rather refined ransom note, issued by fax from Alice Springs, Australia had been received but, fortunately, not responded to by Gould. He had agreed to give Raszer a day or two to extricate Sofia before notifying the FBI. "Who in their right mind," he had asked Monica, "would demand ransom on a girl who *wants* to die?"

Raszer reached into his shoulder bag and took a strip of jerky from Monica's neatly wrapped package. He chewed. Who in their right mind, indeed? Then he recalled Mr. X. *"I handle the money, and it's the money that will bring them down."*

SOFIA SIPPED A watered-down Becherovka and waited with the others for Luc. The liqueur was fiery but pleasant, and its herbal ingredients were reputedly therapeutic. None of the others touched alcohol, as they were following the Temple regimen as religiously as Hollywood actresses follow the *Zone Diet*. The fact that Sofia drank (though very little and usually only wine) was taken by Luc as yet another example of her impertinence, what he called her "American exceptionalism." It did no good to remind him that she was American by marriage only. Sofia continued to drink as a modest assertion of selfhood (which was subversive enough), and because she was in pain. Her concession to Luc's disapproval and the Temple's program was to water her wine.

The six of them had gathered at *U Labuti* – At The Swan's – to have dinner and receive a briefing from Luc before the first night in The Powder Tower. The restaurant was discrete, patronized mostly by locals and a short walk from Hradcany Castle. Sofia was dressed a shade provocatively for the occasion, in a sheer white silk chemise and black toreador pants. The blouse lay three buttons open to her skin. She was well aware of the perversity of wanting to look good for Luc. Although he said he loved her best and called her "a rose among thorns," he treated her more like a schoolgirl than a woman and chastised himself and her whenever something like affection threatened to alter the Master-Pupil dynamic. Still, she was a woman and didn't intend to go to the ball in sackcloth. She had chosen the Temple as much as it had chosen her, and she wanted to be the author of her end, so after the meeting on the bridge, she had dressed for the evening. She looked over the sober faces of her cohorts. For just a tick, she felt she'd come to the wrong party.

Sonja, the pale-skinned German woman of 32 had been a successful model and a lapsed Catholic when she met Luc at a seminar on homeopathic healing and he had stirred the ashes of her faith.

Claude, the Alsatian, was 50 and had been the president of a bank that had assisted the Temple with some high-risk investments a few years back.

Robert was Swiss, an Olympic caliber skier and a protégé of Vuarnet.

The whimsically named Lisbeth and Elsbeth were identical twin sisters of 44, erstwhile madams of one of Amsterdam's most prestigious brothels. Just how they had met Luc was the subject of some conjecture among the others.

Each of them had, over the past year or two, been relieved of all material holdings, investments, inheritances and temporal duties by grace of the Masters in Montreal. They had become "stockholders" in a corporation not wholly of this earth.

Luc arrived out of breath and faintly troubled but calmed himself before anyone but Sofia seemed to notice. After they had dined on a vegetarian meal – not an easy thing to come by in Prague – Luc removed a heavy, leather-bound volume from his attaché and opened it with a flourish.

"Tonight we will familiarize ourselves with the equipment. When we have finished, everything will be disassembled and returned to the cache until tomorrow night's commencement." His sipped his water as if between the lines of a speech. "The alchemical process requires three nights and will be consummated on Thursday at the heliacal rising of Sirius. We are employing a modified wet process. We have, of course, tools that our predecessors did not possess, but the methods are eternal. If the *Materia Prima* remains uncorrupted, albification should occur by Wednesday night, and the rest is a matter for prayer. I must remind you again, there is a possibility that some of us will not get through. Let me say this for the last time: *corporeal death without ascension is a possible by-product of failure*, although we are far beyond Grenoble."

He cleared his throat and began, with what seemed to Sofia to be some embarrassment, to pass out six sets of stapled documents in fine legal print. "You've all seen these before," Luc said flatly. "A standard release of liability that extends to your heirs and assigns, in perpetuity, of course. Even the gates to Heaven, I'm afraid, seem to be attended by lawyers these days. If it were up to me, well…" He scanned the group with hard, unblinking eyes. "I have no doubts, nor should you."

Sofia held her pen just above the dotted line. The other five gave the document a perfunctory glance and signed. The arcane meta-scientific jargon meant nothing to her, but she was smart enough to know a disclaimer when she saw one.

"Luc," she said timidly, "I just need to hear one more time. Why should we believe that some formula worked out four hundred years before electricity will—" Luc glared, and she steeled herself for his reproach.

"Sofia," he said, dropping his voice dramatically, "Your beauty and purity of heart are exceeded only by your lack of erudition. To presume that something is irrelevant simply because it is old is the rankest of prejudices. On this very day at the close of the enlightened twentieth century, particle physicists in the world's most sophisticated laboratories are demonstrating the truth of ideas advanced by Hermes Trismegistus in predynastic Egypt. If you continue to assert your qualms, I will send you home to resume your place as the plaything of your Hollywood—" He broke off, leaving a loaded silence. The others lowered their heads in embarrassment for Sofia. "May I remind you all that we will be joined tomorrow by our *auditore*. He is a distinguished scholar, and we are to accord him the greatest respect."

After the others had filed out to the taxi rank, Luc took Sofia roughly by the arm in the restaurant's foyer.

"Are you determined to provoke me or is it just your American insouciance? It is long past the time for schoolroom questions, and you know it." He dug his fingers into the silk of her blouse and bruised her, but Sofia would not cry out. She felt the heat of his breath on her eyelashes and saw desire flash in his eyes.

"As long as I know you want me," she said, "I can't trust you to save me."

# 7

## SALT

*That no rogue may do business here*
*No knave slip in among the rest*
*That all of you unhindered*
*May enjoy the wedding undefiled*
*Tomorrow every one of you*
*Upon the balance will be weighed*
*Whoever is too light reveals*
*What he would fain forget*

– From "The Chemical Wedding of Christian Rosenk-
reutz" (1616), a Rosicrucian alchemical allegory

THE PROSTITUTE STAGGERED into the *Maltezske Namesti,* her
palm pressed to her nose in an attempt to stanch the blood that dripped
through her fingers onto the cobblestones below. She had seen some
rough trade, but the little *krysa* had not purchased with his meager *koruna*
the right to damage the merchandise. She'd met him at *Peklo,* where her
sister tended bar; he'd seemed such a refined gentleman. It figured; the
highest men always seemed to crave the lowest pleasures.

The moon was hidden behind a bank of storm clouds the color of
mercury. She made it across the square and into the public toilet unno-
ticed, then went to the mirror and washed. Once she was satisfied that her
nose was not broken, she began to think about the encounter. He had
asked her to beat him; that was common enough. He had supplied the instrument – a peeled and polished branch of sapling birch – that had told
her only that he was a devotee. The fact that he'd held a prayer book open
throughout and chanted a mass in some strange tongue was odd enough,
but no stranger than the scenarios other clients had devised. It was what he
had said to her just before he struck her and threw the money down that
had chilled her.

"Do you ever pray?" he had asked her as he fixed his tie.

"Only for my children," had been her jaded reply. She had reached up to straighten his tie when he hit her.

"Don't touch me, whore. I am not yet ascended to my mother."

She decided to hold on to the business card she'd taken from his jacket while he lay prostrate on the cold wooden bench. Marta should be made aware of the kind of men who frequented her bar.

A SUMMER THUNDERSTORM greeted Raszer on arrival at the Prague airport. He hobbled to the taxi feeling in far worse shape than would have been his preference. The layover in London was supposed to have restored him, but the session with Pet and the walk-in encounter left him wobbly. The precise nature of all that he'd experienced seemed beyond any understanding at this point. Then there was this ransom business. In spite of ample evidence that the cult was perfectly capable of criminal activity in order to further its ends, he hadn't expected them to be looking for headlines. By its very nature, the thing a secret society fears most is exposure. That single, unassailable fact had saved Raszer's skin more than once, for he always left a trail of breadcrumbs behind him, invisible to anyone who had not been told where to look. No cult – not even the good ones – could survive the heat of a focused inquest. Hence, Raszer offered his adversaries something like the seal of the confession in return for his safety. He had to, for exposure was also the thing that he least wanted.

The driving rain graciously obscured the concrete hulks of Soviet-era Prague that lay along the route to the city. Once inside the old walls, Prague was eternal and unspoiled by the utilitarian banality of Bauhaus architecture. Raszer had last seen Prague as a wide-eyed tourist, in the afterglow of the revolution. Now his eyes were narrowed to slits and it was another city. He had just three days to get Sofia Gould, and that would require sewing the right threads of both trust (in him) and doubt (in the dogma). The most certain method was to affect a sort of transference of her belief from the cult to him, but as any shrink knew, that could backfire.

The cloudburst had ended by the time the taxi reached Wenceslas Square, and the city reemerged radiantly. Raszer paid the driver and walked into the lobby of the Hotel Europa, Prague's legendary art noveau palace. The hotel's best feature was the lovely and ever-buzzing café that spilled out onto the square. The rooms themselves, in some unintentionally Dadaist stab at style, resembled boudoirs in a bordello, but you couldn't deny the grandness of the place. It recalled an era, before the Occupation, when

Prague's café society had rivaled that of Paris. It seemed to Raszer that, under Vaclav Havel's enlightened stewardship, it might come again.

"Welcome to *Praha,* Mr. Branch," the desk clerk said in classroom English. "There is just one message for you."

Raszer peeled open the envelope and examined the card. *Dinner. Restaurant Peklo. 7 p.m. The Director.* He picked up his worn cowhide valise. He took the lift, leaving the garment bag to the porter, and let himself into the small, fourth floor suite that Mr. X had arranged. Whorehouse red. *Perfect.* He tossed his bag onto the frayed Persian rug and looked again at the dinner reservation. Despite Mr. X's cryptic non-answers and a French coroner's report showing that Luc Fourché had been burned beyond recognition on a Grenoble mountaintop, it was by no means certain that Raszer would not be dining with the man Interpol's chief had called the "Pied Piper of Hades."

Whoever his dinner date turned out to be, he had already shown discriminating taste in restaurants. Peklo was one of the priciest meals in Prague, and the most sacramental as it was served in the catacombs beneath a medieval monastery. Raszer made up his mind to go a couple of hours early and do some cramming in the monastery's library. Before work, however, a catnap and a walk – bad ankle or no – to the Old Town Square, where he would find a café while there was a little sun left to burn off any lingering jetlag. He plumped the pillows, fetched the briefing book and flopped down on the feather bed, his mind already morphing around the profile of the man whose identity he had assumed.

Noel Branch had devoted his adult life to scholarly research on the occult subtext of history, specifically, the royal science of alchemy. Like Raszer, Branch believed that a sort of flare had been sent up at the twilight of the 16th century, announcing that humanity was being given a chance to avert its course toward a materialistic, Cartesian view of the universe. Unlike Raszer, however, Dr. Branch appeared to believe that humanity-at-large, in refusing the overture of John Dee and his colleagues, had condemned itself. Thenceforth, only the *elect* would have a shot at the Grail. The elect, who were limited in number and related somehow to the Gnostic conception of angelic beings kidnapped from Heaven by the evil Demiurge in order to serve as his vassals on earth. The boys in Montreal were not populists and Noel Branch served them.

Raszer took out another piece of the jerky, and his brain began to percolate. *Whom does the Grail serve,* the Fisher King had asked Percival. Could it possibly serve the Temple of the Sun?

SOFIA HAD SLIPPED her guard and come to the Old Town Square, despite Luc's warning to keep to quarters. It was nearly three and she wanted to see the astrological clock on the Town Hall Tower strike the hour. The clock read time in three different modes, the large hand on the azure field of the Babylonian time-dial was just past the midpoint of its arc. There were twelve hours in that ancient day; the night was left to the unseen. From Solstice to Solstice, the wheel measured out the passage of seasons. Winter and summer occurred at the same mark – each was a beginning and an end.

Awe was a sensation that Sofia's melancholy rarely let through, but when the gothic models of the twelve apostles came promenading out of the cuckoo's door, she felt as wonder-struck as a child.

The morning thunderstorm had cooled the air and brought out the tourists. The Square was both the geographical and spiritual hub of Prague, and since the Velvet Revolution had become a polyglot magnet for travelers and perennial flower children of all nationalities. A dizzying number of languages could be heard in the course of a single meal. She settled on a table at a small outdoor café where the midday sun would warm her shoulders, and ordered a bowl of potato soup. Adjusting her dark glasses, she propped her feet on an adjacent chair and stretched her doe-like neck, letting her black hair spill over the chair back.

It was no good. She couldn't relax. She told herself it was nothing more than a guilty conscience. An image flickered into memory – she was holding Larry's head in her lap while the mighty mogul cried like a baby over the death of his mother. The closeted vulnerability of powerful men attracted her.

She sat upright and violently shook her head to erase the image and replace it with Luc's version. Lawrence Gould was a philistine, a hater of all that she loved! Guilt had no place in Luc's world. It was, he said, a sentiment visited upon the unredeemable.

RASZER, SITTING IN the shade not ten meters away, caught the gesture that alerted him to Sofia Gould's remarkable presence within his sphere. It spoke volumes about her lack of resolve. Her appearance had changed a bit in the six weeks since her disappearance, but she was no less striking. She possessed that quality best described by the Old English word *fey* – attended by the spirits.

Raszer felt a rush of sympathy for Lawrence Gould's loss. He watched her fidget, sensing that her butterfly attention was flitting from idea to idea in order to avoid settling on something unpleasant. Although it hadn't been part of the plan to encounter her before tonight's ceremony, he could interpret this only as a synchronicity. His mind began to weigh the risk of daylight contact versus the potential yield of making a beach-head, but he cut himself short, recalling a bit of Sufic instruction he'd once received. "Allow consciousness to work. Don't trip it up with directed thought. If you've done your homework, the information you need is al-ready in your mind. Let intuition act upon it and you'll be guided rightly."

HE FOUND HIMSELF standing before her table, a lit cigarette in his hand, though he didn't remember having lit it. A few heartbeats elapsed as her down-turned gaze adjusted and wandered up his torso to his face.

"Forgive the intrusion," he said with a Canadian brogue and just a hint of the academic's affectation. "I think you must be Sofia." She took a sip of water without dropping her eyes from his, and he felt for a moment as if she could see through his pretense. It was always that way when he'd just assumed a new identity.

He extended his hand. "I'm Noel Branch from the University in Montreal. My section chief was thoughtful enough to include your picture in my briefing book. If it's not too bold of me, you have an unmistakeable face. May I join you?" She shook his hand softly and motioned for him to sit.

"You're the observer," she said. "Luc told me you were coming."

"That's me, but I hope you won't take me for a voyeur."

Sofia shrugged. "I'm the experiment, but I hope you won't take me for a guinea pig."

"No chance of that," Raszer said. "It's a beautiful afternoon, isn't it?" He scanned the sprawling gothic square, as if to encourage her to follow his eyes and take in the glory of the place, the scents and sounds she was about to abandon, but she ignored the cue. She seemed to him both oddly listless and utterly focused on an inner landscape.

"I'm playing hooky," she said, the parchment-thin flesh around her eyes crinkling. He wondered how long she'd been without solid food. "Don't tell Luc."

There was suddenly murmuring all around them, and the oiled ropes within the Tower Clock began to creak with resistance. At this, Sofia be-came animated and Raszer tracked her gaze up the fairytale façade of the stonework building. Just below the clock face, the skeletal figure of Death tugged at a dangling line. The twelve apostles came skating out in proces-sion while the Sun and the Moon moved through the purple Zodiac and the chimes *clanged* three o'clock.

"It would seem," said Raszer, "that Death is pulling the strings."

"And opening a door," she replied. "If it was good enough for the apostles, I suppose it's good enough for me."

"They blinded the poor soul that built that clock," Raszer said. "So that he couldn't reproduce it anywhere else."

"Those were cruel times," she said flatly. "Things haven't changed all that much."

"No," he agreed. He turned away from the clock and found her eyes. "But beautiful things somehow manage to survive in spite of it."

"Only if they're soulless," she said, half to herself. "Like a clock."

Although she took to his professorial charade, falling easily into the role of admiring student, he made efforts to keep rolling the conversation gently back to her. She had her own voice and a quiet resolve that was close to stubbornness. Her jaw was set just a little too firmly. It could have been exhaustion or it could have been doubt.

He ordered a glass of red Moravian wine and was surprised to hear her ask to join him. When it arrived, she took an oversized gulp as if steeling herself for something, which she was.

"If it were your time, Professor," she whispered, resting her hand lightly on his, "if you had been called, would *you* be ready?"

He clasped his fingers and thought hard. A wrong answer could cost him, so he opted for the truth.

"I'm not sure, Sofia," he said, "and for that reason, I'm the observer."

She laughed; a nice laugh, mellow and throaty, and she seemed to relax a bit. She swished her wine and swallowed the last of it. "Luc Fourché is the deepest man I've ever known, but sometimes he's a little paranoid. I think he thinks you're here to check up on him."

Raszer smiled. She had set up his next parry. "Montreal insists that each ceremony be witnessed by an *auditore*. Like a NASA launch. If there's a fly in the works, I can stop the countdown."

"But you won't, will you?" she pleaded with a yearning that tore at his heart. "I want out of here so bad. Don't you know—" The color drained from her face like mercury dropping. She doubled over, clutching her abdomen. Her right arm swept across the table, sending the wine glasses crashing to the cobblestones. She gripped Razser's wrist like a victim of vertigo holding on for dear life and her dark eyes flooded with pain. The boisterous café crowd was instantly mute.

"Sofia?" he exclaimed, jumping up and coming around to her side of the table. "Are you all right? Can you breathe?"

She nodded and, with practiced fortitude, drew herself upright, smoothed her white cotton skirt and began to compose herself

"It will pass. It always does. I pray that in three days it'll pass for good. *God!* I despise my body!" She stood and weakly took his hand. "It was nice to meet you."

Raszer watched her eyes narrow and shift their focus to something over his shoulder.

"Bastards!" she hissed. Raszer held her trembling hand and turned guardedly to find the object of her curse.

About twenty meters away, in the center of the Square, a simian-looking thug with a moonscape face held a camera to his eye, its huge lens pointed directly at them. Raszer felt her hand slip away as he surveyed the crowd. A stone's throw beyond the photographer, a short, cadaverous man tucked his head and disappeared furtively into one of the connecting alleys.

"Jesus," Raszer muttered.

He turned back to Sofia. She was as gone as smoke on the wind.

BEFORE HEADING FOR the Strahov Library, Raszer exchanged some currency and called Monica from a payphone, which required about two pounds of Czech coins. Monica picked up on the third ring.

"I'm going to play you Larry's latest voicemail, Raszer. Step back."

*"Tell Raszer I hope the fuck he's in Australia…and get his ass on the phone to me. I thought we were dealing with kooks, not kidnappers. They want ten million dollars delivered to a numbered account in the Caymans. You better be on this, Raszer, or you'll never fucking work in this town again!"*

Raszer had no intention of calling Gould himself. If the Temple had tapped the phone at Empire Pictures, a trace would show a call from Prague and they would immediately suspect Sofia of double-dealing.

"Tell Lawrence that I'm on to the Australian connection."

"Are you?"

"Yeah, well, it's only a white lie. I will be by the time you finish. Tell him he'll receive two more updates by way of you on Tuesday and Wednesday mornings. If I don't get through to you on Wednesday or confirm by then that I'll have her out by midnight, tell him to prepare to make the deposit exactly as they instructed in the ransom note. They want a cash drop in Caymans – dollars to doughnuts they'll transfer it out the minute it hits the account. We should be able to catch it before it comes out the other end. He is not, under any circumstances, to notify the FBI. I'll do that from this end if need be. This is international and the Feds don't have a clue. Tell him that the extortion only indicates that these guys are either crazier or smarter than we took them for. Either way, they're more dangerous."

Raszer listened to the comforting *clickety-click* of her nails on the keyboard as she took it down. In truth, Raszer was stumped by the Australian origin of the fax. The Temple was believed to have adherents in Oz, and it was possible that it was all part of a laundering scheme, but Gould was right, *why ransom someone who wants to die?* If one thing was clear from his first encounter with Sofia, it was that she was no kidnap victim. No, it could only be an effort to divert international law enforcement agencies from Prague, and it seemed, at least for the moment, to certify that Raszer's cover was solid. Nonetheless, he had to check it out.

"Get a hold of my friend Simon at CultWatch in Perth," he said. "Have him check all the chatter circuits; the Net, the occult bookstores, all of it. See if there's any Solstice activity planned for the central desert regions of Australia, all the way across to Sydney." Raszer's once impressive stack of coins was down to two.

"Got it, boss," Monica responded. "What does this have to do with Prague?"

"I don't have a fucking clue, but I'm out of coins. How's our girl Jeanette? Has the professor been a good boy so far?"

Monica answered with deliberate matter-of-factness so as not to alarm him but succeeded in doing so anyway. "She checked in on arrival, Raszer, but it's been almost twenty-four hours. Remember though, it's only eight a.m. there now. Maybe she—"

The line went dead. Raszer slammed it into its nest. There wasn't much more to say, but that didn't relieve his concern. Jeanette Molinieux and Noel Branch had flown to Thunder Bay on a twin-engine plane chartered by Mr. X. They were to have arrived thirty-six hours ago at an isolated cottage on the north shore where Branch was to write his treatise on the history of the Templar movement, with Jeanette as his secretary. A piece of cake for a pro like her. Eight a.m. or not, she should have logged in by now.

PHILIPPE CAUDAL SAT alone at the terminal and with three keystrokes moved $2.5 million from an isolated account in Venezuela to one of the stock funds now being established in Martinique. The French authorities were sniffing dangerously close to the elusive design of the Temple's holdings, and as chief financial officer, it was Caudal's duty – and his genius – to keep the shell game in play.

In a matter of days, every bite of data in every file would succumb to "St. John's flu," a computer virus he had helped to design. The Temple of the Sun was preparing for *L'eclipse Solaire*. As on the eve of every century for the last six hundred years, it planned to go into hibernation until the heat was off. The money would be safely nested in mutual funds and foundations, and the wisdom accumulated during the last century would be cached. Build and wait until the time for both cosmic renovation and earthly restoration had come. That was how to handle the Inquisition – you both outwitted and out-waited them. It was a policy that had kept them alive for six centuries. Only there were some, including Caudal and those in the Australian insurgency, who now felt they had waited long enough. To allow the current directorate to consolidate its power would only insure a hollow victory, with the spoils claimed by the same German overlords who had dominated a millennium of European history and denied the *sangraal* its time.

When Caudal was finished, the bank trail marked on the ransom scheme would lead the authorities not to the renegade Australian faction that Montreal was so keen to neutralize, but straight back to its own nest. It mattered little if Gould actually paid; Caudal expected he wouldn't. The American detective would push enough buttons to give the police all they needed, long before Montreal got wise and took him out.

Caudal moved another half-million to a numbered account in Brunei and relished, for the moment, having his hands on all the strings.

# 8

## SULFUR

THE UGLY LITTLE watermark on the ceiling came into focus as Jeanette registered a new sound. She'd been lying there, on the cabin's cold plank floor for the roughly three hours since Noel Branch had cracked the back of her skull with a Smith-Corona typewriter. She could see, hear, and smell weakly, but she felt nothing, nor could she move or talk. Although she was unable to lift her head, she knew that her assailant remained crouched in the corner eight feet away, naked and shivering. He hadn't stopped whimpering for even a moment, and it was that, as much as her paralysis, that made the situation intolerable. Now she heard the *snap* of a twig outside and she prayed, please God, let it be the fucking Mounties.

They were easily a half-day's drive from anything like a real town, but in spite of her profound vulnerability and the likelihood that her cranium was filling with fluid, Jeanette had not yet sunken into complete despair. The ability to accept altered realities was one of her gifts. She reasoned that even if the sound outside had been nothing more than a raccoon, Professor Branch seemed disinclined to harm her further and would probably summon help when he came down from whatever drug it was that she had given him. What effect all this would have on Raszer's mission was another issue, but she couldn't process that right now. A floorboard on the front porch *creaked*, and her hopes rose with her pulse.

Along with the briefing book she'd been given by Mr. X's driver, there had been a small packet labeled "Prof. Branch anti-anxiety medication." Inside the packet, along with eight gelatin capsules, there had been a note explaining that Branch was a mild agoraphobic and often became agitated when away from his familiar space for too long. There was concern that he might panic and demand to be taken home before the time was right. Since the professor, having had some nasty reactions, shunned all drugs, it was recommended that she simply open one or two of the capsules into his tea if he got out of hand. The note had been signed "X."

It had been, of all things, the hooting of a nearby spotted owl that had driven him to distraction. He paced about, refused to write and when she rubbed his shoulders to calm him, he became aroused and asker her for a blowjob. That's when she'd offered to make him tea, and that's when everything had gone haywire. Whatever was in those capsules had been seriously toxic to his system. He had torn off his clothes, screeching that he was, "cooking from the inside out." He babbled in Latin (or something like it) and ripped out his brittle hair by the fistfuls. When he wasn't on his knees howling, he had chased her about with a partial erection, shouting *'Le droit seignur! Le droit seignur!'* He had tackled her beside his writing table and torn at her collar. That was when she bit him on the shoulder and, in kind, he had taken the typewriter and hammered her cold.

The screen door opened with a rusty whine, and there were footsteps. She realized at that moment how much judgment is handicapped when feeling is gone. She was unable to tell anything about the size or weight of their visitor, or his degree of stealth or urgency. The lake breeze carried a trace of his cologne. She knew her mind must be going because she couldn't identify the scent.

The footfalls ceased. Jeanette somehow knew that he had dropped to a crouch just behind the crown of her head. The scent was stronger now, and she could hear him breathing aquatically, as if behind a mask. She rolled her eyes to the top of her head, but it was no use.

*"Mahabyn, Professor,"* she heard him say just before she picked up a whiff of gun grease and powder. "You've made a mess of things, Noel," he said, pulling back the hammer. "You'd better go before I shoot you. It'll be far worse if they find you here."

Jeanette waited breathlessly for the Professor's response, for it would be her only indication of whether this intercessor represented rescue or damnation. There was nothing. In the face of the gun, Branch's whimpering had stopped and there wasn't a sound. Then, in the diction of a punch-drunk fighter, she heard him say, *"Noooo...ih c-han't be you..."*

Her field of vision shifted as the stranger lifted her head, and she sensed that he must be probing the gash on the back of her head with the tip of his finger. He set her back down gently, and once again, her eyes were on the water stain above.

"You're in very bad shape, darling," he said, and she detected no irony, "and there's not a hospital for five hundred miles. You know what good spies do when they're caught, don't you?"

Now, finally, Jeanette gave up hope. Her last ditch defenses had always been either mercenary femininity or kung fu, and here she was, unable to speak or move a muscle.

"You're going to die now," he said softly, "but I don't want you to be afraid. Try to think of it as the embrace of a long lost friend."

She saw the fine stream of fluid arc above her head and fall weightlessly on her breast. She knew the sight well, the purging of air from a syringe. With every secret muscle, she struggled to break free of the useless corpse she was imprisoned by, and with her eyes...if only he could see her eyes...she pled and promised to be a good girl, if only—

She watched her murder, once it was forgone, from the perspective of the water stain on the ceiling. *It really does happen like that...dying; in the third person, like a dream.* A five-inch hypodermic, thick as a knitting needle, was plunged into her left breast and slipped easily into her heart. Then, as the pulse that had been pounding ferociously against her eardrums ebbed, he seized her wrists and began to drag her from the cabin and out along the dilapidated pier that broke the opaque surface of the icy, northern bay.

Only an ember of consciousness remained as he rolled her gingerly off the pier and into the black water, but it burned in the hardiest sector of her brain. Curiosity. *Let me see my killer,* it demanded. With dimming eyes, she watched her long red hair blossom like sea grass about her head as she dropped. He was watching, too. He wore a popular Halloween mask, an image of the Canadian Prime Minister. The eyes behind the mask were unmoving, hard focused but not entirely without sympathy.

*Vetiver,* she thought absurdly, as her heart stopped beating...that's the scent. Vetiver.

# 9

## MERCURY

*An immense superstructure of falsehood is built upon a slender foundation of truth...*

– Sir Richard Francis Burton, 1848

RASZER CLIMBED INTO the taxi and directed the driver to the Strahov Monastery. He was thinking about Sofia's attack in the Square, about why no pathology had shown up on her medical report. All he had was Gould's mention of "plumbing problems," and her doctor's assertion that her periods had stopped. He wondered if it was possible that she had cancer or had convinced herself that she did. He even had to allow that she might have faked it. She *was* an actress and talent always sought expression. If her pain was real, it introduced a motive that he hadn't been prepared to contend with. Ask the Buddha. Religion wasn't only about deliverance from evil; it was about deliverance from suffering.

Therein lay a possible clue to the appeal the Temple held for well-endowed and aging Catholics. Christian atonement would only go so far in relieving real pain. All the money in the world couldn't buy you out of terminal cancer, or even terminal *ennui.* Suppose the sect was offering a rarefied form of euthanasia for those who could afford it, those both sick with the world and just plain sick. For the spiritually inclined, a resurrection on Sirius might seem a more attractive gamble than being cryogenically frozen five miles beneath the Utah desert. The mythical oceanfront property in Miami, complete with angelic choirs. Then, Raszer gently reminded himself, there was a chance that it was all true.

As the taxi rumbled across the Legil Bridge toward the south end of the Castle District and the orchards of Petrin Hill, Raszer again opened the "Operation Rudolph" appendix to the briefing book Mr. X had given him. He turned for the first time to the Technical Data section at the back of the manual. His stomach dropped. Was this some sly joke? He'd expected

English (Branch's language), or possibly French but not this. The entire thing was encrypted in John Dee's *Enochian,* an admixture of sigils and Roman characters arranged in a way that could only be pronounced in a fit of glossolalia.

*"Dumb ass!"* he blurted, and slapped his hand to his head.

The taxi driver shot a glance in his rearview mirror and shrugged, evidently thinking he's hit a pothole.

*"Prominte,"* he said. "The roads is not very good."

"No, no— *prosim,"* Raszer apologized. "It's okay."

He returned his attention to the book. Of course, he, Noel Branch, a philologist and an expert on Dee's evocations, was supposed to be able to read this. These were presumably the alchemical incantations with which they intended to conduct their experiment. He'd surveyed enough of Dee's grimoires to recognize some of the sigils and a handful of angelic words, but he had neither a computer program nor a week with which to decipher the rest. John Dee, arguably the western world's first great cryptographer, had wanted to be sure that he and the other members of his hermetic fraternity could operate covertly. Whether he had help from the angels of the watchtowers was a matter for conjecture. Raszer sighed audibly and the broad-faced driver again flashed a worried look in his rearview mirror.

The old red bus leaving the bridge in front of them farted carbon monoxide, a bluish cloud that the river breezes smeared over the west bank of the Vltava, where three children – two boys and a girl about nine – played tug of war in the amber sunlight of late afternoon. A salmon pink ribbon dangled from the girl's strawberry hair, its bow undone.

Raszer sat forward and racked his eyes to her form. He flushed as he recognized the delicate arch of her back and watched her, in a gesture he knew well, raise her chin with pride after managing to pull the two boys to the ground. For just a tick of the cosmic clock, he was absolutely certain that it was his own daughter, Brigit. The taxi lurched off the bridge and mounted the hill, leaving the mirage behind. He rubbed his eyes and dropped them back to the text. Scattered letters in one of Dee's magical acrostics were highlighted to form a single name: *URIEL.* Raszer recalled that it had been Brigit, at the age of six, who'd taught him how to look at those 3D "Magic Eye" pictures that exasperated so many adults. She was still teaching him, from four thousand miles away.

The Strahov Monastery occupied the highest point in Prague, and as the taxi labored up the steep hill through the surrounding apple orchard, Raszer felt calmed by his proximity to a community of believers. He was not a "religious" man in the sense that people mean that now. But that word, like so many other good words, had been devalued by fraud. No person who admired the Middle Ages as much as Raszer did could fail to be moved by a unity of faith such as still can be felt in certain monasteries.

The holy citadel had been founded in 1140 by an austere Catholic order known as the Premonstratensians and had managed to withstand wars, pestilence, The Reformation, the Nazis and the Reds. Its defenses had finally been breached by market capitalism. In order to subsidize the upkeep of their marvelous libraries, the good brothers had leased the cavernous catacombs thirty feet beneath the foundation to a wealthy Italian family. The family had transfigured them into a fancy restaurant and disco, and further profaned the subterranean sanctuary by calling it *Peklo*, the Czech word for "Hell." In a little under three hours, he'd be dining there with a man who might or might not find the setting familiar.

After a stroll through the cloisters, Raszer leaned on the balustrade that overlooked the orchards. Then he retired to the men's room. He felt late afternoon jetlag coming on and tried to revive his wits by doing a little meditation in the quiet stall, succeeding only in lulling himself to sleep. A cough in the next stall woke him after a few minutes. He staggered to his feet and wandered dreamily into the Great Philosophical Hall where three stories of bookshelves rose to a vaulted ceiling of deepest azure.

Raszer approached the tall, tonsured librarian and tried out his Czech.

*"S'dovolenim. Dobre odpoledne. Muzete mi rici prelozit anglictina—"*

The monk raised his palm politely. His hands were enormous, the fingers tapered like candlesticks.

"You may speak English, sir," he said, "but I appreciate your effort."

"An English translation of John Dee's *Claves Angelicae,* if you have one; or the Latin, if not."

The tall monk nodded and smiled sagely. In any place but Prague, Raszer thought, the request would have elicited an empty stare. After retrieving the enormous leather-bound tome, he escorted Raszer to a sunken carrel in the rear of the great hall and left him in peace.

For a fledgling visionary, Raszer's method was doggedly scientific. He considered what he'd learned from the LAPD crime lab to be as valuable in its own way as what he'd learned from his first real guru at the tiny Vedanta Church in Hollywood.

Even apparently supernatural occurrences, like seeing his daughter on the banks of the Vltava, were sifted warily as evidence. It was how he kept his bearings. He feared that if he simply followed his nose, it would lead him through the looking glass, although that's where he was going like it or not. All he could hope for was that he would know he was there when he arrived.

The *Claves Angelicae* was a book of angelic "keys" delivered by John Dee for the purpose of summoning any of the forty-nine governors of the spirit world. Once they had answered your call, you were at liberty to ask their counsel on any number of great issues, but though your insight might be elevated by the celestial session, you were right back on the street when the time was up. Among mortals, only Enoch had managed to grab hold of the seraphim's hem and hitch a ride.

He opened his briefing book to the "Operation Rudolph" section and set it to his right. Then he began to scan the *Claves* in deliberately rapid-fire fashion, looking for common threads. After an hour of fruitless search, he absently turned a yellowed page and recognized the shape of a single three-word phase that occurred repeatedly in his manual. He drew his finger down to the 18th century English translation of the passage. It was a description of the physical properties of angelic beings, as related to Dee in a fever dream by the archangel known as Uriel.

The gist of the passage was that all matter was shot through with divinity; that human flesh, if properly forged by the alchemical process, could be converted to a sort of divine potential. The centuries collapsed like the folds of a fan, and Raszer heard the voice of another hero, the physicist David Bohm, lecturing at Stanford on what he called "zero-point energy," the hidden potential within the dark matter of space, the dark space of matter. John Dee's symbol for this energy resembled a little whirlpool in the vast ethereal sea, a "disturbance" in the warp and woof of space-time. *An angel.*

Raszer's hair stood on end. Approach by reason or approach by faith, pilgrim – either way, you come to God. A sensation flared in his solar plexus, curious and disturbing. Raszer felt the proximity of death and the feeling aroused him.

"Closing time, sir" the librarian said. Raszer slammed the book shut as if he'd been caught with pornography. Viewed from the sunken carrel, the monk looked even taller. He smiled and stepped down to retrieve the volume. "You may want to consult the Library of Ethiopian Texts at the University."

"Really?" Raszer was baffled. "What do John Dee and Ethiopia have to do with each other?"

The librarian stepped back, resuming his lofty height. "That same angel Uriel who revealed the Monad to Dr. Dee also escorted the prophet Enoch to Heaven. You'll find the account in the Ethiopian 1 Enoch."

"Do you suppose Uriel would be inclined to pick up another passenger if one knew how to call him?

The monk chuckled darkly. "Words have power; this is affirmed in the first verse of John. A clever man can always find a way to make them serve his will. But if his purpose and God's be not the same, it may not be an angel who will answer his call."

Raszer wandered numbly out of the cloister. He dropped onto a small stone bench and lit a cigarette. He was not normally a deep smoker, but now he allowed himself to pull the sweet, hot smoke down into the pit of his lungs so that its narcotic resin could feed the tiny veins that stoked his brain. He suddenly had a great desire to call his daughter.

THE DIRECTOR HAD chosen a table set into an alcove carved from the living rock of the catacombs. A sheer curtain of spring water ran artfully down the concave rock surface behind him and masked the noise from the main dining area. His right profile was highlighted by rosy candle-light reflected from the quartz-speckled rock.

Raszer stood for a moment in the foyer and surveyed the place through his faux-bifocals. He turned to the hostess, pushed his fingers through his thickly oiled hair, and nodded. He followed her past the mostly unoccupied tables and over a small stone bridge beneath which the subterranean stream gurgled.

Craftsmanship was in evidence everywhere. The tables were of rubbed, thickly lacquered rosewood with inlaid pearl, and the chairs, with their delicately bowed backs, were fine enough for a playboy's pied-a-terre on the canals of Venice. Illumination was reverent, but subtly suggestive in its pinkness; the light sources were neatly recessed in the cavern ceilings.

The hostess slowed to a halt ten feet from Luc's table and motioned to Raszer. "*Monsieur* Fourché," she announced, "Dr. Branch has arrived."

Raszer's throat seized as he peered through the humid miasma of candlelight at the man who'd just been presented as Fourché. Other than the generic similarity of Gallic features, the slight and impeccably tailored man before him bore little resemblance to any of the Luc Fourché's pictured in Interpol's files.

A thousand possibilities laced across Raszer's cortex as he considered his next move, and felt his pulse accelerate. *Relax, soldier,* he counseled himself. Noel Branch, a college professor, would be expected to know the reputation but not the man.

He stepped forward into the light and extended his hand as Luc rose from his chair. *Monsieur Fourché,"* he said, in his best foreign service French, *"d'apres votre grande reputation, uh...il est pour moi un honneur que d'vous rencontrer."*

Luc tipped his head in false modesty and motioned for Raszer to sit. *"Merci beaucoup. Mais, cependant le fruit de mes travaux n'est inspire que par ma passion...*and now, please have a seat, Dr. Branch. We can continue in a language you speak more fluently. How do you find the Europa?"

"Honestly, it's a bit noisy for my tastes," Raszer replied. "I confess I was surprised that we chose something so *exposed*."

"The surest way to be found, Professor, is to hide when there is no need of hiding. You can sleep, as the French say, 'with both ears.' We are well protected." He gave a nod in the direction of a table not visible from the restaurant's entryway. There, in near darkness, sat the two men Raszer had seen in the Square; the fat one with the cratered skin and the small, ferret-faced older man who looked like a stiff. The later turned as if his ears had been burning and offered Raszer an unsettling, thin-lipped smile."

"They don't look like good company," Raszer said. "Ex-KGB?"

"Belgian *mercenaries,"* Luc replied. "The hungry-looking one, Bandeur, is old enough to have been in the Congo. He is without pity. They say he buggers his victims after he kills them." He chuckled dryly and handed Raszer a menu.

"I'll make every effort to stay behind him then," Raszer said, accepting the oversized bill of fare and laying it open on the table. "Has it come to this, then? Paid killers in the avant-garde?"

*"Come* to this?" Luc chided him. "When was there a time when we did not require protection? You live in an ivory tower, Professor, so you can be forgiven your naiveté about the necessity of unsavory bedfellows, but philosophically, you surely know that in this fallen world, light and dark coexist symbiotically."

Luc's English was nearly flawless but accented in a gentle, almost melodious way that made Raszer think of Marseilles. He processed the statement for a moment, dropped his gaze to the menu and then responded.

"I'll venture to say," he said, "that both my published writings and my private affairs reflect an understanding of that symbiosis."

"Yes," Luc agreed. "It is well-known, Professor Branch, that you are a long way from salvation."

Raszer located an entrée and glanced up at Luc. "Perhaps *Monsieur,* that's why you are the priest and I the altar boy."

"Indeed." Luc reached into an inside pocket of his Italian suit and produced a number of Polaroids. "Then it might be prudent to keep your hands off the communion wine." He flipped across the table a snapshot of Raszer at Sofia's table, his hand resting on her forearm.

Raszer lifted his palms in contrition. *"Mea culpa.* I went for a stroll and recognized her from the dossier. She is lovely—" Luc arched an eyebrow. "—and devoted to you, I might add."

"No matter," Luc said with a grunt. "You are not to have contact with her or any of the others. The six candidates have been under my training for months in what is a highly experimental course. The *Alchemical Endura.* You are to observe them only, as any interference would undoubtedly affect the outcome of the experiment. Is that clear?"

Raszer closed his menu. *"Absolumente,"* he replied. "The *Endura* was the Cathar sacrament in preparation for bodily death and spiritual transfiguration, encoded, some say, in the Voynich Manuscript. Have we adopted their rite?"

"Only what is useful. The Cathari and the Templars both sought the *renovatio.* Both suffered the flames. The inquisition has a great interest in keeping us bound within these prisons of flesh." Luc summoned the waitress. "If you are going to have something to eat, we should order so that we will not be disturbed further."

Raszer glanced at the waitress, a robust bleached-blonde in a white tuxedo vest and lifted his own hand to hold off her approach. "Just one thing, Luc. May I call you *Luc?"* The Frenchman blinked slowly to indicate assent. Raszer tipped his head subtly toward the gunmen in the corner. "Speaking of dark bedfellows, would you happen to know if Operations assigned one of their kind to me? I would have sworn there was a man on the plane…a very tall fellow." Raszer thought he saw the hint of a smile.

"I am not privy to everything Operations does, but they do not take chances." He took a genteel sip from his crystal water goblet, then dabbed at his thin, almost prissy lips with his linen napkin.

Raszer swept his eyes over the table for evidence of wine. He was only fifteen minutes in and he needed a drink badly.

"You must know," Luc continued, leaning in conspiratorially, "that there is a schism; the Australian faction," he settled back. "It's only out of courtesy that I did not have you frisked. It is possible that Montreal assigned someone to insure your safe arrival. From your description, well, God help you if it's Josef De Boer and you give them any cause to doubt you."

Raszer kept his eyes riveted on Luc and flexed his fingers to bring the waitress. She moved toward them with the grace of a gymnast, surprising for a girl of her height and sturdy, Slavic build. Her bleached hair was bunched up into a palm crown at the top of her head, the dark roots planted in her scalp like the trunk of an old oak. Magnificent green, cat's eyes were set in a broad, fair face into which the blood rose when Raszer turned to her, smiled and gamely attempted Czech.

"*S'dovolenium…mluvite anglicky?*"

"English, German and a little Italian," she said, and then glowered at Luc. "Not French."

"Christ," Raszer said reflexively, "everybody puts the Americans to shame." From the corner of his eye, Raszer saw Luc tilt his head quizzically, and he knew he'd just slipped. He was not an American. His heart rose into his throat. "We *Canucks,*" he added, "at least try to master schoolboy French." He seemed to have bought a reprieve and opened the menu. "How's the duck?"

"It is de-boned, sir, and served with polenta and a sauce of Calvados made by the monks." She hesitated when she saw Raszer admiring the beauty mark on her left cheek, just to the left of her upper lip. "It is good when it's eaten pink."

"I'll have to have it then," he said. "You seem to know the room."

She turned to Luc on one heel and rested her order tablet on her hip. "And you, *Monsieur,*" she said. "Your usual penance?"

Luc's brow furrowed just slightly. "I will have the turnip broth," he answered brusquely. "Hot; not tepid, as last time. And some wine for my guest. With duck, let's see…a good *Côtes de Rhone,* not that Moravian piss."

She nodded smartly and snapped her book shut. When she'd left, Raszer turned back to Luc.

"You're not having dinner, *Monsieur?*"

"When we're in this phase," Luc replied. "I try to share the privations of my acolytes, and, in any case, I ceased to eat flesh on the day I came to understand that flesh begins its decay from the instant of birth."

"But you seem to be an *habitué* of this place, *non?*"

"I come for the ambience, not the food, and to escape the odor of the Czechs. Most of them, that is—" The wine steward arrived. "Ah, here is your wine, Professor," Luc said, scrutinizing the vintage. "Now I think you will be more at ease."

Raszer had not been aware that his nervousness showed. Luc, whoever he might be in truth, was an estimable man. There *was* something pious, almost papal about his bearing and certitude, but there was also something utterly amoral in the blackness of his eyes. There was a name for the look, *antinomian;* one that considers himself above all laws and moral constructs in the pursuit of the pure. He poured Raszer's wine, but none for himself.

"So," he began, once they were again alone, "you've no doubt read the brief. How much has your dispatcher told you of what lies in store this week?"

Raszer took a mouthful of wine and rolled it around his tongue. He had prepared for the question but hadn't yet settled on one of a half-dozen prospective answers.

"Relatively little about your methodology, beyond what I can deduce from your choice of location…and of me, as your *auditore.*"

Luc snorted. "You flatter me, Dr. Branch. Perhaps you flatter yourself, as well. I did not choose you. You were selected by the Golden Circle, especially Caudal. If it were left to me, there would be no *auditore*. You would be back screwing students and playing the hermetic dilettante in Montreal. What is it the Americans say? Those who can, do, and those who can't—"

"—*Watch,*" Raszer said, lifting his glass. "Well it's good we've established that. As much as I admire your spiritual courage, I have an equal disdain for zealots." Luc said nothing, remaining expressionless. "Now, I see that you're using Dee's evocations. Tell me how you have advanced our science beyond *La Serre*. Frankly, I'd have thought we'd come up with a more elegant way to give up the ghost than bullets and belladonna."

"Oh," Luc said, relishing the *tête-à-tête* as only the French can, "we have."

*"Je coute, Monsieur."*

Luc leaned in close enough for Raszer to smell a trace of sen-sen. There was something wax-like about his skin that gave Raszer the eerie sense that his host had been struck from a mold. But the eyes. The eyes had been designed by some demonic doll maker for the purpose of seducing souls.

"Professor Branch," he said in a stage whisper, "after two millennia, we have located Enoch's Portal. We are going through the wormhole."

"Interdimensional travel?" Raszer asked, trying to mask undue awe.

"As it has always been, though no one knew to describe it as such before the last century. They spoke of spheres and sephirah, aeons and planes; concepts that the linear, hierarchical mind could grasp. Space exploration was the material analog of this thinking. Somehow though, I think the great ones – Trismegistus, Simon Magus, Plotinus, Dee, and yes, even that rascal Crowley – all sensed that it was an *inner* journey to the source of being. And now, after four centuries of tarot cards and faux spiritualism, we have science as our ally once again in navigating the passage."

Raszer's duck arrived under an ornate sterling silver hood that the waitress removed with a flourish. As an afterthought, she slid Luc's soup dish in front of him and waited for him to pronounce it hot enough. He touched the tip of his index finger to the surface of the broth and grimaced. It had been microwaved to the temperature of molten lava. She turned on her heel.

*"Putain!"* he cursed, as she fled the scene of the crime.

"She seems to have it in for you, *Monsieur Director.*"

"And any man, Professor, who fails to see her as Helen of Troy."

"So, how have you done it?" Raszer asked, piercing the crisp skin of the duck with his fork, the juices running pink. "I'm a good historian and a middling metaphysician, but modern science possesses a vocabulary I cannot deconstruct."

"My process," Luc replied, without a trace of modesty, "is *quantum alchemy.* The Royal Science conducted at the subatomic level. Agrippa and Paracelsus and Flamel were right in theory, but they were wrong in working with gross metals and heat that was insufficient by a factor of tens of thousands. It is the heat of the sun we need, *no less.*"

Raszer set down his fork, the crisped skin suddenly problematic. "You're going to incinerate Sofia Gould and her cohorts?"

"Nothing so crude as that," Luc replied tartly. "You may have heard of the work being done on electron tunneling in the brain; the idea that consciousness itself is a quantum effect. The orthodox scientists will not say it, but I will. What we call higher consciousness is nothing less than the will to unite with the godhead; the *coniunctio,* the Grail of the alchemists. It goes round and round in our brains, taunting us with intimations of the divine but utterly trapped in a closed circuit. I intend to liberate it through the use of the *Casimir Force.*"

"Zero point energy?"

"If you like. Once released from it robotic function, the individual consciousness is distilled to pure spirit and enters *Hilbert Space,* where time flows as easily backwards as forwards. That is the— how do you say it? The dicey part?"

"I suppose I should ask," Raszer ventured, "that is, if you don't mind me playing Devil's Advocate…"

*"Au contraire.* I would enjoy it."

"The Portal you speak of can only be the eye of a very small needle. Dee discovered that or his reputation would now surpass Da Vinci's by light years. What possible force drives the spirit through?"

"*Thanatos*, Professor. What Freud, a Jew misguided by inbred presumptions about the sanctity of life, called the 'death-wish' is in fact the urge to return to the source. Among the *knowers*, his Eros – the mindless imperative to prolong our time in Hell through attachments to other condemned souls – is but a passing blip on the vital signs meter. Death rules."

"There is considerable biological evidence to the contrary."

"Not among our kind, Dr. Branch," Luc countered, sending a distinct chill up Raszer's backside. "Tell me, truthfully, did you ever wish to lie down among the lilies? Have you never tried to end your life?"

Raszer felt his fingers go numb, and for a few moments, he could not so much as lift his glass.

"I do seem to have a problem with nicotine," he offered.

"I should order you into our detoxification program," Luc scolded. "The body may be a trash can, but as long as it contains us, we must trouble to keep it free of corrosion."

"Didn't Adolph Hitler say much the same thing? He didn't touch meat, either."

"Hitler was a visionary with a weak and syphilitic mind. The race will not survive long enough to understand him. But to give your question its due, consciousness will seek to return to its ground. Abstractly, it may follow Bohm's quantum pilot waves and go *zitterbenegung* right back through a singularity in the veil. That veil is the *plenum...the singularity is the way home.*"

"Now I *am* out of my depth," Raszer said. "How can you possibly release that kind of energy without creating your own personal Big Bang?"

Luc pushed his soup aside. "The key, as with all manipulation of energy, is control. That is what three dozen idiot savants in six countries have been working on under my supervision for the past five years. You're quite right. There is a Big Bang, but it's an *implosion.* You will see the device tonight, and I think you will be surprised by its...elegance." Without preface, Luc leveled his gaze at Raszer and said, "I am not the man you expected to meet, am I, Professor?"

Raszer threw a napkin over his duck, which had grown cold. He hated to waste a good meal. He smiled a closed-lipped smile, wishing he had a cigarette for a prop. "I expected only to meet a *compagnon* of the highest order," he bluffed.

"Really? I felt certain I saw consternation on your face when you came in." He let the acuity of his observation sink in for a beat. "Perhaps not."

"A *credente* understands that the physical form is transitory," Raszer said, dancing on coals. "Even an effete academic like myself. But I confess I am curious. The police would have it that a certain *Monsieur* Fourché passed through the gate at *La Serre.*" Raszer reminded himself to breathe.

"He did…and he has completed the circle. *I am Fourché.*"

"Then as a mortal not so privileged," Raszer offered, "I salute you."

"You may find a certain kind of immortality, Professor" Luc said, calling for the check. "It was, after all, your own work on the Voynich Manuscript that provided me with the Rosetta Stone." Raszer swallowed and kept his silence. Neither X nor Stocker Hinge had mentioned this particularly salient fact. "You pointed out that the key might lie in those silly illustrations that every other scholar dismissed as nonsense. 'A theurgic riddle in the guise of soft-core pornography.' I believe those were your words."

"Well then," said Raszer, after a gulp, "my perversity has served a purpose."

"Indeed. As I mentioned, the light and the dark in concert. Come. Let me buy you a digestif. There's a small bar near the entrance. I may even join you to remind myself of how little pleasure it now affords me, in comparison to *Her* embrace."

Raszer stumbled as he made his way back over the bridge. "I'd be honored," he said, his anxiety rising. "After I find the men's room."

The men's toilet was as well appointed as the rest of the place. In the far corner, sat a pale old Czech in a white servant's jacket whose eyes seemed permanently glazed over. He had a hand towel draped over his knee but made no move to offer it.

Raszer leaned heavily onto the marble-topped washbasin, bracing his palms against its sides. He felt overcome with the vertigo that usually preceded his visions, and he cast a forbidding look into the gold-flecked mirror. *Where are you now, Snow White?* He looked down to see that the sleeves of his pale blue linen shirt had ridden up on his wrists, exposing the old scars. Raszer suddenly convulsed and wretched into the sink.

"To be or fucking not to be?" he asked in the hiss of air that left his lungs. The Lady in the mirror didn't answer. Raszer was scared. He'd expected to meet a highbrow con artist, not a rocket scientist. He went to pee, splashed some cold water on his face and headed for the bar, but not before considering a hasty retreat through the kitchen.

A bottle of *Slivovice* and two faceted crystal snifters were on the bar beside Luc, and though the barmaid's wide back was turned, Raszer saw immediately that the cheeky waitress, now outfitted in a snug black waistcoat, was pulling double duty. From her peroxided carrot-top hung a wide hair ribbon of salmon pink. *What craziness is this?* When she turned, he saw that she wore the waistcoat open over a silky white camisole with a plunging neckline.

He crossed the darkened dance floor of what appeared to be a very chic little discotheque, a private cavern unto itself. They were alone but for an aristocratic looking young man who sat alone in a distant booth, nursing a drink. Luc handed Raszer a glass, then lifted his own in a toast. The barmaid smirked.

"You better accept his offer before he switches to orange juice."

"They really ought to find some better help here," Luc opined, loudly enough for her to hear. "It's a travesty to call these people European."

The girl tossed her head dismissively and turned back to Raszer, extending her hand. "I am Marta," she said. "Welcome to Hell." Her handshake was firm.

"Noel Branch," he said. "Hell is looking good."

"American, did you say?" she asked, hearing chinks in his Canadian accent. "I love Americans!"

"Canadian. Sorry. Halfway there."

"Ah, well," she sighed. "As close as I will ever see." She turned her back to her bottles and set to work tidying the area. She had a full, but perfectly pear-shaped bottom, accented by the tapered ends of the long, pink hair ribbon.

"To the *auditore,*" said Luc, still holding his glass aloft. "May you give a successful account of our enterprise."

"To the celebrant," answered Raszer, lifting his own. "If my account secures your place in history, it will have been a success." He took the fiery plum brandy down in a gulp and leaned in to Luc's ear. "May I ask you a pedestrian question?" he whispered.

"Of course," Luc said. In the background, Raszer saw the two gunmen enter the bar and claim a booth in the rear, next to the one occupied by the unaccompanied man, who got up and left without showing his face.

"What becomes," Raszer asked, "of the bodies? It's a little untidy to keep leaving corpses strewn everywhere."

"We're done with that. Where my process is applied, there will be no bodies. Hence, no crime. The centurions will be lucky to find a burial shroud." Luc offered him another shot but Raszer demurred.

"And…" Raszer pressed. "I'm sorry. I feel like a schoolboy, but is there a reincorporation of some sort…once the destination is reached? On Sirius?"

Luc gave him a patronizing but not entirely unfriendly smile. It seemed to please him to have one over on the distinguished academic. He took hold of Raszer's elbow and led him a few steps from the bar. The barmaid's eyes followed, tracking Raszer like a patroness assigned to protect her knight's virtue.

"You're aware, Professor," Luc replied softly, "as an educated man, that when you look into the night sky at the point of light we call Sirius, you are looking back in time; a very long way back. It is no more accurate to speak of 'travel' to Sirius, in the common sense, than it is to say that Enoch was taken up in a 'chariot.' What happens upon the soul's liberation happens in another epoch altogether – the time at which the starlight we perceive was first generated. Do you understand?"

"Not really," might have been the honest answer, but Raszer didn't have the chance to offer it. The dance floor on which he stood suddenly became a nebula of spinning stars set loose by three digitally controlled mirror balls, each one brilliantly reflecting one of the primary colors. Theatrical fog poured from ports in the floor and at the base of the bar. The ancient stone began to throb in resonance with the insistent pulse of a trance-techno groove.

Marta the barmaid, who had her hand on the switch designed to transform the quiet bar into a rave pit, had made an executive decision to end Raszer's tutorial. Luc spun and glared at her, but she simply shrugged her shoulders and shouted above the din.

"Sorry, *Monsieurs!* Club Praha is opening in one hour. I must test system before customers come." She shot a glance at Raszer, who felt certain her labored syntax was a put-on. "You like?" she called. "Is very most techno in Prague."

Raszer nodded his approval and turned back to Luc, who was glowering amid the *sturm und drang.* Jackhammer percussion looped over a mantra-like bass in that incessant, martial Euro-beat that turns even mild-mannered office workers into bacchants.

As if it were quite simply part and parcel of the nightly system check, Marta sprung athletically onto the dance floor and went into a dance routine that was equal parts Tae-Bo and Martha Graham.

Raszer shot a quick look at the two thugs in the booth. They were stiff and expressionless, waiting for instruction from Luc, who was busy giving the finger-across-the-throat kill signal to an obliviously ecstatic

Marta. Raszer leaned back against a wooden buttress, lit a cigarette and waited to see where it was all going to lead. There were worse things to do, on a night when the talk had been of *thanatos* and cosmic cremation, than to watch a big blonde do Salome's dance to a techno beat. He found himself hammering his heel against the floor.

On an exasperated cue from Luc, the older henchman, the one he had called Bandeur, rose calmly from the booth, walked behind the bar and flipped the kill switch. The room returned to its former state. Marta tossed her hair out of her face and marched to her station, her bare shoulders glistening with the honey-sweat of all out exertion. With an oversized wink aimed deliberately at the nonplussed Frenchman, she put on her waiter's coat and said simply, *"Voila!"*

Raszer poured himself another drink and gave her a long look. There was something going on here he couldn't yet fathom. A single bead of perspiration ran from the cleft of her neck down her décolletage, and in a burst of synesthesia, he was able to taste the salt on his tongue.

Luc broke his revelry with an admonition, whispered at close range. "Our work begins in just two hours, Professor. Let us share a taxi to the hotel. As you've just flown in today, you may want to rest before the Tower."

"I think," said Raszer, with one eye on Luc and one on the flushed barmaid, "that if it's all the same, I'll ask our hostess to fix me a cup of tea and make some notes here, while our conversation is fresh in my mind. You've given me a great deal to digest." He watched Luc's eyes narrow slightly. "If I were to lie down at the hotel, I'm afraid I might never get up. If you'll direct me to the site, I'll hop a taxi when the time comes."

"No, Professor," Luc said in a harsh whisper. "You do not 'hop' a taxi to a secure location within the walls of Hradcany Castle. If you must remain here, I will leave Otto with you." Luc nodded in the direction of the younger gunman, who raised his recessed chin slowly at the mention of his name. His face had the dull cruelty of the malignantly stupid. Raszer wondered if a few more minutes of Marta's grace were worth bearing his company. Of course they were, he concluded, for was there any greater *gnosis* than knowing how that single bead of salt-sweat truly tasted? Besides, he had a feeling that she had something for him, something of value.

"All right," Raszer said, nodding an acknowledgment to the man identified as Otto. "Does Otto speak English?" Luc hesitated, and Raszer saw right through his subterfuge.

"No. German and Belgian French, but he'll get you there." Luc shot a warning look at Marta and then back to Raszer, whose own fraud was equally transparent. "Let me caution you, Professor. There is no late admission. Tonight we accomplish the 'Work in the Black;' the cleansing of the physical body in preparation for albification. In the old days, this was the work of purging the body of all carnal desire. You might do well, Professor – even as an observer – to keep your own desires in check."

Raszer leveled his eyes at Luc and squinted hard. "My dedication to the Work is equal to yours, *Monsieur Director,* however different our roles may be. As I said, I'm going to make some notes. After all, someone has to write your story."

Luc stepped back and gave a stiff bow. *"D'accord, mon frere."* He took Raszer aside. "You will enter the grounds via the Old Castle steps and the servant's gate on the east end of the fortress, just beside the Dalibor Tower. Otto knows the way and has the password. Our staging area is a small house at No. 22 Golden Lane. You'll join us there at eleven-thirty."

"Kafka's house?" Raszer noted, having seen mention of the address in a Michelin guide.

"I believe it was for a short time," Luc replied. "Are we clear?"

"Absolutely." Raszer offered his hand but Luc had already spun on his heel and headed out with the gaunt shadow named Bandeur.

Raszer took a breath he'd wanted to take for two hours and pulled a stool to the bar. He reached into his bag and brought out his journal. He did, in fact, want to make some notes. Marta was scrubbing a sink about eight feet away, and Otto was hovering uncomfortably close, apparently unsure of what to do with himself. Raszer pivoted to him and extended his hand, which Otto regarded as if it were a foreign and distinctly repellent object. *What is it with these guys and handshakes?*

"Can I offer you a drink, Otto?" No response. "Well, the…" Raszer nodded toward the distant booth. "Why don't you, uh, stand down for a bit? You'll let me know when it's time to go, right?" Otto nodded with what seemed a dim comprehension and backed off into the shadows. So much for his lack of English.

When Marta came within range, Raszer spoke up softly. "I liked your routine. You ought to consider a career."

"I have a career. Dancing is my pleasure. Stay another hour and you can see the whole show." She made a face. "Without interruption."

"I'd love to," he said, "but I have some business to do tonight."

"Men always say they are 'doing business' when they are up to no good. Especially at midnight in Prague." She gave him an exaggerated sidelong look. "Don't kid yourself that women don't know."

"I never kid myself about what women know," he said. "They always know too much."

Marta threw her head back and laughed deeply, the tendons in her neck taut above the swell of her breast. She had the kind of body that hadn't been much in evidence since the days of Anita Ekberg and *La Dolce Vita,* sumptuously upholstered but remarkably contained. Raszer wasn't picky about women's bodies, but forced to choose, he'd always take soft over hard.

"Then dance with me now."

"I have a bad ankle. I may not be in shape to rave."

"I've got some Nina Simone," she purred.

"Now you're talking." He set a cigarette between his lips and smiled, and he saw the smile have its effect. She rolled her shoulders back and cast a downward glance at his fingers from beneath lowered lashes. Raszer regarded her with fascination, as one would watch a lioness on the hunt. The greater share of men read such gestures as simple come-on, but Raszer had come to read them another way. A door was about to be opened. She lit his cigarette and leaned in close to draw the smoke into her nostrils.

"I may have something for you, Mr. Branch," she whispered. "A man should know who he is doing business with. Where can I find you?"

"At the Europa," he answered impulsively. Now he was sure.

SIX THOUSAND MILES away and seven hours west of the meridian, a naked man sprang from dense forest onto a rutted dirt road in the central Canadian wilderness. Noel Branch had had a bad trip. The Mountie who intercepted him later attested that Branch had moaned incessantly about how a "succubus" had tried to "take his seed." When Branch was found, he was a twelve-mile walk south-by-southwest of his starting point, the small fisherman's cabin on an inlet of Thunder Bay.

As he sat shivering in the Thunder Bay outpost of the RCMP, shrouded in an army blanket, Dr. Branch was stung by flashbacks. He could see her there in his mind's foggy eye, with the small pool of blood coagulated around her pretty head, but he could not for the life of him recall having delivered the mortal blow. What he did recall, with the exaggerated clarity of delusion, was the sound of that voice...*that voice*...and the word it had spoken. "Mahabyn." The old Masonic password. By all accounts, the voice belonged to a dead man. Although as a *credente* of the faith he embraced the notion of transmigration, resurrection of the body was something he'd generally left to the Christians.

At this moment, Noel Branch hadn't a clue as to what sort of mischief had been practiced, but it smelled like a Temple *putsch* of some sort. He felt a deep shame at having once again allowed the promise of literary glory and the spell cast by a red-haired witch to take him out of the center ring. Not currently suspected by the police by anything other than madness, he was invited to use the telephone. He made one call. In his right mind, he would have called his sponsor and station chief, Philippe Caudal, but Branch was not in his right mind. Instead, he dialed the emergency number he'd once been given for Temple Operations in Montreal.

# 10

## METAMORPHOSIS

THE WALKING ROUTE to Hradcany Castle was veined with dozens of steep, narrow streets, as many leading to cul-de-sacs as to the timeless, silent squares that served as hubs in the city's design. Just as in the dark, expressionistic street art that proliferated in the stalls and kiosks of the old town, the eaves of the ancient row houses leaned precariously into those opposite them, as if stooped to share the secrets stored in their attics. The collapse of these top-heavy frame dwellings was prevented by flying buttresses that, in every direction, created the impression of successively diminishing archways, leading to a distant vanishing point that might well be the place you'd just come from. "Kafka-esque," Raszer supposed people would call it. Could even Kafka have envisioned the butterflies that Luc planned to conjure from the cocoons of his six devotees?

Raszer had torn himself from Marta, the Delphic barmaid, to taxi with Otto to the Church of Saint Nicholas on the Little Quarter Square, from where they'd been instructed to hoof it. Just before he'd left, Marta slipped her tongue into his mouth, as if to leave her stinger embedded in him. It was there, all right.

He looked ahead. Looming over the fog-draped treetops of Vojan Park, he could make out the spotlight-bathed profile of the old Dark Age hill fort that had become Hradcany Castle. In the cool bright morning, President Vaclav Havel would report to work there, unaware of the fantastic events of the eve. Raszer would have given plenty to hear his take on what was going on under his nose.

The Malostranska Metro Station was a block ahead, and beyond, Raszer could see the Old Castle steps, ascending into silk-stocking fog. It was only now that he felt the grip of fear on his calves, slowing his stride a bit. This was no coven of silly witches standing naked and flabby in a candlelit parlor, chanting incantations from an Aleister Crowley manual. However misguided his applied science might be, Fourché – or whoever the hell he was – was utilizing advanced quantum physics to effect an alchemical transformation. Raszer had fully expected that the drama in Prague would involve some sort of highly elaborate ceremony leading, presumably, to suicide. Nothing in Hinge's data, however, or in his informant's leaks had indicated that The Temple traveled in circles that could commandeer a castle or commission the design of a "device" that could distill spirit from matter. According to Jung, *alchemy* was a process that took place *within;* the alchemist's vessel – *the amianthus* – was the analog of the soul. There was no analogy in Luc's design. He was preaching the doctrine as literally as a Christian fundamentalist and practicing it like the R & D division of an occult Dow Chemical.

They had mounted the first of five hundred worn steps when an alarming idea flew out of the fog and into Raszer's marrow: what if it was the other way around? What if those, like himself, who took myth as metaphor (though no less the marvelous for that) were the blind ones? What if the whole fucking universe was tiered like a corporate hierarchy, with the grunts struggling to make it to the next level and only those with the key to the executive washroom allowed to use the shower? What if wisdom was just another name for inside information?

The east side of the castle was dark at this hour, and he blindly followed Otto along a narrow easement that ran from the top of the steps to the fortress walls. The moss-speckled stone was damp and slick with a lubricant of misted soot. The tactile sensation of contact with the ancient rock aroused his spirit-sense, and he felt the hair on his arms bristle. Raszer paused and leaned for a moment onto the stonework and visually scaled the thirty foot-plus wall, allowing his fingertips to explore a mortar crack. Ever since his first climbing experience, Raszer had not been able to regard a vertical face without imagining how to get over it. This one seemed climbable with the right equipment. The dampness would pose the danger.

The old servant's entrance was illuminated by a single, bare yellow light bulb. It hung over a recessed iron gate the size of an ordinary door. On Otto's heavy approach, a common looking old fellow, who had been dozing lightly just inside the gate, leaned into the light, giving Raszer a start. The man had on his face the chronically bored look of a holdover from the Soviet era. He stood wearily and, without word or expression, pushed a pencil and a small scrap of blank paper through the bars. Otto scribbled something and handed it, along with a wad of hundred crown notes, back to the guard, who grunted and turned the rusty key.

They were led through a low and dimly lit service tunnel with no apparent terminus. After about a hundred yards of gentle incline, they emerged through a wooden door into a covered walkway resembling a cloister. On his right, through the open stonework, were the North Castle walls. Thirty yards to the left were the massive, gothic buttresses of St. Vitus Cathedral. Two more guards making their rounds and evidently in on the plan noted their progress. Bribes must have cost the Temple dearly, for they appeared to have secured the entire east wing. A greased palm still got you a long way in the old bloc, even here, where Vaclav Havel had made such noble efforts to change hearts and minds.

They proceeded down a cobblestone alley that opened into Golden Lane, a tourist attraction by day. Night and fog had muted the bright colors of the fairytale cottages. Legend had it that Rudolf II's alchemists had once occupied the cottages, but like most everything else, they had now been leased over to the merchant class, boutiques and souvenir shops. Absent of commerce and blanketed by a spectral mist, Golden Lane was the archetypal street of dark dreams; the one run down to elude a pursuer despite the awareness that the only hope of survival lies in waking.

The guard halted at Number 22, gave a perfunctory goosestep and then vanished by an alternate route. Otto rapped twice on the dollhouse blue door and waited. It had begun to drizzle.

Luc's coven was gathered in the parlor of the tiny house, surrounded by the carefully archived artifacts of Kafka's brief tenancy. They sat cross-legged on the floor in a circle, like campers waiting to hear a ghost story. Luc made polite introduction to faces already somewhat familiar from the briefing book. Claude Masson, the banker, looked 50-ish, but older in the eyes. There were deep lines engraved from the corners of his mouth down to the chin. The Klipp twins, Lisbeth and Elsbeth, were attired identically in gray pullovers and black stretch pants, as if by habit since nestling side-by-side as infants. The most striking of their shared features were the slightly crossed eyes that made them look a bit dazed. Robert Perrault, the skier, was impeccably groomed, but there was a hollowness in the neck that made him look like a Romantic-era consumptive. Sonja Kochius, the German model, had skin the color of dough. None of these people, Raszer surmised, were getting enough red meat.

By virtue of both her position in the circle and the Hollywood regality she wore in spite of herself, Sofia stood out as the queen bee. She cast a furtive look in Raszer's direction and dropped her gaze when he smiled.

Luc clasped his hands like a schoolmaster and motioned Raszer to a chair just outside the circle. "Dr. Branch, I would like you to remain close but outside the perimeter of the circle, and bear in mind the protocol we spoke of at dinner. While the Tower is being readied, we have prepared a small 'entertainment' for you."

Luc gestured for his pilgrims to close the circle and then extinguished all but the single candle in their midst. From a bowl of fruit by his side, he took an apple and placed it in the center of the circle. He walked three times clockwise round the group, and placing his hand on the head of each member, dropped his voice to a monotonal chant. The group accompanied him with the unity of a single voice.

> *You are one, you are one, you are one*
> *Child of the child Horus…IATO…exist!*
> *You are one, you are one, you are one with us*
> *SEMELEL…TELMACHAE…OMOTHEM…THOTH*
> *Bring forth the glory; desire the one who desires you*
> *All perfect, all in all in all*
> *AKRON…OH, TRIPLE ONE…AAAAAAAH!*
> *OOOOOOOH! BITREISE…*
> *You are spirit from spirit*
> *You are light from light*
> *You are silence from silence*
> *You are thought from thought*
> *Son of Isis, Son of Man*
> *Seven our number*
> *HEAR OUR CALL!*

Isis. Horus. Thoth. Raszer sat forward, about three feet behind the German girl and fought to retain his center. This was Egyptian incantation, probably from the Corpus Hermeticum, not to be used lightly. It was clear that Luc knew the tricks of the trade, for the modulation of his voice as it invoked the deities had transformed the room – a single candle and a voice. Like Sir Richard Burton in the den of the Hindu snake handlers, Raszer had both to engage fully with the ceremony and keep a certain analytic distance. This was how Burton had managed to both embrace and expose to western scrutiny half of the ancient cults of the Near East.

For Raszer, an actor and a skeptic, it should have been easy but it wasn't. For one thing, a part of him also craved communion; for another, there was Sofia. Gilded by candlelight, as pious as a vestal virgin, she challenged his very sense of separateness from her. He could not make her the object because she was also the subject.

Raszer dropped his eyes for a moment and regained his bearings, but when he returned his gaze to the circle, he saw that the apple had risen from the floor, and was now suspended at exactly the height of the pilgrims' eyes. Luc blew out the candle, cloaking the room in darkness, and Raszer heard the apple drop to the plank floor. A shudder ran from his tailbone to the crown of his head.

Luc had them repeat the exercise three times before he determined that they were ready. With each round he chose a larger and heavier piece of fruit, as if to show off the team's prowess. On the second round, Sofia lost her concentration and clutched her abdomen. The hovering grapefruit veered away from her, and Raszer thought he saw her glance at him. Then, like a well-tutored violinist, she found her place in the score, and the grapefruit returned to center. On conclusion of the third exercise, which involved a melon, there was a knock at the door.

# 11

## THE WORK IN THE BLACK

*But first thou must tear off from thee this cloak
which thou wearest, this cloak of ignorance, origin of
every evil, chain of corruption, tangle of darkness, living
death, sensation's corpse the tomb that thou draggest
along with thee. The robber in thine own house...*

– Corpus Hermeticum

THEY WERE LED through a trapdoor in the guard house and
down a tight spiral of fifty steps to another narrow passageway. The pilgrims marched single file, heads lowered, in the manner of monks going to
vespers. Not a word was spoken.

After the small miracle he'd just witnessed, Raszer needed to relocate
his center. On the plus side, he was beginning to feel like Noel Branch.
The transformation was occurring and after tonight, he wouldn't have to
work so hard at his charade. As he brought up the rear of the procession,
his eyes probed the darkness for possible escape routes. He reasoned that
the Temple could not possibly have paid off every guard on night duty,
and that the west wing of the castle compound offered potential sanctuary.
He could not predict whether Sofia would welcome or reject his interces-
sion when the time came, but the key might lie in whatever had caused her
to lose her concentration during the grapefruit levitation. He hoped not to
take her against her will. The true craft lay in exposing some chink in Luc's
armor; manifest evil, outright fraud or downright silliness in his dogma that
would open the devotee to a radical shift in perspective, as if she could
suddenly see that the emperor was naked. Given what he had just seen and
felt, that wasn't going to be so easy.

They ascended another winding flight of steps and entered the darkened first floor of the cylindrical structure known as the Powder Tower, so
named because it had served to store the castle's gunpowder long after its

halcyon days as an alchemical lab. There, the escort guard left them, and
Luc motioned silently for the group to proceed to the second level. Raszer
had not spent one moment trying to envision the alchemical apparatus, but
naively expected some serpentine arrangement of glass tubes and globes
and six dozen Bunsen burners. What he saw mounted on and above the
Tower's circular stone floor took his breath away.

The main feature was a crowning metalwork spiral of about twelve
feet in diameter, coiled like a flugelhorn and forged of some exotic alloy
that gave off a faint electro-magnetic radiance. It resembled a giant roll of
solder, though shiny and elegant enough for the Guggenheim. As they en-
circled it and took their assigned positions, Raszer hastily traced the metal
tubing with his eyes.

The inner core terminated in a bulge that, in turn, connected to and
was supported by a roughly six-foot high, iron pedestal that looked a bit
like the central shaft of a periscope and was mounted on a massive septa-
gonal steel base. At about five feet up the shaft, just below the coil's inner
connection, the steel shaft was joined to an eighteen-inch cylinder of tempered glass or crystal. As thick as it must have been to support the huge
coil, it appeared to be completely transparent. He could see no distortion
in the glass and could not tell if it was solid or hollow. Luc took a position
next to the upright shaft and waited for his troops to settle.

The outer end of the spiral narrowed to a slit, like the fluted top of an
organ pipe. From there emerged six long cables of fiber optic material,
each of which reached their terminus at one of the six lecterns arrayed
around the contraption. At this point, the cables were separated into three
strands that ended in electrodes. These were clipped neatly to the lecterns,
like headphones at some bizarre museum of science and industry display.

The six initiates took seats on the high stools beside their lecterns.
They seemed to know their assigned positions. Studying their pious faces,
lit from above by the golden spill of the mother spiral, Raszer half expected then to open their hymnals and sing *A Mighty Fortress Is Our God.*
From the base of the central shaft emerged a cluster of electrical cables,
leading to a remote console at which stood a young man whose demeanor
would have suited a Silicon Valley laboratory. Observing his lab coat and
Bill Gates haircut, Raszer felt a mordant laugh coming on. It was a backyard cyclotron, an assemble-it-yourself atom smasher, batteries not included. He could envision it in the next Christmas catalogue from
*Hammacher Schlemmer.* Whatever humor there was in it was short-lived and
diminished to horror as he watched each of the six test subjects methodi-

cally affix the electrodes to their earlobes and ankles. The third contact was left to be attached later.

Luc directed him to a captain's chair placed again outside the circle, not far from the console. Then he began, as before, to pace the perimeter as he spoke.

"You may recall, Professor, that the concept for the *Tree of Ysa* was circulated to one hundred of your academic colleagues shortly after the 1990 conference in Zurich." Raszer kept his eyes on Luc's. "It was ridiculed then by many of them. I believe your reaction was more politic, but equally dismissive, no?"

"True," Raszer said, not having a clue and increasingly concerned about the quality of Mr. X's dope. "But I am prepared to stand corrected."

"In respect of your role as witness to its maiden voyage and as an unwitting contributor to its design, we will summarize the *modus operandi.*" He motioned to the technician. "Dominic, the floor is yours but keep it brief."

"The concept of a spiritual centrifuge," began the technician in a glottal accent that could have been Bavarian or Austrian, "dates to the late 13th century and is credited to Albertus Magnus. Da Vinci made suggestions in the 15th, but the alloy could not be forged for another hundred and fifty years. The first prototype was built here, in Bohemia, under the patronage of the Imperial Hapsburgs but succeeded only in producing a better Pilsner beer." Raszer fought to suppress his disbelief. "A modern variant," Dominic continued, "utilizing radium isotopes, was constructed in 1939 by German scientists working under Rudolph Hess and was tested with human subjects at Bergen-Belsen in 1942. It failed."

"Perhaps," Luc noted dryly, "their cause would have been better served by developing an atomic bomb."

Raszer saw, or hoped he had seen Sofia's chin drop just slightly. *He's got her split down the middle.* There was the chink and the link with the age-old right wing establishment of Europe. Luc was cribbing from the Masters, but he stood not in the grand tradition of western magi like Dee and Bruno but in the line of royalist necromancers like Cagliostro.

"You see," Luc added, "The Reich's theoreticians failed to grasp the connection between the original design and the Cathar documents, although there is evidence that *that* is what Hitler was digging for at Montsegur. Please conclude, Dominic."

"The problem with our own prototypes," said the pasty young man, "was consistency. We had proven that a single magnetic monopole, fired into the neural microtubules, would cause instantaneous dematerialization.

The issue was repeatability. The monopole is the most ephemeral of sub-atomic particles. The answer lay in making our subjects a part of the machine. We—"

Luc cut him off. "Thank you, Dominic," he said brusquely. "We must proceed." Raszer swallowed a surge of disgust. There was more than a bit of Auschwitz in the technician's dispassionate delivery. "Lest you be offended, Professor," said Luc, "by the scientific argot, I'll remind you that our six voyagers have undergone the most intensive program of spiritual discipline imaginable. Were they not possessed of the *will to ascend,* none of this paraphernalia would be worth the shoes on your feet."

Raszer glanced down at the worn brown loafers he'd chosen for his role and nodded. A light rain played rhythmic figures on the Tower's convex roof and somewhere down below, the baying of a hound echoed in the castle's moat.

"Science," Luc concluded, "has always been the ally of learned men. It only fails when it becomes its own end. The redoubtable Dr. Dee used chemistry to effect his alchemy and we, his heirs, make use of the most exquisite truths revealed by particle physics. Death alone has never been enough to set free the 'Glorious Body.' We came to be imprisoned in these worthless skins by way of a demonic intelligence far beyond the comprehension of most men. It will take an equally profound intelligence to insure that we are returned to our source in the Fullness."

Luc turned to his adepts and extended his arms, allowing Dominic to slip off his suit coat. The technician then produced from behind his console a long purple robe of great antiquity and draped it over Luc's shoulders. Fourché approached each of his pupils individually and spoke *sotto voce,* while Dominic fussed with a group of what looked like valves located on the trunk of the pedestal. As he opened the last of them, a string of air bubbles rose into the inexplicable crystal tank. Water.

While Dominic fiddled, Raszer roamed the area with his eyes. Power for the apparatus and for the tiny cones of light illuminating the console and lecterns must have been battery generated. They wouldn't be using the castle's power as precise control of the voltage had to be critical. If he could find the power source…

There was no visible exit other than by the way they had come in, but he found it unthinkable that the designers of the tower had not devised some other means of escape, particularly since the place had been used to store gunpowder. It was difficult for his eyes to adjust to the velvet darkness since each time they wandered back to the glowing Tree of Ysa, his pupils contracted.

Something chirped – a timid shriek – up in the rafters, beneath the conical roof. Bats. Raszer pivoted just slightly to polarize the glare from the machine and raised his eyes to the tower's peak, waiting for some grainy detail to emerge from nothingness. Little by little, he made out the ghostly form of moving and faintly illuminated fog snuggling against the old wood plank roof. Descending from the cloud were the barely perceptible rungs of a ladder. The roof must have been raised lightly from the cylindrical stone structure to allow for air circulation and sunlight, as well as providing egress for the bats. It stood to reason that the ladder was there for maintenance of the roof, but did it continue on down the exterior of the tower as well? The St. Vitus Cathedral chimes struck thirty minutes before midnight, stirring a lone bat to flap its wings and sail across the blackness.

Dominic was drawing a length of thin, flexible plastic tubing – the type used in hospital IV's – from one of a number of small ports in the pedestal. He unspooled it gently across to the lectern occupied by the German woman, Sonja, and attached it by way of a pre-fitted clip, leaving about eighteen inches free. He did the same with the other five, and on completion, the six taut cables resembled the struts of a carousel, with the Tree at the axis and the pilgrims on their painted horses. The loose end of each tube came to a pencil-point, and to this terminus Dominic attached syringes of some wholly original design. Raszer got up from his chair and stepped forward for a closer look, aware that Luc was eyeing him.

"A question, Professor?"

Once again, Raszer was unsure how much he was supposed to know, so he took an oblique approach, recalling Luc's mention of the "elixir."

"If you don't mind," he replied, moving to within two steps of Sofia and pointing to the hypodermic needle now being fitted to her syringe, "may I assume that this is the means by which we make our subjects, as Dominic mentioned, a 'part of the machine?'"

Luc's brow rose in annoyance. "In a technical sense, yes," he answered as Dominic slipped the first of six, four-inch needles under the papery skin on Elspeth Klipp's wrist. "The elixir that will flow tomorrow from the Tree is the *Milk of Isis*. Its effect is to make the body superconductive so that it can, in fact, draw the *digitaria seed* up from the core of the accelerator and into the matrix of consciousness. It is a two-stage process. Tonight's dosage is a cathartic, a pure solution of mercury salts and niacinamide, distilled in our Geneva laboratory, to purge the remaining toxins from the system. The Scientologists use a poor man's version of this treatment. The six will consume nothing but distilled water tomorrow, to flush the waste, as well as the trace strychnine in the mix.

"Tomorrow night our voyagers will receive from the core an elixir that is the product of five centuries of alchemical research. Over the following twenty-four hours, it will shut down all cognitive function in preparation for the *Consolamentum,* in much the same way as the privations of the 12th and 13th century Cathar *parfaits* did. Only we accomplish in one day what formerly required two or three months of willful mortification. When the 'milk' has done its work, everything that sustains this insult we call 'life' will have been leeched from the tissues, and we are ready, as the priests used to say, to 'give up the ghost.' The physical body is shed like a pupa; it can no longer hold the butterfly captive. As of Wednesday night at this time, all that will remain of these creatures is the will to divine union, and that...that is to be consummated on Thursday with the coming of the Queen."

Raszer edged closer to Sofia, who was now being tapped into the machine. Her chin was tucked against her breast; her shoulders rose and fell with rapid breathing. She winced as the needle entered her vein. Raszer found himself thinking, *Do you believe in God, the Father?* He answered himself, *At this moment, I don't know.* He inched closer to her. *Do you believe in the resurrection of the body?* Again the voice inside him answered, *I don't know.*

He was now directly behind her. In two strokes, he could pull the needle from her vein and reach for the combat knife beneath his trouser leg, and...and what? Throw her over his shoulder and carry her up a four hundred year-old ladder like Tom Sawyer rescuing Becky Thatcher? *Do you believe in life everlasting?* Fuck me, he thought, *I don't know!* But she does...

Luc came to her and cupped his right hand under her chin, lifting her eyes to his. "Sofia, my sweet *stella maris,* do you now know whose praises you sang as a young girl? Do you know whose sweet milk you crave when you summon her spirit into your cold statuary?" He cried out suddenly. *"She is the ONE!"*

*"She is the ONE!"* the pilgrims cried in unison, and Raszer flinched.

*"She is the intercessor!"* Luc chanted, pivoting around, arms raised.

*"She is the intercessor,"* they repeated.

*"She is the one who will return us to the Sun of our true birth!"* he sang.

*"She is the one!"* came the echo once more.

Raszer traced an exquisite pain, like a hairline fracture from the depths of his bowel up to his temples, as Dominic methodically tied the remaining star-children to their new umbilical cords. Not one of them – Lisbeth Klipp, Claude Masson, Robert Perrault, Sonja Kochius – betrayed

with his or her expression the slightest trepidation. Never had Raszer felt
so utterly impotent. He was about to stand witness as six people began the
process of dying. There was nothing so terrifying as technology in the
hands of madmen. And yet, in his breast, nesting right alongside the terror,
there was a desire that frightened him even more; namely, if there was even
one chance in a million that this worked...*Do you believe?*

There had been a time when Sofia's place was his own. They had
rushed him to the hospital with his pulse already down to a faint and er-
ratic murmur. His mother had torn her best linens to shreds in an effort to
stem the bleeding. Even after they began the massive transfusions, his will
had failed to rally. He might have died that night, at the age of nineteen, if
his father hadn't come. His father — whom Raszer's mother called "the
wandering Jew" — had been summoned from his pied-a-terre in the city,
and Raszer, in his delusional state, had mistaken him for a prophet.

"Stay with us, Matthew," he'd said, his big hand on his son's forehead. "I know she's beautiful, but keep her waiting for a while. Otherwise,
you'll never learn her secrets."

Between that stark revelation of his father's understanding and his
mother's chanting of the rosary, he'd been pulled out.

Luc went in turn to each of the acolytes, whispering some private
salutation that brought tears to their eyes. Only when he reached the skier,
Robert Perrault, did Raszer catch a few stray words. "...suffering
is...end...no...hospice...are loved by your Mother." He strode to the center of his morbid maypole, just beside the trunk, and raised his forearm
and three fingers in the fashion of Jesus' blessing.

"Now begins the Consolamentum."

On cue, the six commenced a unified drone, issuing simultaneously
from throats and sinus cavities, not unlike the nasal chanting of Tibetan
monks. Luc continued, now both high priest and shaman.

"The work of man and his pomp..."

They answered him. *"Let them be defaced!"*

"His buildings..."

*"Let them become caves for the beasts of the field."*

"Confound his understanding with darkness. For why?"

*"I repenteth me that ever I made man!"*

"We are the children of Sion..."

"We have carried the graal and will carry it fore unto the final assum-
pion."

"We are the progeny of the Firstborn."

He drew from the folds of his robe a *sistrum,* an ancient, rattle-like instrument of Near Eastern origin. As the chanting continued, he shook it, setting azure beads into a locust-like vibration against the strings, and called, "Come Isis, Come Baphomet, Come Isis."

The pilgrims halted their chant to respond in kind. Raszer flashed a look at Dominic at the console and saw that he was gingerly pushing forward a small lever. All eyes rose to the distended crystal fish tank in their midst, in which the water was being slowly displaced by a clear and viscous liquid. As the fluid rose, something began to rise with it. At first, only a few locks of ruddy bronze hair were visible, undulating like seaweed. Then a fierce, toffee-skinned countenance came into view. It was the severed head of some primitive quasi-human, bearded and faintly Cro-Magnon. Blunt, bony stumps protruded from his temples, and the eyes had the slit pupils of a goat.

The pilgrim chorus cried fervently, "Heee, heee, heee...show us SHE..."

Luc bowed to the head of Baphomet and elaborated, "Oh blessed and ancient child of the dark star, show us thy other!"

Raszer blinked. The man behind the curtain had pulled off a pretty neat trick. Was he looking at a hologram? In answer, the head began to turn, bobbing gently in the still rising fluid. It floated seamlessly round to reveal its opposite, the face of a proud queen with bold features and skin like the patina on weathered brass. Raszer exhaled, "Holy shit," the only sentiment remotely fitting. The face was not quite as he might have shaped it, but then he had not been the artist responsible for this particular embodiment of the Eternal Feminine. The eyes were oversized almonds of deep cocoa brown, canted downward toward her mid-nose in the Asiatic pose. All the features – nose, mouth, ears, neck – were elongated in the exaggerated manner of Egyptian sculpture. She was staggeringly beautiful and more than a little familiar.

Luc lowered his arms and absolute silence followed. The pilgrims bowed their heads. Not even a car horn sounded outside the high fortress walls, as if the entire city were under a spell. Luc motioned almost imperceptibly to Dominic, and Raszer's peripheral vision registered the movement of another lever. The fluid began to empty from the tank, and with it, the head submerged. Raszer tracked the simultaneous flow of six individual currents along the taut lengths of semi-transparent tubing. Unless there was some sleight-of-hand, Sofia's arteries were about to receive the same, clear solution in which the head of the Queen had floated.

The bells of St. Vitus announced midnight. On the third chime, inexplicably, the Tower bats began a mass exodus from the vented roof that continued until the stroke of twelve.

Raszer saw the Klipp sisters shudder in tandem. Sofia's trance was momentarily broken. By the time the twelfth bell had struck, the vessel had disgorged itself completely. The technician stepped crisply to assist Luc in disengaging the six from their tethers. Raszer had been in Prague for less than a day, and already he had failed once to protect Lawrence Gould's wife from an assault on her person. There couldn't be another attempt. Gathering his acolytes into a huddle, Luc began a benediction.

He stood in the center and drew from the pockets of his robe a small wooden icon of Christ on the cross. With ritual precision, he extended his arms and pivoted the circle, offering the crucifix to the lips of each pilgrim. Claude Masson was the first, and Raszer expected the banker to make a gesture of propitiation, a kiss perhaps. Instead, he spat on it. Raszer flinched, surprised at how deep the tremor of offence ran. By any measure, this was profanity. Luc came last to Sofia, and Raszer guessed that some combination of dry-mouth and lingering fear of damnation left her unable to muster more than a dribble. Ignoring her failure of nerve, Luc held the cross above their heads and was suddenly shrill.

"Redemption is a lie," he shouted, "that has made us slaves for two millennia. Jesu-Horus, avatar of Isis, you spoke the truth. The elect need never die. Blessed are the perfects, for they shall see God."

Raszer's soul ached as they filed stiffly out of the Tower. He stood for a moment on the parapet, relishing the slap of the damp river wind against his face. The wind was real; for the moment, he could be sure of nothing else. Luc Fourché had stuck together so many different belief systems in order to make up his liturgical pastiche that Raszer no longer had a fix on which one was primary. A whispered promise of space age salvation had drawn ritual-starved moderns into some kind of neo-Cathar sect. There had been a mythological "bait and switch;" Isis for the Virgin Mary, if indeed they had ever been archetypically distinct. Up to that point, the cult was on ground that was more or less familiar to Raszer. Even Bernard of Clairvaux, the patron of the Knights Templar, had heard in Mary's approach the footfalls of the Goddess. But the rest? Monopoles and Manichaeism; an "elixir" that starved the body of nutrients… This seemed a heresy against life itself.

*This is how they get you,* he thought; *in the gap between the familiar and the utterly unknowable.* No one who ever boards an airliner can ever be certain that it will leave the ground, and yet it's only neurotics that try to disembark before takeoff. Once we're aboard, some fatalistic mix of pride, ignorance and hope keeps travelers in their seats. Or maybe...maybe it was just the desire to fly a little closer to home.

# 12

## THE ROOT OF EVIL

PHILIPPE CAUDAL ALLOWED the thought of ordinary suicide to linger for a moment in his mind, and then just as quickly dismissed it as cowardice. In twenty odd years of high stakes financial chicanery, he had not lost his wits, and he was proud enough to believe he could still prevent the unraveling of the plan that he and the unnervingly clever Stocker Hinge had put into play, with a little help from the L.A. detective. He cursed blind fortune. Fortune was not supposed to play a part when you knew how to play the numbers. "Everything is numerology," the Master had said. "The man who masters numbers masters the world." Beyond that, Branch was an inveterate womanizer and the girl was supposed to have been an expert. She must have done something stupid; when great plans go awry, he mused, it was usually for the basest of reasons.

It was midnight in Prague, six p.m. in Montreal. By Wednesday at this time, Raszer was to have had his allotted three days, and those three days were to have allowed Caudal time to finish setting the trap for his former colleagues. The money trail was circuitous enough to convince the authorities of a Temple ploy to collect ten million dollars in ransom money and pin it on their Australian rivals. As an inducement for Gould to take the threat seriously, Caudal had prepared a massive, programmed sell-off of the Empire Pictures stock he had been quietly and methodically acquiring through the Temple's mutual funds. He considered it his finest work.

The Montreal organization would be tied up in criminal litigation for years, and those years would allow the true heirs of the Temple to reclaim its leadership. Caudal had harbored enough money to tide himself over during a lengthy hibernation as he had no intention of ever becoming a public witness against the Temple of the Sun, despite his assurances to Hinge that he would come forward once the trap had been sprung. He had no such intention of throwing the baby out with the dirty bathwater.

Now, some act of monstrous ineptitude in the Canadian wilderness had preempted the plan. Noel Branch was in the custody of the Canadian *Sureté,* and it could only be a matter of hours before Operations determined that someone else was in Prague. More ominous still was the fact that he was just now finding out about all this, not from Branch, not even from Operations, but from a man on the outside. When Stocker Hinge had heard from Stephan Raszer's frantic secretary that there'd been no contact with the girl, they had first examined every scenario from dead beeper batteries to bear attacks to the possibility of Jeanette's betrayal. As a last resort, Hinge had suggested that they use a journalist friend of his to query the Provincial Police in Thunder Bay about any unusual goings-on. That was when they learned that the Mounties had been holding Noel Branch for hours.

Caudal knew better than to try and contact Branch himself, and he knew why the professor had not called him. Neither man could acknowledge the other in the presence of outsiders, let alone the RCMP. Caudal's pulse hammered the glands in his neck. He knew by heart the telephone number that Branch must by now have called – the same number all senior Templars were instructed to dial if apprehended by the police. Only the insiders, however, knew the number's true locus: Defensive Operations. How long could it take for them to trace the treason to him?

Any executive knows that the worst thing that can happen when a crisis is raging is to be left out of the loop. It can only mean one of two things; that one is considered unworthy of inclusion or that one is suspected of fomenting the crisis. Caudal was Number Three in the Temple's emergency notification protocol, yet he had not been notified of the fact that his own assignee, Dr. Branch, was not in Prague. Walking hunched past the gilded, late afternoon oaks along his familiar way to the offices of Savana Investments, Caudal watched his shadow grow longer. He ran his tongue around the inside of his mouth, but it failed to replenish the moisture that had been siphoned out by the fear in his belly.

The detective was as good as dead. He exhaled sharply and tasted iron on his breath. He needed time to think and detoured to a favorite café off the park. He collapsed into a chair at a table facing the boulevard and ordered a cup of tea.

THE PLOT IN which Philippe Caudal had cast himself was workable precisely because of the intensely secretive nature of his organization, though he also owed a debt to the discretion of the Swiss banking system and to the proliferation during the last few decades of a virtual United Na-tions for tax exiles. The Temple of the Sun, as French and Swiss investigators were just beginning to discover, was not monolithic in form, but consisted of a widely distributed network or watertight shell operations with a superstructure that was all but invisible. It combined the outreach and missionary zeal of a grass-roots political crusade with the amorphous inscrutability of a sophisticated intelligence operation. The current members of the Golden Circle, many of them former spooks, had learned well the lessons of espionage. The doctrinal core of the Temple had existed since the dawn of the 17th century, but the present day shape of the Order could be traced to the mid-1980's and to the transforming influence of the Master himself.

It was in 1990, at one of the exclusive ceremonies at the chateau in *Aix-en-Provence,* that Philippe Caudal had first encountered Luc Fourché and his young protégé, the man introduced as Paul. Caudal did not consider himself an intellectual, but he had a quick mind and a passionate desire to put his mathematical skills in the service of a true leader. He was the sort of man who suffers during peacetime. From the moment Fourché, resplendent in his white silk robe, had touched the radiant tip of the sword to his shoulder and dubbed him a *chevalier,* Caudal knew he had found his purpose.

The growth of the Temple had reached a critical stage; Fourché's operations were, even then, too complex and far-flung to be properly managed by his loose-knit, boiler room gang. He needed a permanent *Golden Circle* – a board of directors operating under appropriate corporate by-laws and sworn to secrecy unto death. He needed expertise, and he needed to get the hell out of France, where he was now the target of three separate mail fraud investigations. Most of all, he needed someone who understood the power of numbers. Everything was in the numbers, from the deepest secrets of the Masonic art to the deceptive randomness of a license plate.

Caudal engineered the move to Montreal and the set up of Savana, as well as sixteen other front companies. The trustees of the Golden Circle were selected with the assent of the hereditary leaders of the *Grand Loge Alpina* – the Gnomes of Zurich – and the heads of the old families of the *Valais,* a permanent aristocracy that had survived both the Revolution and the wars of the last century. Their pedigrees were beyond challenge, but though they took the oaths and swore to defend the Temple as vigilantly as had their 12th century forbears, Caudal sniffed early signs of a political agenda, one with a distinctly Austro-German odor.

His suspicions were borne out when they prevailed upon Fourché to allow in eight former officers of *Service d'Action Civique,* known as SAC, the secretive, paramilitary arm of the royalist right in France, and by any number of measures, a holdover from the Vichy Regime. The old counts and barons justified their inclusion as a defensive measure. Caudal was no democrat, but it irked him to see the Masonic craft once again hijacked in service of would-be tyrants. It wasn't long after the move to Canada that members of Q39, the Quebecois equivalent of the SAC, were minding the store. Fourché had assured a worried Caudal that he could keep them reigned in.

At first, the atmosphere in Montreal was heady, and Fourché had seemed the unchallenged pontiff, but the trustees, who still had titles and vast fortunes to nurture, soon grew tired of his apocalyptic urgency. In the early spring of 1993, Fourché informed them that he had received revelation from the Great White Lodge that the *conflagratio* was about to commence. The Seven Entities of the Great Pyramid at Giza were preparing to suspend their stewardship of the planet. It was time to abandon ship.

It had seemed to Caudal that, for the eve of Armageddon, there was a surprising absence of panic in Montreal. Fourché announced plans to travel to Egypt to witness the Solstice departure of the Masters and receive their instruction on the coming exodus. Although Philippe Caudal had good reason to suspect treachery was afoot, he didn't warn his mentor, for to do so would have exposed his own sympathies. Luc Fourché never returned, and the titular leadership of the Temple fell to a pretender, one in the pocket of the royalists.

But if the priests had become plotters, the parishioners still believed. Any church is sustained by tithes, and there was no doubt that huge sums of money flowed into Temple accounts each time one of the elect passed blissfully on. Fourché's charismatic style had drawn followers by the hundreds, and so, Caudal now mused over his cold tea, they had given him enough rope to hang himself.

A new plan had been approved in April 1993, by the Swiss and German trustees, one that would increase cash flow exponentially. Until then, the Order's accountants had to wait patiently for an investor to expire before they could commandeer his or her assets. But suppose that ten, twenty or more true believers took the plunge at once? A mutual fund traded in human souls.

Philippe Caudal watched all this happen; even profited by it. They set him up in a Morin Heights chateau; they gave him unprecedented control of the books. In October of 1993, the Montreal Temple staged *The First Voyage*. A selection of major "stockholders," many of them near death anyway, swallowed poison and passed through the veil. Some had to be "helped" to the path.

Philippe Caudal was a man of prudence and patience, well aware that these were not the attributes of a hero or a martyr, but he was also a believer. The instrument of his belief had been Luc Fourché, the only man who had ever made him feel nobility. If the Lodge had placed its faith in Fourché, then it mattered little that a walking death squad by the name of Josef De Boer had been sent with him to Egypt, purportedly for his protection. Fourché had surely transcended his murder, and Caudal's patience had granted seven years to avenge him. It would be done.

He drained his tea and paid the check, having decided on a plan. He would go preemptively before the Circle, feigning ignorance of the events in Thunder Bay, and announce that he had uncovered a treasonous liaison between the notoriously inconstant Professor Branch and the mercurial cult mole known as Stocker Hinge.

# 13

## THE RED QUEEN

RASZER WOKE THE dozing night porter and ordered a double Armagnac before entering his hotel room. The rainy whisper of traffic noise from Wenceslas Square, drifting in through the big French window, settled his saw tooth nerves a bit. He paused, just inside the door, to examine the room for change. His worn leather valise was exactly where he'd left it, parked in the middle of a faded Persian rug. The maid had turned down the bed. Monica was waiting, nine hours and sixty-five hundred miles away, on the screen of his laptop.

Eight taxicabs had been idling, pre-arranged, in the fog at the Malostranska Metro taxi rank, just a short walk from the Old Castle steps. One taxi for each of them, though he and Luc shared a destination. It was a common but effective ploy, insuring that anyone tailing them would have to choose one cab and lose the others, and it had been an unexpected godsend. Raszer had looked on as Luc led a dazed Sofia to her taxi and eased her in. With his hand on the door, he had leaned in and said, "Promise me you'll stay in tomorrow. You must rest." Just before Luc withdrew, she had reached out to seize his wrist, and Raszer had seen her mouth the words, "Come with me," but Sofia had gone back to her quarters alone.

The billowing night fog and Raszer's knowledge of the city's layout had then allowed him to execute a simple detour that might prove to be the key maneuver of his mission. After crossing the Charles Bridge, as Luc's taxi rumbled east toward Wenceslas Square, Raszer had directed his driver to slow and make a soft left turn north on Karlova, following the cab with the license plate 2UTZ70. As the driver threaded the narrow lane, Raszer watched Sofia Gould emerge and mount the steps to an old Renaissance rooming house known as *U Zlate Studne* – At The Golden Well. A shortcut returned him to the Europa right on the heels of Luc, who bid him a curt goodnight, expressing no desire for post-game analysis.

The Armagnac arrived, oddly enough, with two glasses. Raszer lit a cigarette and pondered the tray. Probably a European convention, the presumption of a rendezvous. He took from his case a custom-built Phillips palm module that served as a jam-free Internet connection and patched it to his laptop. He heard a sigh escape his windpipe as he exhaled bluish smoke.

He hadn't faced this particular moral dilemma in his work before. On past assignments, the stray had presented a discrete target, and he had brought her into sharp relief by identifying with her to the exclusion of the other lost souls who surrounded her. Of course, they were all someone's children, husbands or wives, but he wasn't being paid to be the Pied Piper. It was important not to develop a savior complex. But here in Prague, he was looking at six human beings whose hearts would stop sometime after midnight on June 20. Even if the infernal machine could transmute flesh into pure energy – even if *Notre Dame de Lumiere* herself was looking down on them from the Dog Star – the whole foundation was rotten. He knew it was rotten, not only because the enterprise was based on a virulent hatred of everything truly human, but also for the simplest of reasons; he did not at all like the man who called himself Luc Fourché. This was becoming a police matter and he knew it. As he punched in a ten-digit password and dialed his secure chat lounge via a hopscotch pattern of way stations, he began to consider how to bring in the cavalry without risking Sofia.

He stared blankly at the screen as the little smiley-faced razor icon popped up and stealthily cut the seal to his private e-chamber. Monica's design; it evidenced a mastery of graphics software attainable only by assistants with too much time on their hands between assignments. Double doors swung open with a *creak,* and behind them stood a crudely animated 3D version of his leggy assistant, wearing a veil and dancing something that looked like a Moroccan Macarena to the accompaniment of canned computer music. It brought a smile to his weary face and that, he was certain, had been the intended effect. He logged on and received the first of her messages.

"Hello, Raszer. You've been off the grid for a while. New variables to discuss. NOW. M."

He had just begun to type a response when the laptop burped and Monica herself logged on. Now they were live, and if the routing strategy worked, secure. She took command of the screen.

"i'm here, raszer. bad news from thunder bay. mounties picked up noel branch in the woods, 12 miles s. of the cabin. half out of his mind. no sign of jeanette. no word, either."

Raszer typed:

"How did you learn this?"

"from stocker hinge. he used a journalist who has the sureté wired. he went to the mounties after i pushed the panic button. raszer, i'm worried."

Raszer:

"Not sure that was a smart thing to do. There are Q39 members in the Surete ranks. One phone call and I'm over. Does hinge know if they checked the cabin?"

"no. doubts branch could lead them there in his shape. he thinks jeanette burned us. maybe even mr. x."

"Not a chance. He doesn't know her. She may be a groupie, but only for the right band. Let's bring Hinge online."

Stocker Hinge was not only a brilliant cult analyst but also a skillful operator in the murky world of cops, informants and beat reporters. He was well known to the law enforcement community, and this – and only this – had persuaded Raszer to proceed on his mission without a face-to-face. He had seen Hinge in the flesh only once, at a seminar in Toronto, and pictured him as a lanky, laconic academic in his thirties. Hinge had been digging into the Temple of the Sun for two years, and he had gotten into places that not even the French had plumbed.

Hinge shared Raszer's practiced avoidance of the police, but for his own reasons. The French, Swiss and Canadian authorities were nominally cooperating, but in fact were tripping over each other like Keystone Cops in their desire to be the first to untie Luc Fourché's Gordian Knot. Hinge feared as the police drew closer to the holy of holies, the Temple would pick up their scent from a mile away and shape-shift before he could complete the puzzle, something he desperately wanted to do. Raszer suspected he had a book deal pending. With Mr. X turning evidence, he had gotten closer to the heart of darkness than ever. Raszer knew that Hinge was using him as a probe, but that was okay. It served both of their purposes. Despite the fact that the two men were strangers, Raszer had come to feel a certain kinship. They were both men looking for their own shadows.

He tossed a burning shot of Armagnac down his throat and lit another cigarette. Monica came back.

"I've paged him, raszer. If he's in the office, he'll log on in a minute. Everything o.k. there?"

"Wouldn't know where to begin, but beam me up, Scotty is not far off. Any more on the double eagle symbol?"

The computer *bleeped* a warning tone, and Stocker Hinge joined the conference, via a voice-transcription program that rolled out his words as he spoke them.

"There was a rich man from Nantucket..."

Raszer:

"Hi, Stocker. You sure it was wise to contact the police? Do they know you/the institute are involved? And where is Branch now?"

Hinge:

"I know very little. They turned Branch over to his doctor. Suffering some sort of psychosis or drug reaction. Said he was bewitched. Stephan, if I hadn't checked, you wouldn't know that your cover is conceivably blown. Be gracious."

"I warned her about the drugs. Shit."

"Better worry about yourself, mon ami. I can't find Mr. X, either. We may have a problem. What's the situation there?"

"I'll cut to the chase, Stocker. They've built an atom smasher that uses human fuel. Must have cost 5 or 6 mil in R&D and manufacture. It shoots magnetic monopoles into neural circuits and sends 'em back to ground zero. How did your man forget to mention this detail?"

Hinge was ordinarily fast on the uptake, but now there was a long pause.

"I have a bad feeling. Think I've been used, Raszer, which means you're in great danger. Tell me more. Tell me about the Director. Who is he?"

"My take is this, Luc Fourché is whoever Montreal designates as the golden boy. Don't know if there ever was a real one. This guy is a top-drawer brain. What do you know about Enoch's Portal?"

The screen went pink, indicating no input. An updraft from the street swelled the gauzy, white curtains into living form. The whole night is a dream, he mused. He went to the open window to make certain it was only that and then returned to the bed.

Hinge's words again filled the screen:

"Is that where they say they're going? I've underestimated their ambition. According to the Temple's dogma, and other Masonic lore, our Sun and the 'Second Sun' – Sirius B – are the poles of a single cosmic organism. Interdependent, with energy flowing between them like alternating current. Enoch's Portal is the name some give to the shortcut from one to the other. A doorway to Heaven. Amazing. You say that the machine looks like a cyclotron?"

"With a little Rube Goldberg thrown in. Actually kind of beautiful."

"Stephan, forgive the melodrama, but if this is what it seems, you are utterly expendable. It is entirely possible that governments, even corporations are involved in this. You already know that your NSA looked into the Voynich Manuscript, which is one of the links. Did you ever hear of the Montauk experiment? The OSS in the 1940's?"

"Disappearing battleships or something. You're not suggesting they wound up on Sirius? Listen Stocker, I think it's time you told me who Mr. X is. If I can't throw a wrench in the pipes tomorrow, I'll have to bring in Interpol. Time to break the seal, Stocker."

"I can't, mon ami. You'll end up getting me killed, and Interpol will only undercut your leverage, which is that you may be able to trade Sofia Gould for your silence on this ransom business. Her best chance is for you to stay solo. Forget the Czech police. If it's gotten this far, they have friends on the force. I need time to figure out Mr. X's game, but it's clear you're part of it. As for Jeanette, she's either dead or been converted."

Raszer had, by now, allowed for the former, but he would not believe Jeanette had betrayed him. He momentarily forgot to swallow the caustic brandy he'd taken into his mouth and stared at the bed for a few moments before typing.

"What do you know about Australia? That's where the ransom note was faxed."

"I don't know anything. What do I think? I think it's a red herring. Interpol knows there's a big temple faction down there. The faithful believe that the aboriginals experienced the same astral visitation ages ago as the Dogon people of Mali. It's most likely to divert attention from Prague or wherever the cash is going."

"What are they really after, Stocker?"

"The end of the world as we know it. The *Renovatio*."

Raszer lifted his fingers from the keyboard and kneaded the tight skin on his scalp. Another gust of damp night air blew in form the square and brushed his perspiring back like a wing, raising a shiver. He sifted the information back and forth through his cortex like gold dust through a sieve.

"How did your Mr. X react to the news that Branch was in custody?"

"He plays poker everyday with other people's money. His voice doesn't give much away."

"Any chance we can still make use of him?"

"Only if he's been honest about his raison d'etre, but either way, your cover's blown. Make a deal for Sofia and come home."

"Too late for that, Stocker. Any idea where Mr. X keeps his office?"

"None. He uses a pay phone. Never e-mail."

"But he knows exactly where you are, doesn't he?"

Hinge missed a beat. Raszer blew a cloud of smoke across the room and continued hammering, the Powerbook now bouncing on the well-used mattress.

"Why kidnapping? That's low-rent, high-exposure crime. It doesn't fit. It's as if they wanted to get caught."

"You're the sleuth... I'm just a sociologist."

Raszer punched out his second cigarette and stalked across the room to pull the drape. The street was damp and quiet. Wenceslas Square was a long way from Times Square. The fog had muted all color to gray; only the hookers and strays beneath the streetlamps had any definition. A plume of smoke rose from a black Mercedes parked at curbside and merged with the mist. The angle of Raszer's second story window was too steep for him to make out the smoker. He returned to the screen.

"I need to talk to Mr. X, Stocker."

"He won't deal with you. He's a one man snitch."

"He dealt with me in St. Casmir, didn't he? You don't want this girl's death on your conscience, Stocker. Or mine. You gave me cover. Don't leave me naked here."

"His name is Philippe Caudal. I can't tell you any more."

Raszer relaxed for a moment in the embrace of one existential certainty. With this information, his value alive still exceeded his value dead, at least until tomorrow night. Christ he needed sleep. There were three items left on his agenda. With Hinge having logged off, he continued to Monica.

"Did you get all that?"

"let's give this to Interpol, Stephan. I don't like it at all."

"It was two cops that did the shooting in Grenoble, Hinge is right about that. But we will do this. Encrypt this entire transcript using a leapfrog code; maybe #22. Delete all names. At the closing add, 'Hradcany Castle, Powder Tower, June 19, Midnight.' Print it out and fax it to Hinge. I want <u>him</u> to send it Western Union – no fax, no FedEx – to that prosecutor in Lyon; the head of the task force. It'll take them half a day to crack the code. If I'm not done by then, I'll be ready for them to save my ass."

"why stocker? and how will i know if he sent it?"

"I want to know if he's hedging. You can confirm through WU in Lyon."

"roger, captain. anything else?"

"I need a shadow. Can we afford an Alpha Corp man?"

"only if you want to erase your profit margin altogether. their rates are way up."

"My margin will be zero if I'm dead. I'm outgunned here. Get a man outside my door within three hours. Try to get me a family man, a churchgoer; somebody recommended by our network. Ask that he be discrete and discretely armed. I think I have company downstairs."

"shit. I'm on it, raszer."

"Last, but not least; Lawrence Gould. Here's my status report..."

Raszer typed out the brief message and then waited as Monica dialed his client. Gould picked up the phone at 6:30 p.m. PST. She conveyed Raszer's brief message, *"She is okay, but there is risk involved. Signal intent to comply with ransom demand subject to an 'independent verification' of your wife's safety. Then do nothing. They will not get your money."*

"Tell your boss," Gould had replied grimly, "that I received another fax from Australia this afternoon. It says my wife will die Wednesday night if the funds have not cleared by the close of business that day. It says that any interference by police or private agencies will seal her fate."

After assuring Gould of Raszer's progress, Monica came back to her anxious boss and informed him of the latest fax and her research findings.

"you asked about australia. i got something from cult-watch. one of the aboriginal elders in alice springs is a town councilman. he said a caravan of winnebagos came rolling into town two weeks ago, and there's a conclave of german druids down there. that's it so far."

Raszer wished Monica goodnight and took himself offline. He poured a last snifter of liquid amber and pulled his boots off, unstrapping the sheathed seven-inch blade from his ankle and placing it under his pillow. He peeled open the hidden, inside pocket of his gray cotton shirt and removed the ultra-slim gunmetal cigarette case that contained his "sewing kit" of seven surgical steel needles in minutely varying sizes, each tipped with a different formulation of the paralytic. It was only by the size of the needle that he could gauge the potency of the poison – the smallest would stun momentarily; the largest would kill instantly. Nested beside the two needles were two identical steel tubes, about two-and-a-half inches long and no greater in circumference than a piece of straw. They had been modeled, on a reduced scale, after the blow guns used by natives of the Brazilian rain forest, and they delivered the darts with remarkable precision. Raszer went to the closet and deposited the kit in the room safe. Then he fluffed his pillows and laid back on the featherbed to phone his daughter, Brigit.

She *had*, she said, been trying to contact him with her "thought waves," but only to secure his approval of her choice of subject for her 4th grade geography project, Ayers Rock, a two-hour drive south of Alice Springs, Australia. Once again, a synchronicity. This is what happens, Raszer thought, when one is riding the curl of the wave that is itself the unfolding of time. He told her that he was nestled on a featherbed in a dollhouse red room in a golden city, which was true enough. He did not tell her that he was safe and sound, because as a man whose life involved a great deal of subterfuge, Raszer thought it sane and right for there to be one person in the world to whom he never lied. Instead, he told her that the better angels were watching both of them and wished her goodnight. He had just racked his body out and begun to drift away when he heard a knock.

He withdrew the knife from its short-lived nesting place beneath his pillow and crept silently to the door. He cracked it open to the end of the chain. She'd changed her clothes, seasoned her body with a pungent herbal perfume and donned a stunning henna-colored wig with long French braid, but Marta, the barmaid, would have registered through any disguise. Raszer opened the door and stepped round from his defensive position. He re-sheathed his knife, which she observed passively on entering.

"Expecting trouble?"

"Not so soon," he replied, scanning the hallway after her. "You didn't happen to come in a black Mercedes, did you?"

"No," she said. She stepped to the French window and pulled back the drape ever so slightly. "I'm only a waitress. But there is a man down there, in the back, whose fringe benefits are better than mine." She let the drape go and turned to him. "Will you offer me a drink?"

"Have you seen him before?" Raszer locked the deadbolt and crossed to the desk, where the Armagnac rested. "The man downstairs?"

"Only in my...how do you call them? *Night-meers?*"

Raszer poured her a drink and handed it over the desk. "Lucky for us the porter brought an extra glass. Do you tend bar here, as well?"

She took the liquor down, Russian style – in a single gulp. "No," she replied, "but I am known to the concierge."

Raszer squinted hard and gave her a glancing once-over. The lace-up boots came almost to the knee, leaving a good ten inches of sturdy but nicely shaped thigh before the hem of her cordovan leather skirt. She wore a matching brown vest, bound across the breast with thongs. There was something about the whole ensemble that suggested a fifth century warrior queen ready to receive the general in her tent. Of course, he thought; a girl like this would be known to any European concierge worth his tips.

"And you're also known," he said, "to *Monsieur* Fourché."

She set down the snifter and walked to within an inch of his chest. "Do you trust women, Mr. Branch?" she asked to his face.

"I let you into my room at two in the morning."

"I asked if you trust them, not if you desire them."

Raszer smiled. "Let's see. I trusted Miss Buzzo, my fourth grade teacher. I trusted my mother, when she was sober. I trusted my wife. Big mistake..."

She tossed the French braid over her shoulder and laughed as lustily as she had in the bar. "They can be cruel if you deny them what they really want, Mr. Branch. But if they are on your side, they offer protection that no man should be without."

Marta scooped up her glass and held it out for a refill. Raszer obliged, wary, but undeniably intrigued by the presence in his life, at this particular moment, of such a sybil.

"Your English is head of the class," he observed. "Why do you put on the act for *Monsieur* Fourché?"

She sat on the foot of his bed and drew her right knee languorously up to her chin, revealing, an inch at a time, the tender underside of her thigh. Raszer saw no evidence of underwear.

"Knowledge is a little like a knife," she answered. "Sometimes, I think, it is better to keep it hidden until you need it, no?"

Raszer replenished his own drink and swung the plain, wooden desk chair around to face her. Then he sat down and leaned in, his lips close enough to her bare knee to caress it, his nostrils near enough to smell her essence through the perfume. He knew he was being seduced but had not yet decided what to do about it. Soon enough, things would decide themselves.

"You said you had something to share with me, Marta," he whispered. "About my business partner, Mr. Fourché."

"He beat up my sister last night," she said, matter-of-factly. "He's a pig."

"Your sister, is she—"

"A prostitute. Yes," she cut him off, as if to spare him the awkward inquiry. "I introduced her to him. He has special needs."

Raszer shook his head. "I was only going to ask if she was all right." He dropped his head for a moment and contemplated the Byzantine design on the faded carpet. "So that's why you've got him on the defensive," he conjectured, half to himself, then raised his eyes and looked at her deeply for the first time. "Strange, isn't it? How even a man who can keep state secrets can be compromised by an itch? How badly did he hurt her?"

"She is okay. It is not the first time she has seen this kind of thing…but he frightened her. His eyes. She was sure that he could just as easily kill her as slap her." She swallowed the rest of her Armagnac and her body registered its quality with a shudder that ran to her toes. "Now she can't sleep. She says that the Devil is in Praha." She lowered her knee and bent over to set the glass on the carpet. Raszer studied the rawhide laces that crisscrossed her bodice and felt himself getting dizzy. As she straightened, she placed a hand on his knee for balance and regarded him through the unkempt bangs of her Queen Boedica wig.

"So, I have given her my bed and my Doberman for the night and—"

"And you," he said, "have no place to sleep."

She stood, brushed his cheek and moved back to the window, running her hands over the back of her skirt to smooth the leather. A winning move. Raszer knew it was all over but the ref's call.

"You need protection tonight," she said, her back to him. She touched the drape lightly as if to drive home the message. "And I can give it to you." The muscles in her calf were as taut and strong as the shank of a longbow.

"I don't doubt you can, but protection always comes at a price."

"And wisdom..." She turned her head and her green eyes flashed.

"Even more expensive."

"Then I offer you a bargain," she said, wrapping the curtain around her lower half. "Two hundred American dollars and I'll spend the night with you."

Raszer gave a short laugh and got up to light a cigarette. "For a minute there, I thought—"

"You thought what?" she asked. "That the poor Czech girl would throw herself at the rich Canadian businessman for a chance to get out of town?" She released the curtain and waggled her finger at him. "No. I am not looking for a husband, Mr. Noel Branch. And I am not a whore. But what I have to give has value." She aimed her finger at the half-empty bottle of Bas Armagnac. "You pay a good price for that cognac, yes? Would you not pay as much—" She came forward, head cocked, hands on her hips. "—for something like me?"

"It's not a moral judgment, Marta," Raszer replied, blowing the smoke into the strobing blades of the ceiling fan, "but I've found that when you pay for *sex,* that's all you get. Now, *information*...that survives the morning after."

"Then let's call it information," she said, popping the first of her vest laces out of its hook. "Or if you wish, a contribution to my tuition at the University. I do not intend to be a waitress forever."

Raszer set the burning cigarette in the ashtray, put a hand around the small of her back, and with the other, undid the next two laces.

"If it's for the cause of higher learning, then I'm your man."

FATALISM HAD BEEN Raszer's best defense since emerging from the black fog of depression six years earlier. When the world seemed too bleak to bear, he took refuge in the abiding faith that *whatever would be would be,* and one-by-one, he'd seen most of his phobias leave him. This had allowed him to buy into life with something approaching reckless abandon, but he had always drawn the line at love, which somehow seemed a little too close to the death he had narrowly escaped. He could give body and soul to war; to women he gave pleasure – even the occasional epiphany – but he denied his own, most precious favors. He called it discretion, but he knew full well it was fear. It had probably cost him his marriage and daughter. On this night, as rapidly became clear, Marta was out to strip him of his psychic prophylactic.

As Monica had warned, Czech girls had yet to discover safe sex. The Woodstock Nation had come to Prague, stripped of its sentimentality and tempered by the cool, cybernetic fire of a bold new age of ecstasy without illusion.

SHE RACKED HIS body until he felt as if his bones were the soft cartilage of a baby's. She kneaded each centimeter of his skin with potter's fingers, keeping the clay moist with a mouth so generous that Raszer perceived at last how Isis had managed to raise an erection from the emasculated corpse of her Osiris. She awakened places so deadened by shame or neglect that he cried out repeatedly and even sobbed.

"My beautiful man," she called him. *"Moje krasna golem."*

When she had reduced him to compliance so complete that he lay flattened on the bed, unable to lift a finger but with his cock as mean and red as its namesake, she mounted him backwards and fucked him until her red queen warrior cries had diminished to whimpers. He watched her ass rise and fall like sea foam on a part of him that was his, and not his. He was up *here,* in his head, *wasn't he? Think again,* she seemed to say as she lifted, turned round, and kneeling between his legs, took his liquid self into her mouth and down to the deep, hot *athanor* of her soul.

Sleep came with the weight of God's hand pressing him like a seed into furrowed earth. All light, sound and sensation were baffled as fully as if the room had been filled with down. Consciousness, if it existed at all, was aware only of the continual downward thrust.

What woke him was the sudden return of his sense of smell, or possibly the dream of it. Burnt cedar, fig and myrrh, and a soft *thump,* as if he had reached the end of his fall. A feeling of dread alive in his limbs. He raised his head weakly and turned to look beside him.

She was propped up on an elbow, watching him, the chalk white hair framing her ancient face; her withered breasts lay on the pillow like old silk slippers. Behind and through her he could make out the slumbering form of his lover. A flare of pale indigo shot from his eye and burned through the hag's parchment-skin forehead.

She smiled at him toothlessly. "Shut up and listen," she said. "You ought to know me by now."

She kissed his ruptured eye and spoke a verse.

*Her life's in a temple where ash is burned*
*an ark with the sum of what man has learned*
*A juggler, a Jew and a foursquare cross*
*know her as the vessel of Wisdom lost*

*Her death is the door by which you came nigh*
*and speaks with a lovelorn, she-cat's cry*
*Can but be denied if a groom ye be*
*and bring me the gift of that you promised me.*

Just as her diaphanous form began its dispersion into atoms of night, he watched her ashen hair return to its blue-black youth, her wrinkled skin stretch taut and burnished over high Sumerian cheekbones and her breasts retract from the pillow and form firm, ripe plums of flesh. She laughed melodiously and her breath carried the scent of soma. As she laughed, the pitch of her laughter deepened into a masculine register, and she underwent one final transformation. The cant of the eyes lifted and the folds of skin around them filled with the creases of coming middle age. The nostrils widened and the bridge of the nose bowed out like a raven's beak. The lips spread and thinned, the upper lip curling just slightly at the right corner.

Raszer felt the last cubic centimeter of oxygen leave his lungs and simultaneously fill her breast. He was looking into his own eyes, along an axis of indigo light. When he dropped his gaze to see if his own body still existed, he saw full breasts, damp with milk, swelling from his chest. He tried to scream, but all that came out was a guttural moan and a question more felt than spoken.

*Who are you?*

"Why don't you get up on all fours?" she replied, in a voice that was at first his own, "and see how it feels to be a woman." Now it was Marta, who had sat bolt upright, her own features smeared by those of the Other.

He shot out of the bed and flew back hard against the wall. There was a knock at the door.

"Are you okay, Mr. Branch?" said a stranger.

"Yes, I'm fine," said Marta, in Raszer's voice.

As she rose from bed to come to his side, what remained of the vision was drawn into Marta's lungs with her first breath. She came naked to him where he stood, trembling in the corner, and led him back to the bed. She held his head against her breast and hummed old Slavic lullabies until he dropped into sleep.

Sometime shortly after that, in the drizzly pre-dawn light, she got up, dressed quietly and left. On her way out, she stumbled over the snoring hulk of Raszer's new bodyguard — a fat, kindly-looking Czech. She shook him gently awake, as he was on duty, and he seemed to recognize her as a fellow denizen of the dark city. She entrusted to him the business card that her sister had given her two nights before.

# 14

## PUTTING ON THE NAME

*Prepare the meal of perfect faith*
*To rejoice the heart of the holy King*
*This is the meal of the field of holy apples*
*And the Impatient and the Holy Old One*
*Behold, they come to partake of the meal with Her*

– A Kabbalistic invocation intended to invoke the exiled *Shekhinah,* the feminine aspect of God in Jewish mysticism

AS HIS EYES fluttered open, Raszer's first thought was to offer a prayer. He felt lucky to have survived the night without the treachery that he had, in fact, tempted with his imprudence. Whoever had occupied the Mercedes was evidently more guard dog than assassin, although Raszer knew how quickly one could become the other. He tracked the course of a single stray beam of eight a.m. sunlight from its entry at the window to its terminus on the pillow beside him. Marta was gone, and all that was left was her scent and a bed that looked war-ravaged.

The experience would not tolerate analysis. It simply had to be accepted for exactly what it seemed to be. Raszer's "gift," whatever one chose to call it – second sight, mediumship or madness – was not something he pondered a great deal or even particularly welcomed. It had, in some way, led him to his current occupation, but he left it at that. He feared that if he analyzed it too much he'd discover that he was, in some discomfiting sense, possessed.

He was aware of a pleasant itch between his legs and amazed to see that he still had a nearly full erection. It was then that he noticed that his surroundings looked – or felt – somehow different. It wasn't that anything had changed its position. It was more as if he were seeing the room through a pair of borrowed eyes. A distant echo of the hag's words looped around his brain. He decided he badly needed coffee.

He phoned room service and a few minutes later, heard an altercation outside his door. Pulling on the sorry heap beside the bed that was his trousers, he went to the door and opened it without removing the chain. Filling his field of vision was the backside of an immense human being in an ill-fitting gray suit and a ridiculous Iron Curtain Buster Brown haircut that left his neck as hairless as a baby's bottom. The man was engaged in an argument in Czech with the hall porter, and Raszer feared the worst until he was able to pick up enough of the language to realize that the war of words was over the giant's insistence that he be allowed to sample Raszer's coffee before it was delivered.

He unhooked the chain and opened the door fully, which prompted the men in the hall to pause and turn to him.

"Is there a problem," Raszer inquired, at which the eyes of both men went to the most prominent object in sight, the oversized bulge in his trousers. There was a moment of embarrassed silence, after which the giant grinned and extended a hand the size of a small leg of lamb.

"Dr. Branch?"

"Yes," Raszer answered hesitantly.

"I am Juraj Dubrovsky of AlphaCorp Security, Praha Division, but I think you may like to call me George; like your *George* Bush. It is more simple to say. I have been explaining to this man that I must check your food before you eat. You see, it is in my contract."

Raszer grunted and fumbled for a cigarette. Obviously, something had been lost in the conveyance of Monica's instructions. He shook the giant's hand and felt three knuckles pop.

"It's a pleasure, George." He took the coffee platter from the non-plussed porter and dismissed him. Raszer noticed the tiny wooden chair parked beside his door. "George, did your brief call for you to, er…keep a little distance?"

"My most apologies, sir," the big man offered. "You see, I arrived just before four a.m. and you were—" He flashed his horsey grin "—very busy. As it was night and your case was marked 'high risk,' I did not want to leave you alone. Raszer motioned him in, and George sat heavily on the bed. "It is good that I didn't."

"Uh-huh," said Raszer, lighting the cigarette. "Why's that? Did I have a visitor?"

George leaned over and whispered. "A man in a long coat came up just before sunrise," he said. "Too warm for June. I showed him my Dirty

Harry, and I think he change his minds." He reenacted the encounter for Raszer's benefit, flashing his shoulder holster and weapon.

"Yep," Raszer observed, "that must have done the trick." *Well, shit. Goodbye Noel Branch.* "And did you see a girl leave?"

"Oh, yes," he chortled, "a very nice one." He held his beefy hands under his chest and gave the universal "big breasts" sign language. "She left at six, but I insisted to look in on you to see that you were okay. I show her my Alpha badge. We had nice talk. She was much concerned with you. She gave me this to give to you. She said it was from her sister."

George took the dog-eared business card from his shirt pocket and handed it to Raszer. *Philippe Caudal, Senior Financial Advisor. Savana Investments.* The card bore a Montreal phone number. He flipped it over to the blank side. There was a sequence of letters and numbers, written in smeared pencil with a fluid hand. CB 2Z77L63. Too many digits for a license plate and nothing like a phone number. In any case, useful. Knowing how to get to Philippe Caudal might just save his life. He turned back to the bodyguard.

"Did you know the girl who gave this to you?"

"She is freelance," he replied. "Some work for Interpol, some for CIA. She gets around."

"Right," said Raszer. The nexus where espionage and witchcraft were one. "Okay, Juraj; seeing as you've already drawn your six-gun, let's make the best of it. I am going to make a phone call and take a shower while you keep the peace. Then I'll fill you in. Okay?"

"Okey, dokey," said George. "Copy that, sir."

Raszer squinted. "Are you for real, or did I dream you up?"

George rapped on his head. "Real as rain. I don't know what your business is Dr. Branch, but I can tell you this: have no worries. When you hire Alpha through an Interpol protocol, you don't get any Yugos – only Cadillacs."

"That's good, George. Do you pack a cell phone along with that piece?" George slipped a Motorola out of his inside pocket. "May I use it?"

Raszer fumbled in his satchel for the scrap of paper handed him by the little Sufi in the Montreal airport bar. He stepped through the south facing window and onto the fire escape, although he doubted the room was bugged. For all its sinister competence, the organization he was up against also exhibited a certain starry-eyed naiveté. Did they really believe they could vaporize six people in the middle of Hradcany Castle? Still, no chances. He surveyed the alley below. A teenager had ducked in on his way to some intolerable part-time job at a bakery or currency exchange to smoke a joint, and the updraft carried a hint of its sweet bouquet to Raszer's nostrils. *When this is all over...*

He punched the six-digit number into the cell phone's bank and hesitated before pressing, "send." The print above the number read, *Rabbi Scholem, Old-New Synagogue, Prague.* "Should you ever find your self in Prague..." the little man had said. Raszer was now weaving together fine golden threads of intuition, some of them as insubstantial as spider silk. The relative confidence with which he did so was the boon of last night's ineffable encounter. It was not as if he remembered the crone's riddle, the way one recalls a speech or a fragment of dialogue. It was now simply part of an enhanced knowledge base, wisdom received rather than acquired. *"Her life's in a temple where ash is burned..."*

If a psycho-biologist were to biopsy Raszer's brain, it was possible he'd find an odd cluster of dendrites or a membranous chip upon which this verse was inscribed. Or maybe not. All Raszer knew was that the rabbi had to be seen because the rabbi had information, and that information might provide the makings of an antidote to Sofia Gould's death wish.

The sun had not yet risen high enough to illuminate the alley, but out in the Square, it had already banished the night's vapor. He had to move fast, for the sun might tempt Sofia to leave her quarters again. He stooped and peered through the window into his room. George was perched on the bed, finishing off the strudel delivered with breakfast.

Razer punched the phone call through and waited.

*"Dobre rano."*

"Good morning, Rabbi. My name is Stephan Raszer."

"How did you get this number?"

"From a very small man with a very bald head."

THE SHOWER WAS barely lukewarm and little more than a trickle. Raszer dispensed with it quickly; he soaped his body but put off the shampoo, even though his head had spent a fair amount of time between Marta's legs. By way of this omission, she protected him still.

Raszer toweled himself and dressed hurriedly. The rabbi had agreed to see him, having grasped immediately his description of the little Sufi. The connection between these two men of differing faiths was not altogether surprising, and familiar to Raszer from as far back as his dalliance as a young man with the Holy Order of Anthropos. In the sphere of the world, their respective tribes had fought tooth and nail for fifteen centuries; in the sphere of the most sublime truths, they were one, for Rabbi

Scholem, Raszer had already surmised, was – like that other great Jew of Prague – a Kabbalist.

Kabbalah was a Jewish mystical system that had germinated in the Middle Ages and reached full flower in John Dee's Renaissance. Its roots, like those of Sufism, had been nourished from beneath the ground by the Neo-Platonic stream that had fed the Gnostic heresies of Eastern Europe and troubadour France, as well as the Rosicrucian fraternities of Germany and Bohemia. Some renegade fork of that stream, misdirected centuries ago by the dam of intolerance, was now carrying Sofia Gould to her death. Somebody had to row her like crazy back toward the mother current. Kabbalah, based as it was upon the Torah, had never discounted the value of life, as had Augustine's Manichean Christianity. Sofia was half-Jewish.

Raszer asked George to drop his valise, with the laptop, modem and palm unit in the hotel safe deposit vault and wait for him to emerge from the alley. He was going down the fire escape, lest he run into Luc on his way to some Spartan breakfast. In exchange, George was to collect from the front desk an aluminum flight case that contained his emergency cash, a copy of his will and a bare bones climbing kit: shoes, harness, basic hardware and a hundred yards of nylon rope. The reasons for the cash were fairly obvious; the rock climbing gear was a personal touch. Raszer had found that there was always something to climb.

He decided, for now, against sharing his destination with George and instead asked him to follow at a distance of at least half a block. While George guzzled the rest of Raszer's coffee, he was briefed on the rudiments of the case. They were dealing with kidnappers, potentially danger-ous, who would presumably go to great lengths to keep Sofia Gould in tow. The overfed gunslinger took it all in and then asked one simple, but astute, question.

"How much monies do they want?"

"Ten million dollars, George."

"With your permission, sir," said George, after a moment's pause, "I am going to put another two men on standby and tell my wife not to keep dinner for me." Raszer nodded his assent, and they got up to leave. "Mr. Branch? You don't have to tell me. It is not required for me to know, but what is your job?"

"I'm an intermediary. That's all you need to know right now."

The big man laid a weighty but tender hand on Raszer's shoulder. "Do you have a gun?"

Raszer lifted the cuff of his trousers to expose the seven-inch Swed-ish blade. George seemed less than impressed. Raszer withdrew the weapon ceremoniously and pointed out a crack in the wall, about eleven feet from where they stood. By the time George had focused on it, the blade was imbedded two inches deep in the aging plaster. The skill had been hard won for Raszer, whose inborn gifts had not included hand-eye coordination, but he had been fortunate enough to find in the Salvadoran pool keeper a master of the craft. The old jungle fighter had taught a simple maxim, *the knife goes where the eye tells it to go.* From drill practiced to the point of obsession, Raszer had discovered that the eye is an organ capable of transmission as well as reception.

He returned the blade to its sheath, pocketed the money clip and removed from the room safe his "sewing kit." He tucked the case into the inner pocket of yet another custom-tailored shirt, identical to the one he'd worn the previous evening, except that its color was a dusty pink. All his colors were chosen to mask any contraband he might have hidden in the weave, and all his shirts were made by the same old Hollywood tailor who claimed to have stitched the pleats in Humphrey Bogart's trousers.

Raszer ducked through the window and dropped from view.

On the ground beneath the fire escape, Raszer checked his money clip to see if Marta had slipped her fee out while he'd slept. The cash was all there. A heart of gold or dubious business sense. Or maybe – if she was, as George had intimated, a small but regular player in the old European game of kiss 'n kill – it had all been part of the ruse. Whatever she was on street level, she had served as a vehicle for something more.

He rounded a corner and glanced back to make sure his bodyguard had cleared any security Luc might have posted during the night. George was lumbering down the sidewalk, blithely nibbling another Czech pastry. Raszer fished for a cigarette and hoped that, in this case, appearances truly were deceiving. AlphaCorp was the premium security service in continental Europe. Its ranks were filled mostly by recruitment from Interpol, and it retained a fairly cozy relationship with its supplier. Alpha was the only such service whose agents operated under what was essentially the Secret Service pledge; e.g., to take bullets for their clients. Hence, the high price for their services. The fidelity of an Alpha man was considered so secure that it was not unusual for the agency to have men assigned concurrently to both sides of a conflict. This was the European way: *La Balance.* How George Dubrovsky had squeezed into the Alpha stable was currently a mystery, but Raszer had a feeling about him. He was so conspicuous that he could hide in plain sight.

Raszer scanned the storefronts for a FAX sign, for his first errand would be to have Monica send him a copy of the ransom letter as a means to show Sofia the face of her captors. A tiny old tobacconist's shop, squeezed into the gap between two bigger, newer buildings ended his search.

He ducked in low, for the doorway had been built to 17th century human scale. Like the ancient *fromageries* of Paris, the little place was timeless and redolent of centuries of dispensing its sweetly aromatic product. He changed a handful of bills for coins, and, promising the proprietor he'd be right back, he went out to the phone booth to call Monica. She answered on the first ring, despite the fact that it was two a.m. in L.A.

"Have you slept?" he asked.

"Have you?" she replied. He relayed the instructions and the tobacconist's fax number, and assured her that his bodyguard had arrived and was close behind.

"Monica," he added, "did you make a note of the last number Jeanette called in from?"

"Yep, it was from a pay phone outside a Bait and Tackle shop somewhere near the cabin…but in that neck of the woods, somewhere near could mean ten or twenty miles."

"Let's give it to the Mounties," he said. "We can't get involved. I don't know who Stocker used to get his information, but I want to go the same route. There's a reporter named Jacques Denis at the Montreal Standard who did a series of pieces on the Temple two years ago. He hasn't had any fresh meat for along time, so I think he'll take the bait. Use an alias and tell him that you know of a possible homicide near Thunder Bay that may be related to the Temple. Tell him the victim was last heard from via that number. If we're lucky, he'll play the tip out through the provincial RCMP outpost that picked up Branch. If Jeanette is alive, she needs help fast. If she's not… if she's not—" Raszer sighed.

"Listen, I know it's late but see if you can raise Lawrence. He'll think I'm nuts, but ask him if he knows if Sofia's father had a nickname for her when she was little. Anything so long as it's something that only she could know."

Raszer shuddered. He couldn't shake the dread he'd stirred up by allowing the possibility that Jeanette was dead. If she was, it was as likely as not that the man whose identity he wore was her killer.

"Got it," said Monica. "In another four hours it'll be eight a.m. in Montreal. I'll make it the first thing on his desk. Hey, Raszer?"

"Yeah?"

"Which one of those roots in your herb garden is supposed to give you a speed buzz? Is it the one that looks like a yellow penis?"

"No, no, no!" cautioned Raszer. "Don't eat the penis. You'll be out for a day. It's the one with the purple shoots. Boil it for ten minutes and drink the tea."

"If you say so," she said. "Last thing. Stocker Hinge called about two hours ago. Said he knew you were getting near the crux of things and you might need that money that Mr. X put aside for you."

"I don't think so, Monica."

"Well, look… just in case," she pressed on. "The account is at the Czech Bank, New Town Branch. The account number is—you got a pen?"

"Uh-huh," said Raszer, reaching into the right pocket of his khakis. He brought Philippe Caudal's business card into the light and flipped it over. "Shoot."

"2-Z-7-7-L-6-3." He didn't bother to write it down a second time.

Raszer left the shop with the fax in his pocket and signaled George, who had staked out a sausage stand, to follow. There was no sign of pursuit, no sign of the overcoat-wearing night visitor. Nothing out of the ordinary. It didn't add up. The news of Branch's whereabouts had to have reached Luc by now. Raszer plotted the coordinates of time and treachery in his head, achieving only greater confusion. The words of the Sufi poem came back to him. *"The mystery does not become clearer by repeating the question."*

He hopped onward, his ankle somewhat more limber thanks to the previous night's treatment. He hoped like hell he wouldn't have to run.

As he entered the Old Town Square, he began to experience hallucinatory little pops on the periphery of his senses. At first, he thought it might be fatigue, but then, the smell of burning hemp and the sight of a wildly painted, bare-breasted girl dancing to a tin whistle put it all together for him. Prague was the Haight-Asbury of its time, and it was two days to the summer solstice. Europe's flower children were reborn from the forests and tumuli where they'd been hiding for two decades. A poet was president, and it was once again safe to tell the old stories and reenact the ancient myths. A young man in a death's head mask bumped into him and turned to say in French, *"Pardon, Monsieur…are you one of the dead?"* Raszer couldn't resist looking to see if he was missing an earring.

Raszer's destination, however, lay a few blocks beyond the fringe of this archaic revival and into the true heart of a past that leant itself less easily to pageantry. He was headed into the *Josefov* – the old Jewish Quarter, and he was also walking into his own history. Raszer had years ago declared himself a free agent in the cultural-racial draft, abandoning his declarative Jewish-ness along with his father's name, but as so many of his contemporaries learned, long after they had forsaken their menorahs for prayer rugs and ashrams, it is no easy matter to stop being a Jew. He was hoping that the same was true for Sofia.

The stature of the Old-New Synagogue did not rival Chartes or Westminster Abbey, but the first sight of the ancient structure standing firm at the tail end of the 20th century was impressive nonetheless. With a birth date of 1270, it was the oldest synagogue in Europe. In the 16th century, while Elizabeth's court thrilled to Shakespeare's verse and Rudolph II conspired with magi, the Jews of Prague wore yellow circles of shame on their smocks within the circumscribed borders of the ghetto. But here, in this temple, the Kabbalist Rabbi Low had called upon the original article of faith that had moved Moses across the desert, long before orthodoxy had calcified the living, magic words of the Torah. Whether or not his creation, the Golem, was truly laid in the rafters, this was a place of magic.

He entered the synagogue from Cervena Street, through a small, semi-covered court. Despite the midday sun, the darkness was unfathomable until his pupils widened and he was able to perceive a triangle of candle flames surrounding the spectral form of Rabbi Scholem as he stood motionless on the cantor's platform. The silence invited Raszer to step in and quiet his own heart, but his pulse doubled when the rabbi threw his arms out in front of him and began chanting modally in Hebrew, in a voice that instantly found the resonant frequency of the chamber. A wrought iron grille with gothic ornamentation surrounded the elevated lectern. To its side, Raszer made out the form of a bench. He dizzily felt his way to it. For an instant, he could have sworn that the room and every molecule in it were vibrating subtly to the man's held pitch.

He slid discreetly onto the bench, but no sooner had he relaxed than the chant abruptly broke off, leaving an echo to bounce around the temple. One heavy-lidded and thick-browed eye popped open from the platform above and peered at him with the serene ferocity of an owl.

"Have I won the lottery?" the rabbi asked rhetorically. "Or perhaps been elected the new president?"

Raszer realized belatedly that one should probably not enter the sanctuary while devotions were in progress. *"Je mi to moc líto, Rabbi,"* Raszer apologized. "I've come to see a man about a wedding."

"Is there a bride?" the rabbi asked.

"Yes, but she may be a little reluctant to come to the altar. She's been drawn into *sitra ahra.* "

The rabbi cupped his hands. "May I ask her name?"

"Sofia."

"Ah, Sophia," he said, leaning into the lectern. "She has been in trouble since she stole away from Heav'n with God's wisdom."

His eyes twinkled faintly. No one appreciates names like a Kabbalist. The archetypal Sophia was the mother of gnosis. God's daughter, wife, consort; she had so loved his human creation that she chose to abandon Heaven to be with them, only to find herself exiled, her wisdom scattered into the dark places of the earth, like windblown sparks from a great fire. The art of Kabbalah was to gather those sparks and reconcile her to God.

*"This Sofia* is trying to get back to Heaven, as well," Raszer said. "Through Enoch's Portal, by way of a ritual suicide presided over by a first-rate Svengali. I have been hired by her husband to bring her home, but I doubt she thinks of Los Angeles as home anymore. She may die tomorrow if I can't find a way to convince her of her error."

Rabbi Scholem stepped down from the platform, his chin cupped in his hand. He took a seat next to Raszer as casually as one would in a bus depot. He was intrigued. It was not every day a visitor spoke of *sitra ahra,* "the other side," let alone of Enoch's Portal.

"Is she a Jew?" he asked.

"Her father was a Jew, and I think his presence in her is strong."

"Is this... 'ritual,' as you call it, advertised as Jewish?"

"No," Raszer answered. "More like Bogomil dualism with a Star Trek twist. I suppose the liturgy is kind of Coptic. They borrow from the Jews, though."

"And why not," the rabbi chuckled. "Everyone does." Scholem dropped his elbow to his knee, keeping his chin propped in his palm and drumming his fingers on his lips. He seemed eternal, with his silver beard and bold cheekbones, but he might have been little more than fifty. He looked deeply into Raszer's eye and suddenly sat bolt upright, as if stung by a passing hornet. He took a chunk of Raszer's cheek between his thumb and forefinger and examined it, smiling. "Still soft," he concluded. "You are a man newly made."

The rabbi was not unfamiliar with the Temple of the Sun, but it wouldn't have mattered if he was. He knew the species. In one form or another, he'd had to contend with it for two thousand years. He knew a lot but he listened attentively nonetheless, his shoulders hunched and his birdlike head cocked to one side. As Raszer tried to summarize Luc's appropriation of quantum mechanics to effect an alchemical transformation, he became aware that his listener's attention had strayed. Rabbi Scholem was sniffing the air around him like a bloodhound. Without the least bit of warning, he seized Raszer's head in his large hands and pulled it to his

beak-like nose. Inexplicably, he began nuzzling Raszer's matted and un-
washed hair. Releasing him, he spread his fingers like a Persian magus.

"I know that *scent!*" he exclaimed with glee. "She has been to visit you,
the old trollop! You are a fortunate man. Come!" He rose abruptly from
the bench. "Let us walk a bit."

Raszer's lips curled to a grin. He'd hit pay dirt.

Rabbi Scholem's notion of a walk was to stroll the interior perimeter
of the synagogue again and again as they talked, cutting the corners to
make a circle. Seven times they passed Rabbi Low's famous high-backed
chair and seven times they passed in front of the ark bearing the magnificent scrolls of the Torah with the 13th century tympanum above. It was on
the seventh pass that Raszer recalled the line from the riddle, *an ark with the
sum of what man has learned...*

"It is not possible," said the rabbi as he walked, hands spread in front
of him, "to love God *and* despise life. And no Jew, however heterodox,
seeks literal union with the Godhead. This is obliteration and serves neither man nor God, for he does see a purpose in our humble existence...but. But. But!"" He halted, turned to Raszer and raised his finger in
the air. "I think that you are a man who can appreciate a paradox, and this
is one of the mothers of them all. They are not wrong, these people. Misguided...*yes*. Dangerous...*certainly*. Knowledge in the wrong hands is always dangerous. But if they have studied the writings as well as you
indicate, I cannot say with certainty that something extraordinary will not
happen. You see, Mr. Raszer...there *are* portals..."

Raszer shot him a querulous look.

"And Uriel showed Enoch the secrets of the solstice and equinox, six
portals in all," said the rabbi. "The Merkabah mystics knew of them and of
the great wheel – the Chariot – that was able to pass through them. But
aside from Enoch, Elijah, and if one believes so, *Christ*...the Chariot took
no passengers. It is a vehicle of illumination; a means of knowing God. But
to utilize it as a space shuttle is blasphemy."

Raszer stopped and delivered a Steve McQueen squint. "They place a
lot of importance on John Dee's *Monad*. It shows up in their manifestos,
their letters. But I haven't seen it used in the sacrament."

The rabbi paused for a breather. "Well, that would be a little like the
alchemist's *using* gold to *make* gold. The Monad, from what you tell me,
would be the end result of their efforts – the point at which gender distinctions dissolve, all astrological properties merge and union is achieved. The
Monad *is* the Portal. We all pass through it eventually, Mr. Raszer, but not
until God is satisfied with us; not until we have done our *tikkun*. John Dee

was a very bright boy, but did his intellect serve God's design...or the Devil's? I confess, I do not know. I'm not sure that he did either. What I *believe* is that it is possible to sit at God's table, but only if one is invited."

"I get the feeling," Raszer said, "that these people think they have been."

"Have you ever, Mr. Raszer, been in a Moroccan *souk?* The market-place is a maze; a hapless tourist can enter by any gate and be lost within minutes. So, young hustlers have found it profitable to offer their services as guides, collecting a commission on each purchase that the tourist makes along the way. In the end, the dizzy tourist is led out of the *souk*, and spends his last few dirhams to tip the boy for the marvelous journey. Has he been shepherded or shaken down?"

"If he's found the exit," Raszer asked, "what difference does it make?"

"It's the same door by which he entered! He has seen only as much of the *souk* as the guide wished him to see. Saul of Tarsus was right. The passage to Paradise is as narrow as a hair. And the Gnostic *Pleroma* is the womb of God."

"You've made the godhead feminine, Rabbi. Was that deliberate?"

"The Torah does not give God testicles," the rabbi replied. "Did you know that much of archaic myth has it that each human being houses within his brain both male and female embryos. Is it not remarkable that the primitive mind grasps intuitively what the analytical mind vainly attempts to codify?"

"That God is androgynous?" Raszer asked, his eyes widening.

"That God is beyond opposites." The rabbi stopped at a bench where they had started. "And so, we come back to your mention of a wedding."

"Yes, Rabbi."

"You speak of the *zivvuga kadisha?* The alchemical marriage?"

"Yes, I need to free her from this man's spell."

"Who would be the groom?"

"I would, Rabbi."

Rabbi Scholem lifted both eyebrows. "Speaking, for a moment, in the argot of psychoanalysis...that could invite one hell of a *transference*. Are you ready for that?"

"If it will save her life."

The rabbi took Raszer's head in his hands. "I think you are a *mensch*, Mr. Raszer," he said, a knowing smile on his luminous face. "But I think also that there is something you desire, and you believe that your Sofia may possess it. Can you bring her to me?"

"I'm going to try. It won't be easy. She is being guarded very closely."

"Then I will pray for an angel to assist you."

At that moment, the old door creaked open, and George Dubrovsky peeked in to see if his employer was all right.

# 15

## SOFIA

*Wherefore saith Rhasis*
*make a marriage (that is a conjunction)*
*between the red man and his white wife*
*and you shall have the whole secret.*

*The philosopher's stone is converted*
*from a vile thing into a precious substance;*
*for the semen solare is cast into the matrix of mercury,*
*by copulation or conjunction,*
*whereby in process of time they be made one*

*The soul, the spirit and the tincture may then be*
*drawn out of them by the help of a gentle fire.*

  –    Roger Bacon, from "The Root of the World"
1208 A.D.


THE RABBI HAD agreed to see Sofia at five o'clock, if Raszer could get her there, and the ceremony was to conclude at sunset. Raszer was betting that the power of a ritual even more venerable than the Temple's would begin to reintegrate her, but it was a huge gamble. He knew that a metaphysical counterpunch alone would not sway someone so in love with the poetry of death or so thoroughly mesmerized by her guru. This was a woman who had probably not had animal fat in her diet for months and whose body had therefore ceased to metabolize protein. She was quite literally starving. It was the same prescription followed by the mystics of 16th century Spain. Shut down the sensory organs one by one until all that is left is the voice of God – or the Devil impersonating God. The hopeful news was that this condition also left Sofia very open to the power of suggestion, and Raszer intended to suggest just how tainted her Temple was.

Back on the street, Raszer queried George on what he'd observed during his vigil outside the synagogue. Nothing more threatening than a gaggle of salesmen had passed by. Raszer guessed that whatever protection Luc had hired was concentrated around himself and Sofia. He had to keep reminding himself that even if Luc knew about Branch, he could only know Raszer's identity and purpose if Mr. X – Philippe Caudal – had told him, and Caudal would thus be admitting his own treachery. He briefed George on the likelihood of high security at Sofia's *pensione, U Zlate studne,* and his desire to get her out under the noses of her keepers and without a skirmish, if possible. He had to harbor for a while longer the hope that the Temple would not risk its foundation for the sake of one rich girl.

They took separate taxis, via the river road around the north end of the Quarter and down toward the Charles Bridge. Raszer wanted to avoid the crowds and the scrutiny of the Old Town Square. Sofia's rooming house was five minutes from the east side of the bridge. In the cab, Raszer made a call from George's cell phone to Monica. She was not only awake but animated.

"I got through to Gould, Raszer. I think he upped his dose of Zoloft 'cause he seemed unusually calm. Or maybe I woke him up. Anyhow, he's giving you until tonight to get her on the phone to him. He moved the ten mil into a ready account, but he sure doesn't like it. *'She's dead to me either way.'* That's what he said."

I don't think 'calm' was what you heard," Raszer said. "Sounds more like despair; at least his version of it. What else?"

"He says that Sofia's father called her *'little Hok-ma.'* He doesn't know what it means. Do you?"

Raszer pumped the air with his fist. "Good work. *Hokhmah* is Kabbalistic Hebrew for 'wisdom.' Wisdom always seems to be a woman."

"Tell me something I don't know."

The taxis arrived, and Raszer and George met up at the end of a narrow lane leading to Karlov Street, which was buzzing with vendors and street folk. George was to go on ahead and check first for any heat around the inn. He came back minutes later, panting and grinning like a Boy Scout.

"A guard is posted at the entrance, but he is one of ours…Pavel Zloty."

"You're kidding," Raszer said.

"Well, it is a small town, boss…and we are the best. Anyway, that is the bad news. The good news is that Pavel is an idiot. I know. He is my brother-in-law. Give me five minutes and then go around the back of the building by the little alley where the musician is playing. There is an entrance through the kitchen. I will take care of Pavel."

"He can't be the only one they've got on her."

"No," said George, "now they have me. I'm going to relieve him."

"You can do that?"

"It's an old Alpha trick, but Pavel has only been with the agency for a month. I think I can get away with it."

Raszer shook his head. "It can't be this easy. If I do get her out, we'll head right back into the crowds at the bridge entrance. There's a taxi stand on the north side. Try like hell to keep the heat off until Sofia and I are in the cab. We'll head south as if we're going downtown, but I'll have him detour east across the Legil Bridge and then back north to where we started. There's a little café on the riverbank, underneath the Charles Bridge. It's safe and out in the open. Do you know it?"

*"Na dum Kafka.* It is very romantic, with the white swans floating—"

"That's the one. I need about thirty minutes with her if I can get them. Then we go back to the synagogue. That's the time to call in your extra men. After that – if it all works – we go straight to the airport."

The degree of George's comprehension was difficult to ascertain. No matter how serious the matter being discussed, he would not stop grinning. To an untrained eye, it might have seemed a sign of stupidity, but Raszer had been around enough Eastern Europeans to recognize it as a genuine, if somewhat disconcerting, display of respect and humility.

"Be prepared to cover me if there's trouble, but for Chrissakes try not to shoot anyone."

"Yes, Professor," he answered grinning. "I will, as you say, try like hell."

George had been gone for a minute or two when Raszer noticed a stall across the narrow cobblestone street selling brightly colored, traditional Czech peasant scarves. He walked over and bought one in an ornate red print. As an afterthought, he paid the man for a common, gray Czech worker's cap and slipped it on his head. He eased his way into the river of tourists promenading through the ancient lane, and from thirty yards away he caught sight of his man, casually kibitzing with Pavel on the steps of *U Zlate studne.*

The cook's entrance to the inn was obscured behind an enormous dumpster, but the smell of pork gave it away. He stepped quietly inside.

A small mustached man was rolling out dough for bread in the kitchen and took only slight notice of him. Raszer casually pulled an apron off a nearby rack and put it on as if reporting for work. *"Dobry odpoledne,"* he said, nodding shyly in the Czech way. The man returned his nod and kept on rolling. Raszer slapped his forehead as if he'd just remembered some unfinished business and hustled past the baker and through a swinging door that led to a connecting hallway, removing the apron as he went.

The front reception area was tiny, but fortunately, the clerk was occupied with a guest complaining bitterly about the plumbing. Raszer slipped into the foyer and casually took his place behind the unhappy lodger. From here, he could see diagonally into a sunroom that faced the street and had been converted to a dining area. Raszer's pulse hammered his throat. Seated at a window table not more than ten feet from where he stood were Klaus Bandeur and Otto Scheipp. They were in profile, their small table facing the street. As with Raszer's late night visitor, they were overdressed for the weather in dark gray, pinstriped suits and narrow-brimmed fedoras. It was beginning to seem as if he was dealing with reptiles. Bandeur glanced nervously into the foyer every four or five seconds. From where he sat, he would see anyone who entered or left by the front door. Raszer pulled the brim of his cap down and dodged to the left each time Bandeur turned. A space opened before him, and he found himself suddenly facing the desk clerk who cleared his throat and said, *"Prosím?"*

Raszer stepped forward with a shudder of relief. He leaned in close and could smell the lunch hour Pilsner on the man's breath. With the side-long look that begs discretion, he spoke confidentially, hoping the clerk would respond in kind.

*"S dovolením.* I am American. I am the brother of one of your guests, a Miss Sofia—" It suddenly occurred to him that she had probably not registered under Gould.

"Yes?" the clerk said with a sly helpfulness. "Miss Lawrence."

"Yes. There has been a family emergency and I must contact her. It concerns our father. Do you have a house phone?"

The clerk pursed his lips. "No, sir. I can ring her room." He said it clearly and far too loudly. "But she has asked not to be disturbed."

Raszer grimaced and lowered his head. The clerk's tone was as good as a summons. He waited for the rush of air from the dining room. Five seconds passed. He would not be so lucky a second time. He cast a sideways glance out the front door, which was not visible from where the henchmen sat. George was pointing at his brother-in-law's cell phone, and Pavel was protesting whatever was being proposed.

"Sir…*Můžete mi pomoci?"* said Raszer. He returned his eyes to the clerk and slid a hundred dollar bill across the counter. "She has asked me to come…but her *husband*—" Raszer nodded toward the café. "—might not approve."

The clerk smiled conspiratorily and picked up the phone. There, in a nutshell, Raszer thought is the difference between Europe and the States.

*"Mademoiselle,"* the clerk whispered discreetly, "your…" He looked to Raszer.

"Noel Branch. Please tell her it's urgent."

"Mr. Noel Branch is here on an urgent matter. May I send him up?"

Raszer bounded up the narrow stairs to Room 11. She was in a white cotton nightgown and shuffled back from the door with a lassitude that might have signaled drugs if he'd not been aware of her malnourishment.

She smiled wanly and swept her arm in the exaggerated manner of a *grand dame* to welcome him. "Did you come to take me shopping, Professor?" There was a coy sweetness he hadn't noticed in the Square.

"No, Sofia," he answered gently, "though that might be fun. But I do have quite a story to tell you if you're in the mood for one."

"I love stories…" she said, clutching her abdomen as another mysterious spasm shot through her. "Do you mind if I sit in bed? I'm a little woozy."

"That's my favorite place to hear a story," he replied. He took a seat on the windowsill so that he could survey the alleyway. Then he fixed his eyes on her.

"I'm not going to the Tower tonight, Sofia, and neither should you."

"Why not?"

"There's a civil war going on for control of the Temple in the 21st century. It's got a lot to do with money and power, and not a lot to do with salvation. Luc figures he can pull a *coup* with his machine, but it's not ready. *I know.* The used my research to build it."

Sofia drew her legs up under the nightgown and shivered. "I know it's not foolproof, Professor. Neither is prayer. Does Luc know you're here?"

"No, but there are a few things Luc doesn't know. Remember what I said about stopping the countdown? The Temple is struggling to earn some legitimacy as a church and get the Inquisition off its back. The last thing they need right now is a debacle like this."

The corners of her mouth drooped. She seemed almost crestfallen, a child who hadn't found what she wanted under the Christmas tree. "No," she protested. "You can't do this now. It's not right. I'd rather die on a broken merry-go-round in a king's castle than back in fucking Bel Air. I don't like this story at all."

Her closet door was half-open, and Raszer noticed that hanging on the hook, in addition to her robe, was a compact cat o' nine tails; a purse sized edition.

"Why are you so hungry for the transit? Why so anxious to die?"

"Because life hurts, Professor. Haven't you heard?"

He nodded toward the conspicuous cat o' nine tails. "You don't seem to have a problem with pain."

"That's different," she said. "*I* decide. Sometimes it even makes the real pain go away for a while."

Raszer nodded his understanding. "I know. I get it. When I was a kid, I could stick pins through my skin without feeling a thing, but I couldn't stand to get shots. Later on, when the hurt was a whole lot deeper than polio shots, it used to comfort me to think of dying."

She sat forward on the pillows, her lips slightly parted. Raszer the Actor had tapped into Raszer the Man and hit a vein.

"So why are you trying to save me, Professor? You're one of us."

He came to sit on her bed, keeping a chaste distance. "Because there's something else, Sofia," he said. "Not technical. Something about the liturgy itself; about Luc. And the goddess he's trying to conjure to take you home." Raszer was riffing, and about to take a huge gamble, but she was listening. "Did Luc ever happen to mention her name?"

"There are lots of names, Professor Branch. But she's 'Mary' to me. She's always been Mary to me."

He put his hand lightly on her knee. She didn't stir.

"Your father was Jewish, Sofia. I know that from your profile. Did he ever tell you the story of the Shekhinah?" She shook her head. "No, I didn't think so. The Jews tend to keep her well hidden, even from half-Jews, like you...and me." Her forehead creased. "In the Ancient of Days, God had a wife; a consort. *The Shekhinah*. She was the trustee of God's wisdom. She *was* wisdom. Like most women I have known personally, she had two sides. She was the Matronit, Queen of Heaven...your *Mary*.

"But she was also Lilith, who coupled with mortal men to make demons. That was okay, as long as she was *with* God. In the beginning was the Word, Sofia, and the Word was *with* God. They made holy love in the Temple every Friday night to consummate their union. *The* Temple – the real thing – the one that gave its name to the Knights Templar. And in the Holy of Holies, behind the veil of their bedchamber, the great secret was revealed: *she and God were one.*"

Raszer paused to see if he was in her head yet. There might be a knock at the door any moment.

"So?" she said.

"But the people, they couldn't see what happened behind the dark veil, and they took the Shekhinah for their own private dancer. They began to worship her as a goddess in her own right, and they had a special weakness for her Lilith side. God tore the Shekhinah from his heart in grief and anger, and condemned her to wander in exile until the people could see the truth. Out of sorrow, she split into her two aspects. Life…and Death; Light and Darkness. And when you call for the goddess, you never know which one is going to answer. Are you sure you know where Luc is taking you, Sofia?"

She folded her arms in front of her and rocked back and forth. "Why me?" she asked. "Why did you pick me to tell?"

"Because," Raszer said, cupping her chin in his hand, "when I watched the six of you with Luc last night, you were one who did not seem sure."

"And what is your angle, Professor?"

"That civil war I mentioned," he replied. "I'm on the other side. Get dressed, *Little Hokhmah*." Her eyes widened to circles. "There's someone I want you to meet. Give me an hour. That's all I ask."

Leaving through the window was not an option. They were three floors up, and there was no fire escape this time. He hid her luxuriant hair in the red scarf as best he could and pulled the worker's cap down low over his eyes. If they could pass as a Czech couple for five seconds, they might fool the Dobermans downstairs. When they reached the landing, Raszer saw, to his great relief, that George had managed to bump his dim bulb relative for a moment. He caught sight of Raszer and Sofia and beckoned frantically. Shaking his head "no," Raszer shepherded her toward the rear exit instead. He shouldered into the swinging door that led to the kitchen and met equal force on the other side. The desk clerk shot him a forbidding look and raised a finger to protest.

Raszer offered a shrug that said, "busted," and backed away from the swinging door. A heavyset cook barreled through, scowling.

There was a *screech* of chair legs in the dining area. Shadows danced on the wall leading into the foyer. It was ten feet from where Raszer now stood to the open door and George's protection. No time. He wrapped Sofia under his right arm and tangoed her to the exit. Inches from the threshold, Raszer saw a blur of gray wool on his left, and Sofia lost her footing. And made a serious mistake.

For an instant, she turned her head and looked into the yellow eyes of the old thug, Bandeur. An instant was enough. She was seized by a spasm of pain. The gunman's arm dropped in front of her like a railroad gate. At the end of the arm was a waxy hand and a ring finger bearing the twin-eagle insignia. Raszer gave discretion a moment's thought, then powered straight through the blockade and past George's linebacker form onto the landing. George immediately moved his body into position between Bandeur and the fleeing couple. Raszer skated Sofia down the steps and didn't look back. They dove into the streaming crowd.

George's body spanned the width of the inn's doorway. He turned his back to the thugs, extended his arms and braced himself against the door-frame. Bandeur grabbed hold of the hair at the nape of George's neck and snapped his head back while jamming a knee into his coccyx. George went for his shoulder holster, but took a brutal blow to his left shin from the steel-toed boot of Otto Scheipp, who was now in the mix. His knees buck-led and he let out a Czech war cry strident enough to stop the pedestrian traffic on the street. He stumbled forward onto the steps as the gray emi-nences shot out of the doorway. Then, in one seamless motion that was amazingly fleet for a man of his bulk, he spun about, dropped to his knees on the third step down and leveled the snout of his .38 at the two thugs.

For ten seconds, he was able to hold two targets at close range, just enough time for Raszer and Sofia to clear the first corner on the way to the bridge. The men had the faces of carrion eaters, but guileless they were not. Bandeur feigned right as if to flee, and in the split second it took George to see the fake, Otto leapt into the crowd, pushing over a fruit cart and the old woman who tended it. No apology was offered.

Klaus Bandeur gazed calmly into George's eyes and saw fear. That predatory sense was perhaps his most marketable skill. He reached matter-of-factly for the pocket of his suit coat. George twitched, and twitched again. He clicked off the safety and waited. He'd rarely held a gun on any-one, let alone shot it. Time suddenly had a viscous quality. Bandeur's fin-gers clasped the object in his pocket and drew it out. An unfiltered Gauloise. He set it between his dry lips and smiled.

"Do you have a wife?" he asked.

George nodded warily, his finger still trembling against the trigger.

"Go home to her," Bandeur sneered, "and fuck her for me."

George rose gingerly from his knees. The exquisite pain in his shin had just begun to ebb. When he spoke, the fear was still there but, it was now spiked with indignation.

"Please turn and put your hands together on the railing, sir. Do just as I say." Bandeur spat a missile of loose tobacco at George's well-polished boots. George stepped to the landing, looming a full seven inches over

Bandeur's head, and put the muzzle to his temple. With his free hand, he pulled a set of handcuffs from their harness. "Go ahead, *azzole,*" he said, more than loud enough for nearby by onlookers to hear. *"Meke my day."*

Someone in the crowd hooted, and George turned briefly to accept the acclaim. "Yes, I have a wife," he returned to whisper in Bandeur's ear, "and two daughters. And it is my job that feeds them."

He cuffed Bandeur's wrist to the railing. Backing away, the grin returned to the moon face. He pardoned himself before the crowd, and then lurched into an ungainly trot in the direction of the bridge.

THEY WERE DOWN to the Legil Bridge turn-off before Raszer allowed his spine to curve into the cracked leather of the taxi's rear seat. They'd leapt into a cab, with Otto Scheipp not more than ten yards behind, and Raszer had watched through the rear window as Scheipp scanned the crowds in search of them, his Neanderthal brow knitted in some form of thought, his eyes displaying little knack for picking a target out of a melee. If that was the meanest heat the Temple could put on him, Raszer thought, he might just pull this off. As for Big George, he'd surely acquitted himself. He was owed a year's supply of strudel if they got through this together.

Sofia was looking at him with a look of consternation. "Did you just kidnap me?" she asked. "Is that what that was all about?"

The taxi had now crossed the Legil and was heading back north on the river road toward the Charles Bridge. Raszer decided that now was as good a time as any, and he pulled the fax from his inside pocket.

"It was probably about this." He handed her the ransom note. "You're worth a lot of money. That little prick would've shot the Pope for ten million dollars."

She gave the fax a perfunctory look, seeming less taken aback that Raszer had anticipated. "How did you get this?" she asked suspiciously.

"An ally inside." He turned to her and squinted. "Did you know?"

She turned to look at the passing riverbank. "I wasn't crazy about the idea but I liked being worth something to someone."

Raszer studied her profile, following the curl of her ear to the flushed cheek and the classic line of her jaw. If you only knew, he thought.

"I think I should go back, Professor," she said to the river. "Or whoever you are." She regarded Raszer over a bony shoulder as if just beginning to see his true face. "I've made my bed. Am I free to lie in it?"

"I think," said Raszer, "that you should hold that question for now. We're going someplace and wait for a friend. Try to trust me for just a little while."

THE LITTLE TAVERN'S outdoor section consisted of six or seven tables arranged on the sloping, pebble-paved bank of the Vltava. It was, as
George had said, one of Prague's beauty spots, with the statue-lined
promenade of the Charles Bridge arching overhead and the entire city on
display, but with Otto on the loose and George missing in action, Raszer
decided against drinking *al fresco*. He chose instead a small table against the
rear wall with a view out the front door. Out of respect for Sofia's regimen,
he ordered her a mineral water and himself a Pilsner.

He lit a cigarette. To his surprise, she tugged it gently from between
his fingers and took a deep drag.

"Sofia," he began, "I know this is a lot to—" She raised a palm to
hush him.

"How did you know my nickname, *Hokhmah?* Nobody but my father
has ever called me that."

Here away from Luc's candlelight and atmospherics, he could see her
ordeal had taken its toll. Her fine, cream-colored skin was a little jaundiced.
Her eyes were bloodshot and rimmed with dark circles. Still, it was the
kind of face over which poets found themselves at a loss for words.

"I didn't know your father," he replied. *"Hokhmah* is wisdom. Wisdom is Sofia. I'm a professor of philology and I like to play with words."
She seemed unconvinced. "When did you start having that pain? It seems
bad."

She sipped the mineral water silently for a moment before answering.
"When I was thirteen. About the time I got my first period."

"Have you seen doctors?"

"Dozens. And dozens of their humiliating and awful tests. They say
there's nothing wrong with me physically. My favorite diagnosis was this
bearded shrink in Quebec City. He told me that I was 'at war with my re-
productive system,' and he sort of implied that deep down I wanted to be a
man." She laughed to herself, and Raszer laughed with her. "I lost my faith
in medicine a long time ago, Professor. I lost my faith in almost everything.
Until Luc."

Raszer took a drink and was suddenly very aware that he'd held his
bladder for three hours. "I'll be right back," he said. "I'm going to use the
loo. Stay put. They're still out there, Sofia, and they're not nice people."

Sofia looked through the open door at the sunlit spill of the bank,
and glimpsed a flock of white swans gathered about a little girl who was
feeding them breadcrumbs. A sigh escaped her. She remembered a Mont-

real park and the feel of her father's calfskin glove folded around her tiny hand. She rose from the table and walked out the door with her eye trained on the little girl with the pink ribbon in her hair.

Thirty feet above, Otto Scheipp fought his way through the swarm of peddlers and tourists to the south-facing railing of the Charles Bridge promenade. He scanned the riverside for a flash of the red scarf, as it had not occurred to him that his prey might have removed it. He, too noticed the swans at the bank and would have dismissed them instantly if he'd not seen the thin, raven-haired woman approaching them. He pulled a walkie-talkie from his suit coat and spoke in rapid German. After the relay of instructions, he leaned heavily into the black, wrought iron railing, keeping a watchful eye.

Raszer hustled out of the latrine to find the table deserted. He cursed and was about to query the bartender when he caught sight of her kneeling alone among the swans at the bank. He rushed to the door and, remaining in the shadow, cleared his throat twice. When she failed to turn, he cleared it a third time with a guttural, *"Hokhmah!"* Gaining her attention, he flagged her back into the tavern, casting an eye about for pursuers.

"I read in a tourist guide that the swans of the Vltava go back at least sixty generations," he said, taking her arm. They were here when John Dee was here. It's too bad we can't ask them if Luc got the formula right." They slid back onto their barstools. Raszer was beginning to worry about time and George, but he had to handle the moment as if it were eternal. "Tell me, Sofia. Would anything have changed your decision about leaving life?"

She sighed. "Oh, I don't think so. I've always been a bad fit. When I was little, people told me I was pretty, but I didn't feel pretty. When I grew up, they told me I was bright but I felt dark. Marrying Lawrence Gould was my last shot at making a life my mother would approve of. We even tried to make a baby..."

"And?"

"I'm no good at that, either. My plumbing just doesn't work. Luc says some of us were born by mistake. We were never meant to be physical."

"We were never meant," Raszer said, taking her fingers in his hand, "to be *only* physical. But life isn't a mistake. He offered a nod to the river-bank. "Ask the swans."

Juraj "George" Dubrovsky had taken the prescribed route to the rendezvous, but had been delayed behind a fender-bender. He was out of breath as he hurried down the slope from the Three Ostriches Restaurant and followed the bank to the tavern. He crossed in front of the open door for just long enough to catch Raszer's eye, flash him a grin and give an America-style, "thumbs up." Raszer returned the gesture and signaled a request for two more minutes.

George walked a few feet away and dropped to a crouch on the grassy bank. He followed the movement of a barge as it passed under the bridge, barely clearing the low arch, and his gaze continued until he spotted Otto. He was leaning against the south railing looking bored and stupid as he sucked on a lollipop. Otto's attention was focused on the taxi rank behind the tavern and so, for the moment, had missed the biggest target in sight. George slowly stood, turned away and slouched as inconspicuously as possible back to the tavern door. Raszer was paying the check.

"Go now! Out the back!" George barked, drawing his pistol and flashing the bartender his AlphaCorp badge. "Police matter," he commanded, in Czech. "Please to let these two out the rear." The bartender complied with a shrug, and George hustled his charges through the kitchen door and up the worn steps to the upper bank. He flagged a taxi to pull forward and thus out of Otto's range.

"I will see you at the church," he promised once he had them in the cab, causing Sofia to mouth, "Church?" "I am going first to try and deal with that pig on the bridge."

As the taxi pulled away, Sofia scooted to the far end of the backseat and stared at Raszer, her black eyes circles of confusion.

FROM WHERE HE stood, George could see the span of the Charles Bridge. Otto was gone. George kept his .38 unholstered and pivoted around, suddenly feeling very exposed. He made a mental calculation of how long it would have taken Otto to sprint over from his lookout on the bridge. Impossible. He decided that the best course was to retrace his steps in hopes of confronting his adversary in the tavern.

As he started back, he was suddenly aware of a burning sensation in his left shin. At first, the feeling was a little bit like the bite of a horsefly, followed instantaneously by the prickly numbness of a limb falling asleep. Almost immediately though – it couldn't have been more than a second or two – it flared into a venomous attack on the entire left side of his body. He wheeled around and fell to the concrete with a *thud*, causing a woman waiting at the taxi rank to shriek. An elderly man next to her cried out, "He's having a stroke!"

Gasping for breath, unable to move or speak, George rolled his eyes to the left and saw his monumentally tall assailant in the midst of the small crowd gathered nearby, wearing – as he had on the previous night – an overcoat far too heavy for June. He heard someone call for a doctor; then he passed out cold.

Josef De Boer turned and strode casually away, pocketing the tiny stun gun. He knew it would be four hours before Dubrovsky uttered a word.

# 16

## THE HIEROS GAMOS

*I sing in hymns to enter the gates*
*of the field of apples of holy ones*
*A new table we lay for Her*
*a beautiful candelabrum*
*sheds its light upon us*

*Between the right and left the Bride approaches*
*to holy jewels and festive garments*
*She has seventy crowns, but above her the King*
*that all may be crowned in the Holy of Holies*

*All worlds are formed and sealed within Her*
*but all shine forth from the 'Old of Days'*

—   Isaac Luria


THE GRANITE STONEWORK sparkled like rose quartz in the late afternoon light. It seemed to Raszer almost as if the luminosity within the sanctuary had sought out the chinks in the ancient mortar. He stepped from the taxi and offered his hand to the suddenly recalcitrant Sofia, who stared at the building with something less than wonderment.

"What is this place?" she asked warily. He stooped and peered into the cab. She had scooted a little nearer the open door.

"This is also a portal, Sofia. A very old one."

She set one white-stocking clad leg on the street, but only one. It occurred to Raszer that, like a drug addict, she feared coming down.

"Not a synagogue," she protested, under her breath. "Not even my father dragged me here. And I know what Luc would say."

Raszer left his arm extended to her. "Then Luc understands less about the origins of his own temple than I would have thought."

She shuddered and her eyes bore through him. "I need to see Luc. This doesn't feel right." Using the taxi's doorjamb as a lever, she jettisoned herself out of the seat and flew past Raszer's arm. He leapt after her, threw her over his shoulder and handed the fare to the driver, who hadn't been so entertained in months.

In the cloister just outside the synagogue's entrance, he set her down and raised both palms in a plea for forbearance. "Don't you get it, Sofia? I *know* you. Shit, I *am* you." He ripped his cuffs open, pushed his sleeves to the elbows and held his wrists out to her. She looked down at the tender scars that had never healed quite right and her eyes flickered with comprehension. She allowed herself to be led, dazed, into the temple. Neither of them noticed the long, black Mercedes rounding the corner a block away. The sun had disappeared behind a bank of clouds; it was beginning to drizzle again.

"Ah," a voice called from the darkness, "the reluctant bride." Raszer pivoted clumsily to find its source in the vaporous candlelight. The rabbi stepped forward and held out both hands. He was outfitted resplendently, not in rabbinical black, but in a flowing white gown set around the collar with sapphires. His yarmulke was embroidered in gold.

Raszer kept his arm around Sofia. Her tongue was stilled for the moment by the realization that she had been expected. "Rabbi Scholem, this is Sofia. I don't think she's interested in becoming observant today."

"Well then," the rabbi responded, cocking his head, "we will adjust our expectations. My daughter…" He bowed to Sofia and moved immediately to break the barrier of touch by placing his warm hand on her head. "All we wish today is to show the Sun the face of his lost sister Moon. Consider it a benediction before you leave us again and deprive Him – and the world – of your beauty." He drew the tip of an oiled finger down her forehead and across the bridge of her nose. She sniffed and reflected, as if she recognized in the balm some familiar essence. "You revere the Sun, do you not, my child?" According to your master's teachings?"

"The first sun is a baptism of fire," she answered, without affect, as if reciting from the manual. "And the second sun is home."

"Home to whom?"

"Home to the Chosen," she replied, with a slight hint of embarrassment.

"Well," said the rabbi, "I shall have to consult the burning bush about that."

Without taking his eyes from her, Rabbi Scholem raised a finger to the center of the chamber, and a lamp was lit at the cantor's platform. The serpentine voice of the cantor emerged from the veil of silence – not as an "event" with a marked beginning, but as if someone had slowly turned up the volume on a sound that had been there all along. In accompaniment, the rabbi softly clapped his hands in a rhythmic four-note phrase, while circling her in a subtle dance.

A faint rosy glow issued from the dais just behind and to the right of the cantor and blossomed within seconds into an image that seemed almost holographic. Apparently suspended about two feet in the blackness was the image of an altar unlike any Raszer had seen. Its shape was that of a perfect cube of about two feet square, and as the glow increased in intensity, its outer surface became transparent, revealing a second cube within. The inner cube turned on a corner, rotating slowly on some unseen axis.

A new sound, a tambourine softly beating out the rabbi's clapped four-note phrase, joined the cantor from left of the cube and gave rhythmic foundation to the unanchored chant. Raszer peered through the rouge penumbra and discovered that the accompanist was a monk, cloaked in the humble garb of the Franciscan order. He raised and shook the tambourine for seven beats as the cantor climbed to a small crescendo, and behind the cube there emerged a third form, that of an equal-armed cross, a sort of sacred "plus" sign. This was the archetypal symbol of the conjunction of the male and female principles. It was also, like the double-cube, a sign associated with *Malkuth,* the tenth of the ten *serifah,* or emanations by which, according to Kabbalists, God made his nature manifest in the world of matter. *Malkuth* was woman clothed with the sun, and she was also – in that strange, ever-morphing lexicon of mysticism – the *Shekhinah,* the beloved consort of God, over whose tragic betrayal God wept on the eve of each Sabbath. Tonight, if the ceremony occurred as advertised, she was to be called home – if only for a cosmic instant. Rabbi Scholem stepped forward and put his arm around Sofia. He turned to Raszer.

"We have preparation to do. Allow us fifteen minutes, will you?"

Raszer nodded and as the two of them walked off into the blackness, Sofia looked back to him, as if for approval. Raszer gave it with a soft closing of his eyes. There it was. The transference had begun, and Raszer had been bequeathed a huge new responsibility. He could have spent the fifteen minutes pondering that, but there was a phone call to be made. He stepped outside to the small courtyard and pulled out George's cellular.

"SEVENTH INNING STRETCH," he told Monica. She offered no acknowledgement of his levity. "I've got her for the moment, but I need two things. Call Lawrence Gould and tell him I hope to have her to a safe harbor within two hours. See if there's a London flight tonight. If not, first thing in the a.m."

"Done, Raszer."

He watched the fog roll in through the cloister. He could hear the heaviness in her voice and girded himself for a punch in the gut. "Okay." He took a moment to light a cigarette. "Did you score with that reporter? Any news on Jeanette?" He heard her suck in her breath.

"It'll be in the Provincial papers tomorrow. Jacques Denis told me…they pulled her from the lake an hour ago. No cause of death yet; the coroner has her right now. He thinks they'll move to arrest Noel Branch any time."

Raszer collapsed against a stone column and slammed his forehead into its ribbed surface. *"Goddamnit!* What the hell am I dealing with? This is more like fucking Watergate than *Heaven's Gate."* He felt the paralysis of rage flow through his extremities and knew that nothing would disable him faster. "Okay, *fast,* get me this number in Montreal." He pulled Philippe Caudal's crumpled business card from his pocket. Two minutes passed as the call went through their switchers. Raszer squatted and felt the prickliness of sweat breaking on his forehead.

"I'm putting you through, Raszer, but I don't know…"

A static-ridden voice came on the line. "Savana Investments. How may I direct your call?"

"Mr. Caudal, please. An urgent matter involving his investment in Prague."

"I'm sorry, Monsieur Caudal is no longer with the firm. I'll transfer you to his associate. Who may I say is calling?"

"Never mind. Goodbye." Monica broke the connection instantly.

"Fuck," Raszer said. "They got to him. They must have." He emptied his smoke-filled lungs into the fog. "I've only got one more idea right now. Find Stocker Hinge. I think that account Mr. X set up for me is supposed to receive the ransom money. I think that somehow – I haven't figured out how yet – Noel Branch is supposed to be the courier. It's a double-bind and I'm in the middle. If Hinge has any other way into the Temple leadership, he can tell them that I'll continue to play my role. All I want is Sofia. I don't think Lawrence Gould will pay, but maybe I can buy some time."

"That's the other thing, Raszer. There's a message on Stocker's private line. A death in the family. His mother, I suppose. I can't reach him, Raszer, and I'm not sure anymore that I trust him."

"Then call the main number at the Institute and have them find him."

"Are you sure?"

"Yes."

For a few moments he remained there, squatting in a shroud of mist, his right arm curled back around his neck like an orangutan, the cell phone enfolded in his left hand. He let the whole business drain from his mind. He had to, for Sofia's sake. A gentle tap on his shoulder stirred him, and he turned to find the rabbi beckoning him inside. Inside was good; inside was sanctuary.

Outside the gates, in the back seat of a vintage Mercedes limo, Josef De Boer sat with the recently liberated Klaus Bandeur, calmly working an acrostic. It was in moments like this, with time on his side and the kill within his grasp, that he was most truly relaxed.

When Raszer stepped inside and beheld the synagogue ablaze with candlelight from every sector, his sense of dread was tempered. The rabbi took his arm and led him to the far side of the chamber, about thirty feet from the dais where the altar still hovered. There, in a pool of darkness between the candelabrum, Sofia stood draped in a diaphanous white silk, the slight, almost boyish curves of her body perceptible beneath the folds. She was crowned with a simple garland of waxy green leaf, and on her forehead had been painted an equal-armed cross that reflected the larger one before her. Her feet were bare and she was trembling, but the rabbi had apparently won her provisional consent.

"Will you take Sofia's side," Rabbi Scholem asked, "and bring her to me when I call for her?"

Raszer took his place while the rabbi ascended the platform and stood behind the cubicle altar. Its glow turned his white robes rosy pink. For now, the cantor and the monk stood silently, heads bowed. Raszer felt a buzz at the base of his skull. To the right and rear of the dais, in a place unexposed by candlelight, he made out the vague form of another human being, or more precisely, the auric outline of a human form. He couldn't tell if it was male or female, standing or seated, but the color of its corona was violet.

The rabbi drew from beneath the altar a square of white silk and laid it across the surface. He followed with a red one of the same size and placed it diagonally over the first, then concluded with a third layer of white. He rested his palms on the silk and spoke, at first in English.

"Lord, most merciful and radiant. We call you forth from the fullness of the Pleroma and humbly ask that we may call you by your true names, and with the laying on of them, begin to restore to you your beloved, Sofia. Lord, as the north wind rises in Paradise, let it bring into this chamber, and from its very substance, the true agent of the Philosophers. *AZOTH*, that we may make use of it in the manner prescribed by your servant, Enoch-*METATRON*. Lord, we wish to waken the moon. We wish to lift her up that you may again behold her countenance. Lord, weep no more."

The cantor and the monk were joined by a third, reedy voice from the shadows in repeating, *"Lord, weep no more."*

The rabbi's face, lit from below, bore an expression of timeless grief. It seemed to Raszer that he was having a genuine dialogue with God.

"Lord, I am angered, for one of your own has been led into *sitra ahra* by them who do not perceive the unity of *solve et coagula*. Here, where we dwell, the body is bereft without spirit and the spirit is bereft without body. Lord, hear us. Guide us as true groom in this *coniunctio*, the *zivvuga kadisha*, the sacred chemical wedding. Send forth the sephiroth *tif'ereth* to meet his bride. Lord, hear us and guide us in the practice of that true alchemy, received from you by Enoch in the *old of days*, by which the spirit ascends to you in *solve* and returns to the body in *coagula*. Lord, condemn not our pride, for we know that here today we make only a beginning."

He paused and dropped his head to the altar, and when he rose again, the same equal-armed cross was emblazoned on his forehead in luminescent red. He raised his arms high and four voices chanted in unison, *"Bring forth the bride!"*

The monk began to tap out a new rhythm, this time a repeating seven-beat phrase: tat-tat │ tat-tat │ tat-*tat-tat*. Artifacts of reverberation found Raszer's ears from behind and above, lending to the impression of a troupe of tambourinists. The cantor then wove a melody through the beats – distinctly Middle Eastern, almost like *qawwali* in its ornamentation – its tonal center shifting in a way that made its locus elusive.

Raszer glanced at Sofia. She was looking at him from a deep place, her eyes moist with tears. As he took her arm and walked her forward, he had the queer sensation of being both brother and groom, though not father.

The rabbi's incantation continued to ricochet around Raszer's brain, but certain words, phrases and emphases were beginning to assemble themselves into a nucleotide chain of meaning. At first, he doubted what he was experiencing, as someone who has swallowed a hallucinogen for the first time doubts his transformation until a veteran affirms it. The sense was of a neural telegram being tapped out in his heart and delivered to his mind. He knew for the first time exactly how the Temple of the Sun had so tragically misconstrued the sacred code. *You can't go home again.* The mystical experience was more like energy moving up and down a Tesla Coil, the dynamic more like that of a perpetual motion machine. *Solve et Coagula.*

Mist and Water. Spirit and Substance. Our bodies provided a way station for the spirit between its journeys, and the pain we bear exists to incite the spirit's wanderlust. But we are *always* to return to the world. To reject life, to reject the world, as Luc and his companions sought to do, *was* a blasphemy. The human form is itself the temple.

At that instant, he became aware of overtones in faint counterpoint against the cantor's voice. The sound was so unlike any human voice he'd heard that at first he failed to realize that it was coming from the little sprite he'd glimpsed behind the platform. The violet form was now mounting the platform occupied by the other three. As it emerged into the strobing candlelight, it was revealed as a child – no more than five feet tall – wearing a Sphinx-like mask that, like Janus, looked both forward and back. Three, four, then as many as six silver spheres the size of billiard balls emerged from his robe, and the little person began to juggle them with uncanny speed and precision. Knitted in gold thread on the front of his worn and patched purple robe was the iconic form of the *simurgh* or *avis hermetis,* the philosopher's bird, the Sufi symbol of the soul's flight to God. And so there they were: the Moslem mystic, the Christian mystic and the Jewish mystic – the reactor core of Western faith – gathered on one stage and embracing the same sacrament. An impossible notion fluttered through Raszer's mind, and a coiled energy moved up his spine, bringing a welling of tears to his eyes.

The rabbi approached and anointed Raszer's eyelids, then gently motioned for him to step back from Sofia's side, so that he might escort her to her place before the altar. He remounted the platform, and a voice of almost fearsome *gravitas* issued from his lips. The matrix of the language was Hebrew, but laced with words from another tongue, another country; words like, "CAOSGI TABAORD SAANIR OD CHRISTEOS YRPOIL TIOBL BUSDIR TILB NOALN PAID ORSBA OD DODRMNI ZYLNA ELZAP TILB PARMGI PERIPSAX." Could it be Enochian? Was it the same linguistic key with which Luc hoped to unlock the secrets of the Temple? He wondered if Sofia could see what he now saw – two coins of the same denomination, superficially so alike. Except that one was a counterfeit.

When she had reached the altar opposite Rabbi Scholem, he drew from his left and right two large rings, one white and one red, each about eight inches in diameter. They flickered in and out of the reality field in a way not wholly material, like primitive movie effects made by scratching the film to allow the light of the arc lamp to pass through. Their movement across the altar had a jittery, quantum quality. The rabbi held them at her eye level, at first about two feet apart, and then brought them together while keeping his gaze fixed on the narrowing space between them until his eyes actually began to cross. His voice rose in pitch and intensity and now functioned as the libretto for the orchestration provided by the others. At the instant the rings made contact and overlapped, all fell silent.

In the brief lull that followed, Raszer became aware of rain on the roof and a distinct out-of-body sensation. Then there was a crackling hum that seemed not to come from any point source, but from everywhere. In less time that the eye is capable of perceiving, an arc of pure golden light shot from the nexus of the two rings into the center of the cross on Sofia's forehead and impelled her head back in a spasm. With the speed and instincts of a surgeon, the rabbi set the rings on the altar and came around to her side, calling Raszer to assist him in her support.

"Mr. Raszer, I need you *here* now."

But Raszer did not respond immediately. He couldn't. A part of him suddenly understood why Jesus, in John 20:17, had uttered, "Touch me not," to the Magdalene. For Raszer, at that instant, stood upon the platform, looking at himself through the eyes of Sofia Gould. The rabbi snapped his fingers, and he found himself again in his own body, walking to her side.

Cradling her head in his large hand and pressing his lips to her ear, the rabbi said, "Do you want to be with the Sun, child?" Sofia nodded mutely. "From this moment on, it is with you and in you always."

There was an echo of sound and light in the chamber that filled the two-second eternity of a dream. After that, the three of them were alone on the dais. Rabbi Scholem cupped his hands around Sofia's chin.

"So...how do you feel?" he asked, with the earthy warmth of a family doctor. She raised her eyes to him and placed a hand on her abdomen in wonder.

*"The pain is gone..."* she answered. "Am I dead?"

AFTER SOFIA HAD dressed, the rabbi saw them into the court and gave a little bow as he whispered, "Shalom." Sofia took his gray head in her hands and kissed him on his bearded mouth. He looked at her admiringly and smiled.

"Ah, to be a young man again."

He turned and walked back into the synagogue without a backward glance. Raszer held Sofia in his arms and she crushed her head against his chest, murmuring, "Thank you..." Through the cracked door, he could see

Rabbi Scholem extinguishing the candles with a routine perfection that was pure Zen. Just another day at the office.

"We're going home," Raszer said, but as the last of the words left his lips, he felt cold steel dig into his left temple, and heard her muffled scream as she was wrenched from his arms.

"Good evening, *Professor,*" he heard a dusky, Germanic voice say. "Why don't we get you out of the rain."

Once his captives were secured in the back of the limo, De Boer turned for one last look at the synagogue and spat on the street. There was not a soul in sight. He motioned to Bandeur in the front seat, and the Mercedes pulled away from the curb, rubber rolling across wet stone. In the obscuring dusk and drizzle, De Boer did not perceive the tiny masked figure crouched behind the hedge that flanked the building's west entrance.

# 17

## THE CRUX

THE MORNING FOG of June curled up under dew-misted chaparral in the canyon behind Raszer's house. Monica thought she spotted a mule deer dash through the scrub and vanish behind a fennel-covered rise. She had been trying for two hours to reach Raszer, but there was no answer on either the borrowed cell phone or his palm unit. She had something to tell him, and she had a lump in her gut the size of an orange.

She was desperate for coffee, so she turned from the kitchen window and lit the Bunsen burner under Raszer's old French *Conna*, a bubbled glass apparatus that looked like it belonged in Frankenstein's lab. At home, she had a German drip machine, but when at his house, she did it his way.

The front porch *creaked*. At the front door, a knock followed; three raps, *tat-tat-tat*, then nothing. She assured herself there was no reason to be jumpy and set the pitch of the flame where she wanted it.

When she arrived at the screen door, the porch was empty. There was a boy on a skateboard in the cul-de-sac and a Mexican gardener trimming a hedge, but no one was close enough to have knocked.

She stepped outside. *"Hel-lo?"*

An envelope whispered against the rough pine at her feet. She examined it quizzically for a moment before picking it up and opening it. It was a telegram — one that could evidently be delivered without signature. Her eyes hurried across the halting text.

```
Fourché alive. Christmas in June. No cops
in Prague and Raszer will get the girl.
Send them to Savana.
```

THE ROOM IN which Raszer found himself was dank and dark as a sewer. His blindfold had been removed, and he had been bound to a vertical water main, his arms wrenched back so that his biceps were fully extended, their soft, blue veins swollen from constriction, his wrists tied behind him. They had trussed him in a seated position and removed his shoes and socks so that his heels and buttocks were now resting on cold, cracked concrete that was alive with some foul smelling seepage from the over saturated ground below. He could almost track his body temperature dropping degree by degree. He'd slept little and eaten nothing all day, and something wriggled over the arch of his left foot and began to move up the inside of his trouser leg.

He heard no telltale creaks from the floorboards above. The thought that he might be abandoned in the hellhole was somehow more terrifying than the prospect of being confronted by his captors. Had they taken Sofia back to Luc? He found it hard to believe that a man as shrewd as Fourché would proceed with the work under such disruptive circumstances, at least not until he knew if Raszer was acting alone, but he now understood that this crew was driven by exigencies that lay well beyond the pale of ordinary human concerns.

There was not the faintest whisper of traffic noise to give a clue as to his location, but the brevity of the journey suggested they were within the city limits. The centipede had paused and was resting just below his knee, so his attention now turned to the awareness that little if any blood was getting to his hands. He'd lost all feeling in them. A cold, thick hemorrhage of panic spread within seconds from his intestines to his neck, and he instinctively began to run a sort of "tape loop" in his mind – a mantra he'd once learned from his Vedantist teacher. Holiness existed in the subatomic fabric of even this awful place, so the swami would have said.

After a few moments, his heartbeat slowed enough to allow a single coherent question to enter his mind, a question common to servants, knights and Sufis. *What is expected of me?*

Raszer's ears hungrily seized on a faint sound from somewhere opposite him. He ran the texture of it back and forth in his brain for analysis. It was the moist *creak* of freshly polished boot leather. He was not alone. There was a sudden rush of damp air around his head, as if the wings of some great bat had gone into motion, and then a bolt of pain shot through his skull as his pupils contracted in the glare of a flashlight.

"Let's make a deal," whispered the husk-dry Germanic voice behind the flashlight. "I will consider leaving your tongue attached to its root if you tell me who provided your cover." Josef De Boer stood no less than six-foot-six and taller still in his boots. His cheeks were sunken and cadaverous, their flesh like old paper.

"Counter-proposal," Raszer answered with what little pluck he could master. "I'll let you crawl back in your hole for a few centuries if you tell me who was on the grassy knoll."

The formless figure shifted his weight and sighed. His exhaled breath reached Raszer with the stench of decaying tomatoes. The next thing he heard was the *crack* of the flashlight against his own skull. A moment of unconsciousness must have followed because when he became aware of sensation again, it was of the ferocious mushrooming of pain behind his eyes rather than the initial impact. Blood trickled down his temple. The flashlight's beam was back in his face again, forcing his pupils to contract once more, redoubling the pain.

"You may have hoped," said De Boer, "that I would be a cultivated man. I am not. I am not impressed by will, only by power. You appear to have little. Now, I will ask you again, who provided your cover?"

Raszer swallowed the bile that was moving up his esophagus like molten lava. "I can tell you this; if you harm the girl, the only cover you'll have is a white sheet. Guarantee her safe passage home and you can hold me hostage for the ten million."

De Boer laughed with a chuckle that sounded like kindling newly lit. "Now what, I wonder, would you be worth to the man you've no doubt already cuckolded?"

"Not to him, asshole," said Raszer, readying his bluff. "To the United States National Security Agency." That sounded reasonably genuine, Raszer thought.

Josef De Boer thought differently. He moved the flashlight aside and leaned in to Raszer's ear, revealing a malevolently banal profile of ferret nose and lipless mouth. There was something grotesquely tender about the way he lingered, taking in his prisoner's scent. Raszer shuddered.

"Bandeur will enjoy fucking you after I've killed you," De Boer whispered, and then he clamped his yellowed teeth onto the outer rim of Raszer's ear, bit down and shook his head as furiously as a wolf on the kill. The howl continued to empty from Raszer's windpipe even after he'd blacked out again. Within seconds, consciousness flooded cruelly back into his circuits, and he heard De Boer spit the torn piece of cartilage across the room.

"I am a single-minded man," he continued, "so don't presume we can 'get acquainted' and strike some sort of deal. I don't have the patience for torture, but you *will* tell me what I want to know. I have found no more effective way to make a man value his life than to let him watch himself die very slowly."

De Boer drew a stainless steel instrument from his overcoat and removed the sheath. The blade of the oversized scalpel curved like a scythe.

"You've heard the old expression," he said, polishing the blade on Raszer's pant leg, "'the death of a thousand small cuts.' You may not know that it was, in fact, a nasty torture practiced by the ancient Chinese upon traitors to the Empire. Now, inflicting one thousand cuts would be a great deal of work, so I have refined the technique to require only four. Two here, on the neck just below each ear…" He made the described incisions so quickly that Raszer was not aware of them until he felt the throbbing of the blood. "And two more…*here.*" This time Raszer prepared for the pain. He sucked in a bellyful of the basement's foul air to stifle his groan as, in two strokes, De Boer bisected the veins that ran down his biceps.

The incisions were each about an inch in length and no more than an eighth of an inch deep. The blood, thick and claret-colored, oozed rather than spilled, which was the point. *Christ,* Raszer thought. *I have got to slow my heartbeat!*

"Depending on your fortitude," De Boer explained without affect, "it will take you from forty-five to sixty minutes to bleed to death. Most people cease to be coherent after about thirty. There is a microphone positioned just over your head. Don't summon me for chitchat. I'll most likely cut your throat and get it over with. Until then *Monsieur…*" He began to back away. "By the way," he added sardonically, "I understand that toward the end one experiences something akin to sexual rapture. Everything has its opposite, doesn't it?" He cackled and the dry kindling burst into flame.

He wiped the scalpel on Raszer's shirt, pocketed it and turned to go. Raszer's forearms were already sticky with blood and the trickle from the neck wounds had made its way to his solar plexus. Before De Boer reached the door, Raszer called out.

"Are you a believer in this Temple, Mr. De Boer, or just a whore like me?"

De Boer strode a few paces back in Raszer's direction. "I am chief of Defensive Operations for Europe, so I suppose a nominal faith in the enterprise is required. I gather from your accent that you're an American so I doubt you'll understand. By raising the peasant to the stature of a prince, you people have succeeded in subverting the natural order. The race has been so bastardized that we've lost the favor of the gods."

"And who," Raszer asked, his strength flagging, *"would* find favor?"

"I serve a long line of princes." De Boer turned again to exit. "I don't make the error of thinking myself to be one of them. Their mission is as it always has been: to recover the true source of power. When the world has been burned clean of its filth by a baptism of fire, the way may be clear for them to rule again. Consider that while you bleed to death."

As the door closed and the last photon of light dipped into black ether, Raszer glimpsed De Boer's world for an instant. It was a black and white world, drained of color, devoid of music. It was a world in which trees didn't whisper secrets and birds didn't prophecy. A world stripped of that dancing background radiation that the Hindus call *Brahman*. A world where Raszer hoped never to live. He went back to his mantra and somewhere along the way, he said the prayer he used to recite as a boy before going to bed.

SEVEN TIME ZONES west, Philippe Caudal had awakened after a fitful night and brewed his filter coffee as he had every day for the last seven years. He had tried once again to reach Stocker Hinge by phone for an update on Stephan Raszer's situation, and had again received the voicemail message informing callers of a "death in the family." He didn't believe it. Stocker Hinge did not seem the type of man to desert his post at the moment of truth, even for his mother's funeral, but he also didn't believe that Hinge could have so quickly become the victim of a Temple vendetta. Hinge, as far as he knew, was still perceived by the Temple leaders as an overzealous but ultimately harmless researcher who occasionally got his nose up the wrong crack. He had sometimes, in fact, been useful to them because he was inclined to mislead the police and the press in order to maintain his privileged access to the sect. They were far more likely to try and buy his collaboration. That was the possibility that concerned Caudal.

He had not wavered under questioning by the other six members of the Golden Circle. In truth, they had given him a curiously polite audience. He told them simply that he had dispatched Professor Branch to Prague as per the approved protocol; he had the documents to prove it. It was only later that he had learned through a Temple plant at the *Institute pour l'Observation de Nouvelles Sectes* that Stocker Hinge had dispatched Branch to the North Woods in order to put his own proxy in Prague, the better to gather material for his exposé. Caudal had maintained his ignorance of the proxy's name and occupation, because he still hoped, if all else failed, to use Stephan Raszer to implicate the Circle in the extortion scheme.

Caudal had left the grilling feeling as if he might have pulled it off, but then he found that he'd been frozen out of his computer, and hence, all access to Savana accounts worldwide. Worse, he'd been given a sealed letter, written not on Savana letterhead but on Temple parchment, granting him a leave of absence from his duties as chief financial officer. Whatever relief he had felt drained away like ice water through his veins. He had quickly left the office and gone straight home.

He sipped the coffee absently and thought. If the Temple's hackers spent enough time in his computer, they would eventually retrace the zig-zagging trail of bank transfers he had plotted to lead authorities from the ransom note to the main Savana account. Along that trail, they might discover the tangents that, if followed, would blow open the Swiss banking system and its collusion with both the Nazis and the old families of the *Valais*. He had wanted for the whole thing to take some time, allowing him to complete his disappearing act underground. He had also hoped that by making Montreal trip over its own greed, rather than going public with long-guarded Temple secrets, he might ultimately be revered as a savior of the faith. Now time had little meaning. Despite the knowledge that his phones were very likely tapped, he sat down to compose a fax to Jacques Denis at the Montreal Standard, the journalist who, in the past, had come closest to the truth. Upon finishing, he clicked the "Send" icon and reached for his coffee. His fingers never got to the cup.

The first blow came from directly behind and drove through the flesh between his shoulder blades, severing his spinal cord. After that, he felt little. Seventeen more wounds were delivered before the hail of blades let up and his head was allowed to fall forward onto the desk. His eyes remained open, but his lips were closed and relaxed, his face strangely serene in the computer screen's flickering blue light.

The robed and hooded assassins withdrew, all but for one young man who placed his fingers on the keyboard, inches from Caudal's scalp, and typed in the command to un-jam his computer. Once in, he went online and entered the Savana Investments control center, where he calmly initiated a massive programmed sell-off of the Empire Pictures stock that the multitude of secretive funds had been systematically acquiring over the previous four months.

LUC FOLLOWED OTTO Scheipp through the front door of the safe house and into the parlor. His eyes went immediately and warily to the tall, aging man who was emerging from the basement. Though they had never met, there could be no doubt that this was the man they called the Viper; Josef De Boer, Head of Defensive Operations, former advisor to SAC, and before that, enforcer for the loose-knit cadre of ex-SS agents that had formed the Bavarian Lodge of the Temple. Luc had no more liking for him than he did for the rest of the Austro-Germans who now ran the show. They were a necessary evil.

"Where is she?" Luc demanded, foregoing all pleasantries.

De Boer bowed and gestured toward a bedroom off the narrow hall-way leading from the salon. "Follow me, *Monsieur*. The American is down-stairs. I expect to have a confession shortly."

Sofia was shackled by the wrists to the cast iron foot of a four-poster bed. The décor in the room – all tawny browns and bronze – suggested a permanent, museum-like state of readiness for the arrival of a count or a diplomat. There was a spittoon in one corner and a brass chamber pot atop the armoire. These had been Luc's quarters during his first survey of Prague five months earlier. He stepped into the bedroom and looked her over with disgust. She was a poster child for existential despair; the eyes hollow, her hair disheveled and her skin gone completely sallow. Clinically, she was also beginning to starve. And yet, like an abused child that none-theless runs to Daddy at the first sign of acknowledgement, her mien brightened a bit at the sight of him.

"Oh, Luc!" she cried. "Thank God, I thought I'd die here."

Seeing De Boer stationed in the hallway, Luc closed the door. "This is what you were before, *ma cher*…and this is what you've allowed yourself to become once again – a whore for any man with an agile tongue."

She slumped like a rag doll on the hardwood floor, her wrinkled dress bunched around her scrawny thighs and her chin laid on her breast. He squatted beside her and seemed for a scant moment to consider some ges-ture of tenderness. Her tacit lack of contrition changed his mind. He grabbed hold of her hair and yanked her head back fiercely.

"Have you nothing to say to me? Nothing, after all the secrets I've shown you? The new soul I've given you?" Her glassy eyes rolled back to white. He drew back his arm and backhanded her across the mouth, hard enough to split her lip. "I knew you were inconstant. I *should have known* that you were incapable of true desire. You are a Jewess after all, aren't you, my Sofia?" He slapped her repeatedly across the face until blood ran from her nose and mouth. Then he seized her and kissed her full on her bruised lips. "I should renounce you! I should let you die at the hands of that animal outside. But I keep my promises. I've promised six to The Lodge, and six will be delivered."

He called for De Boer, and the door swung open immediately. "Un-shackle her," Luc ordered. De Boer hesitated. "Do it! You want a confes-sion before he dies? I'll get you one."

Luc stood aside while her chains were freed and pulled a mono-grammed silk handkerchief from the pocket of his suit coat to wipe his forehead. "Give me your gun," he commanded De Boer. He grabbed a fistful of Sofia's hair and hauled her up from the carpet.

The cellar door opened and Raszer struggled to lift his head. They had torn the dress from her shoulders and the tattered fabric hung loosely about her waist. She was half-naked and bloodied, and the sight of her made Raszer sob with rage. Luc prodded her down to the fourth step and reached up with his free hand to switch on the bare bulb that dangled overhead. He took the gun from his pocket and propped the barrel under her chin.

"Are you with Interpol?" he asked Raszer, digging the steel into her flesh.

"No." Raszer was barely audible.

"Canadian police?"

"No!" he howled. "Let her go!" Luc grimaced and fired the pistol into the ceiling. Sofia's knees gave out while Raszer strained helplessly against the ropes. His head fell back against the pipe, and he whispered, "But I can get you ten million dollars."

"Even if I believed you, it's too late. I'm going to give her what she came for."

Raszer's chin dropped to his chest and the world went black.

"TAKE HER PICTURE," Luc said to Otto, when he emerged from the cellar. "Just the way she is. Fax it to her husband, then clean her up." He turned to De Boer, who had now been joined in the living room by Klaus Bandeur. "You, bring her to me at the site. No later than ten. Leave the pig here to guard the American until he dies. We'll get nothing from him."

"And tonight," De Boer inquired, "will go as planned?"

"With some adjustments," Luc replied. He took an envelope from his inside pocket. "Here are your instructions for the move to Strasbourg after the ceremony. Nothing, *nothing* is to interfere with tonight's work. Nothing is to upset their concentration. We have not spent years and millions to abandon the project now, and though I expect it's beyond your under-standing, we *have* made a contract with the Ascended Masters. Six were promised *and six will be delivered.*" De Boer's jaw tightened. "After we've concluded, we will exit through the Number Three sewer, which empties at the bank, six hundred meters north of the bridge. Dominic will assist your men is disassembling the machine and crating it for the move."

Luc turned crisply and headed for the door, brushing past Otto with-out so much as a nod. Just before stepping outside to the waiting car, he turned back to De Boer. "I trust you've taken care of the police?"

"But of course. They will all eat fresh pork on Sunday."

"And the bodyguard? Did you kill him?"

De Boer chortled contemptuously. "One does not murder an AlphaCorp agent unless one wishes to start a war, but he would not have the faintest idea where to begin looking. And Alpha men are strictly prohibited from action without direct orders from their employer."

*"Bon,"* said Luc, headed through the doorway. Turning, he cast an admonishing glare at Sofia and raised an index finger. "There is only one Temple," he said, "and only one Lodge. You will thank me in Paradise."

RASZER KEPT ONE open eye on the blood flow from his left arm, the one closest to his heart. Under textbook circumstances, he might have been able to use *hatha* yoga to get his pulse down below forty, but this wasn't in the manual. The only thing he had been able to manage was to hasten the clotting of his blood with applications of his own saliva, something he'd learned from his Hopi tracker. This required repeated attempts to land a projectile of spit on the wounds. When his mouth dried up, he tried self-hypnosis, which produced an unintended side effect. The half-remembered voice of his crone came back to him. Now that he was halfway to the shadow-lands, he was on her turf.

> *...Can but be denied if a groom ye be*
> *And give me the gift that ye promised me...*

*The gift?* What had he promised? He'd been the groom for her at the alchemical wedding; he'd let her enter his very soul. What more was required of him? His concentration blurred. It was so goddamned cold. He heard a door *creak* and open upstairs, then slam. There were no more footfalls. His extremities were already numb. The darkness began to pulse and atomize, and the atoms formed geometric neon sculptures. *Fuck me, I'm hallucinating. If I hallucinate, I'll fly, and if I fly, my pulse will race and I'll be dead in twenty minutes.* But oh, how he wanted to unshackle his mind and let it float free for just a few moments...

...he was moving upward from the narrow end of an infinitely immense conical chamber – something like the Guggenheim Museum on the celestial scale. At each level of his ascent, the tower was outfitted with a 360° choir loft, and each loft was filled to capacity with human creatures singing boldly from the same hymnal. The music sounded vaguely like the *"Ode To Joy,"* from the final movement of Beethoven's Ninth, but strangely muted, as if heard underwater.

The lower lofts were stocked with common looking folks who, despite their station, were singing their hearts out. Scattered among their ranks were odd little assemblages of uniformed cops, nurses, doctors and even some Hassidic Jews.

As he rose still higher on his invisible elevator, the faces and the dress became more gentrified but still recognizable as individuals. He thought he caught glimpses of the Kennedy family, Grace Kelly and Charles De Gaulle. Priests vigorously shook holy water over the sea of heads, not a drop of which touched him. At what first appeared to be the highest levels, he saw tier upon tier of the European aristocracy, identically attired in royal blue gowns and with homogenous features that seemed to betray a common ancestor. Their performance was considerably more unified, but lacked the raw enthusiasm of the lower levels.

Appearing as "choir masters" for the royal ranks were papal figures in golden robes that shone like the sun. His mind's eye entered a milky cloud that formed a kind of dome, yet he continued to ascend. The music became grander and clearer as he broke through the vapor into the true upper echelon, where the conical tower opened into its broadest aspect, one that seemed as expansive as Heaven itself.

Here, the choirs were composed of angelic beings, arranged according to the classical hierarchy, from archangels and principalities, rising to virtues and thrones; all overseen by the blinding magnificence of the cherubim and seraphim.

Through and within the radiant fabric of music, which was now as much sight and touch as sound, Raszer could hear and feel his heart pumping blood through his veins. He experienced a womb-like sensation of warmth flooding his entire being as it merged with his astral self for the final, soaring leap to the uppermost choir where he would surely look God in the eye.

As the celestial lift came to a halt and the snow-blindness induced by the angelic radiance abated in the sudden, stark clarity of the summit, Raszer began to violently shake his head as if to dispel the horror of seeing, arrayed about him, the entire elite of the Third Reich, led in song by the little Austrian house painter himself. Hitler turned from his conducting to observe Raszer's awe. He threw back his head with a sardonic laugh.

"I am the Light! No man sees Heav'n except through me!"

He conducted with his right hand, while his left offered the Grail to Raszer, whose scream of defiant refusal issued from such a deep fault in his soul that it cracked the very foundation of the tower as he plummeted down to the Hell from which he'd begun his journey...

…the door at the top of the stairs suddenly flew open. In the halluci-natory half-light, Raszer saw a large human form come hurtling down the short stairway and roll to rest with a thud and a groan at his feet. The overhead light came on with blinding intensity, and it was only then that he knew he was conscious.

At the top of the stairs, he beheld a sight that far surpassed the heav-enly choirs in beauty. *It was George,* grinning stupidly from ear to ear. He bounded into the basement and stopped only to deliver a kick for good measure to the unconscious side of beef known as Otto Scheipp. Otto did not move. George knelt beside Raszer in the sticky pool of blood, utterly at a loss.

"My God, Professor; what have they done to you?"

Raszer was so euphoric that he felt he could run a marathon. *"You're God, George!* God-fucking-god-you are," he rambled. "Prometheus is un-bound, you beautiful bohunk!! Have to make some tourniquets. Boy Scout stuff…need clean sheets." He gestured to Otto. "Where's the other one? Frankenstein?"

"There was only this one," he replied, setting to work on the shack-les. "Upstairs sending a fax. The girl is gone." Raszer absorbed the news. George nodded toward Otto. "What should I do with this garbage?"

"Put him right back where I was. If he comes to, knock him out, but don't kill him. I'm going upstairs. Bleeding like a stuck pig." Raszer made the mistake of getting up too fast, and he staggered back against the wall. His legs were dead and the blood loss had vacuumed his brain. "Holy shit," he gasped.

"Let me help you, Professor."

"It's okay, Get my land legs. You take care of him before he rouses." Steadying himself, Raszer made his way over to the steps, where he turned back to George. "Juraj, how the hell did you ever find me?"

George gestured with his head toward the room upstairs. "You will see up there. It's…I don't know. I think…some kind of angel."

The living room was the scene of a very recent melee. Lamps and ta-bles were overturned, and in the middle of it all stood a grave looking Czech of George's weight, though these pounds were distributed over a six-foot, three-inch frame. Raszer guessed that this must be the back-up George had called for. In his hand he held a sheet of blank paper, on which three Polaroid photos of a battered Sofia had been hastily taped. Raszer nodded a greeting, and then gestured to the paper. The Czech, in turn, pointed at a fax machine that lay on its side in the hallway.

"Did it go through?" Raszer asked.

The man shrugged apologetically. "English…I don't speak so well…"

"The fax. Was – it – sent?"

"I think so," the giant replied. "Was in machine."

*"Jmenuji se* Stee-van Ray-zer," he said, offering his hand. *"Tesi me."*

"Good to meet you, too," the guard reciprocated. "Petyr Dubrovsky, brother of Juraj." He surveyed Raszer's gnawed ear and blood-soaked shirt. "You need *doctor."*

Raszer realized that he must look considerably worse than he felt. "You're elected. Can you give me a hand? Clean sheets, some boiled water and antiseptic…er,*antisepticky*…right? If you can find it."

They located the bedroom where Sofia had been chained, and Petyr jumped into action while Raszer peeled the bloody shirt from his torso. The cuts were not critically deep, but deep enough to have prevented a good clotting, what with his muscles stretched by the shackles. He cursed at the sight of the blood continuing to seep. De Boer had gone straight through the arteries; he would need stitches. Stitches meant a doctor and a doctor would insist on a hospital, and while he was receiving a transfusion of A-positive, Sofia would be receiving the second dose of Luc's elixir, the one designed to "shut down all cognitive function."

George lumbered into the room as Raszer was applying a crude bandage to his neck. "What happened, George?" Raszer asked with a bit of grit. "Why weren't you at the synagogue?"

George bit his lip, and his brother stepped in. "He was in hospital. They shoot him with… some kind of poison. He call me to join him at *Na dum Kafka* to go with him to synagogue. I find him on street…like dead."

"Bastards," Raszer said, grimacing as Petyr tied off his upper arm. "Listen guys, I'm going to need a doctor. An old fashioned one with a practice in his home. Very discreet and very fast. Maybe someone associated with Alpha?" George shot his brother a look and Petyr nodded.

Raszer glanced at his watch. "We have very little time. Let me put it this way; we've less than two and a half hours to prevent the Apocalypse. George, see if you can find me a clean shirt in the wardrobe over there. Something, anything snug."

George fumbled in the armoire for a moment, and came out with a black turtleneck pullover. Like the handkerchief, it bore the LMF monogram. "Will this do, Professor?"

"Sure, why not?" Raszer's laugh was full of irony. "And one more thing, boys. Find me a *klobasy* stand on the way." Raszer was suddenly voraciously hungry. While George went to make a call, he hobbled into the elegant master bath and searched the medicine cabinet for iodine. He found a single, smoked glass bottle bearing the old skull and crossbones symbol. He took a whiff and opted to wait for the doctor. He closed the cabinet, avoiding the mirror.

On a stray impulse, he reached for the scabbard belted to his right calf and found it empty. His knife had been confiscated, but his needles were still lodged in the hidden pocket of his bloodied shirt. He slipped them into his khakis and tossed the shirt into the tub. Then he took just enough time to sponge the blood from his torso.

George leaned in. "I have a doctor for you. A good man. He delivered my babies."

"Good," Raszer said, "then he's used to blood." He pulled on Luc's turtleneck, wincing as the fabric passed the wounds. Then, he turned to his comrades. "Now, where is this *angel?*"

They stepped into the empty darkness of a semi-rural area on the edge of town. The rain had stopped an hour earlier, but the ground was saturated and the air had turned much cooler. Raszer scanned the area, registering nothing but George's old Lincoln Continental and, a few yards off, a little moped leaning on its kickstand.

"Where is that *chlapec?*" George asked rhetorically, meaty hands on his hips. "I asked him to stay put."

"Who?" Raszer asked. "The angel?"

There was a rustling in the bushes behind them. Raszer stiffened and a moment later, a third stocky Czech came lumbering out, zipping his fly and looking blithely unabashed.

"Ah!" said George. "There we are now. Professor, may I introduce my brother-in-law, Pavel…the lookout."

Raszer pushed his fingers through his matted hair, squinting in disbelief. It was the same Pavel who, only a few hours earlier, had been guarding Sofia on the Temple's payroll.

"The lookout," Raszer observed dryly. "Right." He took George aside. "This is not family hour, Juraj."

George placed his hands on Raszer's shoulders. "No, Professor," he said. "Is okay. Pavel wants to work for the good guys."

Raszer laughed. "You know, Juraj, first I would have said Prague was Paris in the 20's. Then I thought it more San Francisco in the 60's. But you know what? It's starting to look a lot like Mayberry."

George rolled his lower lip out in puzzlement and had just moved to speak when they heard the moped sputter with a kick-start. All four of them turned simultaneously.

"There he is," said Petyr. "That's the one who led us here."

"I'll be damned," said Raszer under his breath.

The little man throttled the moped off the shoulder and rolled into the dim light of the streetlamp. The bi-directional Greek mask he wore made it difficult to tell if he was coming or going. It was the little juggler from the synagogue and how many midget Sufis were there in the world? He rolled to a stop in the middle of the street and gave a "thumbs up" that George returned with a grin. Then he puttered off on the little two-stroke, lifting the mask at the corner and calling, "Hi-ho, *Silver!* It's *fool's* gold they're after, my friends!"

Like that, he was gone. Once again, Raszer was struck by how small a man's world became once his path was chosen, for there was now no doubt that it was the same little man he'd encountered in the airport bar.

"Professor," said George, "he followed the Mercedes from the *synagoga* and then returned to tell the rabbi of your peril. When Petyr and I arrived, we found the two of them praying. He brought us here. Do you see *now* what I mean about angels?"

"Oh, yeah," Raszer squeezed George's arm. "He's not the only one."

SLOWLY BUT SURELY, the fresco was being revealed to Raszer. He had long accepted intellectually the existence of other worlds, alternate histories. You had to. Otherwise, how could you possibly believe that God had really spoken to Moses, or that Einstein had glimpsed the shape of the universe while on an autumn walk? Only now, though, was he beginning to see that there was a strange cast of characters with cosmic E-tickets who moved freely among those worlds.

THE DOCTOR WORKED much more quickly than his training demanded, and he warned Raszer sternly that the stitches were not up to surgical standards. He offered his firm opinion that the blood loss was sufficient to warrant a transfusion and that Raszer's ravaged ear was vulnerable to all manner of infection, despite the generous shot of antibiotics he'd given him. At the very least, he admonished, Raszer ought not to move for a few hours. Petyr Dubrovsky, who confided – to Raszer's alarm – that he was a provisional member of the Praha Police Force, assured the doctor that this was a police matter, requiring his discretion.

The four of them left the clinic at 9:25 p.m., and made a beeline for the nearest *klobasy* stand, where Raszer sated himself on the sweet, smoky grilled sausage. For the moment, he felt invulnerable, like Odysseus under the aegis of Athena, but he knew that he would soon enough be mortal again.

# 18

## RESTORATION

*At present, earth humans do not fully comprehend their upcoming pattern. Hopefully, this new Sirian model will help them learn how the earth was created as both a spiritual and physical entity.*

*The earth, as with all the planets of the solar system, is surrounded by a Spiritual Hierarchy composed of beings called Angels, Archangels and Ascended Masters. Their sole purpose is to act as spiritual mediators for the eight interdimensional evolutionary energies. These mediators transfer these energies through the appropriate interdimensional portals, for example, the upcoming photon-belt...*

— from the Internet site SPIRITWEB, as received by
    "channeling" from the Sirian Ascended Master
    known as WASHTA

LUC SANK INTO the backseat of the limo, biting at his lip. Like Philippe Caudal – like many of his *compagnons* in the Order – he had little stomach for spontaneity. For Templars like Luc, the world operated according to a scientism that was, essentially, sympathetic magic. Things were plotted, ordained, destined or divined but never chaotic. To see it any other way was to concede that God did not play favorites. The American – whatever his purpose – was an element of chaos and had introduced an unwelcome variable into their undertaking. Now that he was out of the way, the game could continue according to divinely revealed plan.

He glanced at his watch. Within twenty minutes, Bandeur would be along with a chastened Sofia, and they were then to rendezvous with De

Boer and the rest of the force brought in to secure the castle for the night's penultimate ceremony. Many of them were former SAC operatives, but at least one was a current captain in the Prague Police Department. It was all covered, but still, Luc was apprehensive.

He pushed the toggle to raise the automatic window and kill the flow of damp, night air. In the vacuum, his senses targeted the source of his uneasiness. An herbal cologne wafting from the broad shoulders of the limo driver, a man who had come in from Geneva along with the beefed up security force. It was a distinctive scent, one that he knew well from another time and place, and particularly from a long night spent soaked in fearful sweat in the bowels of the Great Pyramid. It was coincidence, of course. It had to be. But Luc was no more comfortable with coincidence than he was with chaos.

He sat up and fixed his tie as the castle's bulk came into view. Appearance mattered. He was both a mystagogue and a master of ceremonies, and people took the whole business more seriously when it came from a man who carried himself well. He was the successor of great men, and like most successors, he was keenly aware of the need to live up to the past.

HE RECALLED HIS last communication with the White Lodge; channeled to him via the Genevese oracle he trusted most. It had counseled him to be pragmatic and to understand that the earthly affairs of the Temple would sometimes be in the charge of men less elevated than himself, men like De Boer and the current regime in Montreal, the offspring of Masonic congress with barbarians. What mattered was that *the work* be allowed to continue. In return for his agreement to remain in their service, the Germans had funded the *Tree of Isis*. It wasn't the ethics of the experiment's funding that disturbed him. If the gold of a few hundred thousand dead Jews could be used to finance an exodus of enlightened souls from the prison of matter, it seemed to him fittingly symmetrical. Israel had once fled the tyranny of Egypt. Now, a new Egypt would flee the dominion that Israel had established over spiritual discourse on earth. Although he knew that his Sofia would beg to differ, Luc did not consider himself an anti-Semite. He thought of himself, rather, as a new Moses; a man who would lead the Jews out of bondage to the evil Demiurge, *Yaweh,* and back to the true Egyptian wisdom that was their primal creed. And that was how he had justified to his crypto-Nazi overlords his inclusion of a Jewess in the chosen circle of six. *Now*…now, he had to wonder.

THE DRIVER EASED the limousine to a curb two blocks north of the assigned drop-off, and Luc sat forward, his finger in the air, ready to protest. That finger remained aloft, in fearful salute, as the driver casually turned around and removed his cap, the scent of Vetiver blossoming from its sweat-dampened band.

*"Bonsoir, mon ami,"* the driver said, but the voice seemed to issue not from his lips but from those dark, commanding eyes that Luc had loved and dreaded during his time as an acolyte. "Have you enjoyed wearing my name?"

"It's impossible," Luc whispered, his throat dry as a husk. "You're…"

*"Au contraire,"* the driver retorted. "Everything is possible. I bring good news from the Ascended Masters. The planet has entered the photon belt and the time is ripe for ascent…but not from Prague, *Jean-Paul.* We have selected the place of the firstborn: *Uluru.* Tonight we settle a few old scores. *Tomorrow…"*

"Do I still," Luc asked breathlessly, for it was he who had played Judas to his master, and kept the silver, "have your favor?"

The driver replaced his cap, turned and put the car into gear. As he drove the last two blocks, he recited a poem.

"There once was a young prince of Thrace…who wanted to share the King's grace; the King said, fair's fair, you may saddle my mare…and go to the wars in my place." He pulled to the curb and dutifully hopped out to open the door for his protégé. "Not a word," he whispered, holding the door. "Everything as planned, or you and De Boer will both be food for the fish by midnight."

AT A SMALL table next to the sausage stand, George reached into his pocket and retrieved Raszer's Swedish Army knife. He rocked the alderwood grip on his fleshy palm and turned the blade in the light a few times before handing it over.

"I took this off the fat guy when I disarmed him," he said, referring to Otto, who was probably forty pounds lighter than George. "You would miss this, no?"

"Yes I would," said Raszer. "Thanks." He lifted his trouser leg and slipped it into the ankle sheath. It was only a knife, the blade a scant seven inches, but it had been forged from the steel of Viking swords and shone like a jewel. It was its beauty more than its lethality that made him feel armed. He finished off the sweet, grilled sausage and wiped his hands. George, Petyr and Pavel were all working on their second of three.

"Now that you know who I am and why I'm here," he said, address-ing Petyr Dubrovsky in particular, "let me tell you what I need."

"We are ready to clean up Dodge," offered George. "Like the Earp brothers."

"Right," said Raszer. "Petyr, you're on the police force. I want to give you a chance to bow out before you violate any regulations. Not every-thing we do will be—"

"This is Praha, Mr. Raszer," Petyr interrupted, waving off the precau-tion. "I have a day job, and I have a night job. Like a farmer and his wife, the two do not meet except at dawn." The bun stuffed in his mouth muf-fled Pavel's laugh.

"I'm concerned about the police, though," said Raszer. "Somebody – maybe a lot of somebodies – is getting paid off or these people could not be operating within the castle."

Petyr Dubrovsky set his sausage down and clasped his hands. "It is…old country and new country. We try, with President Havel, to make democracy…like U.S. We try to clean up departments. Is much better, but some things still smell bad."

"Do you know anyone in particular who stinks?" Raszer queried.

"I will see what I can find out," said Petyr, and the others shrugged.

"I'm going to need a gun," said Raszer. "A high grade military target pistol with a long barrel and a laser sight. And a silencer." Petyr rolled his eyes to George.

"He is registered with Interpol," George whispered hoarsely to his brother, as if in confidence. "I think he is, okay." Raszer couldn't help but observe that the Dubrovsky brothers sat with their fingers identically inter-laced, each gesticulating ardently to the other with the opposing thumb.

"I don't intend to shoot at anything living," Raszer said, interrupting the parley, "if that's your concern, but *you* might have to, so, uh…talk amongst yourselves and make sure you're all right with this. I need coffee."

He got up and wandered over to the *klobasy* stand, where he could observe the three big Czech's from the rear – Petyr in the middle, George and Pavel on either side; all three of them crammed onto one tiny alumi-num bench. He took his black coffee and sat back down, inhaling the acrid vapor of the morning's brew warmed over.

"We have the gun for you," George announced, the brothers having emerged from their huddle. "Pavel will get it from the company arsenal. What else?"

"We're going to need two battery-powered spotlights; at least 2K. The brightest you can carry portably. He scanned the men. "Have any of you done any climbing?" The question was met with blank stares from the three guys in undersized suits. "Never mind. It's show time. Pavel, you'll get the gun. *And* ammunition. George, you retrieve my stuff from the hotel. Petyr, you're on belay for me. That means you're my lifeline." Petyr returned an uncomprehending stare. "Don't worry, I'll explain. Petyr and I will go ahead and survey the north grounds. You two meet us in one hour at the bottom of Chotkova Street, near the river entrance to the Royal Gardens. The old zoo. Petyr…" The part-time cop looked up from under thick eyebrows, one of them raised just slightly. "Would you give me your hand?"

Raszer trained his right eye just above the bridge of Petyr Dubrovsky's nose. Petyr laid his arm across the table, as if preparing to shake, but Raszer grasped his fingers and curled them tightly in his own as a sign of their bond. "I'm going to disable this death machine if I can. That will set them back at least twenty-four hours. You'll be with me. George and Pavel; you'll each take one of the two east side exits from Hradcany: Dalibor and the Old Castle steps. When they come out, you hit them with the lights and make as much noise as you can. We want Sofia. That's it. When it's over, Petyr, whether we get the girl or not, you get on that radio and call in your friends on the force. Whatever happens, I'll go with you and file a full report. Can you find me a commander who's clean? And a safe place away from headquarters?"

"I will take you," said Petyr, squeezing Raszer's fingers with a vice-grip, "to the cleanest man and the safest place in Praha. Every Tuesday night, Mr. Raszer, President Havel takes late dinner at his best restaurant, *Na Rybarne* on Gorazdova Street in the New Town."

"Best carp in Prague," Pavel piped in. "Only place for good fish in town."

"He celebrated there on the Tuesday night he got out of prison," George added, "and he has been doing it ever since. For good luck, I think. His cabinet is there and some movie people and press; sometimes to three in the morning."

"I'm going to make my report to President Havel?" said Raszer incredulously. "Hey, I'm a big fan, but—"

"No, no sir; to my uncle. He is Captain of Police, *Nove Mesto* district, and in charge of security when our president does this crazy thing. You can trust him."

"Jesus, I love small countries," said Raszer, releasing his hand. "Small countries and small hotels…the world could do with more of them."

"DAMN IT, RASZER. Call!" Monica barked. "Call, call, call." She sat at the keyboard, in what they had dubbed "the communications cupboard," like some cyber-Sybil, trying to conjure her boss from the computer. She had the telegram, with its cryptic warning, and she had some information from Jacques Denis, the Canadian journalist, considerably less cryptic and even more troubling.

In 1996, the *Centre pour l'Observation de Nouvelles Sectes* (CONS), the cult watchdog agency that had provided Raszer his cover, had quietly declared bankruptcy in Quebec Provincial Court, the consequence of fighting more than forty lawsuits filed against the group by everyone from Scientologists to New Age weight loss gurus. As per the usual procedure, the foundation's assets, including its letterhead and phone numbers, had been offered at auction by the court, in case any wealthy philanthropist should want to play white knight and keep the lights burning. There had been three bids, the highest of which was made by a soft-spoken lawyer representing St. Lawrence Equity, one of fourteen local companies that Denis had connected to Savana Investments, the nexus of the Temple's network. Whether he knew it or not, Stocker Hinge had been working for the very group that he was investigating. Now, he was missing in action. One by one, the Temple was taking Raszer's operatives out of action. Now they would come for him, if they didn't come for her first.

Had Raszer been carrying anything that emitted a recognizable radio frequency – a satellite phone or a pager – she might have been able to trace him. But here she was, with a cabinet full of 21st century hardware and a boss who insisted on a 19th century *modus operandi*. Before the next assignment, she was going to insist that he get the goddamned implant.

*"Please, Raszer,"* she pleaded to the computer screen, as if into a crystal ball. "Don't do anything macho and stupid…"

# 19

## THE PATH OF THE BLOOD

THE LEAST CONSPICUOUS approach to the massive north wall of the castle compound was from Chotkova Street, upward through a steeply terraced slice of primeval forest, and then into the *Kralovska Zahrada* – the Royal Gardens. The Gardens had been there since the reign of Ferdinand I in 1535 and were now a sprawling public park. The recent heavy rains and ever-present night fog were both a blessing and a curse for Raszer and Sgt. Dubrovsky. A blessing because they had driven away all but the most intrepid dog walkers and park bench gropers; a curse because the saturated ground mucked up everything and the drizzle would make an already dicey climb more hazardous.

Entering the gardens, the two of them crouched and padded along behind a tall hedge that bordered Stag Moat, a deep channel of rainwater that separated the park from the castle wall. Along this boundary, Emperor Rudolph had once kept his private zoo, and tales were told of terrified greens-men who, while clipping hedgerows, were confronted by panthers and leopards wandering loose in the moat.

The Stag Moat ran at about a 30° angle to the fortress and formed a triangle of land that came to its apex just before the cylindrical form of the Powder Tower jutted from the main wall. That meant that the exposed 180° of the Tower, which was built *into* the walls of the castle, was entirely accessible from the Gardens. That was the good news. The bad news was that the Tower's stonework had seen much better days. Along with the oily veneer of city rain and mud that greased the structure's masonry, Raszer could see that any number of the two hundred pound bricks looked precariously loose. That would mean uncertain holds for his wall anchors. As he stood at the Tower's base and scanned the sixty feet to the one-foot gap between the raised roof and stonework, he could make out numerous notches for his toes. This kind of climbing was less about gear than muscle. He turned to his disbelieving partner, who stood holding Raszer's flight case and a coil of climbing rope.

"Okay, Petyr," Raszer whispered. "I'll free climb – that means, without belay – to that big bulge under the roof and sink the anchor. I will thread the rope and feed the end down to you. Tie it into your harness like I showed you and coil the slack like this. Then I'll go over the lip. I won't get more than one shot, assuming I can see to aim, but if I hit the sweet spot it ought to do the trick. If I slip, take up the slack fast. *Rychly*. Do you understand?" Dubrovsky nodded soberly. "Let me down easy. My ankle is all messed up; it won't bear much impact. They probably have all their guards on the east and south walls. They'd never expect us to do anything this dumb. If anyone does show up, tie off the rope to that tree over there and cover me until I can climb down."

The river wind dropped just long enough for them to hear a faint electronic hum from within the structure.

"We'd better move," Raszer said, pointing to a spot near the Tower's summit where a pale reddish glow tinted the stone. "That's the place; right there."

Petyr tilted up to the niche where Raszer planned to insert his aluminum anchor and attach the carabiner through which his lifeline would pass. Both men stepped into climbing harnesses and Raszer knotted the rope through his ring, hanging the rest of the one hundred foot length of rope from his side.

"I'm off, partner."

Petyr handed Raszer the military pistol they'd procured from the arsenal, and anchored himself against a cherry tree whose roots had grown into the Moat's wall. He drew his own pistol from its shoulder holster and scanned the soundless park. Visibility was no better than twenty feet. Almost anything – a man or a black leopard – could approach undetected.

Raszer could see that Petyr was nervous. "The darkness is your friend, Petyr. Just fold yourself into it."

Raszer ran through a mental systems check. He was running on adrenalin rather than carbohydrates, and that was dangerous. If he'd eaten more though, he would have dulled the knife-edge of his will and tempted failure in another way. In any case, it was not going to be easy with stitches on top of muscles that would get stretched and racked out by the climb.

He eased the long barrel of the pistol into his harness and placed his hands on the ancient, seeping wall. His fingers found a notch in the missing mortal and he cast a look back to Petyr. He'd arrived at the last station where an alternative course was conceivable, and if he'd seen any trepidation in the cop's eyes he might have backed away. Seeing none, he began his ascent.

At sixteen feet, he forced the Stealth rubber toe of his right climbing slipper into a tiny divot in the rock and tried to power himself up to the next finger crack. He heard a sickening *crunch* of cartilage from his ankle. Raszer pressed his face and fingers into the cold stone until the wave of pain passed. At thirty-eight feet, he reached the crux, and the bulge in the tower wall compelled his torso away from his center of gravity. He was now leaning ten or twelve degrees out from the stone, and his toehold was weak. He took a stab at wedging two fingers into a quarter-sized notch two feet above and to the right. The throbbing wound in his right bicep tore open and sent the foretaste of nausea to his tongue. For a few dizzying seconds, Raszer was certain he'd lost it. From forty feet, a fall would surely break bones, maybe his back.

The nail on his left forefinger split down the middle as he curled his hand into a mortar chink and used the moment's grace to reposition his right shoe. With both extremities on his right side wailing their objections, getting over the hump in the wall became a matter of sheer grit. He ripped through calloused fingers and frayed tendons, powering himself over the bulge and within reach of the spot where he'd decided to place the anchor. He thought about Petronella Pope's creed, *pain is a vital sign*. Right. Unless it's a preview of death.

He sunk the camming device into a deep recess, where it flared and locked against the wet granite with a satisfying bite. Like his knife, it was beautiful technology; no silicon, no plastic, just steel against stone. After he'd passed the loose end of the rope through the carabiner and sent eighty feet of slack skittering down the wall to his partner's hands, he let himself hang free for a minute to slow his heartbeat. Dangling like a mist-shrouded cocoon, he began to hear Luc's voice from the reverberant chamber below. For an instant, he was spellbound, and that puzzled him until he realized that it was as if he was hearing Luc's voice with Sofia's ears.

"The host we are about to receive will begin our transformation into *Beings of Light.*" Raszer swung in and pressed his ear to the stone. "Our auras will be visible even to those from whom such things are usually hidden."

Raszer found his grip and pushed himself above the anchor to the rim of the tower. His fingers dug into the pitted stone and he prayed that his upper arms would bear his weight over the lip and into the shadowy gap beneath the rotted gable of the wooden roof. With a deep moan and the rip of another three stitches, he was up.

"Do not mourn the world we leave behind," Luc continued. "Man has become a werewolf and will eat the bitter fruit of his own decay. As the planet on this glorious night enters the photon belt, we prepare to be borne up by the angelic choirs, traveling at super-photic speed in our new bodies, to the place of our birth."

For the moment, Raszer found himself grateful for Luc's rhetorical excesses. The spiel was giving him time to position himself. Furthermore, the Sofia *inside him* was not buying it. He hoisted his chest onto the rim and locked his toes into a good-sized crack six inches above the anchor.

The fog lay under the roof only slightly less thick than it had the night before, but he had a reasonably clear shot. Sofia was in her assigned place; her back to him and shoulders slumped. Raszer scanned the perimeter for De Boer, but neither he nor any other thugs seemed to be present in the circular room. Not good. If they were stationed at the exit points, they would be able to get to him more quickly. He glanced over to Dominic, the Silicon Valley stiff at the console, and saw him push the lever that would bring the head of Baphomet-Isis into the magic window.

Raszer put the laser sight to his eye and rested the barrel on the lip of the rock. As the fluid began to rise into the crystal tank, he brought the shimmer into the sight's focus and settled the crosshairs on the goatman's furry brow as it revealed itself. Unconsciously, he put his weight down hard on his right ankle in order to fix his aim.

A bolt of pain shot through a nerve ending, and he suddenly felt faint and lost his toehold. The gun barrel slipped off its perch and *clinked* against the stone, stirring into flight a phalanx of the Tower bats. Raszer scrambled out of range. A prickly sweat rose to the surface of his skin, and a curse slipped beneath his breath. Luc had stopped talking. Raszer looked down at Petyr, who'd dug his heel into the soft ground and instantly taken up the slack. *Dress rehearsal,* Raszer thought.

As the bats settled, the St. Vitus church bells began to chime the midnight hour, providing Raszer a cover that probably qualified as divine intervention. He'd lost valuable time, but he was able to again locate the floating head within the sight just as the fluid filled the last inch of the tank. The head turned to its opposite and once again displayed the face of Queen Isis, Regent of Sirius, pilot of the celestial boat. In moments, she would divest herself of her milk, turning her disciples into zombies.

Raszer had one shot, and his hands were shaking badly from the exertion of holding himself in position. Dominic reached for the fluid release lever just as the royal forehead floated into Raszer's crosshairs. He blinked away a rivulet of sweat. Her mouth gaped open in fury, and her eyes found him where he lived, becoming the shiny dark lures of the Woman in the Woods. "Sacrilege!" she screamed in his head. "Justice," he replied, and squeezed the trigger. The turbulent flapping of a hundred batwings nearly drowned the explosion of glass and the moan of twisted metal as the machine's upper section was deprived of its base and came crashing down on the trunk.

Raszer caught only the flash of fluid spilling out from the ruptured vessel before the kickback of the pistol threw him off his perch into the night air, taking with him eight feet of slack line. The rope cinched violently against the carabiner, slamming Raszer into the tower's wall six feet below, sending a bolt of agony from his right elbow to his brain. The impact wave shot through the forged steel anchor and loosed it from its firm grip, ripping it through two inches of weak and age-corrupted stone. Raszer, dangling thirty-five feet above the ground, felt his lifeline slipping away.

"I've got you," Petyr called from below. The big Czech backed against the cherry tree, the rope tautly threaded through his harness. "I'm bringing you down."

Raszer rappelled inch by inch down the wall, his heart threatening to break through his thorax. He was within twenty feet of the damp and forgiving earth when the rope went as taut as a cable and broke his descent. Raszer pushed himself away from the stone, turned and squinted down for some sign of his comrade through fog thick as smoke in a brush fire. All he could see was ten feet of rope vanishing into an impenetrable cloud. There was a gunshot – the muted *zhip* of a silencer. The rope slackened and he plummeted another six feet before it cinched again. A second shot and the loose end – Petyr's end – of the rope snapped through the mist like a bullwhip, whistling through the carabiner as Raszer plummeted the remaining fourteen feet to the ground. He brought his knees to his chest and rolled against the tower wall, gripped by a dread as disabling as the climax of a nightmare.

The St. Vitus bells reached twelve, and Raszer slithered into a notch behind a small, blooming shrub. He aimed the target pistol into the void, both arms shaking, no target in sight. Then, the brim of a fedora emerged from the vapor, followed by the blunt profile of the Bavarian viper. De Boer approached Petyr's body cautiously, the butt of an AK-47 braced against his shoulder, his finger on the trigger. He stood over the corpse and fiercely kicked the ribs. Raszer burned inside even though he knew

Petyr was beyond pain. Two more shots rang out in rapid succession on the perimeter of the garden; then a third, a few seconds later. De Boer cocked his head to listen for the result and, hearing nothing, called out clearly but calmly, "Bandeur? Is it clear?" There was a pause, and then a voice baffled by the fog, responded, *"Oui."*

Raszer wrapped his body tightly around the bush and propped himself on his elbows, doing his best to steady the pistol. He aimed the gun at the broadest part of De Boer's gaunt torso and pulled the trigger. Nothing happened. He frantically opened the chamber. Empty. There had been one fucking round in the gun, probably left over from its last use. He had assigned Pavel, the idiot brother-in-law, to procure the ammunition. *I'm as dead as Petyr,* Raszer thought. Like a child, he tried to wish himself invisible.

De Boer wheeled around and called for backup. Oddly, no one rushed immediately to his side. He advanced cautiously to within ten feet of Raszer's position, his ghoulish form flickering in and out of the veil of fog. It was impossible to place him.

Raszer dropped the pistol. He fumbled for the knife that lay against his calf, a weapon he was far more comfortable with. He prayed for a predator's patience as the Viper fixed his rifle on the trembling bush. Raszer cocked his arm against the castle wall and took a long breath. He let the knife fly, and then he must have closed his eyes for a second. When he looked, he beheld the old assassin standing stock-still and contemplating the object that protruded from his solar plexus. Deciding to ignore it for the moment, he raised the rifle once again, though somewhat shakily, and simultaneously, two more dark-suited accomplices materialized at his side. Raszer pressed his forehead into the mud and prepared to die.

As if in a dream, he heard a shot explode from somewhere off in the dense fog on his left. Then, two more shots from the same direction. Raszer lifted his head and peered through the branches. The two new arrivals had been dropped instantly. As for De Boer, the bullet had seared the back of his wool overcoat and buried itself in his heart. He staggered and shot off his last round, its missile ricocheting wildly off the tower wall. Then he pitched forward and crashed to the ground, driving Raszer's knife to the hilt.

Raszer didn't dare move. He wanted to howl, but he waited for what must have been ten minutes, extending not one tendon. The interior of the Tower was eerily quiet but for the sound of something being dragged across the wooden plank floor. There was no sign of either George or the idiot and Raszer feared the worst.

When he could stand it no longer, he left the bush and crawled on hands and knees to the body of Petyr Dubrovsky. He peeled back three layers of clothing and pressed his ear to the heart, though it was clear from the cop's glazed and fully open eyes that he was long gone.

Moving to De Boer, he squatted and carefully rolled the corpse onto its back. He removed his knife and wiped it clean on the killer's gray over-coat. He fished through the pockets until he found a wallet and hastily stuffed it into his pants. As he backed away from the body, Raszer thought he perceived a shiver of life. He raised his arms in the air and plunged the knife again and again into De Boer's still heart. Finished, he sat back onto his haunches and let the weapon drop to his side. Without so much as a tremor of air or earth, there was suddenly another human being at his side and a gun at his head.

"Don't turn around," said the voice, its tenor muffled by a scarf or mask, and only the slightest accent detectable. "Take the girl and leave us. Your work is finished. Keep all you've seen in your heart until you know its meaning." The instant that the pressure on his temple was lifted, both the voice and its source were gone.

Raszer knelt cautiously to pick up his knife, then rose slowly and kept walking until he had cleared the moat and was out of range. Only then did he look back into the silent park for some clue. The fruit trees were draped with wispy strands of mist, like spectral Spanish moss, and he became aware for the first time of the garden's fog-muted colors of scarlet and periwinkle blue. From somewhere amid the impressionistic blur, there came a whimper, and then, a voice.

"Professor? Whoever you are…" she said. "I don't know where I am…"

She seemed to materialize from the cloister of cherry trees, groping like a blind peasant girl, the damp hair falling in ringlets onto the shoulders of her long, white robe. It reminded Raszer of his first impression – the photograph on her husband's big mahogany desk. At that moment, George and Pavel came puffing up from the east. None of the pilgrims, they insisted, had emerged from either the Dalibor or Old Castle exits. They'd exchanged fire with a contingent of hired guns, including Bandeur, who'd stormed up from the riverbank at the sound of Raszer's shot. There had been only that brief melee, and then everything had gone as quiet as the grave.

In the fog and the dark, it was hard to be certain they had hit anyone. There had even been a moment when it seemed there was a *third* team at work, firing on both sides at once. But what had happened here, they wanted to know. Where was Petyr?

Raszer gripped George's wrist. He had some answers but he couldn't attend to the questions right now. All he could do was to watch the girl move slowly toward him and wonder by what sort of necromancy she had come to be delivered into his hands.

# 20

## AMFORTAS

*There exists an experience in which the longing of separated Be-
ing for remerging with the integrity of Being is satisfied, as it
were, in the most mature and complete manner. This experience
reveals to us that in complete and unlimited identification, total
insight and utter happiness, lies the end of the "I" death.*

*It is by no means accidental that at the very heights of meaning-
fulness, happiness, joy and love, the spectre of death inevitably
appears with particular clarity.*

– Vaclav Havel, *Letters to Olga*

     \*      \*      \*      \*      \*      \*

*All genuine problems and matters of critical importance are
hidden beneath a thick crust of lies…*

– Vaclav Havel, *Living in Truth*

RASZER FELT LIKE a photographic negative as the taxi lurched
off the bridge into the New Town and navigated the dark streets to *Restaurant Na Rybarne*. Two people had now died in his service, both for the sake
of a girl who had rejected life. Everything was reversed. He wondered if he
had the strength for the formalities that would now be required of him.

The cab pulled to the curb opposite the restaurant, and Raszer raised
his eyes to see two of Prague's diminutive squad cars with lights flashing. A
pair of burly plainclothesmen stood guarding the front entrance. Raszer
gently lifted Sofia's head from his lap and rolled himself forward with a
mighty groan. He made a vain effort to straighten himself. His shirt – Luc's
shirt – was muddy and stained with a killer's blood; his hands scraped raw

and encrusted with his own. The Werewolf himself could not have looked more suspect. And then there was Sofia, dazed and anemic, looking like Saint Joan without a cause.

Pavel, who had led the taxi from the wheel of George's old Lincoln, jogged back to open the door for the two of them and offered an arm to grab hold. George remained, for the moment, in the Lincoln, hunched in grief.

Raszer stepped from the cab and into a tight huddle of cops and state security men. He took his passport and investigator's license from his back pocket. He stammered in broken Czech that he was a private detective, there to see the captain of President Havel's guard and to report a homicide and breach of government security. Pavel's efforts to mediate did little to clarify the matter. Just as the agents seemed ready to take Raszer to the nearest squad car, George appeared in their midst. He dropped open his billfold to display the AlphaCorp badge. His eyes were rimmed with red, but the quaver in his voice telegraphed anger and urgency as much as grief.

"*Prosim,*" George insisted in his own tongue. "A police officer has been killed defending an assault on Hradcany. My brother, Petyr Debrovsky." There was murmuring among the junior officers at the mention of the name, and a stone-faced plainclothesman stepped to the fore. "Please take us to Captain Jan Debrovsky," said George. "These people are my friends. The have news of great importance to the president."

Raszer put his arm on George's shoulder and felt the remainder of his stitches give way. A young, uniformed man was finally sent to fetch Captain Dubrovsky. Minutes later, he emerged with a stout, gray man in shirtsleeves, introduced to Raszer as "Uncle Jan."

"Is it true?" the captain asked of his nephew. "Petyr…"

"Yes, Uncle," said George, "and the man who did it is lying dead in the Royal Gardens. I think…" George scrutinized the uniformed group surrounding them. "…we should explain inside."

Captain Dubrovsky placed his hands on his hips and looked his youngest nephew up and down. For a minute, the appearance of the disheveled American at his side, and of Sofia, just now emerging from the taxi, seemed to argue that these were the last people in Prague who ought to be allowed within a mile of the president.

Raszer took DeBoer's wallet from his pocket and held it at arm's length while displaying the Swiss identification. "This is the man that killed your nephew, sir."

They were ushered down a short flight of stairs and through a bright red door into a foyer draped with decorated fish netting. There was a small bar at this level, and the four of them were directed to wait at the landing with a security man, while Captain Dubrovsky descended another flight to what Raszer presumed was a private basement dining room.

After a few moments, he returned to lead them down into a modest beer hall, with varnished picnic tables and whitewashed walls etched, in black marker, with hundreds of epigrams and celebrity autographs, including those of Paul Simon and Milan Kundera. On the far side of the room was a bar, around which a small crowd of habitués was gathered convivially with the President of the Czech Republic. This, Raszer thought, was Havel's way of keeping his common touch, for the people surrounding him fit no definition of courtier.

The captain left them to wait at the threshold and made his way through the clinking cocktail glasses. Havel exhaled double-plumes of smoke through his nostrils, and cocked his ear to hear the whispered message, his expression turning dead sober.

"My friends," said the president, rising from the barstool and clearing his throat, "I'm afraid we'll have to call it a night. Some rather important business has come up." He turned to a young aide who had been drinking at his side. "Rudie, would you assist Jan in clearing the restaurant – quickly please."

As the young man turned in profile, Raszer had an eerie sense of *déjà vu*. There was no time to consider its genesis as Havel now made eye contact and Raszer found himself transfixed. He mutely nodded his acknowledgement while the president's erstwhile drinking companions filed past, stealing curious glances at Raszer's wounds and at the striking woman who stood trembling beside him.

Within moments, the window shades had been drawn and the premises cleared save for the president and a plainclothes security chief, along with Raszer, Sofia, George, Captain Dubrovsky and the young aide who Havel had addressed as Rudie. He was a nattily dressed man of about thirty who could not seem to take his eyes off of Sofia, that is, once they had pulled themselves from the monogram on Raszer's bloody turtleneck.

Havel took a sip of what looked like scotch and motioned for Raszer to sit. "Would you like a drink?" he asked.

"I would, sir," Raszer began, walking a few paces forward, "but I had better, um…try to get this out correctly before I sit." Havel nodded for him to continue. "My name is Stephan Raszer." He noticed the security chief making notes. "R-a-s-z-e-r. I'm a licensed private investigator. You can check my credentials with Interpol while we talk. In fact, I'd be more comfortable if you did. This lady's – Ms. Gould's – husband retained me when she disappeared earlier this year."

Sofia, who had been standing stock still in her choir robe, took George's arm and lowered herself to a bench, her mouth agape. Raszer glanced back at her and nodded. Havel leaned forward to get a closer look at the damsel in distress. He narrowed his eyes and a faint smiled crossed his lips.

*"Prague Spring,"* he said, apparently directed to Sofia. She shook her daze when she realized that she had been singled out.

"I'm sorry, what did you say?"

*"Prague Spring.* Wasn't that the name of the film? Havel queried. "Yes, I'm sure of it. Shot here in...1995? I didn't think much of the film, but I couldn't take my eyes off the actress." Sofia lowered her gaze and nodded. Raszer wondered if just now she was starting to envision the tabloids: *B-Movie Actress Discovered In Death Cult.* "Please continue, Mr. Raszer," said Havel.

"Sir, could we order some food for Ms. Gould? I don't think she's— what would you recommend?"

"The bread and garlic soup will restore her."

"Yes," echoed Rudie, the aide-de-camp. "The garlic soup. I'll get it for her."

"I learned," Raszer continued, "that she had enlisted in – and, oddly, was being ransomed by – a neo-Templar suicide cult that calls itself the Temple of the Sun. It's activities during last Christmas may be known to you. Sixteen died in Grenoble." Havel took out a pack of cigarettes and offered one to Raszer, who accepted gratefully and continued after a hungry drag. "Something similar was planned for Prague. It is evident, sir, that the security of Hradcany Castle , specifically the Powder Tower, has been breached by members of this group in order to use the premises for a ceremony that would conclude in the deaths of six adepts, including Ms. Gould.

"I believe I've succeeded tonight in forestalling this event. There's a *machine,* I can't quite describe. Unfortunately, an off-duty police officer, the nephew of Captain Dubrovsky, was killed in the process. A mercenary employed by this cult, a professional killer who I believe..." He handed Havel the billfold he'd taken from De Boer, open to the section containing identities that provided a brief history of the gunman's dangerous liaisons. "...enjoys associations with a number of right-wing secret police organizations in Europe and Canada. De Boer was then killed by—" Raszer took his first deep breath and turned to George, who shook his head.

"I wish it had been me," said George, "but no."

"We don't know, I'm afraid," said Raszer, "but it wasn't any of my men."

Havel pulled deeply on his cigarette and sternly turned to the secret service agent at his side, asking in Czech, "How is this possible, man…The Powder Tower?" The agent bit his lip and promised an explanation of the breach. The president thumbed through the plastic leaves of De Boer's billfold, studying the keycards that would provide *entre* to any number of right-wing boy's clubs.

"This fellow has been running with the wolves, all right. I wonder, Jan," Havel said ironically, with a nod to Captain Dubrovsky, "if *my* adversaries were privileged to enjoy Mr. De Boer's services, as well." Despite his mordant wit, Havel was visibly shaken.

Sweat again broke out on Raszer's forehead. "Mister President. They can't have gotten far in this amount of time. Are there any exits from the castle that might be known only to the guards?"

Havel whispered instructions to his chief of security, who snapped his notebook shut, took a shell-shocked George gently by the elbow and went to dispatch the police and the Palace Guard. Raszer saw his perfectly forged shield of anonymity vaporizing in the white-hot light of a very public inquest, but he knew there was no choice. An entire state had been compromised. Havel stroked his chin and then raised his poet eyes to the ceiling before leveling them at Raszer.

"Mr. Raszer, I am vaguely familiar with this group, and if what you say is true, then it seems you have done this lady and her husband a great service. But I must ask you the obvious question. You were aware of a security breach that threatened our state. Why did you wait until two, possibly three men were dead to come to the police?"

Something in Raszer's unconscious must have balked at answering the question, or maybe it all just finally caught up with him, because the next thing he felt was the buckling of his knees and the collapse of his body to the wooden floor.

When he came to, Raszer saw that they had moved him to a makeshift mattress of chair cushions in the main dining room. Something both firmer and infinitely more comfortable lay under his head. He rolled his eyes back and they were met by Sofia's; his head was on her lap. Her expression was neither compassionate nor reproachful, but tenderly bemused. A doctor was at his side, attending to his stitches, and the handsome but vapid young man he'd noticed earlier looked on from a nearby table. Havel walked into Raszer's field of view and squatted next to him.

"How are you feeling?" he asked gently.

"Better after a Becherovka," Raszer groaned. "Is George okay?"

"He's with his uncle," Havel replied. "We've taken his brother's body to the morgue. Everything is quiet. But the others you mentioned – Klaus Bandeur, the gunmen – no sign of them." A knowing smile crossed his lips. "That last question of mine got you where you live, huh?"

"Sure did," said Raszer. Havel motioned to the barman to bring Raszer his requested libation.

"Ms. Gould has told me that you introduced her to our marvelous Rabbi Scholem." Raszer nodded, studying Havel's sage and wrinkled face, the smile lines deep and resilient in spite of the president's own tortuous history. "Something tells me," Havel continued, "that your interests run significantly beyond playing Cowboys and Indians."

"Wouldn't have made a good cowboy," Raszer groaned, rubbing his throbbing head. "Would've fraternized with the enemy and screwed up manifest destiny."

"Like T.E. Lawrence," Havel observed, looking straight into Raszer's psyche. "You serve the Empire, but only because it serves your quest. You've piqued my interest with your story." Raszer caught the young fellow at the table eyeing Sofia again; it was beginning to bother him. "Oh," said Havel, tracking Raszer's glance, "this is Rudie, my soon-to-be former aide-de-camp. He'll be taking over as cultural attaché at our Los Angeles consulate next month."

Raszer nodded a greeting. Rudy was pale, slack and effete. Not Raszer's type but unsettlingly familiar. "Have me met?" Raszer asked him. "Here, in Prague?"

"I'm sure I would remember. No."

The doctor stood and backed away, pronouncing the patient as fit as could be expected. Raszer sat with Sofia's help and took a generous gulp of the potent liqueur. The stuff was magic, restorative, like flowers on fire.

"I have a thousand things to ask you, Mr. Raszer," the president said, "and I'd like my doctor to monitor Mrs. Gould's condition. May I make a suggestion? Until we can confirm your story and guarantee your safe departure, why don't you and Sofia stay the night as my guests at Hradcany? I'll ask Captain Dubrovsky to bring Juraj around once they've replaced the guard and everything is secured. There are a dozen empty guest rooms and I think we can rouse the cook, even at this hour. I promise you, the West Wing is quite safe."

AS CANDLES WERE extinguished and the staff of the presidential quarters prepared for bed, Raszer asked the floor porter if he could make a call. He'd been remiss about Monica, and she was probably apoplectic.

*"Where on earth have you been?"*

"To Hell and back," Raszer replied. "But I have Sofia, and we're in probably the safest place in Eastern Europe, unless the Temple has planted a bomb in President Havel's chambers. The Czech police are beating the bushes for Fourché and his friends."

"Not Fourché." Monica proceeded to tell him about the telegram and her discovery that the wolves were guarding the hen house at CONS. *"Your* Luc is an imposter, but the real guy may be back in the game."

"Jesus," Raszer whispered, shuddering as he recalled the eerily gentle voice he'd heard in the gardens.

"Well," she sighed, "it's a good thing you've got Sofia, because her husband's out ten million."

"Oh, no."

"Oh, yes. You won't believe what's been going on here. Empire Pictures' stock dropped thirty-eight in less than six hours. Some incredibly far-flung consortium of major stockholders started a sell-off this morning, and then it just snowballed. Then Lawrence gets a fax with an Auschwitz-caliber picture of Sofia, and a note saying that he stands to lose a whole lot more than ten million unless he pays. These guys had this thing wired, Raszer. We tried to reach you but—"

"I know," said Raszer. "Where did the money go?"

"A numbered account at the Bank of Luxembourg, Cayman Islands branch."

"Tell him not to write it off yet."

"I'm with you," she said. Monica was moving at a Grand Prix pace. Raszer guessed she had located the purple tubers in his garden. "And here's the godsend. Our reporter, Jacques Denis, gets a fax – from Philippe Caudal – with a list of account numbers from banks all over the globe, and the last one…it was smeared in the fax transmission…but the account number begins with 'CB.'"

"Caudal must have known they were on to him. I think I'm beginning to understand." Raszer took one of Vaclav Havel's cigarettes from the pack he'd left on the kitchen countertop.

"He also confirmed that they've arrested Noel Branch for Jeanette's murder." Raszer had no immediate response. All Monica heard was the spark of the flint on his old Zippo.

"And Stocker Hinge?" he asked.

"Off the grid."

"Keep on the reporter, partner," Raszer said. "See if you can sweet talk him out of those account numbers in exchange for a scoop. Tell Lawrence he'll get his money and his wife back…not in that order. They've got us on a Lufthansa flight at noon tomorrow."

"You're bringing her in?" Raszer heard his assistant sigh. "Good."

"Yeah," he said. "I'd like to follow this through…see if I can get the others out…find out who the hell saved my ass last night. But Sofia, she's my trust."

"Did you ever consider, Raszer, that maybe there are some things we're not supposed to know?"

"No," he said. "Never. Get some sleep. I'll call before we leave."

As Raszer hung up, he felt the gentlest of taps on his shoulder, a tap that nonetheless scared him half out of his Czech government-issue sweats. It was President Havel, accompanied by Captain Dubrovsky and his bleary-eyed nephew, George. Raszer threw an arm around George's neck and faced his host.

"Like to take some fresh air with us, Mr. Raszer?" asked Havel. "The spires of St. Vitus are beautiful this time of night, and there's something I think you might want to see."

"Of course, Mr. President. Let me get my cigarettes."

"Share mine," said Havel, eyeing the butt in Raszer's fingers. "I noticed you smoke the same brand."

All castles were once earthen hill forts, their battlements raised from the good clay that was itself made of the wheat and the rye, the hoof and the wing, and the blood and the bone of the ancestors. Defense of the tribe was also a defense of something even more sacred than the chieftain's life; the hieratic land in which the local goddess lay curled. That is why, in Europe, the land was inseparable from the kings who defended her honor.

Vaclav Havel was not a king; in fact, he'd suffered greatly to end the rule of despots over the land. But he possessed the *gravitas* of a good king, one who truly knew his enemy. Cancer had knocked him down to one lung and the lesser part of a digestive tract. He'd lost his beloved wife, Olga, and half of his country within the same term of office. And yet Raszer felt, as he walked at Havel's side, that Arthur himself could not have evinced greater fortitude. *En route* to the tower, Havel detoured his small party around to the south entrance of St. Vitus Cathedral. It's twin, one hundred twenty foot gothic spires were lost in the roiling fog overhead, so the view was not quite as advertised. The bells were still.

"Do you know where you are, Mr. Raszer?" Havel asked, mounting the steps.

"No, sir. Not in the sense I think you mean."

"This is the Golden Portal…the original entrance to the holy of holies. Just inside this sanctuary, King Wenceslas – the 'good king' of the carol – was murdered by his own brother. There always seems to be skullduggery involved when man makes a leap toward the divine. Perhaps that's why he invariably falls short."

"But the monument remains," said Raszer, peering up at a terrifying mosaic that depicted The Last Judgment.

"This church," Havel continued, "like Chartes and Reims was built by Freemasons. Since Europe is defined by structures, its history is unfathomable without a nod to those who built them. And those, like the Templars, who stood guard. But the Masons—"

"What happened to them?" Raszer asked. "I've never really understood…"

"I think," Havel replied, "that rot set in when their privileged station became divorced from their craft. Wisdom should be applied to service. I was invited once, as a young student of twenty, to join a venerable Bohemian lodge. I thrilled to the idea that I was to be bequeathed some…*secret.* After attending only a few meetings and detecting a certain elitism, I recall turning to my sponsor and saying *'why isn't all this taught in the universities?'* That Jesus was, for all intents, a Buddhist? That Judaism and Islam are one faith? That Eve did not sin? *'My God!'* I said to him. *'People have been slaughtering one another for centuries out of ignorance!'* My patron regarded me with some condescension, and said, simply, *'Never concern yourself with the fate of the ignorant.'* I think, Mr. Raszer, that secrecy breeds a special kind of corruption, and that privileged secrecy breeds monsters. Come on. Let me show you why I robbed you of your sleep."

They entered the Powder Tower by the door through which tourists walked in the light of day. There were now fresh, young guards stationed at each landing on the way to the third level, and Havel saluted each of them crisply. In the uppermost chamber, where only four hours earlier Luc's voice had invoked eternity, a small team of University scientists was at work deconstructing what remained of the Tree of Isis. Havel greeted them and walked to a roped-off area where the plank floor was still covered with the shards of glass from Raszer's demolition. A small puddle of clear liquid remained amid the fragments. With a nod to the supervising inspector, Havel squatted, dipped his index finger into the puddle and brought it to his lips. Raszer lifted a hand in warning, but the president had already tasted Luc's elixir.

"You must know something I don't know."

"A saline solution," Havel said. "Salt water. What do you make of that?"

"Why," Raszer asked, stepping nearer, "would they go to so much trouble to perpetrate a fraud?"

"Well," Havel replied, "one answer, of course, is money. The assets of their devotees. But consider something else. When the priest raises the communion host before the congregation, asks them to believe that the humble wafer has been transubstantiated into the body of Christ, is he perpetuating a fraud? Or is he, like the old shamans, simply inducing the imaginal state in which miracles occur?"

"There is something else," the senior scientist offered, holding a length of plastic IV tubing in his hands. "There were two venipunctures made in each of the subjects. Two needles and two tubes. It appears that the machine was both feeding and extracting. Diluting the blood with salt water, if that makes any sense..."

BEFORE TURNING IN, Raszer stopped into the kitchen for a glass of water. He was surprised to find President Havel, in striped pajamas, mixing himself a hot cocoa. The glow from the parlor fireplace under-lit his face. Raszer cleared his throat.

"Excuse me, Mr. President," he said. "Did you happen to hear from your doctor about his examination of Mrs. Gould?"

Havel turned, stirring his cocoa. "She's anemic and undernourished, but otherwise okay. He gave her a shot of B-vitamins and a mild sedative, and put her to bed." He set the spoon aside, sipped the cocoa and shook his head. "It's not my old friend, brandy, that's for sure. Would you like me to wake you when Jan reports in? It will be a few hours before he's covered all the exit tunnels."

"Absolutely," said Raszer. He rubbed his chin and squinted hard.

Havel studied him for a moment and then put a finger in the air. "Steve McQueen," he pronounced.

"What's that?" said Raszer.

"*That's* who you remind me of."

Raszer laughed, mostly to himself. "Sir," he said diffidently, "in the *Letters to Olga*, you said that you once had a mystical experience where you...I think you describe it as, *'standing on the edge of the finite.'*"

"Or some equally pretentious phrase, yes."

"Did you ever get a look at what was over that edge?"

Havel smiled gnomishly and took another scalding sip. "It occurred in prison," he began and drew closer. "Men in prison are prone to perverse visions – witness both Marx and Hitler – so bear the context in mind. I had been meditating on a question of physics. The desire to escape a prison cell is so great that one begins to explore, for instance, the universe inside the filament of a light bulb or a grain of dust. I got quite good at it, and one day, I suddenly found myself in a world *before being*...or perhaps I should say, a world of *becoming*. At first, there was quite literally, nothing – not even blackness, just *nothing*. Extraordinary. And then I heard it."

"Heard what?" asked Raszer, spellbound.

"The sound of a woman," Havel answered softly, *"weeping*...as if for a lost child or lover. I'm afraid it scared me right out of poetry and into politics. I've not been able to write since without facing the utter inadequacy of words to express such an experience."

"I have some idea," said Raszer, "what that feels like." He hesitated at the door for a moment, a question as troublesome as a hangnail on his mind. "By the way, Mr. President...what's Rudie's story?"

Havel chuckled. "Ah, yes. Rudie. He's the overweening nephew of a very influential Czech industrialist, an old family with connections. He's actually *Count* Rudolph Svaczech of the Hapsburg lineage, but we abolished the official privileges of title some time back. I'm obliged to find him a 'low risk' position in the government, so I've wagered that would be *cultural affairs* in Los Angeles. The old order is a long time dying, Mr. Raszer. Sleep well. We'll speak in the morning."

AN ANGEL CREPT into Raszer's room at about four a.m. and stood in wing-muffled silence over his four-poster bed. A scrawny angel with long black tresses and small, girlish breasts. *"I need a man,"* she said aloud to the soundly sleeping form under the goose down comforter, though she must have known he couldn't hear. She lifted the bedding and poured herself like quicksilver into the curve of his side.

Sofia put her lips to the notch of missing flesh on Raszer's ear and caressed the wound with her breath. *"Make love to me..."* she whispered. His repose was so deep and well deserved that ordinarily she would have thought discretion the better part of valor and let him be. Not this night. He had denied her the Temple's brand of consummation. Now her body and spirit craved the only other form of death she had known until now.

In the black salt sea of Raszer's unconsciousness, a mercurial form moved toward him like a serpent. Treading silent water, he watched its approach with awe more than fear. He looked to the heavens and saw that the sulfurous stars were falling like meteors into his ocean, one by one. Each of them created a sizzle followed by the tinkling of a thousand tiny bells as it submerged. The serpentine form warmed the waters as it wrapped itself around his lower parts. He was unsure what he looked like below the surface. He might be a serpent, too. He felt himself being pulled under, but the instinctual rush of panic was quickly followed by delight when he realized that he was still able to breathe.

He slid down the length of his sinewy companion until his lips found a warm and yielding place. He caressed the newborn whiteness of her belly as the rest of her form swayed like seaweed in the current, and then brought his mouth down to the wine-cask sweetness of her sex, where the taste of the salt water co-mingled with her own sweet ferment. As she came in an escalating series of spasms that brought foam to the water's surface, he awakened fully with the sensation of being in the midst of a whirlpool. All of the elements about, including the earth matter of their own bodies, were being stirred in a great cauldron as if by some unseen hand. He entered her and the big four-poster rocked like a ship in the Horse Latitudes.

When they had finished, they fell back into the deep, their battered limbs entwined. They could easily have remained that way for a solid day had Jan and his nephew George not returned from their vigils.

A soft but insistent knock on the door came as dawn broke through the east windows of Raszer's room. He sensed right away that he wouldn't be catching up on lost sleep until he got back to L.A. Sofia was out so completely that she barely stirred as he untangled himself from her. He threw a blue dressing gown around his naked form and opened the door.

Havel stood with arms crossed, wearing a long burgundy-colored bathrobe. He nodded good morning to the bleary-eyed detective, handed him a steaming and aromatic mug of black coffee and rolled his eyes rightward to the trio of Rudie, Jan and George. They were huddled in the living room where the previous night's fire still boasted a few embers.

"My apologies," said Havel, "but I thought you should hear this."

"I was dreaming of washing down Baja lobster with tequila and lime," Raszer responded. "I must be homesick."

Havel took Raszer by the elbow. "It appears all but one of our Templars have managed to escape. In addition to buying cooperation from what seems to have been a large contingent of the Palace Guard, they must have been given the plans to all of the old medieval servants' tunnels. Some of the passages were, in fact, designed to permit the escape of the royal family in the event of an insurrection." He took a gulp of his coffee and smiled. "I've often thought they might come in handy if the Communists got back in! We have the airport and all major arteries covered, of course. I'm afraid the bodies of Mr. De Boer and the others are still missing, though we've pulled in that young brute Otto you tied up at their safe house." Raszer frowned and sat down on an ottoman, lighting a cigarette. "But," Havel proceeded, "they've left behind enough evidence to verify everything you've told us."

"What about the head?" Raszer asked. *"Did you find the head?"*

"No head," grunted the burly security chief.

"Damn!" Raszer cursed. "It figures they'd make off with that. *That* I would like to have had analyzed." He thought for a moment. "You said all but one got away. Who did we get?"

"She was one of the subjects, boss," said George, who had been understandably quiet until then. "Her name is Elspeth Klipp."

"The poor woman," Havel explained, "had the presence of mind to duck into an alcove as the party was making its way out. We suspect she was the last in line. We found her cowering in there about an hour ago. She's nearly catatonic. Did you happen to notice if her eyes were crossed before last night?"

"Yeah," Raszer replied. "Both her and her twin sister. Lisbeth, I think...strange pair."

A servant brought in a platter of pastries and a samovar of fresh coffee. George, whose obvious grief seemed to have increased his appetite, dove in to the sweet, sticky *jablkovy strudel* with reckless abandon.

"Bring me the bag, will you?" Havel directed Jan. Captain Dubrovsky handed over a large vinyl evidence bag that Havel unzipped. "They left this behind." He drew from the bag the purple robe that Luc had worn during the ceremonies. "There hasn't been time for anything but a layman's examination. I've asked our curator to stop by at eight, but I've seen a remarkably exact reproduction of this in the museum at the Rudolfinum. And look at this." He brought the robe to Raszer and opened it to expose the inside left breast pocket, on which was embroidered the initials J.D.

*"John Dee?"* Raszer asked under his breath.

"It's a bit of a leap, but if my guess is right, this may be the robe worn by Dee during the time he was Rudolph's court alchemist, before the Hapsburgs' guns ended his Hermetic Renaissance for good, at the Battle of White Mountain. If it's genuine, it says something about the seriousness of these people."

"Oh, they're serious," Raszer said, "but I can't help thinking that John Dee is spinning in his grave. I doubt he would have approved of Spiritual Darwinism."

"Yes," Havel agreed, "it does look as if his adversaries made off with his bag of tricks." Raszer limped to the buffet table and absently overfilled his coffee cup with the strong, pitchy brew. He shot a furtive glance at Rudie, the Hapsburg scion.

"You mentioned pieces missing from the machine. Did you find a remote control panel – a console – on wheels, with levels and knobs?"

The men shook their heads no.

A PRELIMINARY INQUEST was to commence at nine o'clock in a hearing room on the distant west end of the same building. Raszer had obtained Havel's assurance that, at least for now, he could testify "in-camera," in order to protect his anonymity, and that he and Sofia would make the twelve o'clock London flight under secret service escort as long as he was willing to return to Prague in the future for further questioning.

Raszer's garment bag arrived via the state courier who'd fetched it from the hotel, and he found its contents remarkably intact. He picked some khakis and a loose-knit shirt, laid them out but then changed his mind about the shirt. He opted instead for one of his custom tailored jobs, the color of rust on a red wagon. He slipped his needles into the hidden pocket.

Raszer brought his eyes to rest on the nymph sleeping in his bed. She was a vision. It was going to be excruciating to fly to London with her scent on him, only to turn her over to a husband he suspected she did not love. But he owed that much to Lawrence Gould and to his own professional conscience. It was probably a good thing that those twin obstacles stood in the way of his heart's desire because otherwise, he might have asked her to be his wife. It would have been an incestuous union.

Smelling of sandalwood after his shower, Raszer stood at the mirror and averted his eyes from the surface reflection, focusing instead on the illusory space behind it. In spite of his concentration on his task, he managed to nick himself again, this time on the chin. The tiny trickle of blood carried germs of memory. *Don't analyze, just listen.* In the past, his visits from the crone in the mirror had been maddeningly dreamlike, hardly distinguishable from delusion. Her words often evaporated from his consciousness as quickly as he tried to grasp them, but when she had spoken to him through Marta two nights ago, her words carried a living presence and an uncanny prescience. He was struck by the thought that this might be what women's intuition felt like. The thought was followed by another, less fanciful, more disturbing. *Was she the same Lady who spoke to Luc Fourché?*

THE INQUEST WAS fairly perfunctory since so many of the puzzle pieces had yet to be assembled. Raszer's interrogators managed nonetheless to make him feel like Bob Woodward being squeezed for the identity of Deep Throat. The panel was chaired by Havel's national security advisor and also included Captain Dubrovsky, a female representative of the Hradcany District in the State Assembly and a tall, chiseled and silver-gray Interpol bureau chief named Alain Saint-Germain. The Interpol chief had flown in that morning from Lyon where he was said to be assigned to the task force investigating the Temple. He confirmed that his organization was now working closely with the Czech police and secret service to determine the extent of corruption within both the Palace guard and local police agencies. Raszer inquired as to whether the telegram he'd composed to the chief prosecutor in Lyon had ever reached his desk. As far as the agent was aware, it had not.

Little was asked or said about parallel events in Montreal. There were, at Raszer's count, six countries and eleven separate police and governmental agencies currently investigating one tentacle or another of the octopus. You had to give it to the Templars. If diversification was the by-word of modern business, they had done it by the book. As far as Raszer could tell from Saint-Germain's somewhat disparaging tone, Interpol had its hands full coordinating the various investigations. There were all the usual turf issues and language problems, not to mention the fact that most of the investigators were treating the Temple like a Jonestown-style aberration, conveniently skating past the fact that some of Europe's finest citizens seemed to be active members. International banking wasn't Raszer's beat but he was truly afraid the Temple would cover its tracks before the hounds of justice picked up the scent of the money trail. He recalled what Mr. X had said about the scandal making Watergate look like a "lipstick stain." Banks had to be involved, maybe at the level of the P2 and BCCI affairs.

"Stay with the money," he urged. "That machine you have over at the university has to have cost millions to design. Where the hell did it come from?"

He handed over Caudal's crumpled business card and offered his theory about the account number. Saint-Germain gave it a cursory glance and put it into evidence.

"It may have been less expensive than it looked." He had a bit of the Gallic Cary Grant in him and more than a trace of condescension.

Finally they came to the matter of Elspeth Kilpp. She was under heavy sedation at the Diplomatic Health Center. When asked if she knew where her cohorts had gone, her response had been to jut out her chin and hoot owlishly, *"Oo-Loo-Roo…Oo-Loo-Roo…"* Raszer's request to interview her brought a response as close to a rebuke as he would receive from this genteel tribunal. Saint-Germain straightened his Armani tie and leaned in to the microphone for emphasis.

"Mr. Raszer, you have accomplished your mission here and left a trail of dead bodies and a state of emergency that might have been precluded had you not opted to play James Bond. Although we appreciate your co-operation, we are today filing a formal complaint with your embassy and a recommendation that Interpol monitor your enterprises for a period of not less than one year."

Raszer nodded his contrition. He knew that the reprimand would have been far stiffer had an illustrious ally not been hovering in the presidential office just down the hall.

WHEN RASZER RETURNED to the chambers, a glowing Sofia – showered and combed out but still bed-blushed – was breakfasting with Rudie.

"Is it true," Rudie asked, "that all women in Los Angeles are as beautiful as Sofia? She tells me so, but I cannot believe her."

"It's all true," quipped Raszer. "They breed them in test tubes on the Warner Brothers lot."

Sofia reached her hand for Raszer's forearm and shot him a wink. He let her touch linger until his heart began to ache, and then he broke free.

"Time to go, little Hokhmah."

George stepped inside the chamber and announced that President Havel had authorized the use of his limousine and two agents for the airport transit.

"Good," Raszer said, hoping that wouldn't be the last he heard from Havel. He took George's arm and met his eyes. "I hope you're included in the security detail. I can't tell you, Juraj…how sorry I am. Your brother would be alive if not for me."

"Mr. Raszer," George replied, placing his beefy hands on the detective's shoulders, "Peter was a cop. Cops know the odds. He is having a *klobasy* in Heaven. Do not blame yourself, just find those pigs before others die."

"Right," Raszer said, knowing it was a promise that would have to be put off. "Thanks to you, and to your brother, for saving my life."

The big man nodded somberly and then scooped two or three stale pastries from the platter on the kitchen counter. Raszer watched the gentle giant turn away and gobble the pastries furtively, a tear rolling down his plump cheek. Everyone, Raszer thought, handles loss in their own way; some with booze, some with prayer. George with strudel.

"There's something you should do before we leave, Sofia," Raszer prodded gently. He'd been struck by the fact that not once since her rescue had she expressed the slightest desire to phone her husband. Raszer himself had spoken to Gould before the inquest and made excuses for his wife. "She's been sedated," he'd said.

Lawrence Gould had agreed to meet them in London and take his wife home from there, but it didn't take a gypsy to see that there was no future in this marriage. Raszer didn't blame himself. Last night had been "survivor's love," the boon of combat for men and women who had found themselves in the same trench. However extraordinary the merging of their spirits, he could not go, would not go and had never gone after a client's woman. He'd accept her grace without strings. Sofia Gould was a hunger he would have to endure.

The limousine stood waiting at the Matthias Gate on the castle's west end, through which President Havel's staff came to work each day. The man himself was expected any minute. Raszer sat halfway out of the backseat, his feet on the pavement, his eyes trained blankly on the hem of Sofia's dress as she stood on the steps making small talk with Rudie.

His mind was as heavy as the wooly gray skies; the pealing of the St. Vitus bells a death knell for his fallen comrades. If he'd had another ten minutes, he might have gone into the chapel and lit candles by the tomb of Good King Wenceslas. One for Jeanette, one for Petyr Dubrovsky and one for the mission not yet accomplished: making sense of it all.

Raszer glanced up to see Havel jogging down the steps in a gray suit and tie, his arms extended. He gave Sofia a hug and a peck on the cheek, then approached the limo. Raszer rose to his feet and felt his chest swell reflexively with the atavistic pride that soldiers must once have felt in the presence of their king. This was a man he would happily do battle for.

"I've been thinking," Havel said, pushing back a shock of hair from his forehead, "about something you asked me; the connection between these people and the extreme right. It occurred to me that perhaps the same alienation from humanity that would separate a man from his own body would make it possible for him to place a bomb in a childcare center or conceive a 'final solution.' I hope that you and I will stay in touch, Mr. Raszer. My duties at state preclude me from wandering at the moment, but I feel better knowing that you are out there on the path as my *Percival*. Let me know what you find, my friend."

George rode up front with the driver, while the state security men were in the car ahead. Raszer and Sofia shared the backseat. They were each feeling the shyness of new lovers who have enjoyed every intimacy under cover of night but don't feel sanctioned to touch in broad daylight. He wanted to ask her if she'd shared in his revelatory dream, if what had happened between them really was the erotic ricochet of the rabbi's cosmic nuptials. He wanted it to be real this time, not just a projection of himself onto an unknowing other, but he couldn't say anything because to speak would be to acknowledge and to acknowledge would alter everything forever.

Sofia slipped on a pair of sunglasses and turned away from him to look at the passing city. She was the first to speak, and she did so in a voice husky with suppressed emotion.

"I should hate you for being my husband's errand boy."

"I wouldn't blame you," he said. "Would you take it all away if you could?"

"I don't know. I'm in limbo." She sighed. "It feels like the day after Christmas."

"If it makes any difference, it feels that way to me, too."

She turned halfway toward him, her soul masked by Ray-Bans. "If you said the words, I'd leave him. Do you know that?"

A sharp pain shot through Raszer's solar plexus. "I think—"

She reached out and put her fingers to his lips. "It's okay, Stephan. We'd never live up to each other's expectations. And if we tried to…" She leaned in and kissed him fully on the mouth, then withdrew, straightened her skirt and composed herself.

*If we tried to,* Raszer thought, *we'd lose ourselves. If we tried to, we'd fail God.*

Raszer leaned back against the door and admired her, the convent school posture and the gypsy fatalism. She was a searcher – a peregrine like him – a breed that dies in captivity. Where would she end up now that death had been stripped of its lyricism?

Almost as an afterthought, Sofia raked through the contents of her handbag and retrieved a brass key chain bearing her monogrammed "S." "Here," she said, with the faintest of smiles. "Every knight-errant should carry the banner of his lady, right?"

He returned her smile and accepted her pledge. Nothing else was said until they found themselves at the Lufthansa check-in. On the wall behind the counter was a collage of travel posters; in the center of the design, a blow-up of the hillside HOLLYWOOD sign.

"I can't believe this is happening," Sofia said flatly. "That I'm going back."

"It won't seem like the same place," Raszer said, getting their tickets from George. He looked to the poster and laughed softly. The big, ugly wooden letters, with their subtext of transfiguration looked pretty good to him.

Raszer had just handed the tickets across the counter when his ears pricked up. He turned to see a small herd of plainclothesmen approaching hurriedly, headed by Interpol agent Alain Saint-Germain. *What the fuck is this,* Raszer asked himself as Saint-Germain conferred urgently with the two state security agents, casting loaded looks in Sofia's direction. Raszer looked at George who shrugged his shoulders.

"Mr. Raszer," Saint-Germain called out, flashing his badge and talking as he walked. "I'm glad we caught you." The other agents followed in a loose wedge while Havel's men hung back. Raszer stepped away from the ticket counter, instinctively placing himself between Sofia and the approaching pack. "There's been a change of plans."

"What kind of change?" Raszer asked.

"We will be escorting Mrs. Gould to London, *Monsieur.* You may proceed on your scheduled flight." Sofia's jaw went slack. "I assure you, this is for her own safety. We have a French military transport waiting, and we have informed both the lady's husband and the U.S. consul in London."

Raszer lifted an eyebrow in protest. "Ms. Gould is a private citizen. I'm a private citizen. We're going home. I don't think Interpol has any jurisdiction here. Where's Captain Dubrovsky?"

"Captain Dubrovsky is attending to the security of the Czech Republic, Mr. Raszer. This is now an international matter." Saint-Germain took Raszer politely by the elbow and begged a private moment. Raszer nodded to George to stay within earshot.

"All right," said Raszer, when they were a few feet removed. "I know I played cowboy last night. I know I broke some rules—"

"This is not about rules *you* broke, Mr. Raszer," said the bureau chief, stopping Raszer cold. "Mrs. Gould may have been party to an extortion scheme that involved international stock and bank fraud. She has privileged information about criminals who are still very much at large and for whom she is still very much a target. As you correctly surmised, the money paid for her release is currently embargoed in a Czech bank account that can only be accessed by the account holder, *Noel Branch*. That, Mr. Raszer, makes *you* a target as well."

Raszer turned his eyes away and felt in his jacket for his cigarettes. He shot a quick look at Sofia who had slumped against the ticket counter, her arms folded and an expression caught between fury and helplessness. Once he'd lit a smoke, Raszer returned to Saint-Germain, who was a formidable presence. Raszer wasn't sure which was more disconcerting: the pale, nearly translucent blue eyes that were drilling him or the overpowering scent of Vetiver cologne that was wafting from his broad, well-tailored shoulders.

"So you're telling me," Raszer said, "that I could put her in further danger?"

"At the least," Saint-Germain replied, "the two of you should not be on the same flight. Who is to say, my friend, that there isn't a Temple enforcer – someone of Mr. De Boer's lineage – currently occupying a seat on Lufthansa 426? Who can be sure that there is not a small, innocuous looking package in the cargo hold, its contents awaiting the prescribed altitude? You and I risk our lives for a living, Mr. Raszer, but we should not ask others to share that risk."

Raszer shook his head. He was beat on that point.

THE LUFTHANSA FLIGHT had started boarding, but Saint-Germain allowed Raszer a couple of minutes to say his goodbyes to George and Sofia. They were not happy moments. Beyond his affection, beyond his embarrassment and a mushrooming melancholy, there was professional indignation at not being able to escort her properly into the world – to "bring her down." That was as important a part of his work as any. She was weak and shaky and profoundly unsure that she had indeed been rescued, and he had looked forward to their time on the plane. He pulled her to him and folded her in his arms until Saint-Germain signaled him to break the clutch.

Raszer turned to him. "Get her home safely, Saint-Germain."

"I will get her home." The polished silver of his sideburns reflected the midday sun. "Now go home. *Your* work is done, *mon ami.*"

She was pale and trembling as they took her off. She looked back once to see if he was still watching her and he was. When she was about fifty feet down the concourse, she turned again and called out. "I'll see you in L.A. I'll call you. I will!" And then, as she descended the escalator, she cried out, *"You're inside me!"*

The final call for Raszer's flight was announced. He gave George a slap on the back, scooped his shoulder bag off the counter and froze. George wasn't grinning. His brow was as creased as a French philosopher's.

"I was at the inquest," George said. "I did not hear you tell them that the Professor was your cover—"

Raszer drew a long, jagged breath and with it came the voice in the Gardens, and with the voice, the words he'd only just heard. *"Your* work is done, *mon ami."* Of course, he thought. *Of course.* Saint-Germain was as obvious a *nomme de guerre* as Fourché.

He broke into a sprint. With George barreling behind him, they flew down the escalator into the lower concourse, running a good five hundred meters before Raszer's heart accepted what his head had already told him. She was gone, back in the Temple's hands.

Having hustled back to main concourse, Raszer leaned against a ticket counter to get his balance and breath while George caught up. He glanced around to see where he was. It was the Quantas Airlines counter, and on the wall behind it was a large framed poster of Ayers Rock at sunset. Raszer cocked his head and stepped to the counter.

"Excuse me," Raszer said breathlessly. "Does *Oo-Loo-Roo* mean anything to you?"

The agent chuckled and cocked a thumb back at the poster. "You're looking at it. Uluru. That's what the abo's call the big rock."

"Give me that cell phone, George," Raszer said as the bodyguard staggered to his side. He took the phone and punched in Monica's line.

The line rang on. *She must be in the bathroom,* he thought. The bathroom where he'd cut himself...the mirror and the crone. *"The door swings both ways...Death is the door through which ye came nigh."*

Hinge. Hinge had set him up.

# 21

## ULURU

*...for as the Zohar, a thirteenth century commentary on the Torah and the most famous of the esoteric Jewish texts notes, the verb, "baro" – to create – implies the idea of creating an illusion.*

– Michael Talbot, *The Holographic Universe*

\* \* \* \* \* \*

*Aborigines could not believe that the land existed until they could see it and sing it, just as, in the Dreamtime, the ancestors had sung it into being.*

– Patrick Jennings, *Dreamtime Journal*

\* \* \* \* \* \*

*The people of Western history, those still in the dreamtime of pre-literacy, have kept the flame of a tremendous mystery burning. It will be humbling to admit this, and to learn from them, but that too is part of the Archaic Revival.*

– Terence McKenna, *Food of the Gods*

RASZER SHUDDERED AS he stepped from the cramped cabin of the old Ansett Airways DC-10 and descended to the tarmac. He'd taken a Halcyon once aloft from Prague and had managed to sleep soundly through most of the six time zones before a fever had awakened him during the previous leg to Singapore. The stopover had been mercifully brief, but the direct flight from there to the port of Darwin, Australia, two time zones further east, had been turbulent and miserable.

Now, as he walked to the small terminal through what remained of the night watching the vapor trail of his own breath dissipate behind him, he had an oddly startling realization. It was winter. Not a bad sort of winter – rainy and maybe 40°F, and it would probably hit 65° or 70° at noon in the desert – but winter nonetheless. He was in the Southern Hemisphere and everything had been turned on its head. If Luc Fourché and his Templars had, in fact, crossed the equator to complete their transit to the stars, they had, by doing so, insured that the ceremony would by synchronized, not to the arrival of summer, but to the Winter Solstice. Just as had been the case last year in the *Vercors,* on the top half of the globe.

Raszer set as his first priority the purchase of a windbreaker. He did not want to die unfit in a place called Darwin. Once properly insulated, he'd find the office of Outback Adventures, the charter service Monica had booked to fly him to Alice Springs. Darwin was the capitol of the Northern Territory's stormy "Top End," and its only real distinction was as the entry point for trekkers that wanted to explore the aboriginal lands, the empty and arid center of Oz.

Monica's routing had come as close to warping time as air travel possibly can, taking advantage of the fact that though Europe had switched over to Daylight Savings Time, Australia had not yet fallen back to Standard Time. That had shaved two hours off the effect of the trip. The flight to Alice Springs via charter would take just under that, and there was to be a helicopter bush pilot waiting there to take him on to his final destination.

Uluru was the seat of the world for the aboriginal peoples of Australia, and perhaps for certain European mystagogues, as well. It would take an act of grace for him to make it there before the Solstice sun came up on the Rock, but he intended to call on all the angels within his firmament.

He'd already heard from a few.

IT WAS ALMOST four o'clock in the morning and the sole concession stand in the terminal was closed. Raszer saw his poncho taunting him from behind the gated shop window, neon blue with a kangaroo emblazoned on the front pouch. Maybe on the way back he'd buy a matching pair for himself and his daughter, if there was a way back from Oz.

He shuddered at the thought of three more hours of darkness and gauged his fever at about 101°. If it didn't get any worse, his body would remain serviceable, but he had a sick and unshakeable feeling that he might have picked up something truly noxious from De Boer's bite. He glimpsed a dispiriting reflection of himself in a pane of glass as he limped past, his posture contorted awkwardly to avoid aggravation of his sundry wounds. It wouldn't do to think too much about his physical being at present, for he was clearly not in shape for this unanticipated leg of his journey.

Raszer approached the Outback Adventures counter.

"Mr. Raszer, is it? The skinny young night clerk yawned. "We've got a message for ya. Lucky it came through in this weather. Says here you're to call 'Mama' before ya board. Better make it quick, sir."

Raszer had gone beat-by-beat through the plan with Monica before his departure from Prague and refined it further during the stopover in Singapore. She was to contact his friend Simon from CultWatch in Perth, the same fellow who had earlier relayed the report from an Anangu council leader of odd goings on at the national park.

CultWatch had more than a passing awareness of the Temple, as it had found fertile ground in the Catholic communities of the port cities during the early 90's. No one had ever been able to figure out, however, why the sect had strayed so far from the familiar ground of Western Europe and francophone Canada. Now there was a possible rationale. If Central Australia held, as Hinge had suggested, some archaic connection to the cult's Sirius mythos, then the savvy shaman Fourché would have had good reason to cultivate it. Raszer wasn't sure if Simon and his group were aware of any of this, as their focus was on the more practical business of restoring cult "victims" to their families, but he had asked Monica to have him arrange an airport meeting in Alice Springs with the Anangu leader, "Sam" Mirrigau. Raszer's first plea would be to ask councilman Mirrigau to accompany him to Uluru. The second would be that he provide some manpower in the form of a posse of the Anangu rangers who tended the aboriginal lands.

Simon Andrew's cult busters had earned close ties with the Anangu and Pintupi aboriginal communities and their leaders by way of an unusual alliance of interests. The national park that contained Ayers Rock was administered by the aboriginal council under treaties that bore similarities to contracts the U.S. government had made with its country's natives. Over the years, Ayers Rock – like Stonehenge, Shasta and Sedona – had become a telluric magnet for New Age seekers and camp followers ranging from bona fide St. Anthony's to stoned biker brigades and millennial militias. It was the council's job to approve or deny permit applications for any manner of ceremony or observance to be held on the Rock, for Uluru was sacred ground. Tribal leaders did not look kindly on acts of disrespect or desecration, of which ritual suicide would seem to be an example.

Raszer felt sure that if Luc and his tribe had hunkered down somewhere on the Rock, they were operating without a permit. He was counting on that sacrilege as well as his urgent concern for the lives of Sofia and her companions to enlist the councilman's cooperation. Everything had seemed to be in order as of midnight in Singapore, when he'd last spoken to Monica. So why was she calling now?

"Did something go wrong on Simon's end?" he asked her apprehensively.

"No, no Raszer. You're all set. Sam Mirrigau will be at the airport when you arrive. But if your Templars are in touch with their base, they're going to be feeling edgy right now, so don't go there without some firepower."

"I have to be careful about that," he replied. "Remember Waco? Anyway, why? What's happened?"

"Philippe Caudal is dead. Jacques Denis managed to trace his St. Casimir address from the fax number and paid him a visit. Seventeen stab wounds to the back, shoulders and chest. The police have raided Savana Investments and taken a handful of secretaries and middle managers into custody. So far, they don't seem to have the big guys."

"Jesus," Raszer said. "It's all coming down. How's Lawrence Gould?"

"He's as okay as he can be. He's glad they traced his money, and they've put the brakes on the stock slide. But I think he knows he's lost her, either way."

"She's a lot to lose."

"Oh, Raszer," Monica sighed. "There isn't a deeply screwed up woman out there that you wouldn't fall for. Listen, before you go, I finally got something on that insignia – the two-headed eagle."

"Go. They're waving me on board."

"It's Masonic, all right. 33rd degree. But you knew that. It was also the emblem of the Imperial House of Hapsburg. Are these people trying to restore the monarchy? Jesus, what a story that would be."

"And you'd be the girl to write it. Gotta go, partner. Say a prayer."

"I will," she promised. "Raszer, don't be a hero. I'd miss your cooking."

"I don't have the strength for heroics," he said. "And I'd miss you, too."

THE TWIN-ENGINE charter was little more than an old mail plane with a half-assed makeover. Worn leather benches ran the length of the fuselage, and there were two small fold-up seats just behind the cockpit, both of which had been commandeered by the craft's only other passenger, a corpulent Sydney Greenstreet-type in a cheap tan suit, who Raszer figured for a salesman. What a gig: traveling salesman in the Outback. The man took up the width of the plane, and though wedged into an impossible position, appeared to be sleeping soundly, snoring and filling the cabin with the smell of stale beer and bile. Raszer took the rear of the bench and strapped himself in. Conversation was not on his agenda tonight.

The plane dipped three stomach-churning times before finding its altitude. Raszer took the takeoff and the rocky first fifteen minutes of the flight to ready himself for the physical and spiritual ordeal to come. The fever had severely tapped his libido, and he was feeling dangerously close to depression, a state that Raszer had nearly managed to eliminate from his psychic repertoire. He ached with the memory of Sofia's last look, and he ached over the death and heartache he'd left in his wake. The combustion of anger and grief rekindled his sense of mission and reminded him also of what was, beneath it all, a personal reason for coming twelve thousand miles to look death in the face. As much as Sofia, as much as John Dee, as much as any Catholic on his knees with rosary in hand, Raszer wanted to know if there was something that transcended death. The possibility had been dangled in front of him like meat in front of a starveling for more than twenty years. Now, perversely, he was looking for treasure in the hands of a crew of murderous brigands. Sometimes God is glimpsed through a glass, darkly. Even the rabbi had said, *If they have read the texts, I cannot say that something extraordinary will not happen.* Truth revealed through its opposite. An old Sufi trick.

After an hour or so, Raszer slipped into the fitful sleep of the overtired, his brainwaves surging and sputtering with the randomness of the plane's ancient engines. He dwelled on Sofia for a while, on her words and on her sweet, young wine smell, but there was no rest to be found in thoughts of her. It gave little comfort to remind himself of President Havel's discovery that Luc's "elixir" was nothing more then salt water. One way or the other, she would be dead when they turned the lights on the Tree, and at this moment, she had to be close to madness.

Only when his mind's eye began to trace one of the long, deep creases in Vaclav Havel's face did he find some repose. That crease was a kind of fractal – he was certain he would find its macro-scale replicates if he could observe the topography of the world's mountains and valleys from a hawk's perspective. Scientists who studied such things said that fractals were basic geometrical motifs that were common to all levels of existence. *As above, so below.* A crease in a man's face could be a crease in the earth's crust or a wrinkle in time. Havel was part of the landscape. In some way, that was essential to his goodness. Could the converse of that be essential to badness? Chaos theory claimed that one could never accurately predict the weather beyond a hazy probability for any sector of the globe because the fluttering of a butterfly's wings over a field of daisies in Iowa could affect the pressure zones over equatorial Asia, or anywhere else. It seemed to Raszer another way of saying what the Hindus had been saying for ages: *it was an exquisitely woven web.*

But what if one were to somehow "disconnect," and no longer feel the ripples created by the butterfly's wings? Could Luc's *Thanatos* be a result of that condition? Could that person become a murderer, as Havel himself suggested with his parting words? As he drifted, Raszer curled his fingers around Sofia's key chain and that, finally, brought him sleep.

THE PLANE SKIDDED to a halt on a dry runway twenty miles or so southwest of the small desert town of Alice Springs. They were in the "Red Center." The fat salesman barely stirred on landing. His routine was probably so well worked out that he'd manage to get to his hotel room without ever fully regaining consciousness. As soon as the plane depressurized, Raszer could feel the damp, ion-laden air of Darwin being exchanged with air dry enough to burn his sinuses. He pulled his flight case from the luggage rack and stepped off the plane.

There was a faint hint of pink winter sunrise over a distant ridge, but Raszer guessed that the real thing was an hour away. The double-star system of Sirius hung like a lantern about fifteen degrees above the eastern horizon. It had risen before the sun, the "heliacal" rising heralded by the Temple's Egyptian forbears. The air was cool, probably the low 40's, but the wind was down. A neon *Foster's Lager* sign beckoned from the airport coffee shop one hundred yards away, and he made out the wizened form of a man hunched over a table nursing whatever small bit of heat his coffee mug would provide. With luck, that would be Sam Mirrigau.

The short walk allowed Raszer to decompress a bit, and its duration seemed dreamily expanded by the sheer enormity of the emptiness around him. Even in the dark, he could sense that this was the most desolate place he had ever visited.

Sam Mirrigau stood even before Raszer had fully closed the door and nodded in rhythmic greeting. In a theater as empty as this one, the identity of a character entering stage right could not be much of a mystery.

"Mr. Raszer, *it tis, it tis,*" Mirrigau chimed, grinning and exposing yellowed teeth in an ancient and wind blasted face.

"Councilman Mirrigau," said Raszer, extending his hand. "Thank you so much for meeting me at such a time and on such short notice."

The old shaman clicked his tongue like a native and then spoke the Queen's English. "Nonsense, time is never bad or good. I will simply push mine around a bit to accommodate the day's exigencies! If what I hear is true, we have little time to waste. Would you like a coffee?"

Raszer accepted gratefully and the two men sat down with freshly poured cups.

"Mr. Raszer," Mirrigau began, "Simon Andrews has told me that you are not only a talented detective but a man of spiritual gravity, so I will not insult you with my standard grilling. But I feel I must hear from your own lips the nature of your mission here."

Raszer scalded his tongue with the black coffee and shakily set the cup down to answer. He was more exhausted than he'd thought.

"I can't say how they managed it, but I believe that members of a French-Swiss cult have assembled this morning somewhere on Ayers Rock to commit mass suicide; at least six people, possibly more. This group is being pursued in six countries for acts of fraud, sabotage and murder. From what I've learned, they believe that the earth and physical life are without value. They seek, through death, to ascend to the spirit realm. They may intend to use Uluru as a launching pad."

The old man's eyes went dark and he clicked his tongue wildly. "Oh, no-no-no-no-no. *No-no-no-no-no!* This would be a very great wound, a great sacrilege. Uluru's roots touch the very center of the earth and the earth is alive. This is its power. This is what the *piranypa* do not understand. They come here, these Europeans, greedy for the gifts of the *tjukurpa* – our spirit world. Hungry for dreamtime. They hear a little about this and that, and then they take it home in a box. Everything in the box gets broken, and when they open it back in their own country, they don't know how the pieces go together. The world is now full of false shamans who think they understand what Uluru is. They have no idea! It is the place from which the world was born. To use it to deny that world would be a very great evil. The real shaman, now he ascends to the spirit world, but then he comes back to the body. Except," he said with raised eyebrows, "for those who get lost in between. What is your plan, sir?"

Raszer conjectured that the Temple's elitism would lead them to seek the place on the Rock thought to possess the greatest spiritual power.

"That could be many places, Mr. Raszer. There is no 'holy of holies.' Only a *piranypa* would think to organize *tjukurpa* into a hierarchy! But the place of the *altjeringa* ceremonies is *Warayuki*. You may have cause to begin there."

Raszer knew just enough about aboriginal myths to know that *altjeringa* was a name for the ancestral dreamtime, when mythical creatures like Lungkata, the blue-tongued lizard man, had brought all things into being through the singing of their songs. The ceremonies to which the old man referred were shamanistic rituals where the world of the dreamtime was revealed to the adolescent males of a community as a living and continuous process. A young man's first ordeal would culminate in his circumcision, but in a later ceremony he would suffer a deeper wound, one that would symbolically unify him with the females of the tribe and with the mother of all. His penis would be sliced to the root with a sharpened flint and his blood spilled on the porous and fertile earth, beneath which his ancestors slept. He would then no longer think of himself as exclusively male, but in a sense, as one with the androgynous titans who had created his world.

"I think it's safe to say," Raszer suggested, "that they'll have chosen someplace with a vantage point and that it will be guarded – how heavily, I don't know – but we should expect guns. Are your park police armed? And will you lend me a few of them?"

Mirrigau rubbed his chin in consternation. "There's a small force of territorial rangers who could be deployed, but none of these boys are trained for assault, Mr. Raszer. What is it exactly you would have us do?"

Raszer did not exactly know. Getting here had been an act of pure manic will, driven he supposed by a sense of duty, Havel's faith in him and an ache for both Sofia and *Sophia*. That was the sizzle; now he had to define the steak. He had to get operational.

"I don't intend to turn this into Waco, councilman," he said, only half-believing he could prevent it, "or to lead an assault. That would only insure bloodshed. It's only my hunch that these people are up there, and at the moment, there's nothing we can charge them with, other than violation of park regulations and possibly illegal possession of firearms. I'm banking on the fact that they won't proceed with this massacre if they know they're being observed. If you can get me a dozen armed rangers and a megaphone – maybe some local press – we may be able to stop this. First off though, we've got to locate them. Time is very short, and I don't know the Rock, so I was wondering…"

Mirrigau finished his coffee and stood. "Okay, my friend. You have gotten my attention. Come with me."

As they walked to the helipad under a purple sky still freckled with morning stars, the erudite aboriginal leader turned to Raszer and cocked his head. "There is an odd fact you should be aware of – one that may or may not have influenced the Temple's choice of venue."

"And that is?" asked Raszer.

"The Northern Territory of Australia," Mirrigau explained, "is currently the last place in the civilized world where there are absolutely no restrictions on the practice of euthanasia, so long as it is administered by a licensed physician. Were you aware?"

"No," Raszer replied. "I wasn't."

THEY ARRIVED AT the helicopter in advance of the pilot, and Mirrigau alternated agitated glances about the airfield with looks at his watch.

"That boy lives in his own personal dreamtime. He should have been here."

Raszer knitted his brow. "Doesn't sound like a strong recommendation for our pilot, councilman."

"Oh no, no, no, no, no," Mirrigau protested, grinning. "The pilot will be along. I am referring to your guide."

Raszer was thrown. "I was hoping sir, that you…" Two seconds passed while the old man observed Raszer's disappointment, and off in the distance both men heard the echo of sneakers slapping the pavement.

"Ah, no," sighed Mirrigau. "Surely not at my age. I thought Simon had told you. But I am sending our very best man!"

No sooner had the accolade left his lips than Raszer heard panting and saw misted breath break the darkness. To his initial dismay, he realized that Mirrigau was referring to the bony, 20-ish aborigine boy in torn blue jeans and Jimmie Hendrix jacket that was now sprinting his final few yards.

"Mr. Raszer, let me introduce the very late Mr. Miltjan Multijulu, who will accompany you to Uluru."

The young man gasped and bent over to catch his breath before extending his spindly hand.

"It's a pleasure, sir," Miltjan said, smiling broadly. His thick, black shrub of hair stood 220-volt erect on his head in the fashion of the guitar hero on his jacket.

"Pleasure's mine," Raszer said warily. He turned to Mirrigau and whispered, "Are you sure about this?"

Mirrigau winked at his young protégé before leaning over with exaggerated secrecy to whisper back to Raszer. "Don't underestimate him, Mr. Raszer. Miltjan knows the Rock better than any of the Anangu. He has spent…what is it? Twenty nights alone there since his manhood came?"

"Twenty-one," Miltjan proudly corrected his master.

In the midst of their conversation, the helicopter pilot appeared as if from the ether and began preparing the craft for takeoff. Miltjan and Mirrigau exchanged looks of surprised concern, and the old man addressed the pilot.

"Where is Nimbo? We had Nimbo down for this flight, did we not?"

The pilot turned from his preparatory routine and flashed an easy smile. "Nimbo took ill, sir. I'll be subbin' for 'im tonight, 'f that's all right."

"You know Uluru, do you, Mr. ...?" Mirrigau queried.

"Kinsey, sir. Jack Kinsey," the pilot answered. "Like the backa' me 'and, sir. Nimbo was my teacher."

Mirrigau, apparently satisfied, nodded young Miltjan aboard. The pilot followed, and the old man turned to Raszer in confidence for a last word.

"You'll radio me as soon as you think you've located them, yes?" he said softly. "I'll have my men assemble at the park headquarters and be ready to jeep out to Miltjan's coordinates. I will phone our sole local journalist. You may have already made his acquaintance – he was on the flight from Darwin with you." Raszer smiled. He still had a few things to learn about guessing occupations. "And Mr. Raszer, I want no blood shed at Uluru that is not shed to defend the ancestors. The earth there knows its own."

Raszer saluted the patriarch and jumped aboard. "If you don't mind my asking, sir; how old *are* you?"

"One hundred and three, yesterday," Mirrigau responded with a grin as he returned Raszer's salute. "I'll be going *back in* soon."

The chopper took off in the inchoate dawn and Mirrigau turned and headed for the dispatch office, still perplexed about the failure of his usually reliable pilot to show. The desk was unmanned and the office dimly lit by a single light bulb. Mirrigau leafed through the flight logbook and found Nimbo's name entered as he'd directed.

He paused. He felt the disturbance of air, his twig-like finger holding down the page, his dried plum ears twitching. The muffled scuffling of heels on the old wooden floor drew him from the desk to investigate. When he found his pilot, he was facedown, handcuffed to the toilet with a chloroformed rag in his mouth.

ONCE THEY WERE a few thousand feet above the ruddy, low-lying hills, Raszer could see that the formation of dawn was well along. That was not good. As far as he knew, most pagan ceremonies tied to the solstice occurred at the moment the sun's first rays broke the horizon, give or take a minute. He couldn't end this mission, already so costly in life, with the image of swollen bodies, pale against the red dust, particularly not if one of them belonged to the fey child-woman whose talisman he now clutched in his hand. His only hope, if he missed the solar trigger, was that somehow Sofia was of more value to Fourché alive than dead.

The pilot spoke for the first time. "Any idea which part of the Rock you want to head for, gents?"

Raszer turned to his young scout for guidance. "Sam suggested we try *Warayuki*," he said. "What do you think? If you were a crazy European looking for a power spot to die, where would you go?"

Miltjan chewed on the question, then spoke with a young man's earnest authority. "The Euros love the *Walaritja* – the Wave Caves – but if they're knowing the secrets, they will much more go to *Kuniya Piti*. This is the place where Kuniya brought her eggs before going back inside."

"Back inside?" Raszer asked, recalling Sam Mirrigau's parting words.

"In the *altjeringa*," Miltjan answered, bending over to fumble in his knapsack for a piece of fruit, "when the ancestors had finished the work of singing up the world, they went back into the earth to rest. Yes, we should begin at *Kuniya*.

Miltjan retrieved the sticky plum he'd been searching for, and unintentionally removed a plastic sandwich bag that had gotten stuck to his fingers. It plopped conspicuously to the floor. Raszer eyed its slimy, nut-brown contents and offered a guess based upon personal gardening experience.

"Mushrooms, eh? Are they...*edible?*"

Miltjan smacked his lips. "Oh, yes sir. Edible indeed. The books call them *psilocybe subaeruginosa*. We call them song seeds in our language."

"Psilocybin," Raszer affirmed. "Lunch?"

"Do you know them?" Miltjan asked, sensing a co-conspirator.

"Oh, yeah. But it's been a while."

"If we finish our work early enough," Miltjan said, stuffing the bag into his pants, "I plan to spend the rest of the day on the rock. These will be my lunch *and* dinner. They make my dreamings come stronger. The old ones like Sam don't need them anymore, but he does not disapprove. He was young once."

"You've got enough in there for a hell of a dream," Raszer observed.

"Enough for a friend," Miltjan giggled.

As the copter climbed and the air thinned, Raszer found himself drifting into a brief, dreamless sleep. He was gently awakened by a sound like wind whistling over the mouth of an empty soda bottle, half buried in drifting sands – the wind with a pitch and a personality. It was a moment

before he realized that the pleasant and utterly natural sound was coming
from Miltjan's half-open mouth and dry, parted lips.

"What's the tune?" Raszer asked.

"I'm singing up the country, boss," was the boy's cryptic reply.
"Makes the land come up faster that way. We say that an Anangu can find
his way home from any place if he knows his song. The song is also part of
his dreaming."

Raszer shot a long glance out the chopper's bubble window at the
curved earth below. The land had wrinkled into a series of successive, rosy
pink ridges that did indeed seem to be rising up, as helicopter and horizon
grew closer. *He doesn't believe the land exists until it appears,* Raszer thought.
*Wow.*

"Tell me about dreamtime, Miltjan. Tell me how you see it."

Miltjan turned ninety degrees in his seat and used his hands to illus-
trate his words with an elegant sign language. "Okay, try this. Dreamtime
was, is and will be. Dreamtime is *there* coming into *here*. The mistake the
*piranypa* make is to think of it as our people's history, like your Book of
Genesis; something dead that happened once and will never happen again.
But each second we live, the world is *becoming*. What we call *tjukurpa* means
to live in that always becoming place. Make sense?"

Raszer smiled and rubbed his bristled and leather-dry face. "I think
so, man. A lot of sense." *Jesus,* he thought. The kid had just dictated the
Cliff Notes for David Bohm's theory of the implicate and explicate orders.
Time and matter are *enfolded* until they *unfold* into what we experience. The
universe is constantly being dreamed into existence. But by whom?

"Let me ask you something, Miltjan. Do the old shamans say that it's
ever possible, in dreaming, to go from here back to there? To go from
what is back to what was before it was, if you know what I mean?"

"Don't think so, mate. Normal folks, they only see what already is.
The shaman, now, he see that stuff *becoming*. He can walk in the crack, but
only the ancestors can go back in. This is a god thing. *We* try to go back in,
we get sucked right down, like shit going down the toilet."

Raszer felt his stomach lift as the chopper dove. Miltjan snapped bolt
upright and thrust a finger toward the front of the bubble.

"Look, sir! Uluru…"

AYERS ROCK, EVEN given its relatively slight three hundred, forty-
five meter height, managed to loom large in this landscape. In nothing,
something can make a big impression, and the Rock was *something*. It was a
perfect natural icon, a massive rust-red Gibraltar that practically begged for

a fleet of Erik Von Dainiken's flying saucers to land atop it. It was thought that two-thirds of its mass was submerged beneath the desert floor, and for endless miles around it, there was sheer emptiness. In the early eastern light, its contours were surreally bold. Miltjan leaned forward to the pilot, who had not asked any further direction and seemed to be heading determinedly toward the west end.

"Say, mate," Miltjan said, tapping his shoulder, "*Kuniya Piti* be *that* way, on the southeast side."

Jack Kinsey answered from behind his dark aviator glasses. "Right friend, but you'll have to save Kuniya Piti for another day. We've got a slightly different flight plan today."

Raszer's mouth went instantly dry. Intuitively, he'd known something was off. Sam Mirrigau's surprise over the switch of pilots. But once again, even with lessons recently learned, he'd ignored intuition and gone on program. A guy thing. He thought about the needles in his inside pocket, but it wouldn't do a hell of a lot of good to paralyze the pilot when neither of them knew how to fly a helicopter.

"Don't think about being slick, either of you," said the pilot. "I've got a forty-four caliber boomerang on me lap and I won't hesitate to use it."

Miltjan looked bug-eyed to Raszer, who shrugged and slammed back into the seat. He knew it was useless to negotiate.

"You people are truly fucking crazy, man. In an hour, there'll be a small army here if no one hears from us."

"Oh, well," Kinsey said laconically. "Wouldn't count on them finding you inside an hour, boss. She's a mighty big rock. Anyway, I'll let that be Mr. Fourché's business. Mine's just to get you there."

The helicopter dropped below the cliff, and Kinsey radioed in that the visitors had arrived. The rotor blades cut so close to the etched red face of the rock that Raszer could nearly touch the porous stone.

"Keep yer socks on, gents," the pilot cracked. "We're almost home."

Five or six hundred feet below, four figures materialized as if from the solid rock. They wore black jumpsuits and held automatic rifles. On a signal from one of them, Kinsey began to bring the chopper down.

Raszer noticed Miltjan. Although trembling, he appeared to be quietly studying the terrain for coordinates. Raszer gave the boy a nod of encouragement, to which Miltjan responded by slyly lifting the hem of his Hendrix jacket to reveal a small pistol parked in his jeans, a .22 for shooting jackrabbits. Raszer shook his head. The small caliber pistol was a bad risk against a .44, especially in the air.

Then it happened. Raszer looked down at the rapidly approaching ground and the guns aimed at them, and he knew a moment of pure *becoming*. He yanked the pistol out of Miltjan's blue jeans and rammed the muzzle under Jack Kinsey's jaw.

"Up, *mate*. Take us to the top of the rock."

Kinsey hovered for a moment, his face revealing nothing. His right hand strobed across his thigh toward the weapon in his lap, and Raszer knew he'd miscalculated. *Of course he knows I'm not going to shoot him while he's flying the helicopter.* But a faster hand, one with long, bony brown fingers, beat Kinsey to it. Miltjan put the .44 to the pilot's temple.

"To the top like he said," Miltjan said with a grin.

"You two are out of yer fuckin' 'eads," Kinsey spat. "I'm takin' her down."

Raszer, his instincts having been temporarily commandeered by an alien intelligence, turned the barrel away from Kinsey's jaw and shot a BB-sized hole in the windshield. It wasn't quite as impressive as he'd hoped.

"Pack it up, cowboy," the pilot said contemptuously, and continued his descent.

Before Raszer could respond, Miltjan had blown a hole in the shatterproof glass large enough to shoot a basketball through.

"Jesus!" Kinsey shouted. "All right then."

Raszer glanced at the men below, who were in disarray. They fired off a volley of warning shots before the chopper crested the cliff, but they clearly had no orders to shoot it down. He saw two of them duck into a crevasse to report the mishap.

"You call it, partner," Raszer said to Miltjan. "Find us a place it'll take them a while to climb to. Long enough for Sam to come through."

"There," said the boy, pointing to a scrubby patch between two enormous, egg-shaped boulders, about two hundred meters to the east. "That's one of my power spots."

Kinsey made a rough landing and cut the engines. He raised his hands in the air and smirked.

"There you are, gents," he said dryly. "Now what the hell do you—"

Before the last words were out, Raszer had inserted a scant centimeter of surgical steel in the soft spot directly under Kinsey's earlobe. With his free hand, he cushioned the collapse of the pilot's head to the console. Once Kinsey was decidedly out, Raszer flopped him back against the headrest and canted his chin upward so that breathing was unobstructed. He slipped the needle into one of the "used" slots in the slim, gunmetal blue case, and tucked it back into his shirt.

Miltjan stared in wonderment. "Is he dead, man? The ancestors won't like it if—"

"No," Raszer replied. "He'll be out for about an hour. He'd be dead if I'd hit an artery and left it there a while."

"Spy shit, man," said Miltjan, impressed. He looked down at the oversized cannon in his own hands and shook his head. "Guns is only good if it's big."

"Small is beautiful," said Raszer.

"What do we do now, man?"

"I want you to try and take me to where we're just above the place where he tried to land. Then, we hunker down and hope for the cavalry...unless another opportunity presents itself."

THE DESERT, PRE-dawn was so fresh, the air so astringent in the fading starlight that Raszer could not help but think how great it might have been to make this vision quest, with this remarkable boy, under different circumstances – when his ankle wasn't torn to ragged fiber, when he wasn't burning with fever, when Sofia Gould was not at death's door. To sit atop the egg-boulders and sing up the sunrise, maybe even ingest a few of Miltjan's mushrooms. *But it's always been this way,* he thought. Too busy surviving to see the dreamtime, to step in the crack between before and after. But then, he had in fact, just been there...if only for a minute.

THE TOP OF Uluru was not as flat as it appeared in aerial photos, and the going was not easy. Miltjan scrambled over the boulders like a goat, but Raszer's ankle was so tender that he was forced to squander his strength by using his arms more than his legs. It occurred to him about fifteen minutes out that they had left Miltjan's canteen in the helicopter and that fever could easily dehydrate him. A cold panic gnawed at him. There was every possibility that he would die here and that he would take yet another life with him.

"This is it," Miltjan called from up ahead. "This is as close as we can get without going down the face. The *Walaritja* caves are—"

Raszer hustled up to his chattering guide and put a hand over his mouth. There was an echo, and it couldn't be coming from surrounding walls because there were none. They were on top of the rock, in thin air.

A trickle of perspiration ran down the bridge of Raszer's nose. He dropped to a squat and put a finger to his lips. The murmur continued. Voices. It wasn't an echo at all. Raszer turned his ear to the wind like a satellite dish and found the source. He motioned silently toward a dimple in the land, about twenty yards distant, where the bare rock appeared concave. He waved Miltjan around to the far side, and the two of them approached the bowl from opposing directions.

Ten feet from the perimeter, there was no longer any question. The depression was acting as a natural transducer, amplifying massed voices from within a chamber far below. Dozens of striations had been water-cut in the sloping stone over eons, some crisscrossing one another, like spokes on a prehistoric bicycle wheel. At the hub, there was an opening – a chimney – and that was where the sound was getting out. They moved into the deeply sloped dish, Miltjan following Raszer's lead, first on hands and knees and then on bellies.

Raszer put his ear to the opening. It was like the hushed chatter of tourists on a group tour of St. Peter's, or the sound of an orchestra tuning. There were random high notes, piccolos playing nervous little runs. Raszer stiffened. There were children down there.

Bracing his hands against the sides of the chimney, Raszer began to ease himself in, headfirst. Miltjan instinctively curled his fingers into the back of Raszer's khaki's and hooked his thumb under his belt.

Once his eyes had adjusted to the darkness, Raszer began to make out, far below, the firefly flickering of hundreds of votive candles. Amidst the twinkling lights were the shadowy forms of human beings, he couldn't say how many. *"Holy shit,"* he whispered in awe.

"Holy shit!" Miltjan howled, as he was seized by the roots of his bramble-bush hair. For a moment, he clung to Raszer's belt, and Raszer was thus hauled from the shaft, his chin raked over the serrated rock, and his fingertips – still tender from the Tower climb – scraped raw and bloody. He found himself and his guide held at gunpoint by four of the jump-suited guards. They had the look of North Africans, probably Tunisians, and they spoke a rough, guttural French as they frisked their captives, confiscating the .22, the .44 and Raszer's ankle knife.

A ROPE LADDER, staked in place by six-inch pitons, ran eighty feet down from an overhang to the massive ledge where Kinsey had originally attempted to land. They were ordered to descend the aluminum rungs, with guards bracketing each of them, top and bottom. It was not a maneuver for anyone with vertigo, as for most of the drop, the ladder hung in mid-air, removed from the fissured cliff face by an arm's length.

When they reached the sentry post, they were frisked again, handed over to a new crew and prodded up a steep, rocky path that cleaved a gorge into the heart of the monolith. In seconds, they were in shadow, and

Raszer understood why the guards, at first glance, had seemed to emerge from sheer stone.

The gorge and path terminated at a large A-shaped fissure that, at first, did not appear to run very deep. The sun had not yet cut above the horizon and the entire gorge was in deep shadow. The orifice revealed nothing beyond its opacity, but once led through, Raszer realized that it was a cave entrance. He cursed under his breath. When Mirrigau and his troops did arrive, they would be searching elevated places, not fucking caves. Raszer looked back at Miltjan, who was looking pretty lost for a fellow who'd spent twenty-one nights on the rock.

"Do you know this place?" Raszer asked.

The aborigine shook his head.

TEN FEET INTO the cavern, flashlights clicked on and they began a forty-five degree descent on a narrow walkway that seemed to Raszer to have step-like gradations, a distinctly non-aboriginal touch. After two or three hundred yards, the path ascended again and opened into a natural anteroom, not unlike Iron Age burial chambers Raszer had seen in more familiar parts of the world. Beyond it and through an oblique opening, Raszer could see the dance of light on the walls of a much larger chamber. They were instructed to remain in the "waiting room," under guard, while the others passed through the portal into the mother cave.

"What will they do to us?" Miltjan whispered.

Raszer eased down to the cavern floor and spoke clearly enough for anyone within earshot to hear. "Just pray that Superman gets here on time, Miltjan."

A shadowed figure appeared, speaking as one who holds the cards. "Superman is in a wheelchair," said the supercilious little Frenchman. Luc stepped into the chamber and regarded Raszer, for once, from a loftier height.

"How did you know I would come?" Raszer asked.

Luc approached and squatted to scoop a handful of red dust, letting it sift through his fingers. "I wasn't sure you would, but then I know you only as an imposter."

"It seems I can say the same of you," Raszer observed.

"Yes, well…in the end, we become the masks we wear, don't you agree? In any case, the behavior of men with human attachments is always predictable."

"How fortunate for you to not be burdened with those," Raszer said. "Where is she?"

"She is here, with us…where she belongs," Luc replied.

A man from the neighboring chamber called out a command in French. Despite the language, it was a voice whose timbre Raszer had no difficulty recognizing, for he had heard it only the day before. He'd already concluded that Alain Saint-Germain was yet another incarnation of the Temple's most notorious shape-shifter, Luc Fourché. When he spoke again, however, Raszer heard a slight *burr* in the "r," remembered from a limerick he'd once heard. He'd considered it, feared it, but until now he hadn't *known* it.

*Tout va bien, Jean-Paul?"* the voice asked. The diminutive Frenchman answered to the name, without removing his eyes from Raszer.

*"Oui. Tout va bien, Commandant."*

The tendons in Raszer's neck twitched as the tall, elegant man he'd met as Saint-Germain rounded the passage into the small chamber. The imposter who had just been identified as *Jean-Paul* turned respectfully.

"We have ten minutes at best, *Monsieur Fourché.* The portal will remain open only while the heliacal arc is visible."

*"Mahabyn,* Stephan. You are a long way from Hollywood."

Raszer stood and accepted the offered hand, though he had no illusion that friendship was intended. He simply had to congratulate the better liar.

"Hello, Stocker. Nice work. You ran circles around me with all those voices. Which one is the *real* you?"

Fourché parroted a perfect impression of Raszer's own voice. "Which one is the real *you,* Stephan?" The erstwhile Stocker Hinge flashed a continental smile, and Raszer understood how he'd be a formidable front man.

"Don't be too hard on yourself, Stephan," he purred. "We've been working undercover longer than you have. Seven hundred years of cloak and dagger…seven hundred years of hiding. You learn, Stephan."

"Can I ask," said Raszer, "who exactly you've been hiding from"

"Don't be coy, *mon frere.* Things haven't really changed much since the fourteenth century. A heretic is still a heretic: a man who sees the world in a way that is utterly at odds with what is acceptable. They may no longer cut out our tongues or burn our villages, but they hound us just the same, as terrorists, tax evaders or most odious of all…cultists. Unfortunately, in the case of the recent stewards of our cause, we have given them all too good a reason to do so. That is about to change for all eternity. We have you, in part, to thank for that."

"Great," said Raszer. "Why don't you thank me by giving me Sofia Gould? You're not going to get her husband's money. Killing her will only bring more heat down on you, and anyway Fourché, she's lost her faith. If she ever had it."

"Sofia is confused right now. *You* have confused her, Stephan, with your considerable charm and your ridiculous rabbi. Judaism was once a great faith, but it is a faith of the earth – a faith of blood and tribe and land. All these things are dead to us. Sofia has a cause to serve. My *compagnon—*" At the reference, Fourché gestured to Jean-Paul who waited anxiously in the shadows. "—was right to have singled her out long ago."

"Your cause is bogus," Raszer said, moving to within inches of Fourché's face. "Your cause is a *jihad* against life."

"Life is a mistake!" Fourché howled, and the certitude expressed was not comforting to a man succumbing to fever and battered from head to toe. "There are many paths, just as there are many histories and many universes. Speak of left and right, light and dark, if you insist on dichotomies, but leave right and wrong to the moralists, who are soon to be extinct. No, Stephan; I'm not going to give you Sofia."

He took Raszer's head in his hands, and the eyes that had been azure became fleetingly translucent, a window to the pale fire behind them.

"I'm going to give you what you really want...*what you came here for.*"

"And what," Raszer asked, his knees beginning to tremble in synch with his jaw, "would that be?"

"Gnosis."

Raszer swallowed a stream of bile. "Not your way, Fourché. No thanks." Raszer squinted hard. "Why did you save my life in the Gardens? Why did you let her come to me?"

"It was all," Fourché replied, "according to a plan greater than either you or I can puzzle out, Stephan. The Lodge is all wise. Look at it this way: the corruption of our Temple has been arrested, the vipers' nest destroyed and you are here because *she* brought you here." He placed his hands on Raszer's shoulders. "Can you say for certain that you would be if not for the time you shared with her? Come. Come with me. Your young friend, as well. Let me see if I can't lend you both a new perspective on *death*. If you hope to transcend it, it helps immeasurably to welcome it when it comes."

Fourché gently took Raszer by the elbow and led him and the party into the adjoining chamber. There was a natural "airlock" separating the two spaces. What appeared at first to be a solid rock wall dematerialized into holographic pixie dust on some manner of ultrasonic signal transmitted by a beeper-sized box in Fourché's hand. As they crossed the threshold into a cavern the size of a cathedral, Raszer gauged the surreal enormity of what lay before them by watching Miltjan's eyes swell in their sockets. That something like this could exist outside the knowledge of the aboriginals almost led Raszer to lapse into thinking the whole thing was an illusion.

The improbable centerpiece in the egg-shaped cavern was a perfect duplicate of the Tree of Isis that Raszer had disfigured in Prague, complete with its operator Dominic, and the remaining quartet of pilgrims from Prague, minus one Klipp sister. Two seats at the wheel were unoccupied.

Raszer quickly surveyed the yawning crypt to its shadowed perimeter, secured every twenty-feet or so by an Uzi-wielding guard. Sofia was nowhere to be seen.

"What have you done with her?" Raszer asked.

"She'll be arriving presently," replied Fourché, steering Raszer and Miltjan along the left-hand wall.

Orbiting the Tree in three concentric circles of twelve each were thirty-six human beings, gathered expectantly as if for some nihilistic Sermon on the Mount. Some of the younger and more limber ones held *falun gong* positions. The older members of the congregation – all of them women – sat cross-legged or knelt. These were the dowagers, the fount of the Temple's wealth. Raszer searched for the small voices he'd heard from above and found three of them, clinging to their mothers. He turned sharply to Fourché.

"Why children?" he spat. "The Cathar *Endura* was reserved for people at the end of their lives, for those who had made their peace. You've perverted their sacrament, you son of a bitch."

"It's *our* sacrament, Stephan. We revere the Cathar *parfaits,* and we use portions of the liturgy—"

"The Voynich Manuscript," Raszer interjected.

Fourché nodded. "But these are different times. These are children whose mothers do not wish for them to come of age in an irredeemably toxic world, to struggle for the illusion of well being only to end up riddled with debt and cancer. Your own daughter, Mr. Raszer, will probably not make twenty without suffering some form of auto-immune disorder, to say nothing of her mental health…particularly given her patrimony."

Raszer stopped in his tracks so abruptly that Miltjan was taken by surprise and plowed into his back. He had never said a word to Stocker Hinge about his youthful brush with madness.

"Who the hell are you?" Raszer demanded, spooked right down to the marrow of his bones. Fourché made the sign of the cross, only with an extra station: forehead, plexus, left, right…and hands cupped above his brow in the shape of a circle. Raszer connected the dots…*was it the Monad?*

"I am with you always, Stephan. Even unto the end of time."

"Bullshit!" Raszer roared, loud enough to alert one of the guards to attention. He pointed at the Tree of Isis, just now beginning to hum and glow as it gathered its charge for the final jolt. "Your elixir of death is nothing but salt water!" He turned halfway to the assembled faithful and shouted, "The whole thing is a fucking show!"

Fourché's strong hand gripped the back of his neck; its thumb and forefinger were right on pressure points. He spoke softly.

"There is not a religion on earth that does not practice *leger demain.* Real miracles are exceedingly rare in this abased world, Stephan. Three, perhaps, of significance in what passes for 'Western history:' Enoch's ascent, the apotheosis of Christ and…" He drew breath sharply through his flared, aristocratic nostrils and let it stand, leaving Raszer to assume that the third miracle was his own return from the house of the dead. "If we are favored, you may see another today."

Raszer and Miltjan were guided to a place in the innermost circle, just in front of a long, low altar, draped with a white cloth emblazoned with a red Templar cross. Upon the altar were four oversized ceramic urns with hieroglyphic design, and two neat stacks of large, earthenware bowls, glazed the color of lapis lazuli, the color of the Queen of Heaven. He ordered them to sit, whispered some instructions to Jean-Paul and a member of the Australian contingent, and then squatted for a moment at Raszer's side. He cocked his head, as if to say, *any more questions, bright boy?*

"Tell me something," Raszer obliged. "Did I ever meet your Mr. X?"

"You met Mr. X," he replied with a smile. "You just didn't happen to meet Philippe Caudal."

Raszer nodded privately. He'd been had every step of the way.

"Caudal, who died for the cause, right?" Raszer asked. *"Your work?"*

"That was Montreal's doing. Philippe's intentions were good but he overreached. He will be remembered as a martyr."

A string of synapses fired in Raszer's brain as he recalled a critical time frame when "Stocker Hinge" had been AWOL.

"And Jeanette Molinieux?" he asked. "How will we remember her?"

Fourché brushed the cavern's dust off his hands. "We are at war, Stephan. All wars have victims. Noel Branch's flight set off a necessary chain of events that led to this very moment. Perhaps it's fitting to consider her a martyr to the cause of your illumination."

Raszer dropped his head. For the first time in many years, he uttered the Eastern Jesus prayer, the simple sentence that had been the sustenance of so many desert mystics before him, the prayer that ends with the words, "forgive me."

"Now," said Fourché, "we will have to resume our discussion in another world. *She* is coming and, as any woman, she demands full attention."

"Just one more thing," Raszer said, as Fourché turned to leave.

"For a man about to have all his questions answered, you're very curious."

"If you've forsaken the earth…if you're building your Lodge in Heaven, or Sirius, or wherever it is, why keep company with all these monarchists? *SAC, P2, Hapsburgs, the Priory of Sion…* What's it to you who rules a wasted planet?"

"Think, Stephan. You've studied the Work. *As above, so below.* I care nothing for earthly power. I can't speak for all, but when we are on earth, we require leave to work without the interference of the ignorant. A lobbyist curies favor with a politician; a knight with his lord. It is a far more straightforward business to secure imprimatur from a monarch than from a so-called 'democrat,' and the lines of authority are never in doubt with fascists, however distasteful their company. I will leave to the Gnomes of Zurich to decide whether the crown falls to the Hapsburgs or to Jean-Paul's Merovingian suitors. I have fealty only to the White Lodge."

"The Nazis? Did you curry favor with them as well? Do you still?"

"We made a deal," Fourché said flatly. "As the American CIA made a deal with the Mafia. Their common enemy? Castro. Our common enemy…?"

"I guess," Raszer said, "that would have to be the Jews."

"Not the Jews, so much as the edifice they had built and the apostasy they embraced. The Jews finally paid interest on their betrayal. In gold bullion. As always, we were able to rely upon the discretion of the Swiss."

At the altar, Jean-Paul and two Australians were preparing to dispense the Eucharistic wine, which Raszer suspected would have chemical similarities to Jonestown Kool-Aid. He watched as, one by one, they filled the lapis-tinted bowls with a tawny, semi-viscous liquid.

Fourché stood and allowed himself to be draped with the robe of the celebrant. Like the altar cloth, it bore the Jerusalem cross. He turned and leaned in to Raszer, as if inviting him to share in a great confidence.

"The communion wine is a solution of potassium chloride and English Yew. It's fast acting and reasonably painless. The Yew causes paralysis and the PCL stops the heart. There is just enough of a jolt to rend spirit from flesh with the necessary force. The rest is the work of the liturgy, the Lodge and the umbilicus that connects us with our Mother. The guards have instructions to abate any suffering with a bullet to the brain, so you needn't be unduly concerned for the children."

Raszer's vocal cords were incapable of response; his sweat smelled of iron and his fever had returned with a vengeance. He had been stripped of his press passes; his observer status had been terminated. He was going to die, too. Paradoxically, the very certainty of that gave him a moment's peace. The deep lapis of the bowls drew his eyes. The color of the Virgin's robe. Like Sofia, like others of medieval sensibility, Raszer had always kept a special place in his heart for the ideal of Mary: intercessor, healer, antidote to vengeful Yaweh. In the silent space that opened in his mind, he caught a glimpse of her lapis robes. God was in there, too; a floating eye regarding him with the mute, expressionless gaze of an infant, or an idiot.

Raszer felt a gentle but insistent tapping on his left shoulder. Miltjan's clenched and trembling hand opened to reveal a fistful of glistening, biscuit-brown mushrooms. He'd stuffed the baggie in his pants, and the tender fungi must have felt enough like a young man's privates to pass the frisk. Raszer raised his eyes slowly from the mushrooms to the boy's grave but remarkably serene face.

"Put your mouth to my hand," Miltjan whispered urgently, "and eat. It is at least fifty milligrams. In twenty minutes, you will vomit *anything* you have in your stomach. Then, you will get very high, but you will be alive. Do it, my friend. Good poison drives out bad."

"Let's hope," Raszer croaked, "for our sake that good angels drive out bad ones, as well."

Miltjan returned a puzzled look that melted into comprehension. "Oh, yes man; it does. We are in a holy place. The ancestors will come…now eat!"

Raszer flinched as the odor of ferment from the mushrooms entered his nostrils, then took a deep breath and sucked the entire heap into his mouth. The heavy alkaline taste was enough to make him vomit then and there, but he bit down hard on impulse. The mushrooms had the consistency of garden slugs, but Raszer had eaten enough French food to deal with that. Miltjan fed Raszer, and then he fed himself. It was all done within a minute's time.

Raszer returned his attention to the main stage, where a few things had changed. The little Frenchman had now filled one of the unoccupied seats at the Tree, whether as reward or punishment he couldn't begin to guess. Still, one seat remained empty and Raszer felt a wave of nausea that was not yet the onset of the psylocibin. *Where the hell was Sofia?* He began to work a little hermeneutic exercise in his head. Excluding Sam Mirrigau's arrival with an army of hell-bent aborigines; excluding divine intervention; excluding entirely the possibility that Luc Fourché *was* divine, how could he utilize the little needles that remained nestled against his chest to bring this whole thing down? A thick bank of what appeared as fog began to billow from the base of the Tree. *Jesus,* Raszer thought, it comes with a built-in fog machine.

Fourché padded to his side for one final appeal. He dropped to one knee and took Raszer's chin in his elegant hand.

"I can make a place in the Lodge for you, Stephan," he purred. "I can give you Consolamentum right now, if you'll accept it."

Raszer observed the thickening fog and looked his nemesis straight in the eye. He was feeling a little giddy. "Are the special effects any better up there?"

"The fog is imbued with pentathol," Fourché replied. "To calm the flock."

"There once was a man named Fourché," Raszer sneered. "Who promised to show us the way." He hiccupped. "He spoke real fine, and his dress was divine…but his feet were both made out of clay." He swallowed a sour belch. "No way, Fourché," he said. "You know what the *real* Gnostics say, don't you?"

Tell me, Professor."

"If you can't trust the priest, you can't trust the religion."

"Go to Hell then, Stephan," said Fourché. He stepped to the altar and took in his hands a large, leather-bound book and held it aloft before the congregation. Was it the Temple's transliteration of the Voynich Manuscript or their gloss on John Dee's angelic evocations?

"This is the book of the Endura!" he boomed, his commanding voice ricocheting off the cavern walls. "MICMA ADOIAN MAD!"

The pilgrims roared their rehearsed response with a fervor that took Raszer completely by surprise.

"ODO CICLE Q`AA: OD OZOZMA PLAPLI IADNAMAD!"

This is the place of the first visitation of the Ascended Masters!"

"ZACAR OD ZAMRAN!"

"This is the place where the first seed was planted, that it might grow within us and bind us to Her; that the elect among us might one day awaken and feel the root within our bellies. That we might seek to return the rose full grown to She who made it!"

Again, the response. "OECRIMI Q-A-DAH!"

The Australian Templars, accompanied by armed guards, were now moving out from the altar into the congregation, carrying the newly filled bowls of terminal soup. They stationed themselves at evenly placed intervals amidst the flock and held the bowls aloft.

A pale streak of color off to Raszer's left caught his eye, the impress-
sion of salmon pink lingering on his retina like a time exposure photograph. It was the fact that the smear of color remained with him even after
blinking that told him he was already beginning to hallucinate, *but its source
was no hallucination.*

A little girl, about his daughter's age, was staring from behind a curtain of chestnut-colored curls. At his glance, she quickly turned back to her
mother, revealing the pink ribbon tied in her hair. Raszer rubbed his eyes.
He was somehow certain that she was the little girl he'd seen on the banks
of the Vltava. She was staring at him again. Her eyes were large jewels of
hazel, and they were talking to him.

Fourché's stentorian voice ripped his attention momentarily back to
center stage.

"What is the true message of Enoch?" he bellowed to his followers.

*"Come! Be like unto us!"*

"What is the true message of the Christos?" he incanted.

*"Come! Be like unto us!"*

"What is the true message of Saint-Germain?"

*"Come! Be like unto us!"*

"THIS IS THE WORD OF THE ROSE ET CROIX! THIS IS THE
CALL TO ARISE!" He threw his arms in the air and trembled with the
practiced passion of a televangelist. A wave of Dionysian hysteria ran
through the crowd as they canted in unison.

*"Torzu! Torzu! Torzu! Torzu!"*

Like offering plates, the bowls containing the poison were handed off
to a "deacon" at the end of each row, who was to serve the communicants.
The pilgrims were exhorted all the while to maintain the pitch of their fervor by continuing to chant *"Torzu!"* In Raszer's increasingly overheated
mind, the chorus took on overtones that cascaded throughout the reverberant chamber. The Tree of Isis, too, was emitting a pitched drone and
beginning to radiate the same phosphor glow he'd seen in the Tower. He
surmised that its passengers had received their final dose sometime during
the night, if indeed it mattered, and were now preparing to be transmuted
– or incinerated – by the torrent of sub-atomic particles that would tear
through their bloodstreams at any moment. Among them, only poor Lisbeth Klipp – who had been deprived of her twin – looked distraught.

Raszer loosened a button on his shirt and slipped his left hand inside.

His belly began to swell as the mushrooms took hold. A foretaste of
nausea entered his mouth, and his gag reflex kicked in. He had to hold it
down until he'd swallowed the poison or he was a dead man.

He glanced back at the little girl, whose forehead was pressed into her mother's shoulder. For the first time, the mother returned his gaze, and he saw dread in her expression. This was not a woman going gently into the night. The communal bowl was passed to her. As she held it in trembling hands, she turned once more to look at him, almost as if to ask his blessing, or perhaps to ask something else. Raszer removed the needle case from the hidden pocket, drew his hand out of his shirt and dropped the case into his lap.

When Raszer looked back at the little girl, the mother had taken her share of the poison, and the guard now motioned for her to administer to her daughter. In a sequence they must have rehearsed, on the off chance that there would be a single moment of grace, the girl took the bowl in her hands and emptied the remainder into her mouth. After she handed the bowl back to the guard, she hugged her mother about the waist, laid her cheek against her shoulder and dribbled the contents of her mouth down the dark fabric of her mother's blouse.

Raszer quickly turned away so as not to direct attention to the small miracle, but not before she rolled her eyes up from her last filial embrace, shot him a faint, wan smile and entered his heart by way of the single, narrow beam of indigo that connected her right eye with his own.

Raszer turned his head down, and his light shone on the little case. Keeping one eye on the altar, he opened it and selected the most lethal of the tiny darts, then inserted it into one of the miniaturized blowguns. The tubes were lightly sealed with resin on the firing end, which allowed them to be hidden temporarily in the shooter's cheek without immediate risk of self-annihilation. Kept in the mouth too long, however, saliva would dissolve the resin, and the rest was a matter of bad odds at best. They were better odds, though, than Raszer figured he had with the wine, in spite of Miltjan's confident folk medicine.

Raszer glanced up. Sofia's seat was still empty. His hand would not stop shaking. He brought the loaded blowgun to his mouth, his palsy so fierce that he nearly missed the orifice altogether. When he had it parked, he put his arm around Miltjan's neck and waited his turn.

The deacon came to Raszer with a freshly filled bowl, dipped a ladle and put it to Raszer's mouth. The acidic fruit juice base stung his chapped lips like a swarm of bees. *Oh Christ*, he thought. It will dissolve the resin in a second.

Suddenly, there was a hand on the deacon's wrist. Raszer rolled his eyes up into Fourché's face. In the moment of his anticipated poisoning, he hadn't noticed that the preacher had stopped preaching. The congregation continued to chant, though some voices had grown noticeably weaker. Fourché locked in on Raszer's eyes and smiled.

"Continue on," he said to the deacon, steering his hand toward a terrified Miltjan. I'll take this one from here."

Raszer narrowed his eyes. "Don't even think of saving my life, Fourché," he said. "You're not the kind of man I want to owe for eternity."

"Oh no, Stephan," said Fourché, hauling him up roughly by his elbow. "I'm not saving your life. I'm saving your soul."

Using his thumb, he wiped the caustic juice from Raszer's lips and led him to the empty place at the Tree.

MONICA SLAMMED THE phone into its cradle and paced. She lit one of Raszer's cigarettes and placed it in the ashtray next to the one she had already lit. Monica had been unable to raise anyone at the Anangu Council Headquarters. She twisted the dark roots of her surfer-girl hair. There had been a quaint, warbled message on the machine informing that Councilman Mirrigau would return all calls of importance "within good time." There was no one at the tiny airport; even the local police were said to be out on call.

She glared at the hand-written sign that Raszer had thumbtacked above her desk. *No Federales! Remember Waco!* It read. "Okay, Raszer," she said aloud. "But I've got to do something."

She scanned across the row of binders on the bookshelf until she found one labeled "NGO's." She opened it, and flipped through to the listing for the International Red Cross in Darwin, Australia. In her present state of knowledge, neither the irony of the organization's symbol nor its country of origin was apparent to her.

RASZER WATCHED HELPLESSLY from his place at the merry-go-round as Fourché continued to exhort his dying audience. He gestured toward the Tree of Isis as if it were the new Ark of the Covenant, and stepped aside with a cry of *"Goholor! Goholor!"* to allow the machine to take the limelight. Raszer, guarded on each side, and with a three-inch hypodermic needle in each of his wrists, looked up to see the magnificent spiral coil atop the machine vibrating so rapidly that it had become a virtual smear of charging atoms. A light erupted from the center of the coil with such focused intensity that it appeared more solid than the machine itself. It was aimed directly at the dome of the cavern, and the narrow chimney into which Raszer had earlier crawled.

Dominic, at his console, had his hand on the largest lever, the one that was designed to deliver the final jolt to those hapless knights gathered at this round table, in whose company Raszer now sat. He had the blow-gun in his mouth, the resin prophylactic rapidly dissolving, but he didn't yet have a plan for its deployment. Maximum effect for minimum effort was needed.

It appeared to Raszer, although his perception was profoundly al-tered, that a number of the older parishioners were already dead or in deep shock. Many were in paroxysms brought on by what must have been ex-cruciating cramps, no less painful that a diver's bends. Somewhere in the sea of writhing forms, Raszer heard a little boy cry out in French, "Please Papa, please! Make it stop!" and in that frozen moment of becoming, he knew where the heart of evil lay: in human self-loathing. Evil was a *meme* implanted in our cognitive systems, like a virus, through every doctrine ever perpetuated about the "fall of man" or "original sin." Evil was the grass is/was greener; it was not living in the unfolding *now*.

Fourché raised his arms to the dome. The deacons moved among the dead and dying, ordering those still able to stand to get to their feet and hail the event they had traded their lives and traveled half the globe for. He announced the arrival of the Mother Ship with a strident cry.

*"Isiteth Vadaik! Ailiater Kecheth! She is among us!"*

He threw his head back and pointed to the apex of the cavern, where the blinding light pulsed with such ferocity that Raszer, his pupils wildly enlarged from the effect of the entheogen, could not look through the pen-tathol-laden fog for more than two seconds at a time. Curiously, the psy-choactive mushrooms had both neutralized and been balanced by the soporific effects of the pentathol, as he was very much awake.

He shot a glance at Miltjan, who had vomited all over his Hendrix jacket, and then regarded the womb-portal again. It dilated to receive the column-like beam shooting up from the coil and in return, began to deliver the goods. The deacons came round to drape white linen shrouds over the shoulders of Raszer and his five cohorts. Fourché approached to deliver a final benediction and locked eyes with Raszer, who at that moment made his one and only choice.

Suddenly a woman cried out, *"It's Her! It's Her! She's come!"* and the others moaned their gratitude. Raszer's attention was torn from his course of action to the ceiling, where his battered senses informed him that a spectral and diaphanous, but distinctly feminine form was gracefully float-ing down along the shaft of strobing light. Miltjan, on all fours and retching again, managed to look up for long enough to register his own amazement.

*Now*, said Raszer's brain. He locked the little blowgun between his teeth and called out for the guard nearest him, who held his rifle at the ready.

"Hey," he said with clenched jaw. "Can you ask Mr. Fourché to come here?"

The guard blinked and wrinkled his brow. In the cacophony, he clearly hadn't understood a word. He edged a foot closer. Raszer tipped his head to urge him a step further.

"What's that?" the guard said.

"I want the C-C-Consolamentum," Raszer said, mush-mouthed. "Fourché…"

Can't hear you, sir," the guard said, obviously irritated as he came to within six inches of Raszer's face.

Raszer rolled the tube onto his tongue and prodded it gently forward between his teeth. From the corner of his eye, he saw Dominic's hand begin to draw down the lever.

"The Consola— The Co—"

Closer still the guard came, and Raszer drew a bead on the solid black pupil in the center of his left eye. "Aw," he whispered, drawing back his lips to expose his loaded teeth. "F-f-fuck it!"

And with the force of that fricative, the dart flew home to its target. The guard staggered back, a needle planted in his eye. Raszer leapt from the stool onto the cavern floor, and wrenched the rifle from the dying man's hands before he dropped. He pulled the left IV from his wrist, then the right. The unbuckling of the leather straps that tethered him to the machine would have to wait for one more important piece of business. He pivoted back to the right, raised the sight to his eye and found the place in Dominic's torso where a heart ought to be.

SUDDENLY, THE ENTIRE cavern was shot through with a blast of white light the amplitude of a nuclear explosion. Raszer squinted and fired off three rounds, missing the heart but hitting Dominic's shoulder, enough to put him off-task for the moment.

Raszer shielded his eyes and stumbled backwards, squinting up through the glare to the Tree's amorphous crown. *She*, The One, the Intercessor, the mistress of the solar boat had descended to the coil and was revolving slowly, her arms held out to her flock, like some divine music box figurine. The lustrous folds of her royal purple gown were just visible through her blinding radiance. Three Temple guards came charging toward Raszer from his left, but for a moment, he could not take his eyes off Her.

The facial features were completely washed out in the brilliance, but in the instant before he wheeled around to face the advancing pack, he caught a glimpse of the raven-black tresses that fell to her silk-covered shoulders. He had no time to consider the wizardry involved. He fired another round and dropped one of the guards.

Miltjan, having puked everything he'd eaten in the last week, staggered to his feet. He found his way haphazardly among the fallen victims, seized the guard's weapon and joined Raszer in a crossfire that silenced the other two guns. Then, wild-eyed, he came to Raszer's side. He quickly undid the wrist straps and looked him in the eye.

"There are more of them than there are of us," he said.

"I know," Raszer answered. "Pray for the ancestors. Can you hear me okay?"

"I can hear way too good. The animal of my dreaming is a dingo."

"Good. Mine's a crow, so I got the eyes and you got the ears."

The *mise en scene* was so thoroughly obscured by light, fog and the hallucinogenic play of their minds that, despite the acuity of their respective power animals, neither tracked the movement across the cathedral floor of the high priest himself. Luc Fourché had his priorities. He strode calmly amid the pandemonium to the abandoned console, pulled the lever and sent the remaining five pilgrims to Kingdom Come.

At one and the same instant, Raszer heard the report of gunshots echo off the chamber's walls. The explosion of flare guns, their brilliant arcs sailing two, three, four at a time on a trajectory across the cave, followed. From the cavern's mouth came random shouts in an ancient language, and Miltjan's face lit up.

"It's Sam!" he cried. "It's the rangers!"

Raszer allowed himself a deep breath. This, more than the transubstantiation of flesh into vapor, was the miracle he'd prayed for.

WITH SCORCHED-EARTH ruthlessness, the Temple guards moved in to dispatch the living with point-blank shots to the head before any could be saved. The Australian acolytes began splashing the perimeter with gasoline, dousing both stone and flesh with equal diligence.

Raszer gripped Miltjan's arm and coaxed him down into a crouch. "It's not over yet," he said, squinting through the miasma for some sign of the small girl who had evaded communion. He found her curled into her dead mother's side, playing possum, but with one eye conspicuously open.

"See if you can make it along the right hand wall," Raszer whispered to Miltjan, "before they torch the place. Hook up with your guys. Tell them I still don't have Sofia." He looked back over his shoulder. The goddess apparition was gone. "Fuck!" he said and swept his eye across the cavern for some sign of Sofia.

The Sirian Queen wasn't the only thing missing from her station. At the positions formerly occupied by Jean-Paul and the German woman named Sonia, the linen shrouds had crumpled to the chair backs, empty of human form, and gave off a faint radioactive glow. Had the little Frenchman indeed gone through the wormhole, or had some high tech hoax been practiced?

The other three were less successful. Two of them – Masson, the Alsatian banker and Robert Perrault, the ski champion – were slumped, still shrouded over their lecterns, physically intact but well cooked internally. Poor Lisbeth Klipp had, it seemed, had good reason to look worried, for as far as Raszer could tell from the evidence of organic matter splattered over various parts of the simmering machine, she had been blown to bits. Of the elegant trickster who called himself Luc Fourché, there was no sign.

Raszer surveyed the entire area. The only visible exit from the chamber was the way they'd come in, and Sam Mirrigau's rangers blockaded that. If Sofia Gould had somehow hovered over the Tree of Isis, then Raszer could only presume that she, along with the master of ceremonies, had been hoisted out through the chimney. If so, it was an event that, despite the mushroom's stretching of space and time, he could not imagine having occurred without his notice. There was only one way to go now, and that was to try and get back to the top of the rock before Fourché and his hostage were spirited away by a revived Jack Kinsey, if not by more miraculous means. Raszer sent Miltjan sprinting to the right to join the posse, checked his rifle load and headed off to the left with the exit passage his final destination. Before he got there, however, there was unfinished business.

Raszer knelt beside the little girl in the center of what had become a ring of fire, one hundred feet in diameter.

"Will you come with me?" Raszer asked, extending his hand.

"I don't want to leave my mommy," the little girl said in French.

Raszer looked at the woman and put two fingers to her neck. Her convulsions had stilled. There was only a faint and fading pulse. Then, that too was gone. All was still in their immediate vicinity, but there was fire on all sides and sporadic exchanges of gunfire continued to erupt. He drew the girl to his chest and held her.

"She's in Heaven now," Raszer said, in the best French he could muster. *"Elle et avec les anges."*

Cradling the rifle under his left arm, he lifted her over his right shoulder and staggered to his feet. He could no longer see the exit passage, but he could see a spot where the smoke appeared to be venting. He took off running for that target, weaving between the bodies of Luc Fourché's victims. Some were still fighting their life's last struggle with *thanatos;* most had already lost. Among the latter was the small boy who had begged his daddy to stop the pain. He was dressed in knickers and a matching jacket that bore the emblem of his private school.

A black-suited guard emerged from the billowing smoke, disoriented. Raszer leveled the barrel of his rifle like a lance and knocked him off his feet. A bullet screamed by his left shoulder and another hit the cavern wall to his right. Sweat poured down his brow in a torrent, stinging his eyes and blurring his vision, but the psilocybin's grip on his mind allowed him to exercise will that he never would have possessed sober. It allowed him to take time. *Time is ours to bend as we wish,* old Sam Mirrigau had said.

Six of Mirrigau's rangers rushed past, headed into the vortex. Raszer took it as a sign he must be nearing the exit. The fiery perimeter was just ahead, and Raszer dove through the flames, the girl pressed against his heaving chest.

A draft of cool, morning air brushed his face. A hint of blue daylight. He leapt, left foot first, into the exit passage, just as the air behind his left ear rippled. A bullet whistled through hair and tissue, burning a wedge through the rim of his ear. His overtaxed ankle finally gave way with a *crunch* as he came down hard on loose rock. He pushed the girl toward the safety of the exit and saw her pink ribbon catch the sunlight just before he pitched into the red dust and blacked out.

# 22

## THE WHITE LODGE

STEPHAN RASZER HAD visited many sublimely quiet places in his life; it was his nature to seek them out -- the High Sierra around Mt. Whitney in the cool pink light of late afternoon, the Utah desert. None of them could compare to the soundlessness of *this place*. Even the hot wind rushing past his ears was without a voice. All around was nothing but pale turquoise the shade of a Navaho rug, and so it was not until he hit a thermal and was suddenly lofted up that he realized he was flying. Rust-colored earth curved gently thousands of feet below, its buttes and plateaus collapsed from this height into the benign features of an ancient face. He felt ballast pulling against his ascent and looked down his body to observe that a young girl lay curled in his arms sleeping, a pink ribbon flapping noiselessly from her hair like a streamer. He was taking her somewhere; that much he knew. He saw Vaclav Havel's face, formed by a series of sharp ridges, and flew down for a closer look. The heavy eyebrows of jagged rock rose and arched, directing him westward.

Over the ridge, the land began to green and soften into rolling waves of mounded earth with occasional stands of trees and Moroccan weaves of wildflower. He began to glean chalky white lines cut through the skin of the planet like giant hieroglyphs, lines that seemed to merge at the horizon.

The tiny, purple-robed figure of a surveyor caught his attention. He swooped down to call to the bearded scholar he recognized as Dr. John Dee. The good doctor raised an arm and pointed west.

Far off in the distance, where earth met sea, he spied a landmass with the shape of an old mantle clock, a head-like hump flanked by extended arms. All the lines in the earth converged upon it, and the keenness of his sight and the certainty with which he soared alerted him to a change in his own form. He looked left and right and observed the polished blue-black sheen of his crow's wings skillfully riding the tailwind. Beneath him, his package was no longer a young girl but a baby, swaddled in white linen. Between his coal black eyes, in the space within his avian skull, a gyroscope spun, generating a frequency that held him on course. It was the only sound he was aware of. As it became more coherent, he recognized it as the first name of God, looping round and round like a tape edit mantra. He knew the moment he heard it that it was never to be spoken.

As he drew closer, the gentle landform on the horizon displayed, engraved in its chalk soil, a spiral glyph. The spiral lay at the center of what distinctly resembled a reclining feminine form. *The White Lodge*, he said in his dream.

He began to hear from afar the murmur of voices and felt some distant part of him being touched. The mound of earth before him heaved voluptuously, and the spiral spun open like an iris. He dove into the blackness – to keep his promise – and heard Miltjan's voice from the other side saying, "Leave him. He is having his 'dreaming.'" It was only then that he became aware of the riot of voices and activity that was taking place all around him. Not long after, he felt himself being lifted and carried out into the light, the old man's cool hand on his head.

From time to time, he felt Mirrigau's long, slender fingers dancing over his face. The darkness before his mind's eye was suddenly speckled pale blue like a robin's egg. He was gliding through an ether that rippled as he flew and seemed woven from threads of light. At the heart of nothing was a warm radiance, the ember of a fire lit long ago, and as he pierced through the innermost veil, the fantastical yet familiar face of an androgynous being of surpassing beauty and tenderness was revealed. Its upturned palms were raised to offer a landing strip, and he swooped in to release the sleeping infant he held securely in his talons. The baby was laid in a nest of sage and wildflower, and opened its eyes to curiously regard him as he flew away. After that, his body was flooded with the warmth of blood freshly pulsing through his limbs, and he awoke in the full red sun of the Australian desert, with Miltjan and Sam Mirrigau at his sides.

"The girl…" he stammered. "The little girl…"

"She be okay now, Mr. Raszer." Sam Mirrigau pointed to a makeshift medical tent surrounded by a small fleet of jeeps and a paramedic van from the Alice Springs clinic. Some distance further, a Red Cross chopper had landed. "And, we found your lady. Mrs. Gould. They are taking her to the hospital in Perth, sir…where you will be going soon." He looked at his watch. "Should be leaving the airport anytime now with Nimbo."

Raszer tried to lift his head but instantly crashed back to earth. "Where was she, Sam? Where did you find her?"

Miltjan broke in, still high as a kite. "They had her in a chamber beneath the big cave. All dress up and out of her head, man."

I have not seen anything like it in my life," said Sam, who had had a very long life. "It was a chamber of mirrors. What you call, I believe, a *camera obscura.*" He pressed his thumbs gently to Raszer's eyelids. "You rest now, Mr. Raszer," he said, "and finish your dreaming."

# 23

## SOLVE ET COAGULA

*And only the Hebrews and the sacred books of Hermes
tell of these things concerning the Man of Light and
his guide, the Son of God,
and concerning the earthly Adam and his guide Antimimos,
who blasphemously calls himself the Son of God
to lead men astray.*

— From the Gnostic philosopher Zosimos

RASZER QUIETLY CLOSED the leather binder of the NSA briefing book and stared absently for a moment into the boughs of a spruce tree that graced the small front yard of his home and office on Whitley Terrace in Hollywood. His mind had been drifting a lot lately; the art of concentration would have to be relearned. The lapses frightened him at first, spawning little demons of worry that the shock and infection he'd sustained might somehow have damaged his brain, but a shrink in Sherman Oaks had recently diagnosed it as post-traumatic stress disorder. That at least gave him the comfort of psychological currency. He was more at ease with the various forms of madness than physical ailments, which somehow seemed nastier and more final. His drift was arrested by the touch of his daughter Brigit, who had come over from the other side of the wraparound balcony, where she'd been drawing while he read. She ran her finger up the stubble on his face and over the V-shaped nick that the bullet had carved in his left ear.

"Bat-Dad," she chirped, alluding to the nearly identical notches in each ear, one from the bullet and one from De Boer's bite. His doctor had suggested cosmetic surgery, but for the moment Raszer thought he'd remain Bat-Dad.

It was the twenty-first of December, a year to the day since the deaths in the Alpine wilderness had first brought the Temple of the Sun the kind of international notoriety that nearly always presages a big fall for anything less than genuine. Six months exactly from the date on which Raszer had nearly lost his head in discovering that, in fact, reindeer really do know how to fly.

It was nearly Christmas. The winter holidays in sunny California were intrinsically weird. Spandex-clad joggers galloped past scrawny Latino Salvation Army bell-ringers, and twinkling lights were strung over succulents bone dry from the autumn drought. Raszer loved it anyway. It was – and he was sure it always had been – a time of pausing, a time when anything seemed possible. Orion's silver belt shone across the heavens on clear night after clear night. Sirius, the Dog Star, was up there, too. Somehow, in her benign radiance, Raszer thought it unlikely that she would ever countenance settlers like Luc Fourché. In L.A. winter, the daylight turns bluish and the late afternoon shadows get longer. The winds that roar down through the canyons at night – even the devilishly hot Santa Ana's – have a ferocity that knows no other season. Brigit would often beg to go to the beach, and then express bewilderment when he explained that one didn't go to the beach in *wintertime*. It had taken him some time to realize that winter in L.A. was largely a metaphorical state.

The forty-odd pages of U.S. National Security Agency summary he had just concluded had come to him after many months of pressing his Freedom of Information Act claim, with co-claimants that included various think tanks as well as an endorsement from the President of the Czech Republic. He'd begun the process while still in a hospital bed in Perth, and he'd continued hounding the Feds through two months of recuperation in a retreat south of Mexicali. He had needed the time to re-orient his visual faculties and learn to live with vertigo. Although the bullet had done no serious damage in its passage through the back of his skull, it had torn up enough nerves to sideline him for a while.

With all he had seen and experienced in Prague and Alice Springs, he had still felt the need for some official certification of the existence of phenomena so far out in left field, something with a U.S. Government stamp on it. So, after being forced to sign an affidavit that made disclosure tantamount to treason and obligated him to years of expert witness duty, Washington had finally released to him the NSA Inquiry Into the Scientific Relevance of the so-called Voynich Manuscript. The study concluded that the manuscript had been composed using an exquisite double-cipher of the type that medieval minds had the time and superhuman discipline to create. It was both a prayer book, whose obscure poetry effectively hid from Catholic inquisitors the heretical nature of the liturgy, *and* a metaphysical how-to manual that appeared to guide its adepts in travel through any number of parallel universes. Sixty percent of the text was pure window dressing, and that dodge had thrown off generations of would-be translators. In order to make any sense of it, you first had to determine which particular words and letters were significant. That required a sorting process that could only now be accomplished by super-computers like those the NSA had at its disposal. How then, had the information been encrypted in the first place, way back in the Dark Ages? The truly mind-blowing thing was that the code seemed to be binary in nature. The baffled chairman of the NSA task force had been forced to admit the theoretical possibility that the manuscript's 12th century authors had received their data *from the future*.

Although the study that Raszer had obtained dated from the 1970's, it also revealed that enough had been known about the *Voynich* as far back as the 1940's to have led to the so-called *Philadelphia* and *Montauk Experiments*, familiar to the Internet's paranoid chat room fringe. In one of those top-secret experiments, an entire U.S. destroyer with full crew aboard had purportedly been made to disappear into another "dimension" and rematerialize unscathed. Quite an effective radar shield. The Navy had apparently deemed the procedure too risky for wartime use, but it left no wonder as to why the Nazis had been cutting deals left and right with the Temple's baronial custodians. As a side note to its discussion of parallel universes, the government's study seemed to allow for the possibility of "walk-ins." Raszer liked that one. Curiously, there was no mention of Enoch's Portal.

Raszer was now one of those rare individuals who had been allowed to peer into the holy of holies. The distinction did not put him entirely at ease. It was a little bit like having a Mafia foot soldier confide to you that he'd helped kill the president. Privileged knowledge carried risks, and as Havel had said, it also created monsters. He was, however, very comfortable with his attitude *toward* the knowledge. So what if you could use quantum physics to blow yourself into a parallel universe?

He looked out at the sun-gilded crests of the pines on the nearby hills, inhaled the bouquet of eucalyptus and wood smoke rising from the canyon and wondered, *was there anything wrong with this one?* God was alive in this domain as well as the next. And even if the other realms were, in some way, more sublime, he had a strong suspicion that killing and defrauding people to get there would have a karmic downside. And so, Luc Fourché, *aka* Stocker Hinge *aka* Alain Saint-Germain and whomever he'd now morphed into, though perhaps a notch above the crypto-Nazis he had conspired to drive from his Temple, would one day face a reckoning with his cosmic Lady. Raszer surely hoped so, for he had come to believe that She was fiercely just.

FOURCHÉ HAD ESCAPED the raid on Ayers Rock through a subterranean passage that only old Sam Mirrigau had been around long enough to know about. Raszer could only guess that Fourché had not taken Sofia hostage because time was short, and she had served her purpose in drawing him there. Among the many things that were still, and would always be hazy, one was clear: Fourché had wanted Raszer to know him and to know his Temple. Of the others besides the young girl Raszer had carried out, one child and four adults were pulled back from the brink of death at a nearby military clinic. The rest had gotten what they'd asked for: deliverance of one sort or another. All but the small boy whose plaintive cry for his father's protection Raszer could not erase from memory. The boy had not asked to die before his fifth birthday.

Old Sam Mirrigau had gone "back in" two months ago. He was now a part of the earth he revered. As for Miltjan, he'd been e-mailing Raszer incessantly; desperate to enlist in what he called Raszer's international dreamtime police.

RASZER HEARD THE phone jingle on the other side of the thick French doors. Moments later, Monica appeared on the balcony with the cordless in her hands.

"It's for you," she said, a tad protectively. "It's Sofia Gould. Do you want me to—"

"I'll take it."

Aside from the brief time they had spent as co-patients in a Perth hospital, he had spoken to Sofia only once since the siege at Uluru. She had told him she had things to take care of, and he'd assumed that meant, among other matters, a divorce. Her husband had gotten his money back and was now pressing a multi-million dollar civil suit against the jailed front men of the Temple, while simultaneously negotiating with their lawyers for the film rights to their story. The Larry Goulds of the world always come out okay. Raszer was certain, though, that Sofia would be changed in some fundamental way.

He took the phone. "Hello, little Hokhmah. How are you?" He listened, his eyes softening at the sound of her voice, and then answered. "I know it well. See you in fifteen minutes, then." He gave the phone back to

Monica and turned to his daughter. "Let's take a ride, honey. There's someone I'd like you to meet."

ABOUT A MILE up Beachwood Canyon Drive, beyond the little Tuscan-style village, there is a monument to whimsy called *The Garden of Oz*. Like the junkyard shrines created by outlaw artists, it was a sanctuary built from colored glass, cheap trinkets and concrete under the hand of a singularly devoted creator. A small plaque informed visitors that Grandma had been one-hundred-and-six when she passed on, having completed this, her life's work. Although the Garden was legally a private backyard, amazed passersby could and did wander in from the road, and were often welcomed with lemonade by the great-grandchildren who still owned the house. Raszer found a shaded spot and parked while Brigit dashed ahead into the Garden, dazzled by the iridescence.

He walked in, pushing aside the low-hanging boughs. Brigit was perched on the "Throne of Angels." He had begun to bow when he heard a voice from behind.

"And I thought *I* was young for you," she said. He turned to find Sofia carefully negotiating the "yellow brick road" in high heels. She was far rosier and more voluptuously beautiful than he remembered, in no small part because she was very pregnant – around six months, from the looks of it.

"The really young ones are the safest bet," he replied. "They don't get themselves knocked up!" She laughed, deep-throated and moist. "Sofia Gould," he announced, "this is my daughter, uh, Queen Brigit the Merciful. Brigit, meet Sofia."

The nine year-old came forward to shake hands and warbled, '*Enchanté.*"

"Well!" Sofia exclaimed. "God, Stephan, she's *you!* She has your mouth exactly."

"Yeah, I know. I'm better looking as a girl." He took her arm and ushered them to a shady bench. "I thought you said you weren't any good at that," he said, nodding shyly at her swollen belly.

"I wasn't," she replied with a wry smile, "until you came along."

Raszer found himself suddenly uneasy. "Sofia…God, I…uh…"

She put her hand to his lips in a gesture he recalled from a similarly awkward moment in the backseat of a limo, six months prior.

"Don't fret, beautiful man. There's only a fifty-fifty chance it's yours, and I didn't bring you here to slap you with a paternity suit." She scooted into the bench. "All I want is for you to be the godfather; teach him, you know, *things.*"

"Of course."

She dropped her gaze to the purple tiles. "I left Larry. Well, I never really went back after London. Everything…I mean *everything* had changed. I couldn't play that part anymore."

"I kind of figured," he replied. "So then, there is somebody new? I mean, you know, the other fifty percent."

"Yeah. You'll see. But Stephan…" Her eyes roamed the shimmering landscape and she smiled as she noticed an inscription from the *Moon Goddess Walking Society*. "There's something I have to ask you. I've read all the stuff in the papers, I mean, about what happened in Australia and the whole money thing…the Swiss bank scandal…all that."

Raszer nodded. Sofia was referring to the fact that not a week had gone by since June that the major northeastern newspapers hadn't run a story on the Temple of the Sun Scandal. It was a big story, but Sofia had her mind on something else.

"I want to know," she asked, "what you think really happened to me in that synagogue."

Raszer squinted. "A lot of things. Some of them you'll probably spend the rest of your life trying to understand. Basically though, I think what happened was that Rabbi Scholem plugged you back into life. You were pretty disconnected."

"Oh, yeah…" She took a folded piece of pale blue stationery from her handbag and opened it carefully. "I wrote this for my mother before I left for Prague. I never sent it. I can't believe it's me talking." She handed the letter to Raszer, and he skimmed its shakily written contents.

> *I can't stand another day feeling scared of my own shadow, Mom. The pain in my insides is so awful. The doctors find nothing but I know it's a signal. I know I have to leave, Mother. I really do believe my life is a mistake.*

Raszer folded the note and handed it back to Sofia.

"No more pain, right?"

"No more pain, Stephan. Sometimes I still get scared. You know – things that normal people don't even think about. That's why, well… Come see where I live. You can meet the presumptive father. Will you, Stephan?"

"Of course," he replied. "You know I love intrigue."

She picked up her handbag to go, but stood pensively, pushing her fingers nervously through her thick hair. "Stephan, could you have loved me? I mean, like a husband?"

He smiled softly. "It wouldn't be hard to love you, Sofia. Not a bit. But I don't think you really want a husband, and the last thing I need is another neglected wife."

"Next life, huh?"

Raszer nodded. "Next life for sure."

*"For sure."*

"Oh," he added, fumbling in his pockets, "before I forget." He handed her the key chain she'd given him in Prague, and they walked silently to their cars.


CROWNING THE OLD HOLLYWOODLAND settlement that had once boasted Charlie Chaplin, Mary Astor and other luminaries of the silent screen as landowners was an expensive villa known as Castillo del Lago, built by Bugsy Siegel in the days when money mixed with money, no matter its source. It sat perched in the shadow of the HOLLYWOOD sign and held a commanding view of the old reservoir called Lake Hollywood and the L.A. basin, all the way to the Pacific. Raszer had never been there, but after they'd passed the last gated estate and mounted a steep grade to the top of Mulholland, he knew that's where they were headed. From such a perspective, it was still possible to see what Hollywood might have become had it not consumed itself with a syphilis of the soul: terraced hillsides, rows of Roman cedars, ancient-looking stone steps and rambling fortress walls. Then, as now, show people had been inclined toward the esoteric. Chaplin had reputedly been a practicing kabbalist; his home a few hundred feet down the canyon on Temple Hill Drive, had been built to resemble the aerie of a Persian magus. Within a square mile or so of real estate, a stunning array of spiritual societies were headquartered: the Gnostics, the Rosicrucians, the Freemasons – even the Scientologists, whom Raszer was disinclined to include with the more venerable clubs.

It didn't surprise him that Sofia had been drawn here. So had he. They might have made a great team, but Raszer was a man for whom attachments to anything but truth always spelled peril. As they approached the gates of the villa, he felt a wave of profound sadness wash over him. She pulled her yellow 450SL convertible around the semi-circular driveway and into the shade of a rose pink portico.

Brigit's only comment was, "God, Daddy. I thought *we* were rich."

"There's always someone richer, baby."

Sofia beckoned for them to follow her in. Raszer felt a creeping uneasiness he couldn't quite peg. After all she'd been through, after splitting from her mogul husband, he'd somehow expected her to cultivate a *slightly* more ascetic lifestyle. But she wasn't, after all, the same as him, although for a few moments in a Prague synagogue, he had known her as himself. She guided them into an impressive three-story atrium that had been recently and very expensively decorated in the latest Santa Fe shabby chic, and then through a set of French doors into a library.

"You guys make yourselves comfy," she said. "I'll go get the master of the house and we'll have a drink on the veranda."

Raszer nodded and flashed a slightly nervous smile. He wasn't sure, in truth, that he *was* enjoying the mystery.

The library, too, appeared to have been stocked by a high-class decorator. All the classics were represented, all the bindings crisp and new. The small selection of more worn volumes were all Czech titles, among them curiously enough, Gustav Meyrink's John Dee fantasy, *The Angel of the West Window.*

Mounted on the wall above the shelf was a replica of a family coat of arms. Its centerpiece was the ancient Austro-Bavarian emblem of the double-headed eagle.

The fog of intrigue was beginning to disperse, leaving behind a more puzzling clarity. Raszer had long since concluded that the "line of princes" alluded to by Josef De Boer referred to whatever lineal strain remained of the Royal House of Hapsburg, the same folks who had shut down John Dee's Renaissance and thus foreclosed on the spiritual transformation of Europe. Through the confluence of royal bloodlines and political interests, they had allied with certain old houses of France, among them the so-called *Prieure de Sion,* who were audacious enough to claim consanguinity with Christ. But it had been an unholy alliance from the start. It had engendered, over the centuries, all sorts of pretenders and false prophets, and it could be argued that Adolf Hitler was one of them. The two-headed eagle had recently become a fashion statement in S&M fetish boutiques and skinhead tattoo parlors. Now it had arrived on Mulholland Drive.

On the whitewashed pine coffee table, Raszer spied a clothbound "baby book," the kind of journal in which new mothers record things like "baby's first toy," "baby's first word," etc. He flipped open the cover, drawn by what impulse he could not say.

Handwritten on the blank front leaf in a flowery but masculine script was an inscription.

> *Each child conceived of genuine devotion is a gift to the Goddess*
> *– LMF*

LMF. Brigit took Raszer's hand as he closed the book's cover.

"You okay, Daddy?"

"Yes, sweetheart," he answered distantly. "I'm fine." As he spoke, he heard Sofia clear her throat, and Raszer was not entirely surprised to find her at the side of the newly appointed cultural attaché for the Czech Republic's Los Angeles consulate.

"Stephan," she said softly, "you remember Rudie from Prague, don't you?"

Raszer shook Rudie's hand, but an odd current passed between them. Was it possible that this "industrialist's son," his regal bearing and obvious wealth born of an age-old entitlement, was heir to some Faustian pact? His family had no doubt held sway in Bohemia long before the enlightened reign of Vaclav Havel, and would continue to do so well after. If so, then Sofia had walked right back into the fire. People did that after all, didn't they? Made the same choice again and again until it either affirmed or destroyed them? Or could it be that Count Rudolph Svaczech stood on the other side of the bi-directional mirror, *with the good kings* like Wenceslas, using his pedigree to operate as a double agent? Raszer now understood that the Devil operates by mimicry of our hearts' desires, and that only the knowing heart could see the difference between real and counterfeit.

"What you've been through," said Rudie, curling his slender fingers around the back of Sofia's neck, "practically qualifies you for sainthood, Mr. Raszer."

"Hardly," Raszer answered dryly. "Just a good vacation. Sainthood is for guys without grudges. I've still got a few."

Brigit curtsied as she was introduced, and they were escorted to a magnificent veranda overlooking the lake and the canyon. There was a dry martini and a golden sunset waiting there for Raszer. He guessed he wouldn't be seeing the lady in the mirror for a while, or the woman in the woods. She had gotten what she wanted for now. She was the Queen in whose secret service he would be until the end of his days. And if Sofia was unsure of her child's paternity, Raszer was less so. Whatever the two of them had conceived that night in Prague was to be a gift to Her. In return for his offering, Raszer had earned a life that came in deeper colors; there was no longer a fearful boy in him who craved the dark solace of oblivion. That vein of raw ore had been smelted into a finer sort of metal, which – if not yet gold – held the promise of great worth.

High overhead, a red-tailed hawk circled. He vaguely recalled how nice it was to see things from that perspective. Down here among the mortals, things got pretty hazy. The wistfulness that had seized him outside the gates ebbed just a bit as Sofia took his hand and led him into the sun where they stood without speaking for a few minutes.

From the far side of the veranda, Brigit approached gingerly, one foot placed before the other. A Monarch butterfly had lit on her shoulder and was flexing its wings languorously.

"Isn't life delicious, Daddy?" she squealed, and twirled to display her new brooch. Raszer took a sip of the cold, numbing gin, and his mind was quieted.

"Yes it is, baby," he said, then repeated for his own assurance. "Yes, it is."

The butterfly having flown, he picked up his daughter and crushed her to his chest, delighting in the way she melded herself into him. Of the necessity of his own flawed existence he remained uncertain, but he swore a silent oath that neither Brigit, nor any child he fathered, would ever think of its life as a mistake.

*Fasting is only the saving of bread*
*Formal prayer is for old men and women*
*Pilgrimage is a worldly pleasure*
*Conquer the heart instead — its mastery is a conquest indeed*

– from Sufi teacher Abdullah Ansari

# ABOUT THE AUTHOR

A.W. Hill did not begin to write seriously until his forty-fourth birthday, following receipt by anonymous mail of a well-worn copy of Strunk & White's "Elements of Style." In it was inscribed the epigram: *Only that festers which is denied the light. Right what you know,* followed by the initials, *C.R.R.* Prior to receiving this directive, Hill was a musician, composer and dabbler in arcana, and most recently, a music executive for Walt Disney Studios, in which position he traveled widely on the company's dime, consorted with the idle rich and idled with rich consorts, a few of whom were witches. Hill received a BFA in Film from the Tisch School of the Arts at New York University. He lives in Hollywood with his wife Valerie, his son Nathanael, stepson Eloic and two daughters from a previous marriage, Olivia and Andrea. He likes lemonheads and his favorite color is lapis lazuli.

"Enoch's Portal," currently in development as a motion picture, is his first novel.